A Wild and Ruined Song

Book Four in the HOLLOW STAR *Saga*

A WILD AND RUINED SONG

ASHLEY SHUTTLEWORTH

Margaret K. McElderry Books

NEW YORK · LONDON · TORONTO · SYDNEY · NEW DELHI

MARGARET K. McELDERRY BOOKS
An imprint of Simon & Schuster Children's Publishing Division
1230 Avenue of the Americas, New York, New York 10020

MARGARET K. McELDERRY BOOKS is a trademark of Simon & Schuster, LLC.
Simon & Schuster: Celebrating 100 Years of Publishing in 2024
For information about special discounts for bulk purchases, please contact Simon & Schuster Special Sales at 1-866-506-1949 or business@simonandschuster.com.
The Simon & Schuster Speakers Bureau can bring authors to your live event. For more information or to book an event, contact the Simon & Schuster Speakers Bureau at 1-866-248-3049 or visit our website at www.simonspeakers.com.
Interior design by Irene Metaxatos
The text for this book was set in Adobe Garamond Pro.
Manufactured in the United States of America
First Edition
2 4 6 8 10 9 7 5 3 1
CIP data for this book is available from the Library of Congress.
ISBN 9781665918800
ISBN 9781665918824 (ebook)

*To anyone who had to sacrifice their
childhood
on the altar of things the adults
should have done*

AUTHOR'S NOTE

This book is a work that comes from an incredibly personal place; it is also a work that features fairly heavy subject matter that may be difficult to engage with/potentially triggering for some readers. It's vitally important that we destigmatize the discussion of mental health, depression, and suicide—especially among our youth—and while books are one of the safest spaces we have in which to talk about these very real and serious issues, it's also crucial that you, the reader, be fully aware of and consenting to that exploration. As such, please be advised of the content warnings listed below, provided for your discretion:

Content warnings: anger, arson, blood/gore (moderate), body horror (minor), depression, dissociative identity disorder (similarities), family dysfunction, genocidal acts, grief (loss of sister/mother/father/family members), mental illness, murder, parental abuse/neglect, psychopathy, psychological manipulation, rape (threat/minor scene), suicidal ideation, torture (moderate), violence (semi-graphic), war

A Wild and Ruined Song

PROLOGUE

Nausicaä

~

Yonge-Dundas Square—September

ALECTO HAD NEVER BEEN *one for words . . .*

The ground Nausicaä stood on knew more pain than twice her lifetime. Earth soaked in the bloody history of human and folk wars both. Stone paved over, sprouting buildings in the place of trees, enormous billboards and digital screens hanging like fruit from branches. Vehicles sped by, spewing filth; crowds of people jostled their way from one destination to the next, ignoring the homeless and starving in their paths. Shootings and muggings and stabbings and fear—this was a city just like any other, and Nausicaä could *feel* every bit of the misery that weighed it down, and oh . . . *oh*, the violence beginning to fan to life in the embers of her soul. The rekindling rage that had already left an indelible mark on this world.

Whatever Toronto thought it knew about hurt, she was about to demonstrate far worse.

The Dirge *was a ship that served many a whim, so long as those whims all served woe . . .*

"Take. It. Off," Nausicaä commanded, in a tone just as dark as her reputation. *"Take. It. Off."*

She advanced a step on the person in front of her.

Gone was their previous backdrop, which only moments ago had been Riadne's private lab. Gone was the glowing array Nausicaä had been tasked to attend, and the chanting alchemists, and the body on that altar that Nausicaä had *foolishly* believed to be Vehan.

She'd hardly been able to process the transition.

One moment, she was perfectly fine and heartless, everything as it was meant to be, and Arlo . . . *Arlo . . . oh gods,* no . . .

The next thing Nausicaä knew, inexplicable magic yanked her from happy apathy and spat her out *here* in the Viridian Circle.

A square of pavement surrounded by street, encircled by towering buildings and bright displays and so many colorful lights.

The sound, though—muffled, as though right where they stood existed within some bubble that kept them separate from the world outside, which went on around them blissfully, as if nothing was wrong.

As if Nausicaä's entire world wasn't unraveling.

The floor Alecto knelt on was a glittering sea of black marble flecked with diamond white . . .

"Take it off, take it off, *take it off,* TAKE IT OFF!" she snarled, advancing another step.

The agonies she'd suffered in the course of her life, they flashed through her mind like a torturous reel. Like she needed the reminder of how *close* she'd been to the edge all along . . . how much it hurt every time she had to break and repair just to break again . . .

The screaming returned. It was back in her veins, in her bones, in her *being.*

Heartbreak was an unforgettable sound that tore from the soul like a curse. Nausicaä had thought herself well acquainted with its harrowing key. The loss of Tisiphone had hit so profoundly that it had ripped her, shredded her, destroyed her in every way, and hadn't she sworn to never again let this happen? She'd worked so hard for over a century, piecing herself back together with whatever she could find—scraps of thread and bits of tape, coffee and sarcasm and . . .

"Being with you . . . Nausicaä, it's like everything in the world just stops, and there's this incredible moment of perfect stillness, and you're the only thing I can see . . ."

"I love you, too . . ."

. . . and Arlo.

Arlo Jarsdel, whom this person standing before her in the Viridian Circle absolutely was *not*, no matter how much they might currently look like her.

"Now," Nausicaä threatened, words barely able to fit through the clench of her jaw, and she reached out to take great fistfuls of fabric of an outfit that was just as much an illusion as its wearer. "Now, or I'll take it off for you."

False jade eyes widened. Fear rolled off this imposter in a sour wave.

A shimmering in the air beside them heralded the opening of a portal, admitting first Celadon, then Lethe, then Aurelian and a small host of others onto the scene. Rory Jarsdel and one of Arlo's ironborn classmates, both of whom had appeared alongside Nausicaä, stood blinking in confusion.

The newcomers staggered to a halt upon arrival, every single one of them, to gawk at what was happening, but Nausicaä couldn't spare them a thought.

None of them saw what she did. This imposter she clutched, who was *not* Arlo, but oh, he looked so *exactly* like her, down to the placement of every faint freckle Nausicaä could remember pressing fluttering kisses to only weeks ago . . .

"Arlo?" Celadon breathed to the imposter. "Nausicaä? I . . . what's going on, I don't understand. Where is *Vehan*—was he not wearing his bracelet?"

Bracelet?

Nausicaä looked down at her wrist.

3

At the bracelet she'd been given earlier that evening. At the one she was willing to bet the very confused Rory behind her wore, as well as that ironborn girl beside him, glaring her own suspicions at the imposter Nausicaä had grabbed.

Schemes and bracelets and *this person before her wasn't Arlo* . . . and Nausicaä shouldn't be feeling this utter, profound breaking in her chest. Her contract with Riadne was flawless: her heart for Arlo's safety. It wouldn't void for any reason, not unless . . .

"*No.*" Nausicaä seethed, half-unhinged in growing panic. Panic—panic she shouldn't be feeling because *she shouldn't have a heart to feel with.* "No. This isn't Arlo. Vehan is right here. He's not the one we're missing. But he *is* going to TAKE OFF THAT FACE—IT ISN'T HIS!"

Her imposter flinched at the sudden roar.

"I can't," he whispered in a voice that made Nausicaä want to rip and tear and shatter the world.

Because it was Arlo's voice . . . but it wasn't Arlo.

And a sickening feeling told her this would be the last she'd ever hear it.

Her contract with Riadne wouldn't void, not unless Arlo was injured by that power-hungry queen's hand, or . . .

Or . . .

Or or or or or or or or—

"I *can't* take it off; it's a . . ." Vehan swallowed. He looked around as he spoke, wildly, hopefully, as though Arlo might be just behind them and none of this was as bad as it seemed. "It's a potion? It has to wear off. I'm sorry, Nausicaä. I don't . . . I have no . . . I didn't *know.* She was supposed to come too. She had a bracelet! Nausicaä, I don't know what's happening either. . . ."

Pathetic.

He sounded so *pathetically* apologetic, looked so confused, and almost as though he could possibly fathom heartbreak, true heartbreak . . . and Nausicaä wanted to *burn.*

4

"I'm sorry. I'm *sorry*," he choked out, tears gathering on lashes that didn't belong to him.

A voice you'll never hear again . . .
A face you'll never see . . .
Look your last—you have your heart back, and this. Is. Not. Arlo.

The tears began to fall, silent streaks down Not Arlo's face, and his searching gaze became frantic. "I don't understand! She was *supposed to be here*, she was supposed to come with the rest of us! We *all* had a bracelet. I saw hers, she—"

"How many?"

It was Celadon asking the question, his voice sharp. "How many bracelets did Arlo give out, exactly?"

More tears fell . . . down a face now starting to transform . . .

"I . . . four?" came Vehan's shaky reply, as though he was teetering on the precipice of hyperventilation. "There was the one she had, the ones for me and Rory, and then she told us you made two extra, one for Fyri and one for—"

. . . to transform . . . . and transform . . . until at last the magic that had made Vehan into Arlo dissolved completely to a pile of silvery dust at his feet, and he was himself again.

". . . and one for Nausicaä," Celadon finished in breathless realization of something Nausicaä *didn't want to hear.* "Arlo gave *her* bracelet to Nausicaä—I only made the one extra, for Fyri. Nausicaä was meant to follow on her own accord once her heart was back. She can teleport, so it was one less stress on my magic to have her come on her own. Which meant that the bracelet Arlo was wearing . . ." How pale Celadon's face had become—a face Nausicaä could barely recognize now, though whether that was because she was quickly untethering from reality or because of his newly black-dyed hair . . .

"If you indeed saw a bracelet on her," Celadon rasped, "it must have been a fake." He shook his head hard, a bit like how Nausicaä felt she might be shaking herself, her entire body a vibrating rage so much hotter than anything she'd ever felt before . . . "*Why? Why would she do this*—Vehan!"

Celadon darted forward, knocking Nausicaä aside—though not dislodging her, as if anything possibly could right now—to grab at Vehan's robes as well. His own growing hysteria warped his voice to be unrecognizable, though that could be the *screaming* that distorted all other sound in Nausicaä's ears. "Vehan, you have to tell me everything that happened—spare no detail. Did she tell you *any* hint of what she was thinking—"

"She's actually going to do it."

Nausicaä stiffened.

Everything paused.

Those words were Lethe's, and she didn't understand for shit what he'd just said, but she knew that it meant nothing good.

Not with that look on his face.

Nausicaä turned to glare at the Hunter she'd never once seen unnerved—not like this, not *horrified* to such a noticeable degree. The complexion behind those starlight freckles was paler than usual, and was that actual *emotion* touching his features . . . ?

"Going to do *what?*" she ground out.

She looked around at the lot of them. Lethe, Celadon, Aurelian . . . Rory, Fyri, Theodore and Elyas off behind them, amidst a small crowd of other folk Nausicaä didn't know or care to identify. There was something going on here Nausicaä hadn't been brought up to speed about, too busy enslaved to Riadne's plot, heartless and indifferent. But she was very much the opposite now, and if any of these people wanted to leave this happy little protection circle *alive*, someone was going to explain to her what the hells was going on.

She was a *Fury*, after all.

Former though the title was, no mortal protection circle would be able to withstand the Fire she could still wield.

Lethe merely stared.

There was something different about him, too, she noticed. Not just the pearlescent white hair, which somehow only honed all his sharp, odd edges to an even deadlier blade instead of softening them; not just the intimate concern he currently fixed on Celadon beneath the myriad flex of other emotions. No, something . . . *differenter* than different. Something that felt a lot like the Titans had felt, and . . .

"WHAT'S GOING ON!" she roared, spiraling down a pit that had no bottom. Rounding back on Vehan, she continued to bellow, "*WHERE IS ARLO!*"

Vehan flinched—she still had a hold of him, and her grip had tightened enough that it started to tear his clothing. "She was supposed to be here," he quickly supplied, speaking in a rush like he thought some paltry explanation would absolve the fuck-off lot of them of what they'd done in Nausicaä's absence.

"It was supposed to be a simple swap. Arlo would challenge Lethe for his position as a Hunter, win, and get her memories back in an additional reward to earning an immortal afterlife. Then she and I would swap roles, her fate as a Hollow Star for mine as Ruin, because she would survive it longer than I could, if her soul was meant for immortality. The plan was that Celadon would call us all back here as soon as she became Ruin, and then he'd use the goddess-blessed sword we have to run her through, killing Arlo and sending Ruin back to his prison. But Arlo wouldn't die; she'd go to . . . um . . . Cosmin, I think? And Lethe would go too and retrieve her, and restore her memory, and everything would be fine—"

Nausicaä punched him.

Hard.

Square in the face.

She felt his nose break under her knuckles, and it wasn't enough. What the fuck was he even saying to her? She was incandescent in her outrage, and a measly broken bone wasn't enough.

Growling out an expletive, Aurelian charged toward them.

7

Celadon gasped, stumbling back as Vehan pitched in the opposite direction.

Nausicaä, meanwhile, could only *boil*.

"Fine?" Her voice was just a whisper. "What? Of all the stupid fucking things anyone has ever said to me—the absolute bullshit garbage you just spewed that I can't even *begin* to level with right now—and you think any of it is *fine?*"

Celadon grabbed her shoulder. "Nausicaä, please, we—"

Nausicaä turned to glare him down. He was saved a similar expression of her thoughts on his *fine* plan, though, by a force like a boulder crashing against the hand she threw out behind her.

Stopped so abruptly, Aurelian—no less furious—shuddered against her palm; that was definitely a rib or two broken, but his only concerned seemed to be for Vehan, on the ground, bleeding sapphire from his nose.

"Nausicaä," Celadon tried again.

Nausicaä could hardly breathe. "No," she rasped. "You don't get to fucking talk. I don't want to *fucking* hear it." She pointed to Lethe. "But you. *You'd* better start saying a whole lot of things. What did she gods-damned do, Lethe?"

And still Lethe stared.

A moment.

Two.

When it seemed like he might ignore the question once again, Nausicaä puffed herself up, intent on hurling herself at him, a fight to the death if that was what it took to get any words worth salt to her.

But then . . . "Flamel."

Nausicaä paused.

"Nicholas Flamel. *Arlo* Flamel—not our Arlo, but the original. Nicholas's son—the one who started this all by summoning Pride into the world, and I am *speaking this out loud to you*. Magic hasn't garbled it, hasn't warped it to nonsense the moment it hits your ears. I was

8

very careful in the magic I wove, over even our immortal kin. But I am standing here talking to you plainly about a family I had to wipe so thoroughly from memory that even *I* couldn't recall the whole of it, and Arlo . . . is doing it."

"DOING WHAT?"

"Why, beginning the end, of course."

Nausicaä was going to fucking lose it.

"Lethe," she ground out, and never had she heard such a dangerous tone in her voice before, but what Lethe said . . . it was . . . true.

She *did* remember, now that she thought on it.

All of it—or at least, what she knew about the Flamel family before Lethe had put his curse on the knowledge.

More than what she'd retained before but had been unable to speak.

The Flamels . . . the parts of their history that the Courts had bargained to blot out of memory. The parts of Arlo's childhood that Nausicaä and all the rest of the immortals had learned almost nineteen years ago, back when "Arlo Flamel" didn't mean anything more to her than some hapless mortal girl named after a legend, a girl who'd fucked around with alchemy that she should have stayed well away from, and—

All of it came flooding back.

Nausicaä gasped.

Oh.

Oh, *shit.*

She's beginning the end.

Nausicaä knew exactly what that meant. She'd forgotten. She'd *forgotten* what had made Arlo so damned interesting to the Immortal Realm, but *oh*, did she remember now—Arlo, the first mortal since the original Arlo who'd managed to summon Eos and Moros, the terrible scions of the Immortal Realm's most feared progenitors, the Beginning and End. Servants of the Primordial Others, who'd been chained in punishment to forgotten thrones and left to fester in their tempers for thousands of years . . .

If Ruin didn't destroy her, Arlo's decision to tie herself to these scions had just made her the number one enemy of every single immortal who remembered what those *monsters* could do.

And what they must be after . . .

Arlo wasn't going to survive this life, and she sure as shit wasn't surviving the next, either, when the Immortal Realm was through with her.

After all, they'd Destroyed others for lesser slights than choosing the Titan of Destruction over them.

"No."

She dropped her hand from Aurelian.

"*No.*"

Turned back to Vehan.

"NO!"

And launched her unbridled fury.

"Nausicaä, don't!"

"Nausicaä, stop!"

"GET OFF OF HIM!"

"Nausicaä, please, I didn't know!" Vehan sobbed, full tears streaming down his face. His hands flailed in an attempt to block himself from her assault.

Straddling him, pinning him, strike after strike after strike she rained down on any solid contact she could land. Bones broke; her knuckles tore; her vision swam in her eyes, Vehan flinching and crying and writhing, taking every blow and returning, and that pissed her off even more.

Did they know what they let happen?

Did they have any idea of how deeply her kin feared the Primordial Ones' return?

Arlo was going to die. She was already dead, but now there was no chance—none in all the heavens and hells and cosmos in between—that Arlo would be spared. She'd be Destroyed as soon as she ascended to the immortality they thought they'd bought her.

"This is your fault!" Nausicaä cried—perhaps genuine tears, it was so hard to tell—and she swore for a moment that it was Heulfryn beneath her and no time had passed in 117 years. "This is your fault. She trusted you! *I* trusted you! You were supposed to protect her and YOU LET HER DIE! IT SHOULD HAVE BEEN YOU!"

Arlo had *died*.

Arlo was dead.

She was dead, she was dead, she was dead, she was—"AHH!"

Had Nausicaä broken before?

That was nothing, a fracture compared to what obliterated her now. "THIS IS YOUR FAULT! IT'S YOUR FAULT, IT'S YOUR FAULT! YOU WERE SUPPOSED TO PROTECT HER! WHY WASN'T IT YOU?"

"Nausicaä."

Hands on her—they felt like ice. Her entire body was burning.

"THIS IS YOUR FAULT!" She kicked and screamed and screamed and kicked, and struck out, and burned. The hands that pulled her back—only Lethe could manage such a feat, though that second, far less careful pair that clawed at her was definitely Aurelian's, and there were Celadon's hands as well, and Nausicaä *didn't care.* "THIS IS YOUR FAULT, YOU WORTHLESS BAG OF SHIT! GIVE HER BACK GIVE HER BACK GIVE HER—"

"NAUSICAÄ."

Abruptly, Nausicaä stopped.

She had . . . never once heard Lethe raise his voice in such a way: full of terrible command. And something inside her—the part of her that recognized that very key difference to the immortal before her—made her freeze.

It had been a greater god's command.

She couldn't move, but this didn't stop her rage. It didn't stop the screaming in her head or the vitriol she spilled, the condemnation that was more for herself than for the boy crying blood and apologies on the concrete.

"Get ahold of yourself," Lethe said icily, and Nausicaä was done.

"Get off me," she snapped. *"Get off."*

It took a great deal to break from Lethe's compulsion. To push him away, them all away.

To push herself to her feet.

But she was *done*.

For 117 years, she'd been doing this on her own, and she'd been *fine*—117 years, and yet all it had taken was one moment of weakness to derail it all. One stupid, errant, pitiful thought that maybe, just maybe, it would be nice to have a friend again . . . that maybe, just maybe, she'd repented enough in her dead sister's eyes to be allowed Arlo.

"Get the *fuck* back here, Nausicaä," Aurelian snarled after her, his fury with her only barely restrained by Celadon holding him back.

"You're really going to *leave*?" Lethe sneered.

"Aurelian, *please*—Nausicaä, stop!" Celadon called after her, desperate. "Riadne has seven stones, a Crown, and Ruin; we need you, Nausicaä, *please!*"

Nausicaä, Nausicaä, Nausicaä, Nausicaä . . . she was starting to hate the sound of this name just as much as she'd hated "Alecto."

And she was so, incredibly done—with friends, with people, with caring, with *this*. One hundred seventeen years ago, she'd sworn a promise to this realm. It had managed to distract her from her pain for a while. It had led her to Arlo, and life had become bearable, but now Arlo was doomed to a fate worse than death, and Nausicaä was reminded of the only purpose she should have kept to.

Too late now.

The damage was done, and once again, it was the person Nausicaä loved most paying its exorbitant bill.

She was so fucking, incredibly *done with this*. For now Nausicaä would give Arlo whatever she needed to help her on the unfathomable path she'd chosen. And when it inevitably ended in Arlo's

Destruction, what would rise from those flames would be Nausicaä no more.

She would at last truly become the Dark Star, unfettered.

If the realms thought they knew the taste of her rage, they were ill prepared for her ruin.

Arlo

The Luminous Palace

THE FLOOR THAT ARLO stood on was a glittering sea of white marble
	flecked with charcoal black.

Heroes went through so much hardship.
Heroes were the stuff of tragedies.

To think, if you were a little more clever,
you might have been able to save them both.

I don't want greatness.
I just want things to go back
to the way they were.

We ask for help to put an end to this cycle.
Destroy all the Crowns.
Take power away from what festers in both realms, so that healing
can begin.
So that balance and unity can be restored.

We ask . . .
We ask . . .
We ask
We ask

We're only asking . . .
she chooses
villain
too

Arlo shot upright on her bed, gasping for air like she hadn't drawn breath since her eyes had closed.

When *had* they, though?

She couldn't say.

Just as she couldn't make full sense of where she was right now. It was so dark with the curtains drawn that she could barely make out her surroundings, was able to recognize them as her things only thanks to her UnSeelie night-vision, which meant this had to be her . . . bedroom?

Her bedroom, and her bed beneath her, and she was still dressed in her shoes, her jeans, the cloak she'd won from Lethe, no longer around her shoulders but draped carefully over her body.

Everything she'd been wearing when . . . *wearing when* . . .

A glowing array flashed across her mind's eye.

An altar, surrounded by chanting alchemists.

The smell of sulfur, of iron blood and melted wax and carved stone and *fear*.

Delicious, wasn't it?

Arlo startled so violently her entire bed shook.

The voice that had just spoken, words said directly to her from inside her own head—the sound was her own but deeper, steadier, cooler, was her vowels but wrapped in an accent she couldn't place. Arlo felt that voice like a cloud passing over the sun, and it was this that made her suddenly, acutely aware that it was more than a voice but an entire separate *presence* within her.

"Arlo?"

"Oh my *gods*," she gasped at the sound of a second voice, not at all in her head this time, and startling all over again. Her hand flew up to cover her rapidly beating heart—funny, when only moments ago it hadn't been . . . hadn't been . . . *hadn't been beating at all.* "Oh," she said, smaller, quieter, for the enormity of what had just clicked into place.

The glowing array . . .

The altar . . .

That voice in her head . . .

Ruin.

Twin pricks of dark light reflecting off silver was all Arlo could make out of the person standing tall at the end of her bed. Eyes glowing a bit the way a cat's did from the gloom, and she didn't need a face to know to whom they belonged, even if her observer hadn't spoken.

She'd recognize that woodsmoke-and-steel aura anywhere.

"Nos?" Arlo echoed back, her voice catching raspy on disuse.

And suddenly it all came rushing back to her with the force of a brick wall, everything that had happened, everything Arlo had done and had apparently succeeded at, because here she was, and no one else stood crowded around her bedside like they would be if her plan with the bracelets had failed—but *gods*, this presence inside her. It made her want to claw at her skin, to retch, to shudder and squirm, *anything* to get away from this *wrongness* at the core of her, like some foul slug tracking ooze over her soul.

"Nos . . . uh . . ."

What could she say?

How could she even begin to explain their situation: that Arlo traded her Hollow die for Vehan's Ruin, complicating Celadon's plans with her own, which Nausicaä wouldn't even know about because she'd have only *just* recovered her heart after Arlo's brief death on that slab, and . . . "How long have I been . . . ?"

"Asleep?" Nausicaä filled in for her. Arlo heard her sigh, then flinched from a flare of sudden brightness as a tiny ball of fire flickered to life, spilling warmth and light from a spark in the palm of her girlfriend's hand.

Or rather . . . well . . . she hoped Nausicaä still wanted to be her girlfriend. With Nausicaä's face now thrown into flickering, orange relief, Arlo could tell that her girlfriend had a lot to say about whatever she'd learned in the time Arlo had been out, and none of it *good*.

"Four days." Nausicaä shrugged, an easy action that belied the anger in her eyes. "But I imagine dying is pretty shit on the system, especially when your soul doesn't have anywhere to go. The girl gets whole-ass immortality, every mortal's wet dream, and yet Arlo Flamel decides she'd rather dick around in the highest-stakes match of tug-of-war this glorified schoolyard has ever known."

Ah.

So Nausicaä knew pretty much the lot of it, by the sounds of things.

Which . . . *good*. This meant she'd made it to the protection circle in Toronto, just as Arlo had planned when she'd slipping Nausicaä one of Celadon's bracelets. This meant she'd had the chance to talk to Celadon, Vehan, and Lethe. No doubt everyone was confused and irritated with her, to put it mildly. The original plan, after all, had been for her to return to the circle *with* everyone, to let Celadon kill her and banish Ruin back to their prison, then ascend to that immortality Nausicaä had mentioned.

But . . .

That had been *before*.

Before Arlo remembered what it was that Eos and Moros had tasked her to do. What they'd imparted, just for her, direct and private in her head, right before vanishing back into that portal they'd come through and leaving an eight-year-old girl with an impossible destiny heavy on her shoulders.

"Okay, yeah," Arlo sighed. "I know it doesn't sound all that great. I know you're probably *furious* with me—"

The *shiiink* of a blade cutting quickly through the air paused Arlo's attempt to swing her legs from the bed. Angled flat, the threat of it still barred her to her mattress. "Yeah. Pretty upset with you. But that's a discussion for later. Right now I'm going to need to you stay where you are."

Arlo looked at the blade.

Funny, she noted—how she didn't feel an ounce of fear. Not that she'd ever be afraid of Nausicaä, but looking down at her sword, Arlo knew herself well enough that the complete lack of apprehension for this sharp object in her path was suspicious, to say the least. She almost had to hold herself back from pressing against it just to see her own blood.

And that definitely wasn't a normal compulsion to feel.

Shaking herself out of whatever had come over her, she lifted her gaze back to Nausicaä—firm and resolute, her hopefully-still-girlfriend's expression was a mask of purest adamant.

Arlo frowned. "What do you mean, stay where I am? Why?"

"Because I don't know what to *do* yet," Nausicaä huffed out in frustration. "Because you aren't yourself, Arlo, and the moment you get off that bed, this whole thing just . . . *begins*, and I don't know what I'm going to do about that."

Rolling her eyes, Arlo reached out and swatted the sword from her face. She slipped out of bed and to her feet. "I don't *need* you to do anything, Nos. Nothing but keep yourself alive."

"Oh, like you did for me?"

Irritation scorched sudden and bright across the field of Arlo's emotions.

"Excuse me?" She glared at Nausicaä, who matched the look with a gaze that *burned*. "Listen, I get it, I'm sorry. You're mad at me for doing this. I'm pretty mad at you, as well. You *left* me. We had . . . we shared . . . I *gave* myself to you, and you left me the very next morning to throw yourself like a martyr at Riadne's feet without so much as a warning beforehand. So, yeah, be angry all you want, but don't you dare pretend you have any moral high ground here. You did the exact same thing!"

Tossing her sword aside, where it dissolved into a puff of smoke before it could hit the ground, Nausicaä took a step toward Arlo, curving around the end post of her bed. "Fine, okay, yeah—not cool on my end, but Arlo, this is . . . this is so much *more*. I gave up temporary custody of my heart to keep you safe; *your* thing might actually *kill* you. For real!"

"I know!" Arlo threw back, her blood suddenly boiling—again, definitely not normal for her. She and Nausicaä fought fairly easily when their tempers were high, but this sharp flare of . . . what could almost be *hate*? No. This wasn't her.

This was Ruin.

And *there* was the fear she should have felt before—how easily Ruin could already make her forget the most intrinsic parts of her.

She took a breath.

Her emotions were so much closer to the surface right now, as though her body were attempting to sweat them out or, perhaps more likely, as though Ruin were forcibly trying to expel them. And that simply wouldn't do. She had to get better at holding on to herself.

"I know," she repeated, in a far calmer tone. "And you're right—this *is* so much more. More than you and me. More than whether I live or die. Nausicaä, this is—"

A pulse burst through the air in the room; to Arlo's ears, it sounded like a quiet, deep reverberation of a gong.

Nausicaä stiffened and immediately lowered her gaze.

The presence inside Arlo—Ruin . . . four days wasn't enough for them to react much to anything yet, apparently, not more than testing their influence over her in this conversation, at least. She could feel a sort of attentiveness perk in her that wasn't her own, but Ruin was still caught in the throes of what she assumed to be a sort of summoning sickness, exhausted by the effort it had cost them just to claw through the realms and into her.

19

Arlo, though . . . she'd sensed them, too, before she could see them: the press of cold and deeper darkness against her left periphery, the caress of warmth and light on the other.

"How are you here without a portal?" she asked, eyes still on Nausicaä even as she spoke to the immortal scions that now flanked her. "Oh," she said a moment later, the answer coming to her without needing to be told—the wish she'd made back when she'd still been a Hollow Star filled in all the gaps of alchemy she didn't already know. "I gave you freedom to come to me back when I summoned you as a child."

It was Moros who spoke first—it was always Moros who spoke first, as first before anything had been darkness.

. . . and it occurred to her, belatedly, that this random side note had been pulled directly from Ruin's memories. Sharing a body might give them full access to her thoughts and emotions, but it seemed that bond ran both ways.

That might be useful to know for later.

But for now . . .

"Your earthbound Titan's spawn is astonishingly gifted." Moros's words poured like silken night. "Lethe, I believe he calls himself? It did take us a while to find you again after he erased you so thoroughly from even immortal memory. The dreams we had to comb through . . . the threads we had to chase . . ."

"But now you remember," said Eos on her right. "You claimed your heritage and unveiled the knowledge that concealed you from all, including us. Including yourself."

Ruin's strange anesthetizing apathy rose once more within her.

Despite how profoundly Arlo knew that she shouldn't look, she felt herself sigh and turn around.

Nausicaä gasped in alarm, but still Arlo felt nothing but calm.

It was hard to define the beings to the left and right before her.

Meeting them as a child, Arlo had done her best to keep from looking at either directly. The scions operated like a curse, were more reflections of the Primordial Ones they served than they were their own individuals. And how could anything encompass the End and Beginning?

But Moros was a man built of shadows and smoke and pale citrine eyes, which glowed in a long and pointed face. Eos was a woman of gentle light and dew, and rosy-morning hair, but with hollow sockets for eyes like great devouring pits, horror carved into unparalleled loveliness.

Neither had been expecting her to acknowledge them head-on.

Inside her chest, Ruin stirred into proper curiosity.

"We need to get something straight," Arlo declared, with a command that surprised even her. "You asked me years ago to destroy the Three Crowns and restore balance to the Mortal and Immortal Realms."

The scions merely watched her, confirmation enough of her mission.

"You asked me to become the villain—and afterward, right before you left, you told me that I would need to join forces with the Titan Ruin, the only of the Primordial Ones' children to stand against the others when the immortals rose up against them, earning imprisonment in their parents' fall. You said the Crowns were too powerful, that they were starting to corrupt even immortal hearts, and that the End and Beginning wanted them gone."

Again, they only watched her.

It was a little unnerving, she'd give them that. Moros was surprisingly the easiest to look at; the empty holes in Eos's eyes made Arlo want to shudder and step back.

"But *why?*" she asked them. "I mean, very obviously, I've agreed to do it, because the Bone Crown has caused nothing but harm for mortals, and I can't imagine the two others have done much good for immortals either. But why do *you* care? Why do your masters care? What are they getting out of this, to ask me to do it at all?"

Eos leaned in, and those disturbing holes drifted so close that Arlo could see through to the back of her equally hollow skull.

She was so much less beautiful at this new proximity, and so much more terrifying.

Anxiety shot through Arlo like a jolt of lightning.

And thank goodness. There her fear was, returned—Arlo was still Arlo yet.

"How presumptuous," Eos hissed like steam. "To ask the First Ones to explain themselves to a mortal-born *girl*."

"Very presumptuous," Moros intoned. "But perhaps, given the enormity of what the First Ones ask . . ."

Eos curled even closer to Arlo, and the longer Arlo held that gaze, the more off-putting the scion became. "We *did* tell you already that destroying the Crowns will release both realms from the grip of the bones that make them. And it must be all Three Crowns, made from the bones of the First Ones, pulled from their chests by their own Titanic children. When Urielle, Cosmin, and Tellis rose to power, they took those bones and fashioned them into circlets. They were well aware that the First Ones' magic still resided with them, but they severely underestimated their ability to withstand the negative effects of a Primordial essence. However more resilient, by now, those Crowns have long since corrupted the immortal heads that wear them, just as they do your mortal sovereigns."

"Breaking the Crowns," Moros continued, picking up from where Eos dropped off, "would release their contained power back to its origin. *Balance* would be restored—what was stolen would be returned, and in so doing, the First Ones would again know freedom millennia denied."

Nausicaä snorted.

"So Arlo destroys the Crowns and the Primordial Ones get their powers back, and definitely break free, and then it's just game over anyhow, provided Ruin doesn't fuck it sideways first?" Still not looking up from the ground, Nausicaä added, "Arlo, I can't begin to tell you how much danger you're in right now. The Immortal Realm

22

isn't going to just sit back and let this happen, but let's just assume you *do* manage to break all the Crowns. The Primordial Ones were *bad news*. There's a reason their immortal children put aside their extremely petty and extremely many differences to work together to seal the First Ones' asses to thrones in the middle of fuck-off nowhere space. The First Ones devoured worlds. Ate their own children. Ate anyone who pissed them off, really. Very Goya's *Saturn*. They enforced their *balance* with cruel tyranny and obliterated any who dared to oppose them. It sounds great on paper, sure, but balance? True balance? Is conformity. Repetition. Unflinching *law*—things that leave no room for stuff like creativity and circumstance. Sometimes, life needs a little *im*balance is what I'm trying to say. All of this assuming that none of the deities say fuck it, abandon their treaty, and come down here to smite you in the act—or send something to kill you so they can make your afterlife as short and painful as your actual life."

Frowning, Arlo mused on this. "But the Crowns aren't good either," she said, weighing. She didn't want to restore beings like the Primordial Ones to full power, but her immediate issue was the Crowns—the one Riadne wore, to be precise. It had to be destroyed.

The number of lives it had already ruined, the death it tracked everywhere it went . . . Arlo had known immediately that she wanted to do this, even if she'd also suspected there might not be a wholesome reason behind what drove Eos and Moros after her.

"Far from good," Moros agreed, taking a step forward. Then another. Then another, making a much slower advance on Arlo than Eos, but every bit as intimidating. "Ruin knows no real allegiance. Ruin sides with who will grant them the most opportunity for devastation. The more you tend to that need while tied to them—the more you indulge what they crave—the easier it will be for you to access their *talents* for your own and apply the power of oblivion to your undertaking."

Arlo nodded.

This had been all explained to her forever ago, back when she hadn't been old enough to really consider what it was she would be doing. And everything had been so rushed. Once Lethe returned the memory of it all, she'd chosen what seemed like the best thing to do at the time . . . and now found herself slightly regretting her noble intentions for the details she'd failed to ascertain.

"Yeah, all that I know. But Nausicaä isn't wrong; it doesn't sound to me like the Primordial Ones are the sort of beings I want to unleash back on the realms. Can I not destroy maybe one . . . or two Crowns? What happens if I don't *obliterate* all three?"

Besides condemning the ones who wear any leftover Crown to further suffering and corruption.

It would behoove you to pay attention to wording, child.

Moros smiled, almost as though he'd heard Ruin's scathing words, revealing teeth like black, serrated knives. "The First Ones were swayed to Ruin's involvement in this matter on the reasoning that they would expedite your travel between realms to fetch the other Crowns. They agreed to Ruin because to do would require the strength of a Titan and nothing less, and Ruin's destructive abilities would be best suited to tearing open portals between the realms. The First Ones wish you to break all Three Crowns and release the magic within—but what was it that *we* asked of you, dearest child?"

"A *coup*," Nausicaä interjected with an excited gasp, already having worked out what Moros had been hinting at. "The Primordial Ones want her to break the Crowns; you asked her to *destroy* them. *That's* why you need Ruin—only a Titan's power can entirely obliterate something from existence. You're turning on your masters!"

"Is that what we're doing?" Eos drawled, reeling back into herself and blessedly away from Arlo. "I would rather call it self-preservation. What need have our masters for scions when no longer chained to their thrones?"

"Aw, you guys are dicks—that endears you to me a little more, to be honest. I might actually like you."

"She is correct," Eos continued, ignoring Nausicaä entirely now to turn attention back to Arlo. "It is our wish that you use Ruin's power to *destroy* the Crowns, not simply break them. Doing so will eradicate bone and magic both, restoring balance while also removing dark influence from the realms and, most of all, keeping the First Ones chained. But it must be all three, and it *must* be done quickly. So much time has passed since the First Ones' imprisonment, there are days and nights and days in between where they've hardly any awareness at all. They trust in us, their scions, to steer you true, and will not be looking closely unless given reason to suspect foul play. Take too long, spare even one Crown, and the End and Beginning will notice that there's suddenly far less of their prize than there was before, giving them incentive to investigate, and you will not like what they will have us do to you should they discover what you've done."

She paused to let this all sink in, perhaps noticing that Arlo had gone a little pale green around the edges.

Oh, Arlo was certainly still doing this now that she knew she wouldn't be unleashing an even worse nightmare into play—in for a penny, in for a pound, so the saying went. But it was occurring to her now just how incredibly dangerous this entire thing was, from so many different angles, in so many different ways.

Eos almost looked apologetic to read the worry in Arlo's face.

"I must remind you, too, that this must be achieved before Ruin takes permanent control," she added in a softer tone. "Their annihilation will work even quicker than you do. Even now you can feel yourself beginning to deteriorate, yes? Your emotions working differently. Arlo Flamel beginning to dampen . . ."

Gods.

How long did she have to do all this?

There was a great deal she hadn't considered before jumping into this. She'd made her deal with Lethe, and almost immediately upon recovering the memory of what she'd been charged with, Riadne had summoned her final stone. Arlo had been forced into action, but even so, she'd choose it again, regardless of what she knew now.

The Crowns had to go if the realms were to make any significant change for the better.

To her, that was very much worth the risk of her life.

And again as though Moros could read her thoughts, he nodded his head. "Once Ruin awakens fully, you will not have much time. The sands of your hourglass trickle fast against you. But you will not be alone, young one. This I must impress on you. We will be watching. We give you our belief, but more than this, we give you a reminder."

"Look to the places you keep your heart," Eos gentled.

"And remember what makes you strong," they said in perfect unison.

And with nothing further, as abruptly as they'd come, they vanished into the night.

A moment of silence . . . followed another . . .

"Illuminating," Nausicaä soured.

"Was it?" Arlo asked faintly.

"No." She frowned, then pointed to Arlo's bed. "Rest," she commanded. "You should take advantage of your last few hours of freedom before the morning. I'm pretty sure we were just told we have to court your freeloader if we want to keep them interested and use their magic properly. Busy days ahead of us, lots of destruction. You're lucky that's my specialty."

Arlo looked at her . . . then dropped her gaze to her feet. Somehow, this made it easier when she asked in a small voice that sounded very gratifyingly *her*, even as the severity of what she'd done had finally begun to settle in, "Us?"

"*Tch*—you're not doing this without me. A Dark and Hollow Star, remember?"

Arlo's stomach dropped.

26

"I'm not a Hollow Star anymore, though," she replied, barely above a whisper.

"Yeah," Nausicaä drawled, and when Arlo's gaze lifted from the floor, she saw there was something intimate and kind in those sharp steel eyes that watched her. "It was never the title that made you mine, Arlo."

Heat flooded to Arlo's face.

Sliding backward onto her mattress, she patted the bed beside her. "There's a smart TV in the wall, you know. If I promise to rest, will you lay with me on the bed and binge shows on Netflix and . . . pretend that nothing's happened? That nothing changes when the sun comes up?"

That soon she might not care about doing such things with this girl she loved so deeply right then that she wanted to cry just knowing that she'd forget what that felt like too.

"I'm really mad at you."

Arlo nodded. "Yeah. I'm sorry." She shifted over, making room. "Nausicaä?" she said, quiet and private between them, as the bed beside her dipped and an ex-Fury's weight settled warm and flush against her.

"Mmm?"

"Can I ask you to do something for me?"

"I am notoriously not known for doing anything for you ever, but go ahead, I suppose."

"Please," Arlo breathed, and Nausicaä sobered as she dipped in close, lips hovering with barely a hair's space between them. "*Please* don't let me forget Final Fantasy. I don't know what I'd do if I lost that extremely core piece of my character."

Groaning over a chuckle, Nausicaä grabbed a pillow to swat Arlo in the face. "You're such a dork. I promise to remind you about your one true love, Cloud Strife, on a regular basis."

"Thank you," she replied grandly, then dissolved into laughter as another *flop* of Nausicaä's pillow came down on her.

Let Ruin try their worst; there was no way Arlo could forget herself enough that *this*—these moments of love and softness and *them*—would ever fail to bring her back from no return.

> *Ah, the satisfaction I will derive,*
> *from proving you so very wrong.*

CHAPTER 1

Aurelian

~⌒~

Florida, Present Day—January

Abump in the road made the back of Aurelian's head smack the metal wall behind him, but it was Ten throwing up the contents of their stomach that made him huff out a curse.

"That's so fucking gross!" Rosalie, the pretty blond lesidhe at Ten's side, whined as she lifted her boots off the ground to save them from the puddle of bile.

Aurelian's footwear hadn't been so lucky.

"M'sorry," Ten groaned, dropping their head between their knees to draw great, gulping breaths and grip the short length of their rainbow-dyed hair like a lifeline. The way their impressive ogre bulk shuddered through waves of nausea told Aurelian they weren't over the worst of it yet. "It's the hells' damned truck—why do we have'ta *drive* everywhere? Couldn't we at least use a normal vehicle?"

Tiffin, the ebony-haired violet goblin seated at the far end of the bench she shared with the quarrelling two beside her, snorted. "Pretty sure the hint's in the name, Ten—*armored truck*. The iron in it protects us."

She didn't look to be faring much better, though.

"It makes me want to claw my fucking guts out."

"Grosser," Rosalie chimed in, and despite how she clearly looked ill right now too, her eyes danced with glee. "Fifty dollars to see you try."

"You can keep your Canadian fucking Tire money, harpy—you only get to fool me once with that," they growled, turning to send a kick in her direction, which made Rosalie cackle even more delight-edly, and Aurelian heaved out a sigh.

It was Ivandril who rose to his feet, however, his silver hair bound in a knot atop his head. A sharp turn in their journey made him place a hand on the roof of the truck they were stuffed in to keep him steady.

Between his enormous height and thick strength—both incon-gruous with the standard for lesidhe builds—Ivandril was almost too big for this space on his own, let alone with the six of Aurelian's team. Aurelian wondered vaguely if there was ogre blood somewhere in his family line to account for that.

"All right, everyone, settle down." Waving his free hand in the direction of the vomit, Ivandril sent a pulse of blue-sparking lesidhe magic dancing over the floor and Aurelian's boots to wash the both of them clean. "None of us *likes* being in this thing, but as we've discussed *many* times before, it's a necessary evil. We're nearly at our destination—we need to focus. Ten," he added, calm and measured, deep and soothing, but by no means lacking command. "Will you be okay to fight or do you need to hang back?"

"Fifty *real* dollars if you vomit on a demon," Rosalie challenged under her breath, a waggle of her brows to add enticement—as though Ten needed encouragement to take their girlfriend up on anything.

"Deal!" Ten cried, not instantly recovered, but certainly far less miserable.

Honestly, the newly minted pair was the oddest couple Aurelian had ever met—and curiously perhaps also the happiest.

Too used to this team by now to pause over any of their antics, Ivandril merely shook his head, then turned his attention to Aurelian.

They'd been busy these past four months, all of them.

Aurelian had been working closely with Ivandril to rebuild the Market; to reinforce its protections; to train anyone who was willing to offer themselves up for combat, and himself in this potential role of leader Celadon seemed determined to place him in. It was a role he still wasn't sure he really wanted. Ivandril would be a far better choice, in his opinion. But Ivandril wanted the job even less, and *someone* had to fill the enormous vacancy the Madam had left in her departure. Between Aurelian's personal relationship with their new Night King, Vehan's magnetism bleeding through their bond, and the efforts he'd been putting into the Market lately, the folk there weren't entirely opposed to the idea of his command.

Four months—Aurelian hardly recognized himself when he looked in the mirror now.

Four months' worth of hard, physical labor and fresh air and the Hiraeth's magic. He was healthier now, stronger now, taller and sturdier and far more powerful. He still kept his hair the same, still maintained its lavender hue. There were still his rebellious iron piercings, and the tattooed sleeve of Autumn foliage running from his fingertips to his shoulder blade. And he would probably never lose his slender, lesidhe build completely to his new lifestyle. He was still Aurelian, and with Vehan here at last beside him, neither of them any longer trapped under Riadne's thumb, he would almost say he was happy.

Hard to be fully happy though, when the world was beginning to unravel.

When a queen gone mad with power was on the rampage, and one of his best friends was caught in her clutches in the precarious balance between life and death.

When the very earth was beginning to crack apart, and the demons had begun to spill out in droves. No longer did they lurk in shadows, yipping and snarling along the fringes of their world, slinking through the Hiraeth for scraps. Now they prowled human streets, night or day, in full view of human witnesses.

"Coming up on the Magic Kingdom. I would remain seated—road quality is poor." Jaxon's quiet, steady voice floated back at them from the driver's seat, where he sat with Leaf—the woodsprite Aurelian had picked up in the forest—perched daintily on his shoulder. Seventeen years old and so pale he was nearly translucent, with short, shaggy gray hair and a wolf's tail and ears, Jaxon was the youngest of Aurelian's personal crew, a boy of very few words and somehow better manners than the rest of them combined.

Ignoring Jaxon's advice, Tiffin and Rosalie both lunged for the divide between the truck's cabin and hull to press their faces to the open grate and goggle in eager anticipation of today's destination.

"I'm surprised you're not up there with them," came a soft voice from Aurelian's right—a voice that could still send a shiver through his system whenever he heard it, even after all these years. A voice he knew just as well as his own, one that he would never grow tired of hearing in all their years to come.

Aurelian's attention snapped to Vehan almost of its own accord.

Like magnetism; like a flower to the sun; except it was something even stronger than nature *or* magic that stole Aurelian's time, affection, and focus so completely.

The soulbond between them—just as months spent in the Hiraeth had made Aurelian stronger, so too had it strengthened the connection between him and his boyfriend. The pair of them finally able to *be* together helped significantly, of course, but to have at last the chance to knowingly, purposefully nurture this incredibly rare gift that tethered them to each other?

It was *this* more than anything that had helped Aurelian to flourish.

Did Vehan have any idea how thoroughly, nearly obsessively Aurelian loved him? Vehan sat slightly folded in his seat, one leg casually over the other and arms crossed against his chest. The way his chin was tucked just so toward his collar meant Aurelian couldn't see his shocking blue eyes but could admire the sight of coal-black bangs brushing that golden-tanned nose.

Vehan sat like the very portrait of a romantic figure in human paintings, a fae prince to the letter. And though his comment had been joking, though his posture suggested perfect ease, there was no fooling that thread that tied them together, and no fooling the years of familiarity between them, as well—there was pain in that tone.

There was pain in *Vehan*, constant.

"Every summer vacation, you always wanted to go to Disney World," he said, looking up at Aurelian.

Did he have *any* idea? It was ridiculous that they'd known each other for so long, that they'd been boyfriends for half a year now and rarely out of each other's sight these last four months, and still those eyes made Aurelian's breath hitch every time their gazes met.

And Vehan whined that *Aurelian* was unfairly pretty.

"Mmm," Aurelian hummed, leaning back once more against the wall and turning his head to close a more private distance between them. "What can I say, it *is* the most magical place on earth."

"You just like when they march Kylo Ren through Star Wars Land."

"I am absolutely certain that's not what they call that section, but all right."

It was almost normal.

Almost Vehan, like nothing was wrong . . .

Except *everything* was wrong.

From the world quickly cracking apart to spew out hell from its depths, to Vehan's own mother as the villain orchestrating the entire thing, to Arlo—*Arlo*, who was Aurelian's friend too, but Vehan *adored* her. She'd brought him back from the damned *dead*, and he loved her like a sister. Every word that Nausicaä had hurled at him four months ago in Toronto had been a knife, and Vehan was the sort who didn't need any encouragement to shoulder failings, even the ones that weren't his.

It had gutted him, tormented him, broken him down to his core to take responsibility for what had happened to Arlo.

He'd cried for days after Nausicaä had left, spent half his time trying to get her back on their side, to make things right between them, and the other half—at least the majority of it—consumed with his mother and Arlo.

Vehan was spiraling, and it terrified Aurelian to *see* the effect this was having on his boyfriend's mood, his health, his sanity.

Vehan, the boy he'd loved from childhood, was *hurting*, and nothing Aurelian tried to do could make it better, it seemed.

A low whistle from Tiffin interrupted their moment. "Oh, the humans are going to have a hell of a time cleaning *this* up."

"Looks like we might be a bit late to the party," Rosalie added, far too mildly for Aurelian's liking.

There was nothing else for it—he had to look too, to gauge what he was about to drag his team into.

Peeling away from the wall once more, Aurelian waved the two faeries back to their seats and took their place at the grate; Ivandril came up beside him—in the front seat, Jaxon huffed out an exasperated, "No one listens to me."

True to word, the roads themselves were terrible.

Great fissures had cracked across the otherwise meticulously maintained pavement, some enough to cause whole chunks to jut up like stone glaciers Jaxon had to swerve around to avoid colliding with.

The more difficult obstacle was the mass exodus of park-goers fleeing Disney World's main attraction as fast as congestion would allow.

Honking and beeping and swearing and shouting filled the air; cars were hopping lanes and veering off right into the grass to get around the bumper-to-bumper stream of vehicles on the road leading out of the park. Some people had abandoned their cars completely in favor of booking it out with their families as fast as they could run, and Aurelian didn't blame them.

"Damn," he swore under his breath, peering through the grate up at the park entrance's iconic MAGIC KINGDOM sign, metal twisted and warped and bent this way and that, half of it severed and smashed against the pavement. "I thought the pit was supposed to be up at the castle? How are we seeing destruction out here?"

Since Ruin's resurrection and Riadne's triumph, the Market's tactical teams had been extremely busy chasing what they called "pits"—

34

by-product portals from the Infernal Realm opening up around the world in result of Riadne's dark magic.

There was no clear pattern behind where these portals chose to open, but the team had gotten good at reading the warning signs that tended to crop up beforehand—spontaneous sinkholes and odd changes in weather and complaints of the scent of gaseous fumes.

Unfortunately, once this collection of signs was reported, it was usually too late to do much besides damage control. Most of the time, their teams couldn't get to these sites before those pits sank enough to bleed demons.

And then there was the matter of what—or rather, *who*—was quick to follow the pits' opening.

"We've got eyes," Jaxon noted, and Aurelian bit back a groan.

The human news teams were here—because of course they were—circling up overhead in their helicopters, peeling down the grass just behind their truck. Which meant the human police force wasn't far behind either.

Four months had given birth to a flurry of articles, television specials, and hashtags; posts and reels and TikToks.

Aliens are real—and the monsters are too!

Lions, Tigers, and Faeries—Oh My!

You Won't Believe Which Legends Are True

A magical community that conformed to order, control, and concealment, they could keep well enough from discovery, but masses of demons popping up from holes in the ground and devouring everything in sight tended to draw just a *bit* of attention.

"So, this is *bad* bad, then," said Tiffin, reaching beneath her seat for a case of weaponry and adding a few more daggers to her supply.

It was *bad* bad, then.

Jaxon, who was suspiciously good at high-tension, fast-speeds driving for someone so young, pressed his foot to the gas and sped them ahead of their tail.

There was no real point to glamours anymore, but they kept one

35

on the truck to prevent unnecessary interruptions. Thus disguised, it sailed through the Magic Kingdom's already decimated entrance toll and wove expertly around both debris and traffic, which had abandoned all rules of the road.

Parking was almost laughably easy once they made it around all the congestion. The news reporters on land and the sirens just behind in the distance would take a little bit longer to catch up. "Let's make this quick," Ivandril said, and Aurelian nodded in agreement.

Doors swung open—Tiffin, Rosalie, Ten, Vehan, Aurelian, and Ivandril jumped one after the other from the back. Jaxon prowled around from the driver's side to join them.

Moving to the front of the group, Aurelian turned and fixed them with a steady look. "You know the drill," he said. "We go in, we take out as many demons as we can neutralize on our way, but our first and main goal is—"

"Hey, Kyle's here! KYLE! HEY!" Rosalie called across the lot, waving joyously at another truck that had just pulled up a short way off.

A rebel group—a few had cropped up here and there across the Courts, made up of folk who didn't like what their new High Queen was doing and had taken it upon themselves to do what the Falchion now ignored at her order.

Kyle was an independent sidhe fae here in the Summer Court, whom they'd run into a few times along with his small team of three.

For reasons best known to her, Rosalie liked him a lot—possibly because he hunted down demons in brightly colored Hawaiian vacay shirts with a massive hot-pink crossbow and heavy metal blaring from his iPhone like a soundtrack.

Kyle pretended to shoot his crossbow in Rosalie's direction, winked at Aurelian, then proceeded to unload an absolutely massive contraption that looked a lot like a shoulder cannon.

"I feel underprepared now," Rosalie huffed. "Kyle has a . . . rocket launcher? I want a rocket launcher."

"I want one too," Ten agreed, nodding fervently, and Aurelian sighed through his nose. "Focus," he reminded them. "Our first and main goal is to locate that pit in there and contain the situation as best as possible. We'll give Arlo ten minutes on arrival to show—if she doesn't, I want that pit sealed. And I have a feeling it's going to need everything we brought if the fissures ran all the way out to the main gate, so don't pack light."

Sealing pits was the Market's specialty, the thing that set them apart from the independent rebel groups. It involved a very complicated alchemic concoction that Rory Flamel had designed for them that was essentially a grenade filled with a liquid that would expand and solidify into six-feet-deep solid iron.

It wasn't a perfection solution, but they didn't have running communication with Arlo these days. The pits she showed up at, she sealed on her own once she was done with them, but they never had any warning which pits those would actually be. Rory's grenade was enough of a deterrent for the demons to find a different entry point, and that was just about the best they could hope for right now.

"Everyone armed?" Ivandril inquired, to a round of grunts and nods and *you bet, handsome*. "All right, then. Aurelian, on your signal—"

"Let's go rescue Disney World!" Rosalie whooped like a battle cry before turning to run for the park entrance.

Ten took off after her, their massive axe held aloft as they screamed their way to the entrance as well.

Aurelian's team.

They could . . . use with a bit more training, really; a little more deference to leadership, maybe; a little more practice fighting as a *unit*, for sure. But then, most of the folk tended to forget themselves when it came to this theme park, so Aurelian could only shake his head and follow.

At least they didn't want for enthusiasm, and he had a feeling they were going to need a lot of that too, tonight.

"This has to be the weirdest fucking mash-up of vibes I've ever experienced," Tiffin commented as the group of them pressed through the ticket booths for the Magic Kingdom's main courtyard.

He had to agree.

There was still a decent amount of people fleeing in terror around them. Cast members were armed with all manner of objects for self-defense, screams and cries and curses coming from all of them. It explained why they hadn't run into any demons until this point, not with so much enticement to keep them right here. But Ivandril let out a low whistle, and Aurelian could only gawk—the sheer *number* of them. Humanoid creatures of rotted flesh and fungi and pustules, skittering around, shrieking high-pitched, shrill sounds as they chased down anything that moved to rip and tear and break it apart, gorging themselves on the gore.

Blood splattered garishly across the smooth pavement.

The demons that weren't busy feasting were climbing, roaming, and wreaking general destruction on their surroundings.

Several fires had erupted here and there, spewing smoke into the air, all of this to an ambience of cheerful Disney music, with a backdrop of pastel pinks and yellows and greens, stylized storefronts waving their American flags and their Mickey Mouse banners and winter holiday decor.

Center to it all, off in the distance, was the iconic Cinderella Castle against a cotton-candy sunset.

It was Rosalie's heave of a roar that broke Aurelian from his stupor, drawing his attention to his right, where she'd aimed a powerful blow at a group of demons cracking limbs off a man like a roasted chicken. The massive hammer she carried strapped to her back glinted as it swung through the air, big enough that one worried she'd topple over.

"Three for me!" she crowed.

"The castle!" Aurelian growled, shaking himself out of his head to resume command of the party. "We get to the pit—that's our only priority right now. *Get to the pit!*"

And get to the pit they tried.

This was so much more than Aurelian had been anticipating.

So much more destruction, more danger, more *demons*—they'd never contended with something on this scale before.

Rosalie and Ten weren't the only ones to get waylaid by distraction. It was impossible to make it even a few steps without a demon or five bursting out through broken shopwindows, lunging from meals they were only half through, all rotten teeth and blackened claws outstretched for the kill, clicking and screeching and snapping and crunching.

From the depths of a candy shop off to Aurelian's right, a demon tore from the wreckage.

Swift and hurtling directly for him, it advanced in the *sliver* of Aurelian's blind spot.

Too busy dealing with two other demons that had decided they'd rather a fresh kill than the one they'd been working on, this third he noticed only in time enough to turn . . .

But was saved by a thunderous *crack* that seared the air, shaking through the very earth below his feet.

An enormous bolt shot from Aurelian's periphery, and in an instant, the demon was a scorched silhouette on the pavement.

Nothing but dust.

"Your boyfriend's really fucking scary, Rel," Ten hollered across the street, but that was definitely praise in their voice, along with a little bit of awe.

Damn if they weren't absolutely correct, though.

With no time to spare save the quick kiss he blew Aurelian on the way by, Vehan streaked past him, already pulling more stored-up electricity from a core that was at *least* a level higher than the Three he'd been classified as on his exam.

Four months in the Hiraeth.

Four months of training—proper training, not the torture Aurelian was horrified to learn Riadne had been putting her youngest son through on a daily basis back when they'd been separated.

Four months of a die Vehan was quite good at utilizing, almost as though he was always meant to have it—a Class Four lightning wielder, possibly Five, with a tool that allowed him to exceed even those bounds? Yes, Aurelian was *very* glad it was their side his prince fought for.

Especially today.

The spill of demons here seemed endless, grew more concentrated the closer they managed to advance on the castle.

Main Street, U.S.A. felt like an endless gauntlet, where they swung their swords, their fists, their lightning, their weapons, and for every demon they felled, three more crawled out of the woodwork to attack them.

BOOM.

Aurelian cast a wild look over his shoulder behind them . . .

And caught a burst of streaming fire—Kyle's team tended for hard and heavy hits, with things like their launchers and flamethrowers and bundles of dynamite. It made a mess, but it was usually effective. Today, though, even all that didn't seem to be making much of a difference.

"The flare!" Ivandril shouted over the curved dagger he pulled from a demon's throat. It crumpled to the ground at his feet and was instantly replaced by two more. "Aurelian, send up the flare!"

The flare—right. Aurelian should have thought of that first, should have already sent it up, to be honest. He'd been so absorbed in trying to keep his party alive, *himself* alive, that he'd forgotten protocol.

Another of Rory's inventions, the flare shot red light up into the air, burning like a dying star, and would immediately signal to the others that monitored each mission to send reinforcements.

A precaution, really. Aurelian's team was one of the best they had. They never needed the waiting assistance, and smaller parties meant less human attention drawn where they didn't need it.

But Ivandril was right.

This was *bad.*

The demons didn't usually pour from the pit in these numbers. They didn't usually attack faster than Aurelian and his team could cut them down.

He reached into his pocket, pulled out the crystal vial of blazing red light, and was just about to dash it on the pavement to release their beacon when—

"AURELIAN, BEHIND YOU!"

The bolt of lightning came too slow.

Rosalie's hammer flew through vacant space where a demon's head had just been.

Both Jaxon's and Tiffin's daggers sailed and missed, embedded in the tree beside him.

Aurelian lifted a hand—blue sparking magic formed a humming shield that caught only just in time the demon that had lunged for him, knocking him flat to his back.

Normally, lesidhe magic—connected as it was to the soul—would have burned the demon enough to deter it, but this one was set on its prey.

It gnawed on the shield, snarled and shrieked and clawed around it, swinging wildly.

A hefty thing too—this demon was bigger, solid muscle pinning Aurelian to the ground, its claws caught his arm.

Aurelian drew on the bond between him and Vehan; his shield began to crackle, to charge with his boyfriend's channeled electricity, the humming now an angry agitation that spit errant tendrils of sparks.

Aurelian aimed a blow around the shield, and though it connected, though it had been backed by lesidhe strength and months of training . . . the demon didn't budge. It barely seemed to register the electrified shield *or* being struck at all.

"AURELIAN!" Vehan yelled in warning.

When Aurelian looked, Vehan was already forming another sizzling electric bolt in his hand.

Aurelian pressed himself as close to the ground as possible and sent a quick prayer up to any god that was feeling generous that Vehan wasn't about to scorch him to dust in collateral, another that those teeth didn't snap through his shield entirely . . .

. . . so close . . .

. . . just one more crunch and it . . .

The demon stopped.

It paused, almost comically, blinking down at him. Gradually, it closed its mouth. It lifted its head to scent the air—and just like that . . . it disintegrated, Vehan's electricity raining the demon down on Aurelian as ash.

Carefully, Aurelian pushed himself to sitting and looked around.

A moment ticked by . . . followed by two. . . . All around them the demons began to stop what they were doing and lift their heads as though in consideration of something even Aurelian's senses couldn't pick up.

The park wore down to sounds of crackling flame and ambient music, the scattered moans of the wounded and dying . . .

An absolute standstill—

Then the demons began to shudder.

Began to whimper, to keen, to cower.

One after the other after the other after the other, the hordes of them began to yield, to tuck themselves up almost apologetically and slink back to the pit they came through.

Instantly, Aurelian's veins filled with ice.

He looked first to Vehan, whose eyes had grown wide with a mixture of anticipation and dread. "Rel," Vehan whispered—they knew what this was.

Demons acted like this only around one particular presence.

A presence that hadn't been a threat to them in the beginning, even if her *cohort* made everything so much more difficult than it needed to be. But four months had changed quite a lot for them *all*. Aurelian, Vehan, their bond, his team—all had become so much stronger in this short span of time . . . including the monster that grew inside their girl.

Drawing a breath, Aurelian pushed himself up to standing, about to issue an order for a tactical retreat to the sidelines. Sometimes it was Arlo that turned up in control, and things were . . . fairly depressing, because Arlo was *very* far from okay these days, but her petrifying detachment was vastly preferable to the alternative . . .

To the *thing* she was rapidly devolving into and remaining for longer stretches of time . . .

He opened his mouth—

And that was when Aurelian heard it: the distinct sound of metal scraping through pavement.

A blade being dragged behind the sauntered steps heralded the promise that events were about to go from dangerous to viciously ugly.

"Well, well, well. If it isn't Weather Boy and Grumpy."

CHAPTER 2

Celadon

~~~~~~

THE BOLT OF ELECTRICITY to Celadon's chest was a charge so powerful it hurled him airborne on contact. Painfully, he collided with a nearby pillar, the force of which caused great cracks to spider across its width.

"Phenomenal," Lethe mocked, not far to his right, as he no more than threw out an arm to dash aside the bolt sent in *his* direction. "A bevy of elements at your disposal, and you choose instead to shield with your flesh."

It took a moment for Celadon to pull himself out of shock and channel from his system a current that would have been lethal had it hit anyone else.

"You're right," he growled under his breath as he shakily, stiffly peeled himself off the stone. "What a silly decision I made for the hells of it that wasn't at all imposed on me by necessity."

Chunks of the pillar rained down on him in crumbles.

Lethe issued a sound like a snarl.

Before any more words could be traded on the matter though, another searing bolt flew in Celadon's direction, so quickly he had no other option but to duck for an embarrassingly narrow miss.

"DEFEND YOURSELF!"

"THAT *WAS* DEFENSE! HENCE WHY I'M STILL ALIVE!"

Gods—Lethe was miserable to be with in combat. Or rather, he was miserable when it came to being in combat with *Celadon*.

Four months they'd been training together, Lethe putting Celadon through paces even the best on his guard had failed to keep up with— just Lethe and him darting around the private arena he'd once trained in with his father, hurling all manner of offense at each other.

The elements he'd inherited from his lineage—wind and electricity, ice and earth—coupled with the boosts to his power as the king of a Court, the offspring of two formidable sovereigns, and not least of all his previous life spent as the Moon Celestial, he had quite the repertoire to pull from.

Four months of Lethe pushing him to his very limits, and Celadon felt he could safely claim he'd more than proved his capability to his . . . well, Lethe recoiled to be labeled "boyfriend," but woe to the person who mistook that position in Celadon's life for vacant.

Regardless, Celadon was far from green and frail.

But Lethe, too unused to actually caring about anyone's welfare but his own, was surprisingly quick to agitation the moment Celadon was in even a *hint* of danger.

To be fair though, Celadon had to agree that right now it was warranted; they were clearly in over their heads—or rather, again, that was only Celadon.

Lethe was faring just fine.

Another bolt—Celadon rolled in a skillful maneuver to the side, throwing out a hand as he went, to crystalize the moisture in the air and pull that ice into an encasing shield.

"Better."

As though Lethe were incensed by this defiance, five more bolts shot in quick succession at him, and almost as soon as he'd conjured it, Celadon's shield was shattered to shards.

"Lethe, this is—"

A sixth bolt then, this one smaller but no less painful as it sliced his arm like a blade.

Groaning out, Celadon clasped his bleeding upper arm.

"End simulation!" Lethe snapped out angrily, and Celadon fell back to his hands and knees in relief.

A flutter pulsed through the image of their battleground: the ruins of some ancient Greek temple on a cliff that jutted out over the sea. A place Lethe told Celadon he'd once spent his time long ago between battles—before his captors had taken to locking him up—sitting and chatting with *him*, back when Celadon had been the Moon.

On the second pulse through their arena, the image began to disintegrate, falling away like shimmering dust that vanished before it hit the black-tiled floor.

Panting, Celadon lifted his head to watch as his boyfriend prowled toward him from his side of the room, the cavernous expanse of floor-to-ceiling pure obsidian in which Azurean had privately trained Celadon in his childhood.

His gaze caught on their fading opponent.

Riadne stood in the center of the room, radiant as reality, a cutting force to behold.

Her long black hair—the perfect match to the color Celadon had dyed his in a petty but definite gesture to claim this mirror image he was of his mother as his own—blazed even darker than her surroundings. Her electric-ice eyes were so blue, Celadon felt chilled to the bone under their piercing watch.

What did it say about his mother that there seemed little difference anymore between her living figure and this illusion glaring soullessly at him as it too dwindled to dust?

"Every time."

Celadon's gaze returned to Lethe, who now stood before him with a hand outstretched, his expression livid. "Every time you let her best you—*why?*"

Placing his hand in the one offered, Celadon allowed Lethe to heave him back up off the ground. "I didn't *let* her do anything. What level did you set this scenario to? It was all I could do not to die, Lethe. I barely had time to—"

Something flexed across Lethe's features that could have been worry or could have been nothing for how quickly it sank back below his surface.

"The level is immaterial," he snapped on recovery, a touch defensive. "I could set every parameter to its maximum output and *still* it would fail to accurately match what we're going to have to soon face out in the real world, where I cannot save you from your hesitation with a simple command."

There—the crux of Lethe's constant agitation.

He was afraid for Celadon's life.

He was afraid, because *Celadon* was afraid. It was one thing to pull together a Court from scraps of his deposed father's rule; one thing to win three of the six other Courts to his ambitions; one thing to manipulate strings and send out teams to thwart enemy advances; one thing to declare war on his mother—and another thing entirely to strike her directly with the intention to kill.

Celadon had already lost two parents to Riadne's cursed war.

Barely months ago, he'd lit his father's and adoptive mother's bodies on a makeshift funeral pyre and returned his family to Night. Despite all she'd done, all he'd been working toward since the Summer Solstice that changed everything, Celadon still hesitated *every time* he confronted Riadne in simulation.

Simply because . . . that was his *mother*.

One that actually loved him, beneath layers of madness and twisted intentions and no small amount of generational trauma.

"Celadon."

Gentler now—Lethe's cool, still-water voice was pitched in an intimacy reserved just for Celadon.

It never failed to make Celadon shiver to hear his name spoken like this, like this man who cared for seemingly nothing would set whole worlds on fire for him.

Celadon looked up from where his gaze had dropped to his feet, the feather touch of Lethe's long fingers beneath his chin to guide the way.

Four months together.

Celadon didn't recall the lifetime they'd first shared. Part of the conditions of being reborn was that everything before was forgotten.

He didn't remember his time spent as the Moon Celestial—the greatest honor for a fae whose power was aligned with the night—but the way this bond inside him sang with every touch now . . .

It made his breath catch in his chest to know that because of this invisible tether, they'd find each other in every life to come.

Lethe was his.

And Celadon was very much Lethe's in return, he was beginning to realize more and more every day.

The expression on Lethe's face had gentled too, to match his tone, and Celadon couldn't help the swell of fondness that made a smile curl a corner of his mouth.

"*Thousands* of years it took for you to return to me, Fate so angry with my defiance, my choosing to keep half of Luck's power and claim my birthright as Misfortune, that she held on to *you* as punishment." Lethe's voice had grown whisper quiet, his head bowed slightly so that their noses were a mere breath apart and Celadon could almost feel his words against his lips as they were formed. "I don't know what happened to steal you from her clutches after so long, but she is even more furious for that. Very clearly, given the number of times she's tried to reclaim you, she did not *intend* to give you back." He sighed and dropped his forehead to touch Celadon's, eyes fluttering shut.

Celadon's closed as well, and for a moment, they simply breathed.

"Names no longer record themselves in my Book of Death, Celadon," Lethe resumed a few beats later, though his eyes remained closed, as though it made this part easier for him to confess. "I am at once still Hunter and . . . not. Until my godhood is officially recognized, not only do we have no means of destroying the philosopher's stones without Ruin, but we have only what the other Hunters are willing to risk to keep Fate from stealing you back from me."

He'd explained as much countless times before, whenever something Celadon did frightened him.

Lethe had angered Fate in refusing to return the power he'd been loaned all those years ago when he'd sunk Atlantis and revenged himself on its king. She'd kept Celadon from rebirth for as long as she could without suffering punishment of her own—thousands of years, she'd held on to her grudge, and now she was even more furious with Lethe for abusing his role as a Hunter to strike Celadon's name from the Books of Death, Fate's numerous attempts to reclaim him.

How Celadon felt about being caught between two immortals' ire aside, Lethe was under constant stress now—one of many downsides to what Arlo had chosen to do. Lethe was technically no longer a Hunter, but Arlo wasn't one yet; neither had access to a Book of Death to continue prolonging Celadon's life.

They were both, therefore, relying on Arlo for *many* reasons to pull through with her plan as quickly as possible. As a recognized, unclaimed immortal, the moment she died (if they could manage to ensure death before Ruin erased her soul), if she chose to throw her support behind Lethe—for all immortals had to choose an alliance, Lethe had informed Celadon—it was all the backing he'd need to earn his own status, regardless of what the other deities wished. After all, Lethe was the offspring of a Titan, so with Arlo's help, Lethe would become a Greater God to match Urielle and Cosmin and Tellis in might.

And once Lethe ascended to his Greater Godhood, he'd be able to dole out immortality to anyone he chose—to Celadon, for instance.

Without that godhood, though . . .

"You have to fight back," Lethe continued, his eyes snapping open now, and Celadon's, too, at the steel in his voice. "You're no longer a Celestial, no longer immortal: all the honor of having once been one, but none of the protection that role previously afforded. You cannot give Fate or Riadne or *anyone* such fatal openings by *not fighting back.*"

"I know," Celadon sighed, his irritation relenting. "I *know*, Lethe."

So much stress—he really did feel bad for his partner.

And for himself.

Their current predicament inspired what Celadon was going to generously label as "protectiveness" in Lethe, to an extremely vicious degree. One had better luck now in catching a unicorn than coming within arm's length of Celadon without Lethe imposing himself between.

Reaching a hand up, Celadon placed his palm on Lethe's cheek, far warmer than that frigidly pale skin looked. "It's going to be okay," he said, trying to soothe. "I—"

His reassurance was interrupted.

Across the way, the heavy obsidian doors swung open, and the *click* of Theodore Reynolds's heeled boots echoed sonorously on his entrance.

"So you *do* come down here just to make out with each other," he said by way of greeting, the words wrapped in a playful drawl. "There's that bet lost. And to think I really thought better of you two."

Fyri, the ironborn faerie girl coming in beside him, shook her head with a roll of her eyes.

The *look* Lethe cut Theodore for the comment—Celadon wanted to laugh, but unease bloomed like mold in his chest, spreading faster than humor could contend with.

If Theodore and Fyri both were here, it wasn't just to pop by for casual conversation. Everyone knew he and Lethe weren't to be disturbed in their training sessions.

With Riadne having exiled Theodore to the Wild for his role in aiding the Madam's attempt to overthrow her and helping to hide the ironborn children she'd experimented on—Marked, in further punishment, as her Hunt's quarry—the only way he could set foot in the Courts without attracting immediate death was by keeping to Celadon's domain.

Independent to Riadne's rule, so long as he kept to what was formerly known as Spring's territory, now the Night Court, Theodore and his family could live in relative freedom and safety.

And their conversation back in the Market—after Celadon and Vehan had rescued Theodore and Aurelian and their respective families, and they'd made their escape through Riadne's Egress—when Theodore had confided in him his genuine desire to assume the role of king of the Day Court in Celadon's new world order . . . Celadon hadn't lied back then. Theodore *would* make a good fit for the job, especially if Vehan preferred standing at Aurelian's side as ambassador for the Wild.

So many cogs in motion—it did get a little overwhelming at times, for Celadon to keep track of it all.

Regardless, Theodore was best kept here.

And when Theodore wasn't indulging his expensive tastes by raiding Celadon's wardrobe—as apparently he'd done this morning; those gold-brocade boots and that bloodred blazer were definitely familiar— he was working with Fyri, the rather impressive ironborn in training with Rory, whom Arlo had recommended as ambassador of *their* community. The pair of them served as Celadon's points of contact when he couldn't personally check in with Aurelian and Vehan.

"What is it?" Celadon inquired, stepping out of Lethe's space and toward the advancing party. "What's wrong?"

Theodore grimaced, dropping his playful facade.

The mold of Celadon's unease grew thicker.

"Well, good news and bad news," he replied, coming to a halt a Lethe-approved distance away. "I won't ask which you'd like first—it's the same answer, regardless: Ruin's made an appearance again."

Finally.

"Confirmed?"

Theodore nodded. "Confirmed. It's the real deal. Whatever she's been doing for the past few weeks, she's back on the radar. It only took a mass-scale demon attack on Disney World to draw her out. . . ."

After they'd left the Viridian Circle and regrouped in the Night Palace's medical wing four months ago, Lethe had explained everything as best as he could, how Arlo had challenged and defeated him in combat, winning back her memories from him. Celadon— who'd been curiously immune to Lethe's Gift, thanks most likely to *his* Gift of drawing out secrets of the mind—had never forgotten who Arlo and her father truly were, though he hadn't known she'd summoned the scions of the Primordial Ones, the End and Beginning.

Lethe, Celadon, and his father, Azurean, had been the only three people in mortal existence who knew that Flamels had lived on. After the events just last spring, when Arlo had returned from that fateful café where she'd witnessed that ironborn girl's death, he'd done digging only his unique position could afford him and had learned every bit he could of the Flamels' whole sordid history, which the Fae High Council, to suit their aims, had manipulated so far from the truth it was barely recognizable.

What he hadn't known was the deal Rory had struck with Lethe when Arlo had been just a girl.

No more than eight years old, Arlo had managed alchemy beyond what any other alchemist could probably dream of: she'd opened a portal directly into the prison of the oldest immortals in existence.

Moros and Eos had been the ones to charge her with the task of destroying the Crowns the Great Three had made out of the End's and Beginning's bones.

Terrified for his daughter, that this would put her in even greater peril than she already was as a Flamel under Court supervision, Rory devised a plan.

They would go to the High King and request a mind wipe for both him and Arlo. Claiming that Rory was tired of them having to live their lives like criminals, he and his daughter would submit all memory that they were the last Flamels.

An extreme measure, perhaps, but it would lessen the scrutiny they were under, the careful watch that Azurean and his father had both been tasked with keeping over the family. It would turn attention away from Arlo, and no one would be given incentive to pry into what she could do, all in a way that wouldn't draw suspicion that there was something they were hiding in doing this, should they simply have Lethe perform the wipe on his own.

The High King had been all too happy to agree, had been perhaps hop-

ing for this, Lethe surmised. He'd ordered his immediate compliance—
and here Lethe took great pride in his Gift:

*"But according to my deal with Rory, I was to only pretend to wipe
Arlo's memories, as I'd done for the whole of this realm save the Flamels
themselves, and you and your father. Rory wanted them locked away only
until Arlo was old enough that she could choose for herself whether or
not she wanted to forget them entirely. When it came time to perform the
wipe in front of Azurean, it was actually Thalo's memories I pulled and
bottled and submitted for his council's keeping. Your father, so grievously
dulled by that Crown he wore, had no idea of my duplicity; he merely
thought Thalo a very good actor, afterward, for the sake of her husband
and daughter. The deterioration of their marriage and resulting divorce
was an unfortunate side effect of having so much of their shared history
altered, which I did feel a modicum of . . . well, let's not say 'guilt,' but
perhaps maybe regret. The Flamels had always been oddly . . . welcoming
to me. Thalo would have made an excellent Hunter."*

Now, with Arlo's memories unsealed to her, with her claiming
them and returning knowledge of the Flamels to the world, she'd
remembered the task she'd been set as a child.

Had taken it up, in addition to their preestablished plot to kill her
while she harbored Ruin before Ruin could usurp her soul.

"With Ruin," Lethe had continued explaining, *"she'll be able to jump
between realms, so to speak, to reach the rest of the Primordial Crowns."*

But using Ruin's powers was costly.

It took a great deal out of Arlo whenever she accessed them for
her own use.

In an effort to preserve herself as long as possible, she'd come up
with the rather ingenious plan to use the *demon portals* to her advantage. The portals were already a weak point in the barrier keeping the
realms separate, so she would have to use Ruin's power and expend her
energy only in surviving the journey.

The problem was—well, manyfold.

They'd had precisely *one* decent conversation with Nausicaä and

Arlo in order to lay this all out the first time their paths crossed at a demon pit that opened shortly after she'd taken on Ruin. Arlo had informed them what she needed to do and what she needed from *them*, in support of this.

It was more than just finding a way in that Arlo was after—she was to use Ruin's power to completely obliterate the Crowns, not merely break them, and to find them, she needed the *right* way in.

These rifts between the realms opened up in random places, on both ends, and since time spent in the Immortal Realm wore so greatly on her mortal soul—the Arlo part of her they very much needed to keep alive—she had to locate one that would let her out as close to the Crowns as possible.

As close to Urielle and Tellis as she could get.

It was a lot of trial and error.

A lot of convalescence in between the jumps, which might be the reason for her two weeks' absence before today.

Celadon was determined to be ready at each one she attempted, and he would support what she felt she needed to do before making good on their original plan.

But if she started showing serious signs of fading—if the ember of Arlo's soul began to cool and dim to coal to the point of no return—he had to be ready to act, to run her through with the goddess-blessed sword and send her on to immortality and Ruin back to their cage, regardless of how many Crowns she'd managed to destroy.

It had to be Celadon.

For many reasons.

But also for the fact that the sword Arlo had left them, Thalo's blade enchanted by Mab herself, responded best to her Viridian bloodline—a very dwindled thing, these days.

"How much time has passed since report of this sighting?" Celadon asked, already beginning to stride for the arena's exit.

They had to hurry. Arlo might be on their side, but the entity she shared her body with called some shots for them as well. Ruin wasn't half as accommodating to their plans, and four months of constantly wrestling control from them had begun to accumulate in visible ways.

More and more, the person Celadon met at these portals was less and less his cousin.

Darting to catch up to his side, Theodore replied, "Practically none. Aurelian called it in as soon as the Dark Star showed up on the scene. Ruin's only just arrived."

"Perfect. All right, let's move."

Lethe was in luck—between Ruin and demons and Nausicaä too . . . Celadon without a doubt would have opportunity yet to impress him with *shielding*.

CHAPTER 3

Ruin

HOW LOVELY IT WAS to be free of their cage, to stand at last on mortal soil—this paradisiacal war zone of pollution and bloodlust, corruption and greed—among creatures who needed so little encouragement to answer the call to *destruction*.

A minor setback, that this body's soul had refused to cleave in twain upon their summoning, had yet to yield to their occupation even now.

Yoked together as they were, their passions were dampened and hungers starved. How Ruin *longed* for true autonomy: to unleash themselves fully on all this realm had to offer, all it had to break and crumble and fall like worship at their altar.

But it wouldn't be for much longer.

Ruin would win in the end—Ruin *was* the end, inevitable.

And if they had to be forced into the company of any of this world's denizens, Ruin was at least . . . pleased that it should be the first being to have drawn their attention here, that blink of an eon ago. *How lovely it was*, to be

reunited

with

Arlo felt her muscles seize, a chill run through her veins, that familiar wash of nausea that gripped her each time she managed to wrest back control of herself from Ruin. The mortal body wasn't meant to sustain two different souls, let alone ones as powerful as hers and Ruin's.

Not for the first time, Arlo felt a pang of regret for the path she'd chosen to take.

When she wasn't fighting against her own flesh, determined to purge whichever soul it could manage to expel first, she was fighting to hold on to her own sanity, her mind, her passions and desires and morals and goals. Her heart. All the things that made Arlo *her* were beginning to . . . fade a little.

Dulling around the edges.

Care by care, characteristic by characteristic, things were falling away and would continue to do so until eventually they were gone altogether, and then Arlo Flamel would be gone as well.

It was a balancing act that required pinpoint focus to keep evenly aloft. Arlo had to destroy the Crowns—all three of them, complete obliteration. She had to keep enough of herself alive so that Celadon could be the one to end *her* and, in so doing, banish Ruin back to their infernal prison. She had to both court and grow Ruin's power with "dedications" of destruction, which Nausicaä was more than happy to help with, all while maintaining control and the constant fight for dominance, never letting Ruin in command for too long so that she could protect the world and the people she cared about from their devastation. At the same time, she had to make sure she rested, kept up her strength to keep up *her* . . .

At least you have your Dark Star's company to
boost your morale . . .

Arlo frowned.

It was a strange sensation, to have a voice that wasn't her own in her head—and still just as grossly uncomfortable as it had been in the beginning. Ruin was cast to the back of her mind, like she was when Ruin held her body's reins, and their words bobbed up from the depths like rotted apples in a barrel of murky water—along with their wry amusement.

"Well, well, well, if it isn't Weather Boy and Grumpy."

"If it isn't the Dark Star."

"Nausicaä—!"

"*Piss off*, Prince Lysterne."

"*Hey*. You don't get to talk to him like that. Pull yourself the fuck together, Nausicaä. None of this is Vehan's fault and you know it. If it's anyone's, it's *yours*—"

Arlo sighed.

> *So much friction, such delicious frustration—*
> *all these pent-up destructive emotions*
> *in so fragile a vessel . . .*
> *Delightful. Is this what calls you mortals to friendship?*
> *I think I might now understand the appeal.*

Shut up, she pressed back in her mind, and stepped out of the shattered souvenir shop they'd portaled to from the Luminous Palace, onto Disney's Main Street, U.S.A.

Nausicaä was on her in an instant.

"Red—"

Arlo held up a hand to halt her, a pulse of magic radiating outward to physically stop Nausicaä in her tracks.

The more Arlo fed Ruin's power, the more they were able to do. And the more Ruin, as an amalgamation of the Seven Sins, could do, the more *Arlo* was able to do. A whole host of things Arlo could perform now, things that gave her an unfair advantage in any battle, things that would affect even her ex-Fury girlfriend.

That was another of those strange sensations: to care about Nausicaä so deeply that she didn't want her anywhere near this danger. At the same time, Nausicaä was deeply necessary to ensuring Arlo could achieve her goals—no one but Ruin themselves was better at causing destruction and chaos than the *Dark Star*.

As Arlo's cohort of sorts, and again, a very dedicated patron of their altar, Ruin was content to allow Nausicaä free rein around them.

They allowed her to follow where they went like a lethal shadow whenever they left Riadne's cage, shielded and aided them during confrontations. On the one hand, this meant Arlo had to exert herself a little less, save a bit of energy for other things not conducive to Ruin's ultimate goals, but on the other hand . . . just as Nausicaä saved *Arlo's* energy, so too did her help mean Ruin could spend more of themselves on *acclimatizing*.

The more they grew their power, the stronger Ruin became as well, and the harder it was to shove them back from control.

Such a fine and fragile line they walked . . . and Ruin's mercurial nature meant that their mood could change in an instant. It was one of the greatest fears Arlo could still feel that made her worry that as soon as they felt Nausicaä more trouble than she was worth, they would easily do away with her. She might be unraveling rather noticeably these days, but Arlo was still herself at her core; she still cared about what happened to her girlfriend.

But half of her belonged to someone else now, which meant half her capacity for emotion did too. And when that someone else felt, at worst the all-consuming craving for blood and obliteration, and at best the sort of cruel bemusement that led them to pick the wings off butterflies just to watch them writhe in pain . . .

Arlo *was still her*, but everything just felt so much . . . less.

And what frightened her most of all was that there was no telling when the switch would flip, and she would become a new version of herself who *didn't* care if Nausicaä, or Vehan, or Aurelian, or anyone she knew and loved became collateral.

Idly, she wondered if this was a bit how Nausicaä had felt back when she'd given her heart up to Riadne and Lust in order to keep Arlo safe.

"You know I hate when you do that," Nausicaä growled, struggling against invisible restraints, her mouth pressing into a flat line.

There were many other things she clearly wanted to say, opinions that danced in her silver-blade eyes.

She didn't like when Arlo used this magic against her, no, but often didn't fight it with any sincerity. Nausicaä didn't want to risk upsetting Ruin either, though less out of self-preservation, Arlo suspected, and more because she didn't want Ruin to deem her *uncooperative* and force her away.

A flex of anger fluttered across Nausicaä's face as she clamped down on her instincts—then, slowly but surely, she relaxed.

Only then did Arlo release her.

Come now, you can't deny how good that feels . . .
To have such control over something so raw and
powerful as a Fury.

I said shut up.

Arlo pressed forward.

She met Aurelian's gaze—the fire in those golden eyes, the war of defiance and pity. Aurelian never refused an opportunity to challenge Ruin in any way he could. For her? She and Aurelian were friends, and she'd liked him well enough, but did he truly feel such offense for what had happened to *her*? More, she suspected, his anger at Ruin was on Vehan's behalf.

Vehan Lysterne . . . the boy she'd brought back from death, the soul she'd held in her own, an intimacy and violation both. And for that, Vehan was somehow more than a friend, more than family.

He was . . . honestly, if Arlo had to put it to words, Vehan felt a bit like herself in another body now.

"Arlo."

Arms wrapped an embrace around her shoulders from behind. The sudden *slam* of a body against her would have caused the Arlo of before to stumble. Now she could feel it before it even happened, like a premonition.

Still . . . she paused.

Just a moment . . . a flicker of *her* flared just a moment, long enough for her to reach up a hand and place it over the fold of his arms.

". . . Vehan," she echoed back.

An inhale of breath—a shakier exhale.

"You're getting thin."

"Ruin doesn't have much of a palate for food."

Gently, she pried him off her.

It was unbearable, sometimes, how much she missed her friends. Especially since she never felt more herself than she did when she was around them.

Nausicaä hovered on Arlo's periphery, and sometimes she dared getting close when Ruin was in their weaker moments and didn't have it in them to threaten or ward her off. When Arlo was in her stronger moments, rested and able to pull more of *her* to the fore, they'd sit and chat like nothing had changed . . . until Arlo couldn't ignore the devastation that lurked behind those piercing eyes, the panic, the rage . . .

Until Nausicaä could no longer put on her act like nothing was wrong . . . like Arlo wasn't standing on a pinprick precipice, and any way she fell would cost her everything.

She wished so badly this task hadn't fallen to her.

That she didn't share memories with the darkest of Titans and, because of this, could look so far back into their past that she knew exactly why the task *had* fallen to her.

All the way back, to the very first Arlo.

To responsibility . . . *pride* . . .

Ruin chuckled in her head.

Always your forte, that.

She had to press on.

There was no time for ruminating on the past, on what she could and would have done differently, if different had been an actual option.

She couldn't linger—it had taken so long for her to recover from their last jaunt to the Immortal Realm, and a pit this size, demon activity at this intensity . . . if this wasn't what she'd been looking for, it at least had to be close.

The more time she spent trading feelings with friends, the less time she had in control.

Turning from Aurelian and Vehan, she made for the rift between realms, any demon too frozen in fear of her to have fled before her arrival now skittering out of her way, clearing her path.

> *Are you certain you wish to give this up?*
> *The things that bow to us, cower at our feet . . .*
> *does it not feel good*
> *after a lifetime of disrespect?*

What she sought was just ahead, in the center of the courtyard where park-goers could gather and watch the shows performed on the stage right in front of Cinderella's Castle.

A trill of something like relief sped through her—she'd almost made it; the rift was just right there. A few more strides and, regardless of where this portal let out on the other side, she might be able to count this the most successful mission yet.

No casualties by her hand, nothing to draw Ruin into play, her friends all safe and sound behind her—

"HEY!"

Arlo's head snapped to the side.

She had just enough time to spot one of the mercs from the independent rebel squad—someone new, she noted. Bright pink hair, ogre tusks, a faerie girl Arlo didn't know, beside a young sidhe man she'd heard the others call Kyle.

"This is for my brother, you bitch."

Her brother?

Who?

Arlo had no idea, but she could guess—the faerie girl's brother must have been someone who'd fallen prey to Ruin's bloody appetites at some point in the last four months; the reason she kept herself back from her friends despite the good they did her. Arlo sympathized, truly, felt every degree of guilt possible, but that was a *rocket launcher* the girl held aloft over her shoulder, aimed directly at Arlo's head. . . .

"*No,*" she gasped, urged, begged.

"NO!" Nausicaä shouted from behind her, because she knew.

This was the one sure way to draw *them* out . . . No one made threats against Ruin and lived.

The faerie girl ignored them, though, and Arlo could only watch in stupefied horror as the launcher fired with a resounding *boom* like thunder that shook through the earth.

Its missile sailed toward her . . .

And like a sudden bottoming out, a tidal wave crashing overhead, a burst of white-hot fire scouring through her, Arlo fell back, to

make

way

for

Ruin lifted a hand, brushed it through the air in a casual sweep, a flick of their wrist—a simple thing it was to send the missile arcing upward and back around, redirected at the fool of a mortal girl who had really thought them so easily vanquished.

As though a tool of catastrophic destruction could ever be their undoing.

Please, don't hurt anyone . . .

Oh, I think it is too late for that request.

Ruin laughed deep in their throat, spread their arms wide to embrace the delicious heat of the explosion that blew rubble and flame around them . . .

And smeared that insipid faerie into the crater of where she once stood.

Shouts rang out all around.

The purple-haired lesidhe boy launched himself forward in attack, aiming, it seemed, for Ruin—did he know how much he owed Arlo's Fury? That silver-eyed girl, full of such potential if they could only convince her to give herself over completely to the chaos and rage that bellowed inside her . . .

For now she threw herself like a boulder against the lesidhe, knocking him off course.

The pair of them rolled, snarled at each other.

The lesidhe grabbed fistfuls of blue magic wrapped in electricity-like chains. Nausicaä armed herself with fire.

The two of them wrestled—and it saved his life. Ruin would have scorched that boy alive just as they'd done the faerie-girl-no-longer, no matter how Arlo railed against the very idea inside them.

It was all so delightful, truly. No wonder their immortal kin longed so fiercely to return here. Such a pity there would be nothing left of it when Ruin was through—of the Immortal Realm, too, for that matter.

"ARLO!" a voice screamed out behind them, rushing closer.

A voice they knew intimately, a voice that had nearly been their own.

They turned with a smile to greet it, hand sweeping out to the side, and as it rose to extended, the demons huddled on the battle's fringe began to agitate.

Vehan, no!

Very lacking in manners, their almost-host, this mortal boy with hair like the void of their prison, eyes like the exquisite burn of all that electric magic he wielded.

Vehan slammed into their front, tackling them to the stone as the lesidhe would have done. Ruin went only because it amused them. The anger in this boy, the desperation, the grief—they did miss it, but then Arlo Flamel was a delicious mixture of all these things as well. ———

"Give her back!" Vehan demanded, grabbing Ruin roughly by the front of the very nice robe they wore, a cosmic black that glittered like Fate's stars, which Ruin hadn't seen in far too long. "Give her back. I need to talk to her!"

How charming.

What *fun*.

This boy, who rose a fist at them, and stared them down, trembling with the desire to unleash himself, to give himself over to obliteration . . . ruin . . . *Yes*.

But the strike wouldn't come.

It never did.

Not to *her* face; not from any of them.

A twist of their legs caught them up in a rapid maneuver that saw their positions reversed, Ruin on top and Vehan beneath them.

In the background lunged the demons too starved by their journey through the portal to let their fear of Ruin hold them back any longer.

Shouts rang out again. More commotion followed as the battle was renewed.

The rebel group . . . the lesidhe's team . . . they busied themselves with the demons, while Nausicaä—ah, what a wonderful creature she could be at times such as this—peeled herself off the one called Aurelian, with his bloody nose and scorched clothing.

As she waded into the fray, pulling from her core such blazing *Fire*, the truest of that element, to hurl great balls of it at posts with their happy little holiday wreaths; at displays and vending carts; a volley toward the castle in the distance to catch on whimsical turrets.

All for the devastation of it . . .

All for *Ruin*.

She did so like to impress them, to ingratiate herself by means of pretty demonstrations, undoubtedly so that they'd be inclined to keep her around a bit longer—and who was Ruin but obliging to such devotion? Who was Ruin to deny her what she'd want for this, after, when she dedicated to them such glorious destruction . . .

> *Don't kill him don't kill him don't kill him*
> *don't kill him—*

Goodness.

Ruin looked back down at the boy beneath them.

Even if they wanted to—did they wish to? Perhaps. There was always the longing to unmake whatever their hands touched. But this blue-eyed prince would prove useful yet, and Arlo . . .

Here we are, back to friendship, they mused at her. *My original argument stands: not at all worth the meager rewards it affords. . . . How much did it cost you, to project that much will?*

Their host—when she wanted something, really *wanted* something, they were helpless but to comply.

The sooner they were rid of her, the better.

The sooner they got to the rift, the closer they came to achieving this.

Wear her down, last it out—it benefitted them to aid this girl in her fatuous mission. The more rifts they flung themselves through, the more time they spent in the Immortal Realm, the more exhausted their unsolicited companion became. Eventually, her soul would give out, and in the meantime it afforded Ruin the opportunity of immortal prey.

Mortals were all well and good, but the power they absorbed from their *immortal* kin . . .

"She doesn't wish to speak to you," Ruin replied aloud. "Does that sadden you, princeling?" They raised a fist of their own.

Their former host narrowed a glare at them, not electric at all but *icy*, and oh, they had to pause for another laugh—

"Arlo can tell me that herself," the boy said.

And Ruin sneered. "I'll see she gets the message."

"ARLO!"

Curse it all—the boy called; Arlo answered.

Down came Ruin's fist, directly into the prince's rib cage. But these *friends* of hers . . . Arlo was always so quick to resurge in their company, to dampen Ruin's fun. The boy called for her, and Arlo's will *clenched* around them.

Strength thus checked, they could feel the crack of bone beneath their knuckles, but nothing more devastating.

With a sigh, Ruin swung themselves off Vehan Lysterne and began immediately again for the rift.

Time to work your magic, darling . . .

That infamous, cataclysmic alchemy, reborn in this little girl, provided no end of amusement. They might even be sad when this was all over and no form of Arlo Flamel remained.

For now, though, they raised their hands, but it was Arlo they allowed back a modicum of command, to pull from their depths and etch in their mind an array so complex, even Ruin didn't fully understand it—and didn't need to. It functioned regardless, and all that was required of them was the backing of their power.

The rift began to tremble and groan, and gaped open wider, its portal reactivated. A darkness like ink, seething and swirling and gleaming in its depth, waited for them to give themselves over to it, and simply fall . . .

Beautiful . . .

And however much it rankled Arlo to have their awe, she was no less pleased by it.

Ruin chuckled once more, quiet and private and rich between them.

That's a lovely shade of pride *on you—*
but you've always worn it well. Careful, Flamel;
wouldn't want to go the same way twice . . .

67

"Evening, Nicholas."

Flat on his stomach, as close to the floor as he could press himself, Arlo peered between two wooden posts of the railing that guarded his bedroom loft, straining to see who was greeting his father at the door.

It wasn't a particularly large cabin they lived in, deep in France's rolling countryside, where the only thing of even moderate interest that wasn't two days' wagon ride away was a meager village on the other side of the forest behind them.

The main floor was a singular large expanse divided into a sitting room, kitchen, and dining area, with an offshoot in the back where his parents slept, and a door that led to a cramped cellar basement, where his father worked and Arlo was expressly forbidden.

The loft was where Arlo slept—a sliver of space so close to the ceiling that at thirteen he was already forced to stoop if he wanted to walk around.

But it was comfortable up here, private: a bookshelf he and his father had built together when he was eight, a desk where he could sit and practice his reading and writing, as though he still had a tutor to care about such things. A soft bed propped under a small, circular window where he could lie at night and gaze out at the moon and imagine all sorts of things being different about his life, which had once been so grand and exciting, now traded for pastoral boredom.

"Phoebus. Cenavy." Down on the first floor, Nicholas inclined his head to their two visitors, a stiff motion, as he stepped aside to allow them through the door—about as welcoming as Arlo's father ever was to any outsider these days, and not at all the sort of greeting owed to two of the Eight Founders of the Courts of Fae.

Nervously, Arlo pressed himself even flatter to the floor as the pair crossed the threshold and into his house fully.

"Come now, old friend." The High King of UnSeelie Spring chuckled like wind chimes, arms spread wide as though nothing more than a whim was the reason he'd portaled all the way here with the Queen of Seelie Summer as companion. "There's no need for such hostilities. We bear with us no intended harm—Ah, and there she is, Penelope! My dear, if possible, I'd say you are even more radiant than the last we met. Seelie Summer truly outdid itself on you, Princess."

He dropped a wink at her, and Arlo's mother breathed out a laugh that, despite the undercurrent of anxiety, said she was too used to such comments from men like the king, and not any more persuaded by his charms than theirs.

Penelope was a beautiful woman, with onyx-black hair, a smile that bloomed like a carefully unfolding rose to morning sun, and eyes so green, even the sea would envy their sparkling hue.

Folk whispered many things about her, that her beauty was the blessing of the gods they weren't supposed to worship anymore, but Penelope had—never in secret, but quietly enough, and who would tell a Founder's niece what she was and wasn't to do?

Arlo admired her fiercely for it, the confidence his mother carried herself in.

Of course Arlo attempted to emulate this quality that was the reason for the Founders' visit tonight, the reason for his parents' unease and the tension that filled the room like the noxious fumes that sometimes wafted from his father's work. Arlo's dread turned his mouth to cotton and caused his heart to beat like hummingbird wings.

"The countryside agrees with you, love," said Cenavy Lysterne, by way of placid greeting.

Arlo didn't miss the way her summer-brown eyes cast around their house or the slight curl of distaste in the aging corner of her mouth.

His great-aunt had never been overly fond of them back when they'd lived with her in the Luminous Palace, but she'd been sorely cross with their decision to move here, out in the middle of nowhere, to what was practically squalor—it was the only thing Arlo had ever fully agreed with *her* on.

The Flamels didn't belong hidden away like fugitives.

"Enough," Arlo's father interrupted with an impatient growl. "We know why you're here. Don't waste our time with pleasantries. And before you get on with it, you're not taking the boy *anywhere*—he'll serve punishment by my hand, and that will suffice plenty."

Arlo shuddered.

Nicholas Flamel was an intimidating man, no less so as he climbed in years. Tall and sturdy and deep in voice, with fire-red hair and matching beard that ate up most of his face and hung down to his belly. It was the eyes, though, that unnerved the most—a brown so deep it gleamed nearly black. He could level a bull troll with fear when one of his famous glares was inflicted.

They were the same eyes Arlo had inherited, though he was far less effective at wielding them.

Not many people wished to land themselves in his father's irritation, especially back to only last year, when he'd held the title of the High King's Head Alchemist. When it had been his job to investigate and experiment with the limits of alchemy's reaches, and rumor filled his wake with fright and hushed whispers that debated what terrible things he could do.

Not many, but Phoebus Viridian was one who could look at the storm on Arlo's father's brow and dismiss it with a smile.

"*Come now*, Nicholas," the High King repeated, though now it was layered with an intention that could almost be force, the first hint so far of who he truly was: a fae so powerful he'd driven their very *gods* from this world.

Jade-green eyes flashed. Phoebus was handsome, still retaining a great deal of youth despite his many years as one of the last two remaining Founders—all russet-brown hair like new tree growth, the bluebell flush of life sitting high on the cut of his cheekbones, and a smile that held the confidence Arlo had been so foolish in chasing himself . . .

"If we're not to mince words any longer," he continued, taking a step forward, "then you should know it's not that simple a matter. My Hunters sensed it; the Fae High Council has been apprised. It is *known*, dear friend, that on this very day's afternoon, one Arlo Flamel performed dark magic that resulted in the loss of human life."

"With no intention of it!" Nicholas countered, voice pitching even deeper as he puffed in response to the High King's advance. "He is a *boy*—thirteen! The Erinyes have stayed their revenge on his foolish mistake, and so shall you if you know what's good for you, *old friend*."

"Nicholas," Phoebus sighed, as though Arlo's father hadn't been standing there growling threats in his face—treason and insult both, for any other fae. Phoebus shook his head as he spoke. "Oh, Nicholas. As I said. It is not that simple."

Lifting a hand, the High King clicked a loud *snap*, and almost before the sound had faded from the air, a swell of darkness filled the open door at his back.

Transfixed, Arlo watched as that darkness grew, his heart sinking even deeper, fear rising so high it sat acrid on the back of his tongue.

He watched as it began to warp, as it took on shape and spat out a man with long, water-beetle-black hair and eyes the color of the foulest poisons locked up in father's basement.

Long black robes that glittered like the night sky . . . silvery-freckled skin the pallid color of death . . . teeth sharp as a shark's—this was a Hunter, and not *any* Hunter. This was the Hunter *Lethe*.

Arlo's father had told him such stories of this nightmare being that Arlo had been unable to sleep for weeks after, resulting in his mother strictly forbidding the subject for his bedtime.

And here he was, in the flesh.

Lethe swept into the room like a deadly pestilence, those unnervingly bright eyes glaring coolly at his surroundings and the people that occupied them.

Penelope gasped and moved quickly to place herself between Lethe and the narrow twist of stairs that led up to Arlo's loft. Nicholas inflated even further for the threat of what a Hunter meant.

"I would first like to hear it from the boy himself," Phoebus continued, as completely unbothered by Lethe's reception as he'd been by his own. "I would like to know it in *his* words, if you please, Nicholas. What exactly transpired today that pushed a thirteen-year-old boy to recesses of alchemy none before him have yet explored?" Something flashed in his eyes that Arlo couldn't name, but it made him feel a bit like a fly snatched suddenly from flight by a spider's careful web, where struggling would only summon a faster end. "I bring my Hunter for confirmation of truth only. As you know, this one in particular specializes in the art of memory."

All eyes turned to Arlo's loft then—to Arlo, exactly where he'd been lying, as though they'd known he was there all along.

"A crossroads."

"What?"

So surprised was he by the voice that came out of nowhere beside him that Arlo's head whipped to the side, and his gaze found a young woman lain sprawled just as he was, flat on her stomach. She looked not at him but out at the floor, where no one but Lethe seemed to take any notice of her, judging by the way his green eyes flashed when lighting on her face between the bars.

An odd sort of young woman, the way she was dressed, as though from another realm entirely.

Arlo took in her willowy build and long, airy white hair, the soft cut of her jaw and the light pitch of her voice, all of it incongruous with the threat of her powerful aura and the otherworldly gear of black leather that looked a bit to be armor, with matching bracers and leather boots.

The young woman turned her head to blink once at him, slow and judgmental—it reminded Arlo of a cat.

"That's what this is called—a crossroads."

"O . . . kay?"

The young woman rolled her eyes, then followed to roll over with them onto her back. "The decisions you make in the next few minutes," she clarified, speaking to the ceiling, like this was all above her, "will decide which course your life will take into the foreseeable future."

He shook his head, confused. "Who . . . What . . . How did you even get here?"

"Arlo?" The High King spoke.

Arlo's head snapped back to the front. All eyes were on him—all except Lethe, who was staring now so hard at the woman beside Arlo that he feared a little she might be in danger.

His own peril, though, was probably far worse.

At last complying, Arlo pulled himself to his feet and left the strange young woman behind him as he started down the stairs, clasping the loft's railing like a lifeline. He tried to channel any amount of composure he could, to nod in greeting to the High King and his great-aunt without trembling like the leaf he felt like beneath the High King's penetrating gaze.

Phoebus lifted his hand once more and, with a curl of it, beckoned him to them—quite literally.

Arlo felt the air heave around him, and it was all the warning he received—that, and a pulling at his core—before he was suddenly standing windswept and rumpled in front of the most powerful fae in the Eight Great Courts.

Swallowing thickly, Arlo paused only to gain his bearings, then stooped into a deep bow.

"None of that, my boy," Phoebus chimed with a hint of amusement, despite the severity of his expression. "You have heard what you've been charged with?"

Words failing at the rising tide of his anxiety, Arlo nodded so hard his red hair flopped in his vision.

"Do you deny any part of it?"

Arlo shook his head no.

Instead of frowning, which Arlo could practically feel his father doing behind him, Phoebus's gaze took on a glint like eagerness, and he bent a little, so as to better match Arlo's gaze.

He took Arlo's hands in his own and smiled that charming smile he'd used on Arlo's mother.

Arlo understood it now—the reason why she resisted what so many other folk would give their firstborns to possess: that smile was dangerous. *Phoebus* was dangerous, as all cunning, persuasive men in power were.

"Will you tell me what happened, Arlo? Will you give me permission to look within your mind and learn the truth of what's transpired? If you truly meant no offense—if, as your father says, the Erinyes have turned compassion on this act—then I would have it known so that I, too, may absolve you of what our justice here demands in punishment." *Such* a dangerous man. Arlo wasn't certain who terrified him more right now—Lethe or the High King. "Do I have your permission, son?"

A moment passed . . . followed by two . . . Arlo wanted dearly to look behind him to his parents for guidance.

He could feel their unease growing thicker against his back, but the situation he was in was delicate—refuse, and Arlo might be branded a murderer and taken in for beheading; permit, and the High King would learn exactly what he'd done.

Another moment, and then finally, Arlo nodded his permission.

From up in the loft, he heard the disapproving click of a tongue.

"*Wonderful.*" Phoebus's smile bloomed so lovely Arlo almost forgot why he'd been nervous at all.

The High King beckoned Lethe next, with the jerk of his head to Arlo.

74

Would it hurt? Arlo wondered.

How exactly did another person look into someone's mind for memories? Would Arlo know he was there? Would he feel him?

Too soon, a long-fingered hand gripped his chin and tilted Arlo's face to meet poison.

Lethe didn't stoop, as the High King had, to make this more comfortable for either of them. He stood in all his formidable height, towering over Arlo, lip curled ever so slightly to match Great-Aunt Cenavy's disgust.

"I wouldn't struggle," he said like a creaking, and it was all the warning Arlo received before he felt a sensation like cold water flooding through him and his vision darkened to black.

Pitch black.

Lethe and Arlo alone stood in a void of endless night, and at first there was nothing—then there was smoke. Or what appeared to be smoke: pale, whitish wisps that rose up around them, curling in the air.

Arlo watched, entranced, as they spent a few moments dancing and weaving lazily together. He tried to reach out to touch one, but the action earned a painful swat on his hand from claw-tipped fingers, and almost as quickly, the wisps began to knit themselves with purpose.

They wriggled and writhed, coiled and burst—took on all sorts of colors and shades and shapes, painting a scene, until at last Arlo found himself no longer in his small little cabin at all but back in the woods of earlier that day . . . and his stomach bottomed out completely.

The scene was thus:

Arlo Flamel, whom everyone had always agreed was so terribly smart and wildly talented.

Arlo, who at ten years of age was already performing alchemic mastery that full-grown wizards who'd given entire decades to the practice could not achieve. Arlo, who worked closely with his father in his royal laboratory, where his curiosity was always indulged, his father always keen to teach him; who was his mother's pride and joy, her favorite company for tea and walks through the gardens, where she taught him, too, of this and that flora.

What need had he for other people?

His life had been happy and full.

But then, as things tended to do, everything had changed. Arlo's father had grown more and more furtive, more and more paranoid over a new project he refused to let even Arlo know anything of at all. More and more, until one day his father quit them of the palace, of the Courts altogether, and whisked them out to human isolation. And it was here in this tiny village that Arlo realized something very important: he was lonely, and spectacularly terrible at making friends.

The other village children teased him whenever he and his mother came to market to trade for things they needed—his father rarely left the house these days to join them or do it himself.

The children called him pretty. Called him a girl, teased him about his clothing, his face, his hair, his eyes, for being quiet, awkward, short— anything and everything, it was all too different in their opinion, too soft and delicate and fancy for rural life.

On their less kind days, they called him a demon, a devil and fairy— or what humans understood of such things. At first Arlo had been nervous that he'd let something slip in front of them he shouldn't, but no, they simply took in his red hair and hints of former wealth and branded him "other"—a leprechaun, they'd latched onto.

Frustrated, hurt, and no small amount worried that the adults might take their children's teasing for truth and try to burn him at the stake, Arlo had asked his mother for advice.

She'd told him that sometimes people would simply not like him, no matter what he did; that there was no use trying so hard to please every- one, and certainly not the people determined not to be pleased.

For a while, Arlo had taken heed of this advice, had left the other children and attempts to befriend them well alone. Had contented him- self with his previous pursuits of combing through the woods, half in

76

play and half in test of the things his mother had taught him.

He'd kept to himself.

Pushed down his loneliness, retreated into imagination.

For a while, it had worked . . .

Until one day—when Arlo had been collecting interesting stones by a nearby stream, and the village children, in pursuit of their own leisure, had happened across him—it didn't.

"He is a fairy, to be sure, prancing around in the woods all day," Geneveve spat like the curse it was. "Do you know what my mother told me about leprechauns?"

Arlo was certain he didn't want to know.

Geneveve told him, regardless. Taking a step toward him, she sneered in his face, "She said they were evil little fairy creatures that steal treasure and bury it someplace private, and if you catch one, they have to give it over to you."

How quickly events had transpired after this point.

"CATCH THE LEPRECHAUN!" one of the children shouted, and Arlo had no choice but to run.

And run . . . and run . . .

He ran, and tripped, and stumbled through woods where no amount of familiarity could guide his terror.

Stones cut hard into his knees when he fell.

Branches and thorns caught skin and clothes and hair alike.

Arlo was the son of a Founder's niece, of the greatest alchemist of their age and possibly of all time, but he was still just a boy—and talented as he was, he wasn't very fast. Palace life hadn't bred necessity for practice running.

"CATCH HIM!"

"STOMP HIM!"

"GIVE US YOUR GOLD, LEPRECHAUN! COUGH IT UP, FANCY BOY!"

Arlo tried to curl up on himself in protection against the fists that rained down on him, the heels of boots that met his bones.

"WHERE'S YOUR GOLD, DEVIL?"

"GIVE IT OVER AND WE MIGHT LET YOU GO!"

"Aw, is the little baby devil crying?"

Arlo trembled with rage.

He was hurting, humiliated, terrified, and angry—*and that's when the thought occurred, as thoughts often did for him when he was pressed by an impossible situation.*

These kids wanted gold?

Arlo was smart, perhaps smarter than his father had counted on, for it had taken some persistence and great deal of luck, but Arlo had managed once to sneak into his father's basement.

Had learned what it was, in part, that had driven their family into hiding.

The philosopher's stone—immortality, wealth . . .

Arlo hadn't ever put to use what he learned from that chance investigation, had done his best to keep this secret so as to impress his father with his loyalty, when the time inevitably came that he'd have to spill that he knew what was going on.

Arlo was smart.

And incredibly good at remembering arrays.

And if these children wanted gold . . .

It was quite simple, really, to attach in his mind the animus rune like an anchor to the most complex array he'd ever encountered, memorized from his father's journal.

Arlo's intention had been modest: the animus rune would direct the philosopher's stone array's magic to a living target. They wanted gold, and he intended to give it to them—an arm or a leg, nothing too dangerous, and nothing that wouldn't wear off by the time they made it back to the village to cry what their parents would assume to be wolf.

He'd just wanted to teach them a lesson . . . make them stop hurting him . . .

"Do you know what you've done?"

Lethe's question brought Arlo out of the moment, tore his gaze away from the array gone wrong—or rather, *right.*

From Geneveve, lying dead on the forest floor, blood seeping through the front of her dress in the pattern of that cruel array . . .

Oh, Arlo understood.

In the moment, he hadn't. It had all occurred *so quickly*. He was smart, and he was talented, and it had been a recent development in his art that all he needed to do was close his eyes and picture his target clearly in his mind, and his magic would stamp on it any array his brain could imagine.

He'd never used this technique on a living person before and had pictured the array on Geneveve's *arm*, besides, not her chest like a fool—but the dark magic he'd been toying with had taken liberties of its own, and though Arlo had had no idea then, now . . .

"You attached the animus rune on a whim to a profoundly dark array you only just picked up from a book."

Lethe's tone was guarded.

Arlo couldn't tell if he was proud or disapproving or completely apathetic to the situation entirely. All he knew was that Lethe's voice echoed as though Arlo were listening to it both from his mouth and in his head, and that made sense . . . a bit.

They weren't really back in the woods.

This *was* in his head.

"And here I thought the one to figure it out would be your fool father."

The animus rune was no anchor when attached to that strange array, Arlo had worked out on his flight home.

No anchor but a *door* he'd installed, and then swung open wide to unleash a terrible *something* that he could feel in the back of his brain, his heart, his bones, his soul . . . a kind of . . . stretching.

Like whatever had spilled from that door had attached to *him* and was only just beginning to awaken.

"What was your name again, boy?"

"Arlo Flamel," Arlo supplied with a gulp.

His gaze had fallen back to Geneveve. To her lifeless eyes staring

79

sightless up at the forest canopy—gold gleaming bright from her encrusted throat, spilled between lips frozen in a breathless gasp.

"Arlo Flamel," Lethe repeated, the name spoken like loose floorboards as he studied Arlo a moment longer, as though Arlo actually might be interesting. "*Very* interesting—at least, perhaps in time. It depends first on whether or not my former Hunter allows you to live."

What?

"Come."

Almost as soon as he was beckoned, Arlo was pulled from his head.

A nauseating experience—he wanted to vomit, though that might also be from the fresh reminder of what he'd done.

Expectantly, Phoebus commanded attention. "Well?"

Lethe shrugged. "He tells the truth. He had no intention of killing that girl, but kill her he did, in exactly the way you'd been hoping . . . *my liege*."

Phoebus frowned, the first show of discontent this evening, but was quick to recover from the barb in Lethe's words. "'Hope' would be a word poorly chosen, Hunter. Remember your place."

Lethe sneered.

Turning back to Arlo, the High King softened. Still kneeling, back to smiling, he took up Arlo's hands once more. "My boy, I would like—"

"Absolutely not," Nicholas hissed.

Darting forward, he seized Arlo by the shoulders and tore him away from the High King so roughly that Arlo stumbled. "You have your answer. Arlo is no threat, and neither will he be your puppet."

"Now see here, Nicholas!" Phoebus boomed, pulling himself back to full height. A braver man than Arlo would have flattened himself back against his father too. "I have given you my patience and my respect. I have permitted your honorable discharge from my service and a quiet and comfortable life for your family where none should think to disturb you. You have had before that *years* of access to personal troves of knowledge and wealth, and in the span of an afternoon, it is your *son* who's managed to make the progress we've been working *decades* to—"

"YOU WILL LEAVE HIM OUT OF THIS!"

"YOU WILL REMEMBER WHO YOU SPEAK TO!"

"Would either of you care to tell *Arlo* what's happening here?" the voice from the loft interjected, and all heads turned as one to peer up at the railing.

A moment of silence . . .

Followed by two . . .

"Alecto," Lethe greeted, the word dagger sharp.

Arlo drew a breath that hitched on his fear—Alecto, Megaera, Tisiphone. The young woman in his loft was an Erinys, a *Fury*.

"I see they've assigned you your first mission. *Congratulations.*" Lethe spoke it like being forced to eat dung.

Dashing across the room, Penelope yanked Arlo from Nicholas's grasp to wrap him up protectively in hers. *"Please,"* she begged, half in tears. "Please, do not take my son from me—he's only a boy, he didn't mean what happened! He won't ever do it again!"

Alecto considered her briefly before speaking, her tone growing imperious. "I have not come to collect on punishment. You can be at peace, mortal mother. Your son is yours—for now. Whether he remains as such . . ." Her disconcerting eyes turned on Arlo, a color nearly white as her hair. She assessed him a moment longer. "It depends on what you choose, Arlo Flamel."

"Yes," Phoebus snapped, returning to himself from his surprised transfixion. It wasn't every day one encountered a Fury, even when you were a gods-slaying fae sovereign. "That is the heart of it exactly— *Arlo* gets to choose. He is thirteen, is he not? Not so much a boy in need of protecting. Come, Arlo. Would you listen to my request?"

Arlo could feel his mother stiffen.

He could see the anger brewing on his father's face.

But there was that stretching again . . . that stirring presence in the back, back, back of his being, and something inside him poked at his desire to be useful again, wanted again; to *belong*. "All right."

And there was that smile.

That dangerous smile.

"You would like it, I think. It does come with much weight and responsibility; you will be the one a great many look to in admiration and jealousy both, for guidance and assurance. It will afford you everything you could possibly want, though—wealth, power, access to knowledge denied to all others . . . Something a clever mind like yours would make good use of, wouldn't you agree?"

"No," Nicholas breathed; he sounded aghast. Alarmed. *Afraid.* "Phoebus, you cannot—"

"I would like what, exactly?" Arlo asked over his father's plea.

That dangerous, *dangerous* smile.

"Why, your father's old position, I mean. The High King's Head Alchemist—when you've completed your schooling at the High Academy, of course."

Arlo could only gape.

The High Academy—*the* High Academy!

As a descendant of a Founder and Nicholas Flamel's son, his name had been down for the school before he was even born. But Nicholas detested the idea of classrooms, of rigid curriculums and generalized study; he'd been firm in his desire for Arlo to receive personal, private tutelage, and Arlo had always been eager to please him—*loved* his father deeply.

But the High Academy . . . with other children his own age . . . where Arlo might *finally* make a friend . . .

"What say you, Arlo?" Phoebus pressed. "Would you like to return with me to the Courts? Would you like to see what else that clever mind of yours can come up with? What advances you could make in a field that can offer our people such promise of peace and protection?" His jade eyes gleamed. "Would you like to have friends who *want* your company?"

Arlo tilted his head to look up at his mother and the grim set of her mouth.

He looked to his father and the storm blowing wild behind his eyes.

He looked to Alecto . . .

"Don't look at *me*," she told him plainly. "Do it or not, only know this: pursuing this path puts you dangerously close to breaking the laws of magic. This night you escape Destruction—you will not be so lucky a second time. Ignorance can no longer shield you. And I will be watching."

Heart racing, hope running rampant with his imagination: power, friendship, his life not only restored to comfort and splendor but *improved*. . . . He only needed to avoid taking life to keep himself on that straight and narrow—not at all difficult! He didn't *want* to hurt anyone; his father needn't look so concerned.

What harm could he do, if his intentions stayed pure?

Arlo turned to face the High King and gave him a smile of his own.

CHAPTER 4

Vehan

A SLIVER OF MOONLIGHT FROM the gap in the curtains sliced through the bedroom Vehan shared with Aurelian, its single beam cutting across his nightstand to light almost purposefully on the die that sat there.

A clear electric sapphire in color with numbers etched in sparking bright gold—it had changed from the jade it had been as Arlo's the moment it transferred to his possession. And it might be his imagination, might be all the stress he was under playing on his pessimism, but he was almost *entirely* sure when he held it that there was this radiating sense of disappointment, as though the die too were mad at Vehan and missed its original owner.

Sighing, Vehan shifted onto his back, wincing a little when the action pulled at bones that hadn't quite fully mended themselves yet after Ruin's crushing blow to his ribs.

Beside him, Aurelian shifted too, winced a little in echo of Vehan's discomfort.

This soulbond business . . . Vehan hadn't doubted a word of what Aurelian had told him when they'd first returned to the Market from Toronto.

However unbelievable it was—that despite all these people congesting the world, the two of them had found each other—everything about them; all that they'd been through; the way Vehan had sworn he'd been able to feel at times Aurelian's emotions and physical well-being like they were *his*; the way it had felt like an unmooring when they'd been separated those months after the Solstice . . . there was no denying that something far more than ordinary *love* tethered them together.

Beneficial, even, the way it was definitely Aurelian's lesidhe magic that seeped through their burgeoning bond to expedite Vehan's healing process.

Aurelian didn't mind this new facet of *them*.

In fact, he seemed almost excited by it these days—that there was something profound working to keep them together, something that would help them keep the other safe, something they could also use as an advantage in the war to come . . . and that was where Vehan's heart always hitched.

The war to come.

Against his mother.

Vehan stared up unblinking at the ceiling.

"Your ribs are whole again." Aurelian's voice was a faint, deep rumble against the side of his head, his mouth ghosting words along the shell of his ear.

The arm that had been slung low and proprietary over Vehan's hips drifted, fingers drawing feather-light up his bare stomach for the palm to spread wide and flatten to the side where Ruin had done the most damage. "I don't like it when you're injured."

Sleepy Aurelian was his favorite Aurelian.

Or rather, it was among the top ranks. Tied was the Aurelian that walked around their room in low-slung joggers after his morning run, all windswept hair and T-shirt sticking to sweat-gleaming muscle; the Aurelian that split logs for their winter stores with his red-checkered flannel rolled up to his elbows; the Aurelian that sat like a man defeated between his brother and Elyas Viridian, the pair of them chattering happily away as Harlan touched up the purple in Aurelian's hair.

He liked a lot of Aurelians.

Turning his head ever so slightly, Vehan brushed his nose against his boyfriend's.

Still half-asleep and frowning a bit—*pouting* a bit—Aurelian returned the gesture.

"I'm sorry," Vehan whispered. "I don't like it when I worry you."

"I am always worried about you."

"I'm sorry about that, too."

"Mmm."

Just like that, he was asleep once more—exhausted.

Aurelian was *exceedingly* exhausted lately. He did so much, played so many roles so that the Market could continue standing as a safe haven for both the Wild and the folk Riadne took personal exception to. He never complained though, and in many ways seemed to flourish in this new and better-suited environment, but Vehan could tell it wore on him all the same.

Just as he could tell *he* wore on his boyfriend as well.

Softly, Vehan pressed a kiss to Aurelian's hair. "I'm going to get some air. I'll be right back."

"Mmm," came the puff of Aurelian's reply, but hands released him all the same, and Vehan slipped as carefully as he could from their bed.

Threw on some clothing.

Grabbed the die from his nightstand and a packed cloth bag from under the bed, and padded silently out into the hall of the tavern that was his home now.

When the door clicked closed behind him, Vehan dropped back against it and released a heavy sigh.

Arlo barely cared about him half the time, more and more of who she was fading into Ruin with every day that passed. Nausicaä *despised* him. His die begrudged him. The Wild barely tolerated his presence as a Lysterne. And he was going to have to kill his own mother.

To say Vehan had been living more often than not in his own head lately would be putting it mildly. He didn't blame Aurelian for worrying, would be worried himself if their situations were reversed, but after his switch with Arlo had backfired so spectacularly for him, like hells if he was ever going to agree to something like *that* again.

He wasn't sure how he'd rank his current woes, but knowing he

was a large contributing factor to Aurelian's stress—so constantly concerned as he was for Vehan's mental health—was certainly in the running for what bothered him the most.

It made this secret he kept from him—probably the first he'd ever tried and successfully managed to hide from Aurelian's perceptiveness—all the more difficult to bear.

Clutching his die, Vehan peeled himself off the door and strode down the hall, then down the stairs, then out to the porch, where all was quiet and still this time of night save a trio of vampires huddled together at a far table, passing between them a long, glass pipe.

The Market was peaceful at night.

Most of it had been rebuilt after the fire Nausicaä had caused that had nearly obliterated it off the world map, but there was still the odd skeleton or two of old homes and shops yet to be torn down to make way for new.

Vehan passed a few buildings still glowing warm at their hearts, a good portion of the Market's denizens Night-aligned. But there was no one in the streets except for the goblin patrol, which was more than used to him at this point, no longer even bothering to warn him that once he left through that front gate, they wouldn't let him back in until morning.

A small price to pay.

Vehan nodded politely at Randal, one of the goblins on tonight's duty standing guard at the gate's exit, armed with a set of wicked iron teeth to match his iron-tipped crossbow.

Randal merely stared him down until Vehan passed him by—not overly friendly, the goblin guard here, but again . . . *Lysterne.*

Most people were reserved with him. It was only thanks to his relationship with Aurelian that they didn't chase him off outright—which they would, regardless of Aurelian's protections, if they had any idea what he got up to on nights when he just couldn't sleep.

Out through the gate . . .

Into the woods . . .

When Vehan was a safe enough distance away, he finally halted to drop his sack on the forest floor and look down at his die.

In this small clearing not far from the Market's borders, the canopy gave way to open night sky, awash with so many stars Vehan wondered if this was magic or what the night would truly look like if it weren't for all the pollution and light of the mortal plane.

Moonlight caught sharply on the die's glass edges, glinted off the golden numbers as he rocked it in the palm of his hand, waiting for it to warm.

"Come on . . ." Vehan encouraged, his voice pitched in a whisper. It hadn't denied him yet, but he shuddered to think what would happen if it did, stranding him out in the middle of the demon-infested Hiraeth until daybreak. "Come on, that's it . . ."

Slowly, the numbers' gold took on a warmer gleam.

The die grew heavier in the palm of his hand, heated to the touch.

"Thank you," he breathed in relief, and gripped it tight with intention.

What a curious sensation, standing live in a world of stopped time. Vehan had marveled plenty on his first use of this feature, to the point that Luck had interceded to tell him in polite enough but very direct terms to stop wasting *their* time with indecision, to either decide a purpose or dispel the magic and try again later.

It was the same thing he asked of it every night he did this: "I successfully disguise myself as palace staff and pass undetected as Vehan Lysterne for the duration of my visit."

And when he rolled the die to see if his manipulation of luck would be successful, it always landed on the same number, a—

"Hang on . . . *twenty?*"

The number was *always* a five. Vehan had the right clothing tucked away in his bag. He knew the palace like the back of his hand, was very practiced these days at keeping a low profile, and purposefully chose the middle of the night when he knew the majority of the palace would be asleep.

It was always, *always* a five. For the past four months he'd been doing this.

Why was tonight a *twenty*, and did he risk the attempt of a roll? He would get only one shot.

Vehan bit his lip.

And tossed the die high up in the air, catching it in his palm once more when it fell.

Please, please, please, please, please . . .

"Nineteen . . . ," he read aloud dismally.

Now what did he do?

He'd failed the roll—whatever was going on at the palace tonight, if he went, *someone* was going to recognize him. If he didn't go, he'd have to spend his night in a tree, which didn't at all sound appealing, and his ribs gave a twinge in agreement, but was that better or worse than potentially never being able to do this again?

Panic trilled through him at the idea.

To be cut off for good . . .

The same panic, knowing it would be a very long while before he'd get the chance to try this again.

Vehan faltered.

"Damn it," he cursed as he stooped to pull his things from his bag and stripped down and changed.

He had to go.

He'd rolled a nineteen—that had to count for something, at least. He couldn't fail too spectacularly in this mission. Someone would recognize him, but they might not tell, might not believe what they see, for that matter. And more than this, Vehan had already made up his mind about what he was doing tonight the moment he'd left Aurelian in their bed.

Successfully disguised in his Bone Guard attire, Vehan lifted a hand and pressed it flat against the air.

Like every time he'd done this before, a moment passed; then came a ripple.

The first time he realized he was still able to do this had been mere days after initially arriving at the Market. Still bruised and hurting—physically *and* emotionally—from Nausicaä's blame and reeling under the reality that had finally begun to set in, Vehan had run.

Into the Hiraeth, where he'd gotten lost, and he hadn't yet received any tutorial on how to utilize his die, so on instinct he'd called out to the Luminous Egress, desperate for safety.

And the Egress responded.

Riadne hadn't revoked his status.

Despite his betrayal, she hadn't disowned him, hadn't taken from him the title of Seelie Summer's Crown Prince. Which meant Vehan was still a Lysterne in every right; still considered Riadne's son; still welcome home, whenever he wished.

Which wasn't to say he *did* want to go back.

He understood now how profoundly corrupted his mother was, the depth of the abuse he'd been unwilling to admit he and so many others he cared about had suffered at her hand.

But the Luminous Palace had been his home for . . . almost nineteen years now.

And Riadne Lysterne . . . Stripped of everything else that she was, he was still a boy who'd long been his mother's fiercest protector. Some things were hard to shake.

The ripple in the air pulsed outward, a pale, shimmery translucence spreading in its wake.

Slowly, that translucence grew opaque and began to harden until what stood before Vehan was *himself* reflected back in glass—the setting behind him traded, though: forest for the Endless Corridor's stark whiteness.

A moment's hesitation was all Vehan paused to assess whether he truly wanted to go through with this—to risk the discovery he was bound to walk into . . . Shaking his head, he snapped himself out of doubt and into action, and stepped through the Egress back to the heart of Seelie Summer.

It was almost deafening, the sudden silence. The sounds of forest nightlife gone as though instantly smothered.

It was almost blinding, the corridor's glare of brilliance after the Hiraeth's pressing darkness.

Only a Crowned Royal could command the Egress of their Court to open a portal from anywhere they happened to be. Every time he did this, Vehan breathed a sigh of relief that he hadn't lost this too, then immediately choked on the rising guilt—so many people had suffered and sacrificed to get him away from his mother's clutches, and here he was running straight back to her, on more than one occasion.

What the Market would think if they found out. . . . They'd assume Vehan was a spy, accuse him of running their secrets to the enemy, but that wasn't it at all.

Vehan just . . . needed to be here.

To check on things.

He couldn't explain it at first, the pull he felt to return home, like something was wrong—more than the fact that his mother had murdered her former lover for a magical crown and killed dozens of children for the sins she grew as stones in their chests, all to summon a horrific Titan of death and destruction, who was tethered to the best friend he'd left here chained to said mother's tyranny.

Looking around, Vehan relaxed a little in his disguise.

His amplified luck hadn't failed him completely—there, behind Vehan and the mirror at the far back of the circular room, were the guards on duty, but they were so wrapped up in conversation that they hadn't even noticed his arrival. And when they chanced a look his way at last, they must have assumed him on the job, making for his destination, judging by the fact that all they did was quickly assess his uniform, then nod their heads in greeting before turning back to their own conversation.

Another relief.

Vehan released a pent-up breath and made for a door to his right before the guards could find reason for suspicion and assess him a little harder.

Down the halls . . .

Up the elevators . . .

Through heavy marble doors . . .

The Luminous Palace was a much gentler place at night, the daylight brightness dimmed much softer and flickering warmly in the gilt and gold decor.

He knew his path by heart, even before he started doing this.

Back when he'd been a much younger boy, and his mother not quite so hardened against him, Vehan had journeyed it often. He didn't need the sense of *wrongness* in his heart to steer him, but it pulled him along all the same, led him past other guards who barely turned their heads his way, too unconcerned by someone they assumed to be one of their superiors to peer a little closer at him.

Down more halls, through more doors, up one last elevator . . .

Vehan halted at the pale oak wood of another door that was massive—easily three of him abreast and stacked in height as well—but otherwise . . . completely unremarkable.

The last place one would expect to find the most powerful queen in the Mortal Realm.

He paused, just a moment.

If anyone was going to recognize him tonight, surely it would be his own mother.

But then . . .

. . . the reason why Vehan had kept coming back after his initial visit.

Most of the time, he didn't encounter Riadne at all on these trips. Vehan made do with gossip, with poking his head in on her usual haunts and sweeping the palace for nothing in particular, but checking security as well. The times their paths did cross, she never recognized him—either due to her disinterest in him as one of her perceived guards, or . . .

Vehan lifted a hand.

It was madness to seek his mother out intentionally, especially when he knew that someone was going to recognize him on this particular visit—most would place their bets on her. But he couldn't shake this feeling . . . that he needed to come see her directly. And his mother being the one to recognize him would surely have resulted in a critical failure roll for what she would do in result.

It was such a risk, and Aurelian was going to be *so* angry with him for it if he ever found out, but no. Something inside him had compelled him this far; he couldn't say why, but he *knew* in his heart that Riadne was not his threat tonight.

Hoping he wasn't about to be proven the immense fool he definitely was, Vehan knocked softly three times on the wooden surface.

And . . . nothing happened.

And nothing happened . . .

And *nothing*, until—

The door was ripped wide open.

Vehan stared.

Riadne stared back. She was dressed in a nightgown of porcelain-white silk, an opulent gold robe unbound and hanging slightly askew on her body, her ink-black hair freshly brushed and hanging long to her waist, her electric ice eyes positively *freezing*.

His mother glared down her nose at him, took in everything about him, and Vehan's breath retreated once more to the back of his throat in fear. He was about to say something, either in greeting or apology, but at last, Riadne beat him to it.

"Vadrien—what in the *hells* are you wearing?"

. . . Ah.

So it was one of *these* nights.

The nights where Riadne didn't recognize him, but not because his cover was good and not because she spent a good deal of time these days absorbed in her Crown, in her head, in her war, and completely uninterested in her palace staff.

No, tonight was a night she didn't recognize him because when she looked at him, she saw his father.

"I'm sorry," he heard himself reply. "I—"

"Never mind." Riadne waved him off with a click of her tongue before stepping aside, and Vehan took this as both permission and command to enter. "You *will* eventually have to relinquish your glory days to duty, husband. You cannot spend your nights rallying with the guard—you're a king now, and a father besides."

Yeah . . .

Vehan took in his mother's quarters.

This main room was beautiful, understated with its snow-white furniture and solid gold bookshelves, a few matching tables, but otherwise having extremely minimalistic decor. Riadne didn't spend much time in here, seemed to dislike the space altogether and perhaps the memories that filled it—memories such as this, that thrust Vehan into the role of his father and . . . there, stationed by the lit fireplace and awash in its warm glow, a bassinet fit for a tiny princeling, with all its pastel lace and silk and fringe.

Where Riadne had dug it out from . . .

More concerning to Vehan was the swaddled bundle Riadne crossed the room to retrieve from it and lifted to her heart to soothe.

"I . . ." Vehan opened his mouth, began to say *something*, but couldn't.

What *did* he say? To this proof that already—no doubt expedited by the lies she'd dealt in, the stress of the Sins, and the Titan she'd control only for as long as her spirit withstood the drain—his mother was unraveling to the madness that had claimed High King Azurean. The madness that claimed every High Sovereign.

"Hush, Vehan, it's all right."

Vehan startled.

For a moment, he thought she was speaking to him—and she *was*, but the "him" that she cradled now in her arms and beamed down at, like beneath the schemes and abuse and trauma was a

94

woman who might have actually *wanted* to be his mother.

Who loved him.

"I'm sorry," Vehan repeated, a little stronger than he'd uttered it out in the hall, but not by much. "I won't stay out late any longer, Mo—my dear."

Riadne chimed a quiet laugh, high and clear and genuinely humored. "You've always the best intentions, my shining husband." And replaced her bundle of cloth back in its bassinet. "Never mind it," she said dismissively. "Come. We've a council to attend."

With purpose, and without pausing to check if Vehan followed, Riadne strode to the door and out into the hall.

It was the middle of the night . . .

His mother's council, last he knew, was composed entirely of Seelie fae—none of them particularly partial to anything after sundown.

What could they have to discuss at this hour?

Surprised and confused both, Vehan hurried to fall into step behind her. "Ah . . . my dear," he hedged nervously, trying to play into the role that would save him from discovery, but no actual idea how his father had spoken to his mother back when he'd been alive. "In your"—he cleared his throat, embarrassed—"nightclothes?"

Riadne's steps didn't falter, but she did turn her head to raise a brow at him. "I am queen. If I wish to take council in nothing but my riding boots, they will avert their eyes." She tossed a hand out to the side, and a darkness began to curl around her fingers like tendrils of smoke. Her voice took on a layered, deeper quality; she spoke next not to him but to the void that connected her to her prize and looming demise both. *"Ruin, attend."*

Vehan slammed to a halt, immobilized by a flood of dread.

Arlo—she was the one who was going to recognize him, the reason his die required a twenty from him tonight, and if Ruin was in control when she came, his cover was absolutely going to be blown.

In front of his mother.

In the middle of all of her oldest and more powerful servants . . .

95

CHAPTER 5

Nausicaä

————— ⌒ ⌒ —————

NAUSICAÄ SAT ON THE edge of the rift chucking stones into its depths.

It was fully night now. The fire department, the human police, their FBI units—anyone the United States government could throw at this situation, in fact—were still gathered on the scene, attempting to no avail to douse Nausicaä's flames, milling about, taking pictures and collecting anything that would fit into their stupid little plastic baggies for closer examination in labs that weren't going to tell them *shit* about what had happened here tonight, but go off, she supposed.

Just about the only semi-useful thing they'd done so far was set up a perimeter around the rift Arlo had jumped through.

Fenced off, illuminated by portable spotlights, it reminded her of her first real adventure with Arlo, breaking into Hieronymus Aurum's lab almost a year ago now, and Nausicaä felt a bit of nostalgia.

Funny how they'd only known each other for all of nine months, yet it felt like entire lifetimes, and *deities*, she missed her girlfriend.

Deities, she was terrified for her too.

An enormous bag of cotton candy dropped unceremoniously onto the ground beside her. Nausicaä peered down at it coolly, ignored entirely the young man who followed it to sit on the edge of the rift as well, as close to her as he dared, because he had to know she was one wrong word away from booting Celadon Cornelius Fleur-Viridian Lysterne Wayland Herondale *300*-style into this pit after her rocks.

This entire situation was *his fault*—his and his mommy-issues little brother's.

The fucking Titan spawn that sat down beside him was the only reason she didn't reach over and give him a push anyhow. Nausicaä was all for a swift death if things went even more sour than they were, but right now Arlo was still alive and needed Nausicaä to be as well.

Because she sure as shit wasn't going to place all her eggs in hope's basket that Celadon and Lethe's stab-happy plan would be executed without a hitch.

So much had already gone off course.

Not to mention that so much could still go wrong with *Arlo's* plan. She was already dead, technically. If all went swimmingly, the moment they killed her mortal body and Ruin was forced to leave the no-longer-functioning husk that left behind, Arlo would pack off to the afterlife with the immortality she'd won. But if something went wrong in this very crucial stage, when Arlo would have to make her choice about who to back with her immortality, with no memory of what she was supposed to do . . .

If she didn't remember to choose Lethe, she'd be a wide-open target for every immortal's extreme displeasure with her; for thwarting so many plots and secret agendas that all hinged on obtaining a Crown; for slighting the many deities' many advances in favor of an unofficial, illegal god; and *Ruin*. Because a Hunter might have Cosmin's protection, but that would mean precisely shit to the immortals. Scions were far better protected, were directly linked to their deity's power and considered far too prestigious to Destroy. If Arlo didn't have that, she was toast. Nausicaä didn't trust Cosmin to keep Arlo from the Destruction the rest of the immortals would all be intent on delivering.

After all, Nausicaä had trusted her mother to protect her and her sisters, and look where that had gotten everyone.

No.

Arlo was already balancing on a fine-enough wire. There had to be something else they could rely on to ensure she *made* it to the shit show waiting for her after, and not Ruin's obliteration. There had to be another fail-safe to put in place for when this all inevitably went sideways, like everything else so far. A loophole that would help her get her girlfriend out of Ruin's clutches if Arlo couldn't manage to destroy the Crowns before Ruin took over; if Celadon wasn't on hand for the sliver of a window he'd have to run Arlo through, especially in the event that Ruin sprung their permanence on them as a surprise, eradicating Arlo's soul and giving her no chance to *ascend*.

There was always a loophole when it came to magic, always a way to undo whatever magic was used. Ruin might be better than most at concealing the chink in their armor, but it was there, probably staring her right in the face . . . Nausicaä probably already *knew* exactly what it was.

In fact, she was almost certain she did.

It was a feeling, a sometimes-fluttering like a cheeky taunt in her heart . . . and the words that Moros and Eos had left them with, which initially they'd all taken to mean what they understood at face value—*look to the places you keep your heart . . . Remember what makes you strong . . .*

Arlo's friendships helped to remind her of who she was, helped her hold on to important, key pieces of herself. That hadn't been hard to figure out. But there was something about the way the scions said these words . . . something that made Nausicaä suspect there was a little more to it than that.

Something that would be useful, if Nausicaä could just *figure it out*.

"It's not poisoned."

She ignored the self-appointed shitty Night King.

And the self-appointed shitty Night King ignored that in return.

"Arlo wouldn't want you to starve, Nausicaä. I know you're immortal, but you don't look like you've been eating all that much." A bag of spun sugar was a wild choice to rectify that. "You could also consider taking a shower at some point."

Was this an attempt to rile her? To get her to speak to him?

Nausicaä didn't care about all that much these days, sure, but she did maintain her basic hygiene, fuck you very much. More likely, Celadon was just an asshole, but she still wasn't going to acknowledge his existence in any way, and she didn't care if that made her five years old in emotional maturity.

Delicately, Celadon tore off a piece of his own cotton candy and placed it on his tongue, and the three of them sat in blessed silence while he let it dissolve, watching, waiting for Arlo to make her way back through, just as Nausicaä was. As she did every time Arlo dipped into the Immortal Realm, where Nausicaä was banned from following.

Arlo had to search for these Crowns with no one but Ruin to aid her, had to fling herself through every crack between realms that she could in the hopes it would spit her out close to the Infernal Palace, where Urielle kept, or the Sacred Grove, where Tellis lived.

The longer this took, the longer Arlo was forced to share her heart with Ruin, the stronger Ruin became, in result. As they did each time they forced Arlo's hands to take a life, and every time she and Arlo caused mass destruction in their stead.

This entire endeavor was a ticking countdown where Arlo needed to be so *careful*—needed to finish her task before Ruin could smother her out of existence; needed to power them up just enough to keep them satisfied, but starve them enough to stay just this side of manageable; needed to keep enough presence of self and mind so that Celadon didn't get too antsy and use that sword strapped to his back to cut her down regardless . . .

"I wonder what they're making of all this." Celadon resumed his chattiness, casting a look around them at the humans, who couldn't see them at all through the dense glamour he'd woven for their cover, upon his arrival, out of his phenomenal, cosmic powers, expressly so that they could sit here undisturbed.

Tch—if he thought she was grateful for that . . .

Nausicaä had been concealed just fine by her Hunter's cloak.

99

When would he and the rest of them get that she *didn't need them?* She didn't want them. She was doing just fine on her own, stirring up just enough trouble to keep Ruin placated, doing everything she could the rest of the time to keep Arlo grounded in who she was.

"The human citizenry," Celadon blathered on. "It's all over their news, of course, and their social media. It's all they talk about in the streets, on the subway, at work, and at the same time . . . they sort of just continue on. Bills to pay, groceries to spend exorbitant amounts of money on—have you *seen* the price of their basic goods? Eggs, cheese, milk, bread . . . I wouldn't care about demon attacks either if I had to pay a king's ransom just to eat like a medieval-age beggar. I might have to sell the fine silver just to keep buying Lethe the strawberries he likes—"

"Oh my *gods,*" Nausicaä snarled. In one quick movement, she had him by the throat, on the point end of a dagger she'd pulled from her boot. "Do you ever *shut up?*"

Celadon blinked at her, frustratingly unbothered by the violence she threatened.

Which might have something to do with the dagger point at the soft of *her* throat—she hadn't even seen Lethe move, that was how quickly he'd responded to this threat against his boyfriend. And wasn't that just another disgusting piss-off, that Lethe and Celadon got to be a cozy, happy couple while she and Arlo could barely trade pleasantries.

"Would the two of you just fucking go already," she growled, in an even fouler mood, as she begrudgingly lowered her weapon and batted Lethe's away. "You won't have to use your sword on her tonight, so just—"

A rippled passed through the pit's churning depths, a seething sea like blackest tar.

It wasn't overtly obvious, but it was enough to snag Nausicaä's attention, and Celadon's. Not until the groaning that took up next did the humans become aware that *something* was beginning to happen.

Another ripple.

It didn't confine itself to the pit but shuddered through the earth below them.

Orders were shouted.

The human forces gathered into a pack, parting without conscious decision around where Nausicaä and Celadon and Lethe now stood, everyone peering over the ledge at what was going on below.

"She was in there longer than usual this time . . ." Celadon murmured in observation. "Surely that's a good sign?"

Or a terrible one.

Countless possibilities flashed through Nausicaä's mind along with every worry and concern she had about letting Arlo go to the Immortal Realm without anyone but Ruin for protection against Nausicaä's asshole kin. Ruin would either let the immortals fling their worst at Arlo just to wear her down enough that they could break her or aid her in obliterating anyone who tried something, and in result, as they gorged on death and destruction, their power would grow a *substantial* amount compared to the controlled leanness of their current mortal diet.

And that was just if she *didn't* find one of the Crowns she was after.

If she did, she had two nearly impossible fights to throw down against: Urielle, goddess of the mutable elements—Nausicaä's mother, and a whole new field of concern in that regard— and Tellis, the goddess of fixed earth.

There was every chance Arlo wouldn't survive either, so Nausicaä wasn't blowing smoke when she told Celadon off about his sword—every time Arlo went through that portal, there was a chance that if she even came back out at all, it would already be too late. Ruin couldn't be killed by physical means once their possession took permanent hold.

They needed another plan.

What the fuck had Eos and Moros been talking about with their hint?

Another ripple, another shudder—this one so powerful it toppled several of the humans into the others beside them.

One had the misfortune of being too close and cried out in an almost comical fading as he fell to the pit's depths.

And as he fell, the pit reached out for him, quite literally.

Thousands of hands from thousands of arms from thousands of featureless bodies stretched from the tar-like substance that filled it. They bubbled up and burst and receded, clawed and poured and clambered over one another in an effort to snatch the officer from the air and drag him down, down, down with them to be smothered beneath their surface.

The universe wasn't all that agreeable to rifts between realms—even less to the people that tried to hop through them.

"IT'S FUCKING ALIVE!" one officer shouted above the yelling and screaming that had followed the first officer to his death.

A few pulled their guns from their holsters and emptied their entire magazines into the pit, trying their damnedest to defeat Chaos with their standard-issue 9 millimeters.

Nausicaä couldn't help but snort.

The last bullet sailed . . . hit off an unseen force field, and was deflected back, right through the center of the officer's head. And as he dropped too, the pit gave its final shudder, and finally, Arlo broke through.

But it wasn't her.

Ruin had precisely zero fucks to give for glamour—why would they? There was a reason Celadon needed a goddess-blessed magical sword just to cut Arlo down while Ruin possessed her. She was more or less invulnerable. Nothing could touch her unless Ruin willed it, and when Arlo's body dying meant bye-bye to Ruin, too, they were pretty compelled to keep her safe.

Still, it got Nausicaä's back up to see every single gun be whipped out and trained on her girlfriend as the pit expelled her out onto the pavement.

"Orlando PD—freeze!"

Beside her, Celadon raised his sword. "I'll give you five seconds to prove to me that Arlo's still in there or I'll run you through."

Righting themselves, unfurling to standing, Ruin turned their head to examine Celadon.

Tilted it in deeper inspection.

"Hands in the air! Down on the ground or we'll open fire!"

"I SAID FREEZE!"

Then, with a sigh, they lifted their hand, just the one, but not to comply with the officers shouting at them.

Instead, they flicked it in the Night King's direction, and a force like a pulse blew both Celadon *and* Lethe to their backs on the ground several feet away. "If she did not linger, fatigued though she is, that pit would have greeted you instead of stone."

"Did she do it?"

Ruin looked next to Nausicaä. Hand still raised, every bullet deflected as soon as shot . . . hundreds of officers dropping like flies. Nausicaä couldn't help but snag on the thick pool of blood that had quickly begun to drain from the bodies and trickle over the ledge, feeding into the pit and sending the tar back into a clawing frenzy.

"She did not," they replied at last, stealing back Nausicaä's focus. "Though to her curiosity, we did arrive in the fields of Elysium. She wanted to bring you back a flower."

. . . ah.

Nausicaä blushed.

That was . . . incredibly endearing to her.

Nobody'd ever given her flowers before. And it explained the holdup, because one didn't simply *walk* into Elysium and pick a flower. It was a big piss-off to the Eternal Gardeners that tended them, and nobody wanted to mess with those. Nobody except Ruin, she supposed. And her girlfriend.

Ruin reached into the fold of the Hunter's robe that Arlo still wore around everywhere—security, she'd told Nausicaä when she'd asked about it; it helped her remember who she was.

They extracted a beautiful periwinkle-blue flower that looked a bit like a roselily and was so singularly fragrant, Nausicaä felt the calming effects of its scent just held aloft in Ruin's hand.

She took the gift.

"I would have rather it come from her," she murmured, touched all the same, because it *had* come from her, and was the most proof she'd received in probably four months that Arlo was still Arlo . . . still cared about Nausicaä at all.

Ruin shrugged.

"Follow," they bid, and like the trained dog she was these days, Nausicaä went.

Ruin didn't often beckon her anywhere, didn't often acknowledge her at all save for the occasional taunt to see what she would do.

Two steps and Ruin already paused; looked behind them at the mass of dead officers; held up their hand once more to grab hold of the air and *pull*, and Nausicaä was allowed to enjoy the uniquely uncomfortable feeling not of *them* moving an inch but of the world shifting closer, as though on a conveyor belt.

All of a sudden, they were standing in the thick of death. Ruin lifted a boot to press against the side of a russet-haired officer's face. "This one. Collect it."

"Uh . . ." Nausicaä looked down at the body in question. "Whyyyyyy, can I ask? Do I *want* to ask? If you think I'm going to let you use Arlo's body to get your jollies with a corpse, you can—"

"Collect it," Ruin repeated, as blandly as telling her to get milk from the store. "For *Riadne*."

Again Nausicaä paused.

Looked back down at the dead body.

Looked back up at Ruin's waiting face.

"Uh . . . ," she repeated. "That 'why' still stands . . ."

Sighing, Ruin stooped to pick it up themselves and tossed it over their shoulder like a bag of flour.

"Come on, don't leave me in suspense here! Is *Riadne* planning to get some jollies with a corpse? Because—"

"You do know that if Arlo continues to throw herself blindly into these rifts, she will wear past exhaustion *very* soon. One day soon, she will not return with me at all. Why have you tried nothing to save her, I wonder? Why do you do nothing but dabble in destruction, then silently follow and wait? What purpose do you serve her at all, at this point, besides one of burden?"

Oh, she was well aware.

The flower in her hand was proof of it—of the many ways Arlo acted to protect her, make her happy, pit herself against danger for Nausicaä's gain. Their entire relationship she'd been this way: punching Megaera, throwing herself between her and Zombie Heulfryn on the Ghost *Dirge*, the stupid bracelet that took Nausicaä to Toronto instead of her . . .

"One might think your heart still the possession of one of my Sins, for all you seem to care."

Nausicaä's brow . . . furrowed.

That's right.

Lust.

Nausicaä had traded her heart to Riadne in an attempt to ensure Arlo's safety. The condition had been that it would belong to the High Queen only so long as Arlo remained unharmed and alive—and had returned to her the moment Ruin had been summoned, the death of Arlo's mortality triggering the end of their contract.

She hadn't forgotten that experience at all. But what Ruin had just taunted . . . perhaps it was because her mind was already churning over the scions' hint, but suddenly, she was reminded of something that hadn't occurred until just now.

Maybe the something she'd been waiting for, biding her time trying to figure out . . .

Because back when she'd been supposedly heartless, there were flickers of moments where she found herself acting as though she wasn't, not fully.

In Seelie Winter's throne room, when Aslaug had been lost to grief over the death of her wife, and Nausicaä couldn't stand to see her first friend in this world cut down without a weapon in her hand. When Riadne was furious with Arlo for standing up to her, and Nausicaä had seethed—things she shouldn't have felt at all . . . for people she'd given parts of her heart to.

Hmmm.

There was something there, something that she hadn't considered, had forgotten about entirely with everything going on . . .

She had to think.

"Okay, well, you and Riadne have fun with . . . whatever this is," she replied cheerfully, waving a hand at the body over their shoulder. "Hard pass on the invite to join. Arlo, if you can hear me, I'll catch up with you later. There's something I have to do."

Ruin frowned but ultimately didn't care that much what Nausicaä did so long as she kept out of their way.

And that was just as well.

That was part of the plan.

Holding her flower preciously close, she saluted Ruin, then summoned her wings to transport her away.

CHAPTER 6

Ruin

COUNCIL WAS ALREADY WELL underway by the time Ruin returned to the palace. They strode through the War Chamber's twin howlite doors into a windowless room commanded by an enormous table at its very center.

Around this, the Fae High Council and the High Queen's closest advisors were assembled. Riadne presided at the end farthest from the entrance, and all in the room were bent over the top of quite the ingenious map. Spread wide between them, it built itself like a miniature-scale model of whatever part of the world was requested.

At the present, it showed a great expanse of desert surrounding some paradisical city of sandstone and ruby and gold, ripe for the ravaging . . .

Riadne Lysterne, their lady and master, glared at them as they entered. "You took your time," she greeted coolly.

Oh, how Ruin would enjoy watching her *wither* to dust at their feet.

Wordlessly, they deposited the body they still carried into the nearest, velvet-upholstered, high-backed chair, much to the disgust of the High Councillor stationed beside it.

Making quick assessment of their offering, Riadne clicked her tongue. "I suppose that absolves you. Sit," she commanded, brushing a hand toward to the chair on her right.

Tediously, Ruin was obliged to acquiesce.

Was about to stalk for their appointed seat when they noticed the young man in the chair on her left.

Dressed in the guise of one of the Bone Guard generals, his

features contorted ever so slightly by glamour impressive enough that no one would notice what lay beneath, not unless they were looking for that shimmering sheen that was so obvious to Ruin's perceptive eyes . . .

This horde of spineless sycophants wouldn't dare question anything their queen chose to do, but oh, how curious to see that young man looking so distinctly uncomfortable, doing his best to make himself small at his mother's side.

"Well, hello

there,

little

—" prince of their own Court, and no one recognized he was there? Whatever he was playing at right now, he was *so* lucky Arlo had recovered *just* enough energy to wrest tentative control of herself before Ruin blurted out the end of that condemning sentence.

Spoil sport.

Riadne raised a brow at her, mildly interested in what she'd been about to say. But Arlo shook her head, continued for her seat as placid as Ruin had been, and sat without further comment.

Luckily, the queen was absorbed back into conversation, allowing Arlo to press as far back in her chair as she could flatten to shoot a peeved look at Vehan Lysterne.

What are you doing? she mouthed.

He'd better not be here for *her*.

Vehan shrugged, his wide-eyed glance shooting back distress.

"—we simply must work harder," said one of the High Councillors, drawing Arlo's attention to the discussion. "The *Night Court* has been prolific in their appeals to the undecided Courts. If we've any hope of wooing them to our side, we must ply our efforts with considerably more vigor."

They were back at debating UnSeelie Autumn and Summer again, it seemed.

Celadon and Riadne had been hard at work, contending against each other for the support of the remaining Courts. Riadne had won without contest the entirety of the Fae High Council—entirely unsurprising to Arlo, given what she knew from Ruin's memories, of the strings they'd been pulling behind this operation from the very beginning.

But it *had* come as a blow to see Head Councillor Larsen among them, the representative of UnSeelie Spring, who'd been the reason Arlo had been permitted an extension for her Weighing. Seated at the far end of the table, she did look considerably thinner, wane, and withdrawn these days, as did her pointedly silent husband beside her.

Seelie Autumn in Germany and Spring in England had been quick to sever ties with their Council representatives and side themselves with Celadon's Night Court; Seelie Winter in Norway had already been claimed by Riadne prior, and UnSeelie Winter, her father's Court in Russia, had been staunch in their support of one of their own blood.

What remained was two, Japan and India, both rejecting the insistence of their Councillors and refusing the yoke of further Western rule. If the system was to be redesigned, they reasoned, what they wanted was independence.

Arlo didn't blame them.

Under different circumstances, she knew Celadon too wouldn't have begrudged them that, but with Riadne unrelenting, he had to be as well.

"Do you think perhaps we are finished with *asking*, Councillor Sokolov?" Riadne replied, her tone dangerously light, to the ice-eyed, black-haired man who'd spoken—Councillor Kirill Sokolov of UnSeelie Winter, Arlo recalled. "Do you think, *perhaps*, we ought to try now a different method of acquisition?"

Eyes flashing, Riadne drew herself tall in her seat, and even though

Riadne hadn't inherited Winter's gift of ice, Arlo swore she could feel the room dip a fraction cooler.

"It was courtesy, esteemed gentlefolk, that extended *my* Courts the illusion of choice in this matter. If they are unwilling to make one, if they cannot bend to reason as their own Councillors have done, I shall simply have to force decision upon them. Commander Rowan—"

Riadne's gaze snapped to a man on her right.

Aldaine Rowan, commander of the Bone Guard, was a frightening fae. Tattoos scrawled all over his body, blacking out the whites of his eyes; nails filed to the points of claws; iron nails drilled like studs into the sweep of his collarbone. And as vicious as his appearance, his demeanor was even worse. Arlo had been sent on numerous errands with him in tow, and all had ended in blood.

"It seems my display of force in Seelie Winter was insufficient demonstration of my character. This indecision mocks me—how *little* I enjoy that."

Arlo and Vehan both sat a little straighter in their seats, listening intently.

"As High Queen, Master of Ruin, Lady Sin, I will not be made the fool of by my inferiors any longer. The Courts my wayward son has lured under his temporary protection will be returned to my fold soon enough. Two more remain that cannot decide where their allegiance should lie? Then one will fall to make an example for the other. If *neither* will choose their side . . ." She slapped the flat of her hand so suddenly on the table, so loudly, that several Councillors startled.

Silence, then, stretched heavy over the room.

A full minute later, Riadne leaned delicately back in her seat.

"No more the fool," she repeated, deadly in her placidity. "UnSeelie Summer first, if you would, Commander," she said to Rowan, causing him to grin widely enough that the tips of his gold-capped fangs glinted in the room's dim lighting. "And given the maltreatment of my magnanimity thus far, I shouldn't think any warning necessary, do you? Be ready to move at first light."

The meeting was now adjourned, simple as that.

Riadne rose, her chair sliding soundlessly backward, and all around the table, the Councillors and advisors rose as well. They bowed, folded their hands over their hearts in reverence to their High Sovereign, and didn't move a further muscle until Riadne had swept back out of the room.

Arlo knew enough of entitled old fae that she doubted no one had an opinion to share in the wake of the queen just declaring war. Certainly the Fae High Council would be meeting later to discuss what had happened here, the power-hungry queen whom Arlo had heard them admit, in one such gathering, that they'd taken measures to push in the Sins' direction, now giving them a spot of trouble in the terms of their control of her.

Fools.

And cowards, too. No one would say a word—not with *Ruin* still in their midst, which they hadn't been counting on Riadne managing to summon, Arlo surmised. By all indications, they'd been intending to eliminate Riadne themselves as soon as she'd made all seven stones, which they'd hoped to be the ones to control. But then Nausicaä had gone and made herself Riadne's soldier, and none of them had wanted to risk what *she* could do. And now all of them were unhappily here, biding their time, talking endlessly of what could be done to put them back on track with their goals of . . . Court domination, Arlo supposed.

She hardly cared.

There was enough going on without this extra layer of trouble, and when Arlo had mentioned what she'd learned to Riadne, the High Queen had only laughed, was only more delighted to make things uncomfortable for them in every meeting.

One by one, in weighted silence, the group began to gather their books and their maps and their papers, sharing looks among themselves as they filtered out.

When it was only Arlo and Vehan remaining, still seated in their chairs—Arlo casual and Vehan stiff—she turned properly to him at last.

Took in his disguise, which would have allowed him to pass unrecognized by the general guard, not looking too closely at one of their feared superiors, but the fact that he'd been sitting here beside his *mother*, in a room full of very clever and very vicious fae . . .

"So . . . putting your die to good use, I see?"

Hand waving air to cool his face, Vehan wilted with a shuddering sigh. "I failed the roll, actually. A nineteen instead of a twenty. Mother didn't recognize me—she . . . currently believes me to be my father. Which . . . sometimes happens. And no one else really cared I was here. They figured me for security, I think. But I'm pretty sure I would have been made just now after she'd left if it weren't for the overall terror of *you* making all those very scary people look anywhere but over here."

Vehan regarded her now.

Fully.

So deeply that Arlo felt something of her old instincts—the her she'd been before apathy had started to eat at her roots like mold—make her want to drop her gaze to the floor and blush.

Something about Vehan in particular . . . Nausicaä was like the earth to her. She could always count on being able to touch her and find her center. But there was something about Vehan that was just as good, in a completely different way, at reminding her who she was.

She cocked her head at him.

Met his gaze with mild pensiveness.

"Well," she said, "you're lucky I was able to be here. Lucky you came, regardless. Riadne's planning a strike against the UnSeelie Summer Court in just a few hours' time—Celadon should probably know that, yeah? Come on, I'll blend some fancy alchemy with Ruin's formidable cosmic power and send you back to the Market. I'm sure Aurelian's worried sick about you."

"Arlo?"

Arlo paused, mid-rise from her chair. She tilted her head in silent permission for him to ask whatever it was he would ask even if she'd denied him.

"Why didn't you tell me what you were going to do?" He gestured to her person. "With Ruin. Your plan—*our* plan, back at the summoning. You're my friend, Arlo. Probably my best, besides Aurelian. I wouldn't have stopped you. Why didn't you say anything?"

It was something in the way he spoke—small and wounded and light.

Arlo straightened. She could sense Ruin growing bored with the conversation, as they always did when things started taking a personal turn toward feelings. She was also extremely fatigued, nearly flatlining on exhaustion, and all she wanted was a good long *rest*, but . . .

Something.

In the way he spoke.

Vehan was so good at it—at reminding her how to care. Where her girlfriend was very reserved with what she thought and felt, Vehan was an entirely open book.

"Nausicaä blames *me*, you know?" he continued, as though the dam holding back all these thoughts had just blown wide for everything to come flooding through. His chest heaved with barely restrained emotion, and his blue eyes took on a quality like water. "She blames Celadon, and all of us really, but me the most, and that would be fine. I could deal with that if the person that didn't blame me more than anyone was myself, because I promised to protect you, Arlo! I promised to stay beside you. And you promised me the same. But you still didn't tell me. You *should* have told me."

"I'm sorry," Arlo heard herself reply, and was almost . . . surprised to also hear she meant it. "I didn't intend to hurt you or cause you trouble."

Shaking his head vigorously, Vehan made to stand as well. "I'm *worried* about you, Arlo. You shouldn't have to do any of this by your-self—"

"But I do," she interrupted. "I do have to do this by myself."

"But *why?*"

In the back of her being, she felt Ruin's dark amusement, their chuckle of mean-spirited laughter.

Oh, my darling.

She heard them purr.

*That pride of yours—it always was your greatest strength.
No wonder the Sin chose you.*

"It's just the way it has to be," Arlo said aloud to Vehan, ignoring the jab as best she could.

This wasn't her pride. She *did* have to do this on her own. The danger, the strain this entire thing put on her immortal soul—it would have broken Vehan. Or Ruin would have. It was all she could risk just to let Nausicaä as close as she did, because Arlo was weak and wanted her girlfriend around, despite the fact that she really, *really* shouldn't put her in the crosshairs of this parasite inside her. But try stopping Nausicaä from doing anything she didn't want to stop doing.

Arlo was working so hard to hold on to herself.

She didn't want anyone involved more than they had to be, if she lost that careful control before she could accomplish her goals.

"Let's go," she finished, concluding their conversation. "I'm running on fumes, and Ruin's definitely going to give you up the first opportunity they get, so you have to leave. Now. And don't come back, do you understand, Vehan? You can't come back here anymore. Riadne will be waiting for it."

The look Vehan gave her was pure defiance. "Sorry," he replied, squaring his jaw, pulling back his shoulders, affecting the prince who wouldn't be told *no* by anyone. "I can't promise you that. I already made you a different one, and I intend to keep it."

Arlo sighed.

What would her life have been like, she wondered, if she'd had friends who weren't all so frustratingly stubborn?

They stood at the edge of a sprawling lake—Arlo and High King Phoebus Viridian—the water so clear and glassy-smooth that Arlo could see straight to its floor.

It was a beautiful setting, surrounded by lush pine forests and a backdrop of snowcapped mountains, morning sunlight spilling warmly over their peaks, and the clean air only just beginning to take on its first hints of autumn decay.

"You've never been to UnSeelie Spring proper, have you, son."

It wasn't a question, but Arlo shook his head regardless, lifting his gaze from his reflection to do so. "No, sir, I haven't."

As a Lysterne, blood of one of the Eight Founders and a royal, he'd been expected to live in his great-aunt's castle, alongside his mother. His father—whose duty had been first and foremost to High King Phoebus, and who therefore spent most of his time with him—had often brought Arlo along with him to the UnSeelie palace for some hands-on experience with alchemy. But Arlo had never been left to roam the grounds as he'd pleased, and certainly not permitted to take off to explore the Court beyond—his father had *always* been wary of others, even before his philosopher's stone research, and hadn't wanted to risk one of his many enemies snatching Arlo for leverage.

And here Arlo was, walking himself to their clutches willingly— his father had been absolutely apoplectic over his acceptance of Phoebus's offer; he'd stormed from the room and into his lab, and hadn't even surfaced to bid Arlo goodbye come the morning.

High King Phoebus made a sound like mild dismay low in his throat.

Arlo, meanwhile, watched as he plunged a hand into his robes to draw back out a dagger.

"Take it," he commanded, not unkindly, holding the precious weapon flat between them.

A gorgeous thing, this dagger.

The blade and cross guard were so pure a silver that they gleamed an unblemished white in the morning; the knife's grip was made of hundreds of tiny, polished black opals extending to a large chunk of sharply angled obsidian for a pommel.

Arlo had lived his entire life so far a prince, and still he'd never seen anything so fine. Taking it in his hands, he was amazed by its featherlightness.

"A good, solid throw should do it," the High King said next, startling Arlo out of his appreciation.

He blinked up at him, confused. "Sorry, what?"

Phoebus smiled, bland but encouraging. "Go on, lad. Give it a throw! One can't expect something for nothing—there's a toll to be paid for traveling this waterway, and we don't want to keep the Lady waiting for it."

Not a single idea what the High King was on about, but of the vague impression he was meant to throw the dagger into the *water*, Arlo turned himself to the bank slowly, drew back his arm, looked one last time to Phoebus for guidance, then threw the dagger as far as he could.

"Good arm," the High King complimented after a low whistle.

Together, they watched the glinting metal sail in pinwheel spirals, arcing high before beginning descent—and just as the blade was to pierce the water's surface, a woman's deep brown hand shot from the depths to catch it by the blade.

"The Lady is partial to weaponry," Phoebus said like it was a good joke between them, chuckling at the shock in Arlo's wide eyes. "And I do like to keep her happy—no better guard could stand between our capital and the world. But come, Arlo. We don't want to miss our boat!"

About to ask what the High King meant, Arlo was at a further loss when he tore his gaze from the hand, which had lowered once more below the surface, to find a small wooden boat, barely big enough for the full-grown fae and his young alchemist charge, bobbing against the water's shore.

It most certainly hadn't been there before.

"In we go!" Phoebus instructed, as though this was all perfectly ordinary, and moved behind Arlo to usher him forward with a brush of his hands.

Into the boat Arlo climbed. "Wait a minute," he said over his shoulder as he made his way the best he could balance to the farthest plank to claim a seat. "The *Lady*—you don't mean—"

"I do mean! *The* Lady, my boy—of the Lake herself. Guardian of the Realms. And she does not like her time to be wasted, so onward we row."

Taking up both paddles, like he wasn't the High King and history's most exalted fae, Phoebus rowed them out to the lake's center, right where the Lady's hand had appeared moments ago.

Immediately, Arlo threw himself to the edge of the boat, hoping to catch a glimpse of her.

"Oh, I wouldn't do that, Arlo."

"Why?"

There—the water was much deeper out here, but Arlo could see something iridescent flash in its depths like an enormous fish tail alongside a cloud of black-ink-like hair.

A fistful of the back of his tunic reeled Arlo from the boat's ledge.

"Men have gone mad off a glimpse of her alone."

Squaring his jaw, trying to sound a lot braver than he suddenly felt—had that been a glimpse? Would madness set in quick or slow? Would he know?—Arlo replied, "Well, I'm no mere man."

And once again, Phoebus smiled—this time the smile Arlo associated only with danger. "A fact I am very hopeful will prove true, my boy. Now . . ." He motioned to the plank Arlo sat on. "A big breath,

Arlo, and hold on tight—we don't want you falling off between realms!"

"What?"

SLAM.

Arlo's hands scrambled for purchase as from below a force like what he imagined being tackled by a whale felt like threw itself against the underside of their boat.

Never had anything felt so wildly insufficient and fragile as the old, rotting wood that was all that separated them from whatever it was. The boat rocked. *SLAM.* Arlo held fast to his plank. *SLAM.* The High King drew a long, deep breath; Arlo only barely remembered to do so as well before one last *SLAM*, and the boat flipped fully over, plunging them into . . . nothing?

What a curious sensation.

Arlo had braced himself, expecting the rush of water, the sting and press and panic of drowning. There was neither. He wasn't even wet, he realized, when he opened his eyes, which had squeezed shut on instinct, to inspect himself.

"Exhilarating," Phoebus chimed brightly. "Everything in order, Arlo? Did you know, if you hadn't held your breath, you would have drowned the moment we turned? Your body wouldn't even have time to recognize it was dead. The Lady would get to keep your soul for an eternity—how delightfully vicious the merfolk are."

He spoke like this thrilled him too.

Anything Arlo had to reply, though, dissolved like sugar on the tip of his tongue—for just then he'd lifted his gaze from his inspection and what met his sight was a view he was certain would stay with him to his grave.

Catching his awe, the High King grinned. "The Isle of Avalon. Welcome home, Arlo Flamel. And may I say how very pleased we are to have you."

Avalon.

One of the last pockets of the Otherworld still accessible by the mortal plane, besides the Hiraeth. Most had been closed off from access with the banishment of the gods, as they had been the ones to open the doorways that allowed the folk to hide there.

Now, with the gods gone, the Founders had been left to their own clever bits of magic to conceal their cities from human detection.

But Avalon . . .

Avalon was still theirs. Phoebus had married into it with the stunning mortal sorceress Morgana, who'd won ownership of it from the gods themselves; Morgana, who'd been Arlo's father's mentor.

As they glided along the misty lake, Avalon sat in the distance like an isle floating.

The closer they drew, the more there was to see, and Arlo didn't know what to take in first. Castletown Market—the thriving center of the Eight Great Courts—had been built in every shade of green and black; homes and shops and inns and entertainment all stood in splendor, encrusted with emerald jewels and gleaming moonstone, pearl and shining ebony stone. Moss crowned their rooftops. Crept between the grooves in the cobbled streets.

Only when they reached a wooden dock jutting far out into the lake did the mist thin enough for Arlo to see the moonbeam-white face of the Fae High Academy, with all its opal quartz and diamond adornments.

Behind it, like a looming shadow, the starkly black silhouette of UnSeelie Spring's famous Château Noir—the Black Castle.

A group of distinguished old fae Arlo knew only from his father's rantings, in the fine onyx-and-ivory robes that marked them as the Fae High Council, was gathered at the end of the pier, waiting to receive the High King.

They eyed Arlo in such a way he was strongly reminded of a pack of circling vultures.

Phoebus disembarked with ease. The vulture pack fluttered rapidly to engulf him. But before they could close him into their ranks, he bent and offered Arlo his hand, and pulled him easily from the boat, fastening Arlo quickly to his side.

"A full reception," Phoebus said privately between them with a wink. "Have I mentioned how excited we all are to have you here? Councillor Urquhart might even be on the verge of a smile!"

Yes.

Excitement.

Was that what glinted in the cloudy eyes of Councillor Urquhart, the fae man with hair so wisping white it looked to be translucent? Possibly he was over a thousand years old, and definitely that was more the look of *hunger*.

The Council began to trade pleasantries with their High King and to fill Phoebus in on the little that had happened in his short absence.

Arlo busied himself with inspecting the town.

Early as it was, there wasn't overmuch activity on the streets save what seemed to be a fish market down the docks. But inside shops, folk were busy preparing for their day: bakeries scenting the air with spice and warm, fresh bread; woodsmoke from homes stoking fires for breakfast; outdoor vendors setting up their stalls; tailors and milliners and dressmakers fixing their window displays.

On and on the list of waking activity went, and Arlo took it all in as they walked.

How clean everything was . . .

How pleasing a sight . . .

Greenery spilled from pots and climbed up walls and curled between homes. Great trees towered here and there, occasionally forcing their group to part around one in the middle of the street; a house to Arlo's right had been built in a curious curve around another. As Phoebus passed, flowers unfurled to happy, full bloom and moss thickened beneath his heel, the Gift that marked him as an exceptional fae—the Gift his young son Enfys had apparently inherited, but Arlo had never met him to behold this for himself.

They neared the academy's famous glass gates, the school cutting so high into the sky that Arlo felt dizzy to look up at its turrets and spires. The enormity of the Château Noir behind it seemed unfathomable to him; he'd never felt so insignificant in his life as he did standing here, a mere ant, at the formidable foundations of fae society.

"Cenavy!" the High King called, drawing Arlo's attention from the two castles.

He quickly surveyed the right side of the courtyard, where his gathering had paused, and his gaze snagged on glaring pale eyes—belonging to a young white-haired woman in strange black leather, folded against the side of one of the yard's many statues.

The same young woman who'd been in his loft just the night before . . .

Alecto.

A *Fury.*

The one who'd sworn to keep vigilance over his alchemic endeavors, as though Arlo would ever again put them to such horror as what had instigated this whole turn of events.

In an attempt to be friendly, he sent her a small wave.

Alecto, if possible, frowned even deeper at the action and looked away.

"Phoebus," Arlo's great-aunt greeted stiffly upon their party's approach, and Arlo shifted focus to her at last. She'd parted from their collection this morning. Arlo retrieved, she'd returned home instead of setting off for the journey here with them, and Arlo hadn't understood why at the time, but the two who trailed close in her wake cleared that mystery on a glance.

Crown Princess Arina and her twin brother, Hyperion Lysterne.

It was the start of the new school year; of course the twins would be here, exact same age as Arlo that they were. And Arlo felt the sight of them like a physical blow to his gut.

Tall and warmly tanned, with great brown eyes and brilliant copper hair, they were *lovely* fae to behold, and the year of Arlo's absence had only sharpened that.

He'd never been close with either. Arina was too much her

mother's carefully groomed replacement, aloof and austere and constantly looking at Arlo like his human heritage made him mud.

Hyperion was different.

Hyperion was the sort of person one couldn't help but gravitate to, who lit up every room like sunlight and laughed like warm summer nights—charming, popular, intelligent, a proper sidhe prince. In their younger years, he'd made a good attempt at befriending Arlo, but Arlo had been so content back then to let his world and schooling revolve around his parents alone that by the time he realized he might actually like to be friends with this boy in return, Hyperion's advances had finally ceased, and Arlo had no idea how to go about making his own.

"Well now." Phoebus gave a clap of his hands and that deceptive smile Arlo wasn't sure he liked at all. He turned to Arlo and the twins standing in an awkward group, each pretending they weren't eyeing the other in interest. "Here we are, on the cusp of the grandest adventure we ever journey in our lives—school. Ah, to be young again. . . . In my day, we had no such fine establishment as the academy in which to pursue the world's knowledge. Cenavy, do you remember—"

The High King broke off into reminiscing, his focus drifting back to the queen who'd long been his closest and dearest companion, it was well known. The Lysternes and Viridians were so closely entwined that the Courts could all break into odds with each other, but Arlo doubted UnSeelie Spring and Seelie Summer would ever be anything but fierce allies.

An elbow to Arlo's side snagged his attention.

He looked over to find Hyperion grinning.

"They finally convinced your father to let you come here, did they?"

Flushing—because no, Nicholas Flamel had been *furious* with Arlo's decision, had refused to so much as look at him after he'd made his decision, let alone speak—he merely gave a quiet nod.

"Brilliant." Hyperion beamed. "Just you wait, Arlo—if I may be so familiar? Just you wait, you'll love it here." He slung an arm across

Arlo's shoulders, laughing a little at how startled Arlo was by the intimacy. "Son of Nicholas Flamel, greatest alchemist of our time? Oh, they're going to love you right back." He winked. "Come, if we ask it very nicely, perhaps we might persuade our prefect to room us together."

Arlo was almost offended to discover making friends had been this easy all along.

CHAPTER 7

Aurelian

A GENTLE SHAKE TO HIS shoulder woke Aurelian with a start. He shot upright in bed, instantly alert and primed for a fight. For a moment, there was sheer panic, his brain able to comprehend nothing but the fact that Vehan wasn't beside him.

"Easy—it's just me."

Aurelian blinked.

He looked from the vacant spot on Vehan's side of the bed to the sliver remaining of his own side, where his boyfriend sat watching Aurelian with a mixture of guilt and trepidation.

Aurelian loosed a heavy sigh. "What time is it?" he groaned, bleariness settling back in with the receding of adrenaline.

Vehan shrugged. "I'm not sure. Sometime after three a.m."

"You're worried. Is everything all right with your mother?"

He was far too exhausted to pretend he didn't know about Vehan's nighttime wandering. It didn't bother him that Vehan hadn't confided in him about his homesickness, not reasonably at least, but he'd be lying to say he wasn't the least bit concerned—the love of his life, his soulmate, throwing himself into the highest of danger so far from Aurelian's protection.

Between Riadne and Ruin and all the vicious others prowling the Luminous Palace, if he thought it would get him anywhere, that Vehan would actually listen to him, he'd command outright that the visits stop.

But he understood.

Sort of.

Vehan had been his mother's fiercest defender since boyhood, and old habits were exceptionally hard to drop. He knew from experience how impossible it was to extinguish love and caring.

To Vehan's credit, he looked to be suffering only a *mild* heart attack over the statement. Wincing, he replied, "Ah. So . . . you knew all along, then?"

"More or less." Aurelian yawned, patting his heart like he could physically touch the tether anchored there. Falling back against the pillows, he stretched a little, and more than enjoyed the effect he could *feel* this had on Vehan's attention. "How did you get back inside the Market? They don't open the gates until sunrise."

Immediately, Vehan sobered.

He drew himself from Aurelian's side, paced a little in wild thought. "Arlo. She was there—listen, Aurelian? We need to get to Celadon, now. My mother . . . I got lucky with my timing. She was holding an emergency war council, and apparently they're going to make an example of UnSeelie Summer for taking so long to decide their allegiance. The strike is planned for first light—whose first light, I have no idea. Most likely her time zone, which means we have barely *hours* to get ahead of this. We have to warn Celadon."

This was . . . a lot to take in.

Once again Aurelian found himself blinking.

"All right . . ." he said, slow but trusting. Shaking his head and flinging the covers from his body, he swung himself out of bed. "All right," he repeated, clearer. "Let's get to the portal in my office."

"You, ah, *will* be putting some form of clothing on first, yes? Not that I mind, and maybe Celadon wouldn't either, after your little nighttime escapade together last summer, but—*oof*!"

Lobbing a pillow at his boyfriend's head, Aurelian stalked to their dresser.

"Has anyone ever told you you're scary good at magic?"

Aurelian bit the inside of his cheek to conceal his amusement.

The portal they'd established in the private office that had once belonged to the Madam led directly into Celadon's office. Celadon, bolstered by his own exceptional inheritance and pedigree, had created it himself to connect directly to his Egress, but it was Aurelian's lesidhe magic that had placed all manner of charms and wards and protections to keep all but Aurelian, Vehan, and Celadon from utilizing it.

Anyone else who tried would find themselves spat out the other side as dust—as was evidenced by the tiny heap of *some* creature's remains, possibly a mouse, but assassins came in all shapes and sizes, and there was no being too careful with something that let out into the Night King's personal quarters.

"Also," Vehan continued, jumping subjects quickly, as he tended to do whenever nervous, "it's very dark in here, and it's occurred to me that Celadon might actually sleep once in a while. We are essentially sneaking up on my unsuspecting and extremely powerful brother in the middle of the night, in the middle of *war*, to accost him in his bed. Is this smart?"

Aurelian shrugged. "Probably not, but this is exactly the reason this portal was established. He will get over it."

Frowning, Vehan made his way through the dark for the door that led out of the office.

Silently, it swung open to them.

Aurelian could only just make out the scene around his boyfriend's shoulders, in the pitch darkness of Celadon's bedroom. Illuminated by only the wash of moonlight and Toronto's ambience reflected off snow through the far glass wall that overlooked the city, Celadon's enormous canopy bed loomed, swathed in silk and shadow.

"Where do you figure Lethe is?" Vehan hissed quietly between them. "Because I doubt *he's* going to be very happy about—AH!"

The commotion was instant.

Aurelian barely had time to process what happened.

Something large and swift knocked Vehan to the floor as several lights burst to life around the room. Aurelian found himself staring, momentarily stunned, down at the half-dressed form of Lethe atop Vehan, knife pressed hard to the soft of his throat . . .

"Not happy at *all*," Lethe bit out, furious.

It was just . . . that Aurelian had no idea how to reconcile this image.

This young man, pale as starlight, moonstone-bright hair rumpled from bed, emerald sleep pants slung low on too-sharp hips. Ordinary. *Intimate.* There was something that looked like a bite on his shoulder, and this was what had given him pause.

This, and Celadon rising from the bed, the sheerest black robe all that existed to preserve his modesty—gods, what had they just walked in on? It was so extremely weird to think of Lethe in the context of anything this domestic.

Then his brain caught up with *dagger* and *Vehan's throat*, and the growl only lesidhe could produce issued Lethe a warning right before Aurelian tackled him—"*Off*," he snarled, rolling with the god of mis-fortune as the two of them bared teeth and snapped and wrestled for dominance. Aurelian *very* obviously lost, but he liked to think he gave a good effort.

Peering down at them through a mixture of exasperation and calm-ing fright, Celadon kept one hand holding his poor excuse for a robe closed—seriously, what was even the point of that thing, Aurelian wondered through the gap in the cage of Lethe's deceptively strong arms—while the other hand rubbed at his temple.

"*What* is going on?" he asked through a huskiness that definitely hadn't been sleep. "Vehan—"

"FOR THE LOVE OF *URIELLE*, PUT SOME CLOTHES ON!" Vehan cried, hands sealed firmly over his eyes.

Folding his arms over his chest, Celadon merely raised a brow. "This is *my* room—well outside visiting hours, I should add." He straightened on a thought. "Has something happened? Is Arlo all right?"

"Arlo's fine," Aurelian replied, still flat on his back on the ground and sporting a bloody nose. He kicked up at the weight like several buildings atop him, but Lethe had already begun his smug retreat to prowl for Celadon's cavernous walk-in closet. "She's fine," he repeated, rolling onto his stomach. "UnSeelie Summer won't be able to say the same though, in a few hours."

For a moment, Celadon only stared.

Lethe returned from the closet to drape a far more suitable robe on the Night King, in a way that was almost obscene to witness, and Aurelian was never coming here unannounced again.

More suitably dressed, Celadon began at once for the doors of his office. "Come."

CHAPTER 8

Celadon

AS MUCH AS CELADON *hated* the trek through rolling dunes of loose, coarse sand, if pressed to choose one other than his own, he'd have to say without a doubt UnSeelie Summer's Court was his favorite.

Hidden somewhere in the heart of a desert none could name with any certainty—not even the folk who dwelled there—entry to the capitol was permitted only to those who followed, in correct sequence, a very specific set of instructions.

The location could be accessed only by means of a secret portal, established in whichever South Asian country the ruling royal family was from—at the moment, the throne was sat by the Fahim family, from Bangladesh.

The portal would spit the traveler out into an unremarkable barrenness, sand and only sand as far as the eye could see. If the sun had yet to rise, one had to walk in the direction it would; if it had yet to set, they had to walk the opposite. Only when the sun touched the horizon—and no longer than this duration—would the capitol city be revealed through the formidable glamour shielding it, and if one didn't manage to reach the gates in this brief time span, they would be forced to wait out the entire cycle to the next sliver of a window.

"Just . . . a bit . . . farther . . ." Celadon huffed, only partially glad for the cooler temperatures of desert predawn. He was by no means out of shape, but stand in place for more than a couple of seconds, and one would find their feet beginning to sink through the sand, up to their thighs. Quite difficult to walk through, then, even for a fae, which meant their pace had to remain constant. "We have to . . . make it before Riadne . . . gets here."

They had only minutes.

When no response or confirmation of receipt had answered Celadon's attempt at warning the palace of his mother's intentions, he hadn't been able to leave it simply at that and tell himself he'd tried.

Lethe had rolled his eyes and commented peevishly on his bleeding heart, but he would much rather *not* have the weight of an entire Court's demise on his conscience if there was something he could do about it.

And it was easy enough for him to get here—son of the late High King and current High Queen, head of his own Court, Celadon enjoyed a perk or two that expedited the process. But nothing, not even his status, would mediate the hellscape *all* had to suffer in this last leg of UnSeelie Summer's trial—all except Lethe, who seemed more or less unfazed by their terrain; whether owing to his godhood or his powerful body remembering it once used to propel itself through dense water, Celadon could only envy the result.

Envy, and plug on—*minutes*; they had to reach the city's gates as soon as they appeared, or there would be no hope for the Court surviving whatever it was Riadne had planned.

Celadon couldn't see any hint of her forces in the distance, but he knew his mother well enough by now not to underestimate what this meant.

"There!" Celadon cried, pointing directly ahead of them only several paces away.

The first rays of sunlight began to peek over the horizon. The wards around the Court began to shimmer, bend, dissolve . . .

The Flaming City was one of the most impressive feats of fae ingenuity, one of their wonders of the world, in fact. The way it materialized out of nothing into an oasis of towering sandstone carved in the likeness of flame frozen in time. The way light played across the many facets of its surface, encrusted with copper and gold, rubies and garnets and fiery glass—and this was just the fifty-foot rampart wall that spanned the city's limits. Within held far more extravagant displays of their formidable element.

Two guards resplendent in fire-red and yellow-sun robes flanked the city's only gate, great spears of pure gold and exquisite gem work imposing in their hands.

Celadon straightened.

They were so close—and yet nowhere near as close as he'd hoped they'd be able to get . . .

Lifting his hands, he began to wave them. He opened his mouth, prepared to shout his warning if he must, *something* to grab the guards' attention, when—

Boom.

Celadon faltered.

Lethe darted a hand out to latch onto the back of his shirt.

The tremor had hit so suddenly and quickly even the guards in the distance were unsure of what they'd just felt. It had passed like a tremendous ripple, deep beneath the sand. Celadon had felt it; he'd been able to see it in a traveling vibration across the sand's surface, carrying like a wave to break at the shore of the Flaming City's walls.

Looking down at his feet, he frowned. "What was that?"

"Look," Lethe said, speaking for the first time since they'd arrived here.

He tugged on the fistful of Celadon's shirt; Celadon turned his gaze to follow in the direction of his pointing.

There, so far from where they were but no less deadly than if she were right beside them, Celadon could make out that radiance anywhere.

Riadne.

Only Riadne, standing alone atop a distant dune, completely unmoving in her frosted-glass battle gear, all save her unbound ebony hair tossing in the kicks of desert morning breeze.

She was glaring at him.

Celadon couldn't say how he knew this, couldn't see far enough even with his fae enhancements to meet her gaze, but he could feel it. The electric burn of those icy eyes was just as unmistakable.

"Celadon . . ." Lethe spoke in all the warning he had a chance to give before another, far more powerful *BOOM* knocked them both unsteady, nearly toppling them.

The guards on duty were shouting now—calling out in confusion to Celadon, summoning reinforcements, surprised and growing deeply concerned . . .

Other guards began to gather, curious, in the rampart's walkway.

BOOM. BOOM.

What in the hells was going on?

Celadon clearly wasn't the only one wondering this, judging by the way the guards with the spears began to agitate and form a unit with other soldiers now pouring through the gate.

BOOM. BOOM. BOOM—

"*Celadon!*" Lethe hissed, and Celadon didn't like one bit that whatever connection he'd just made about the ripples trembling beneath their feet, he was clearly terrified by it. "Celadon, we have to move. *MOVE!*" he shouted, practically hauling him to a redirected course and giving Celadon so firm a shove in this direction that he nearly planted face-first into the sand.

"*Excuse* me—"

"*Move*, Celadon. Move!" He sounded so desperate that Celadon complied, the pair of them scrambling not for UnSeelie Summer's borders but for the stretch of encircling dunes to their right. "Move, move, move, move," Lethe chanted under his breath, looking half the time behind them in fear, the other half in wild longing for their destination.

BOOM. BOOM. BOOMBOOMBOOM—it was almost like a drumming.

Not a drumming, Celadon mused as he stumbled in their climb for higher ground—not a drumming but a beating.

A sound like a great something hammering against the earth's crust from below it.

"What is she *doing*?"

BOOM—Celadon tripped and fell to his knees. Lethe attempted to haul him to his feet, but Celadon was too entranced by what was going on down where they'd only just been to be much assistance to his own rescue.

For down below, the sandy floor was beginning to cave—to sink into the earth like water through a drain, the pit of it growing, and growing, and deepening, and growing.

The final beat had done it—the tremors morphed into more of a shaking, and it started first as a protrusion in the pit of that swirling sand, something massive and pointed poking through to rise and rise and thicken and rise . . . a *horn*, Celadon belatedly concluded.

Not just one horn, but two.

Cracked and weathered and scuffed black bone, the pair broke through the surface, and Celadon could only watch as they pulled with them a colossal, beastly head. With vibrant streams of flame for a mane and blazing coal for eyes, a snout like a hound's, and teeth each the size of a human toddler, which gnashed and snapped as the creature snarled, struggled for its freedom . . .

Two arms came next—great and powerful and humanoid in shape, thick as the trunks of redwood trees, fingers capped with talons surely longer than Celadon was tall.

Planting its palms flat on the sand, it *heaved* itself the rest of the way through, pulling a body of pure muscle covered in yet more fire for fur, and enormous hind legs like some terrible demonic goat.

Up and up and up Celadon's eyes had to travel just to measure the height of this towering beast, tall as the Titans of old were rumored to be; tall enough that this *thing* could stand flush with UnSeelie Summer's walls and peer easily over.

"*Lethe,*" he gasped when he realized what it was he was looking at. "Lethe, is that an *ifrit*?"

The creature paused a moment upon freedom to breathe deeply the surface air, smoke billowing through its nostrils on each puff of breath and streaming between its bared teeth—stemming from the heart like a furnace that glowed through the taut, grim gray of its hide.

"That's an ifrit," Lethe confirmed, just as frozen in horrified awe as Celadon. "Riadne is putting Wrath's command of the Infernal Forces to use at last, it seems."

This fresh horror was the only thing enough to break Celadon's focus. "I'm sorry," he gasped, head whipping to face Lethe. "'Forces' as in *plural*? As in, there are more of those things down there?"

"More than one? There are *thousands*. Perhaps you are now beginning to grasp the enormity of how utterly your mother outmatches us." His poison eyes flashed on Celadon. "And you will take our training a bit more seriously."

So suddenly that Celadon actually flinched and slapped his hands over his ears to block out the sound, the ifrit craned back its head and unleashed a sepulchral roar that shook the earth's very foundations.

"It's going to *flatten* them!" Celadon shouted over the din.

"Oh, it will do far worse than that."

In the distance, Celadon could see UnSeelie Summer's guards. Their ranks had multiplied; several units had gathered together, drawn from within, frozen in place to stare in terror at what they would have to face and undoubtedly lose their lives to.

An actual ifrit.

Celadon didn't blame the soldier that took one last look at this nightmare and attempted to flee to the dunes.

Attempted—for as large and bulky as the demon was, making their movements less seamless, their eyesight was remarkable.

The soldier dropped his spear to run, shedding armor as he went to lighten his load, but he wasn't fast enough. The movement had fixed the soldier in the ifrit's attention, and gathering flame in its hand the size of a miniature sun, it threw it in a fireball that engulfed the soldier in an instant.

All who watched stood in aghast silence as the soldier screamed and screamed and charred to smoldering remains, quiet once again. How hot that fire had to burn, to reduce a fae of that element to cinders.

Another moment passed.

A breeze kicked by, stirring the sand.

The UnSeelie Summer army turned their focus back to their opponent, all in absolute stillness, and the ifrit watched them in return, almost like a taunt.

Then a shrill, loud alarm began to sound from the depths of the Flaming City, and the spell over the battlefield was broken.

The soldiers charged.

The ifrit *roared*.

Celadon scrambled at last back to his feet, turning to grab hold of the front of Lethe's tight, black shirt, a perfect match to what Celadon wore. "We have to help them."

"We most certainly do *not*," Lethe bit back, eyes narrowing in supreme annoyance. "If you recall, they wanted nothing to do with our protections before now."

Glaring in return, Celadon only pressed closer to the former Hunter. "If we cannot take down even *one* of those things, we stand no hope of winning Riadne's war."

"The two of us, alone."

"A Titan's son and the reincarnation of a moon god born with four different elements at his command? Yes. The two of us alone." Celadon raised a brow. "Don't tell me you cannot lay a simple ifrit at my feet? Whatever is the use of you?"

"*You,*" Lethe snarled, closing the barest space between them to snap in riled displeasure at Celadon's mouth. "I abhor the things I find I would do for you."

"I rather think you love it."

Lethe snorted, a quick huff of breath.

"Not the *task*, I don't," came his cryptic reply, and as soon as sniping it, he tore away to storm down the slope of the dune they'd been attempting to scale. Celadon could only stand mildly stunned in his wake.

Not the task, he'd said.

Not once, despite the many ways he showed how ardently he cared, had Lethe ever said that four-letter word to him. On the spectrum of aromantic as he was, it was only the profound and two lifetimes' worth of relationship between them that had gotten them to this point of emotional intimacy. Perhaps Lethe wouldn't ever proclaim love in the word outright, and that was all right with Celadon, as Lethe was more than understanding of his reservations with the physical expression of their intimacy. But that he'd come *this* close to expressing it, regardless . . .

There was an entire hells-spawn demon wreaking havoc on the Court below.

Celadon could marvel over his boyfriend's feelings for him later.

Rushing down the dune as well, Celadon was glad for the breathable, simple-cotton choice of attire they'd opted for in coming here, making his movements far more seamless.

As he went, he drew on the Winter he'd inherited from his mother to form in the air beside him an enormous, wicked spike of solid ice.

In practice, he could normally amass several, but there was so little moisture in the air out here that he could assemble only one, and would have only the one shot to utilize it.

Celadon and Lethe broke back onto the field at the same time as the UnSeelie Summer army.

Gold flashed in rising morning.

Gem-encrusted spears glinted as they were pitched at the attacking creature.

The ifrit issued another soul-rattling roar as it swiped them from the air, batting them aside as easily as a cat did string.

Lethe threw out his hand; his adamantine claws elongated and wove together into a deadly blade. So armed, he darted, slashing at the back of the ifrit's heels, Celadon simultaneously hurling his icy projectile directly at the glowing in the creature's chest.

Slam—ice struck true to embed in its chest; another roar. It pitched to the side, hands scrambling to remove what was melting in the waves of infernal heat it effused.

Shhiink—adamantine cut through sinew and bone, and the ifrit fell to a knee in the sand, snarling out in pain.

To the other heel now, Lethe applied his blade once more—sliced clean through it, just as he'd done the first, the spray of foul black blood arcing in the sword's wake.

Celadon *threw* himself down to his hands, splaying them flat on the ground.

Drawing on the UnSeelie Spring Gift he'd inherited from his father, he summoned from the earth beneath thick ropes of thorny vines.

They shot from the ground around the ifrit.

Clinging tight to the creature's limbs, they wound and grew upward, constricting as they went. Rope after rope lashed it, weaving together to bind it under its weight like a net and force the ifrit pinned to the ground.

A thunderous *thud* shook the earth as the creature's arms gave way under the strain, collapsing them hard under yet more vines that snaked up and over the ones before.

Restrained at last, but the ifrit was no less deadly and far more pissed off.

Great, black eyes swiveled, about the only thing it could move in its current state, for it to scan the desert for the source of what had assaulted it—and found Lethe and Celadon easily.

"SURROUND IT!" the man who was most likely captain of the UnSeelie Summer guard shouted at his soldiers as they made their approach.

In quick, fluid motion they complied, closing ranks around the ifrit to trap it in their circle, Celadon and Lethe just outside of them.

"FLAMES AT THE READY!"

Soldier by soldier, the circle caught fire.

As fire was the element of this Court, only those fae who could wield it to a Class Three degree could even qualify for *candidacy* for its military. Celadon watched as flame sparked to life in the soldiers' hands. Those deadly flames lengthened, much as Lethe's vicious claws had, until each soldier was armed with blazing swords.

Would this do anything? Celadon wondered.

Fire against fire—and the ifrit's was so much hotter.

"ON MY SIGNAL!"

It never came.

The ifrit's attention broke from Celadon and Lethe, fixed again on its original prey. It eyed each of them with such furious hatred, a burning even fire couldn't replicate.

The captain raised his hand in the air, preparing to direct his army to action—and in that very moment, the ifrit caught flame as well.

A wave of fire like a pulse radiated outward, incinerating its prison of vines, and Lethe had both presence of mind and quick enough reflexes to pull himself and Celadon back just enough that only the tips of Celadon's eyelashes suffered the singe of its touch.

The UnSeelie Summer guard . . . wasn't so lucky.

One moment they stood as flesh and bone—the blink of the next . . .

Just like Celadon's vines, they lay in piles of ash already beginning to scatter in the breeze and mix with the sand.

Pale, Celadon gaped at the scene.

"How do we fight this?" he despaired to no one in particular.

It was occurring to him, on a very deep and personal level, that as the central force at the heart of Riadne's opposition, he was the one leading thousands of innocent people to a sure and similar demise.

They weren't prepared for this at all.

Looking at the ifrit now heaving itself back to its feet, bathed in rippling flame, Celadon was struck by the surety that they could have thousands of years to make the attempt, and even then they still wouldn't be anything close to enough to contend with what Riadne had in store for them.

And just when Celadon didn't think it could get any worse, it did.

It took a minute for the quivering to register as something occurring *outside* of his body. A quivering that became quickly a rumbling, became even quicker specks on the horizon that turned into soldiers clad in horrific bone-white armor.

Lethe latched on tightly to him once again and pulled him protectively close into the circle of his arms as Riadne's Bone Guard poured hundreds thick over the dunes from all around.

Yelling, screaming, snarling, yipping—this army was bloodthirsty, excited, already celebrating the victory they'd won the moment that ifrit joined their cause.

Celadon pressed even closer to Lethe as the army came upon them, but the wall of Riadne's force parted like water to flow around them.

Clearly, the army had been instructed to leave them be, but that didn't stop numerous soldiers from snapping their teeth in Celadon's direction and screaming obscenities and taunts at them as they passed . . .

They advanced on the Flaming City.

Celadon hoped a wild hope that it could fall back to untouchable obscurity before they could reach it—and it might have done. It might have survived this, ifrit and all, if it weren't for what happened next.

A ring of glowing blue light began to carve itself around the city, weaving together runes and complicated equations, all the necessary markings of an *array*, the likes of which only one person would be powerful enough to create.

"*Arlo,*" he gasped, whipping around to try and spot where she might be.

And yelled out in shock when he found his mother suddenly and directly behind him.

Lethe startled as well, neither of them having been aware of her advance, and to make it so close without detection . . .

Arlo stood right beside her in her fluttering Hunter's cloak, eyes glowing the fierce bright red of Ruin's increasing influence.

Lethe tried to move between them, but Arlo lifted a hand—flexed her fingers, and the one-day god froze as though entirely stopped in time.

The array behind them trapped the Flaming City in a similar predicament: dawn had left the horizon, but the city didn't fade; the glamour didn't rise.

And now there were other screams to profane the morning—sounds far harder for Celadon to hear, the dying cries of mothers begging for their children's lives; fathers throwing themselves in protection of their families; folk being cut down in their beds, in the streets, in the corners they'd fled to in hopes of safety . . .

The army had made it.

They tore through the city in a trail of pain and blood, fire and electricity clashing. The sand trembled as the ifrit advanced on the city too, and then there was *true* terror when it crashed into the defensive wall to smash its way through.

"This is your fault, really." Riadne spoke hardly any louder than the breeze, but Celadon heard her. "You ridiculous boy. I applaud your ambitions, your rebellious spirit, but *this* is the reality of the war you are so determined to strike against me."

Roars and screams and explosions and death—the world was *unraveling* behind him. A Court cried out in the throes of death, decimation. All of it, just as his mother said . . . *all of it*, his fault.

Riadne reached out.

Placed her deceptively warm hand on his cheek.

"Enough, my son. Our efforts are far better spent united. It's not too late to join this cause."

Almost of its own accord, Celadon's hand lifted as well.

Placed itself over his mother's, to cradle it close, a show of affection—that immediately turned to ice.

"I would rather burn with that Court," he spat frostily, before tearing Riadne's hand from his skin and throwing it back to her.

Fury blazed in those electric-ice eyes.

Riadne rounded on Arlo, who merely regarded the temper with cool boredom. At the moment, she was purely Ruin.

"Obliterate it," the High Queen commanded, and there at last—a flicker of interest in the parasite that fed off Arlo.

An order to exterminate, with so much of her force still inside? Practically all of the Bone Guard . . . Ruin wasn't the only one caught by the callous waste of this, but the message was clear: she could stand to lose all this and more, and still Celadon was hopelessly outmatched by her.

"I wouldn't linger, darling," Riadne called to him over her shoulder, already making for the portal she used her Egress to open in the air. "Or you will certainly get your wish."

The moment she disappeared through the gaping hole in the air, Ruin unbound Lethe from their spell. He immediately sprang into action, darting forward and snatching Celadon's hand in his own, and spared only a *look* at Arlo before tearing immediately back for the dunes with Celadon in tow.

And Celadon didn't need to ask why.

Obliterate it, Riadne had instructed. *I wouldn't linger.* . . . It fairly spelled itself out.

Arlo raised a hand into the air, leeching darkness from the heavens and shadows and all the spaces in between . . .

Gathering it all into a ball that built and built and built at her fingertips . . .

"Celadon—call to your Egress!"

CHAPTER 9

Vehan

❧

SOMETHING WAS WRONG—VEHAN COULD feel it.

Celadon and Lethe hadn't been gone long in the grand scheme of what they were trying to accomplish. But sitting here in the dim cavern of Celadon's private office, waiting around for his brother's return, all Vehan could think about was every worst-case scenario, which grew more and more grim with each passing second.

"Calm down, Vehan. They'll be okay," said Aurelian in what would normally be comfort and reassurance to Vehan, but right now even his boyfriend's steady, sure tone couldn't soothe his nerves. "Riadne wouldn't hurt Celadon." *Not yet, anyway*, he left unsaid.

Riadne wouldn't hurt Celadon *yet*, not when she thought there might still be a chance for her to win him to her side, not until their war began in earnest. But just because she didn't intend for him to get hurt didn't mean he wouldn't—Vehan was resurrected proof that his mother's temper could get away from her.

"I know, it's just . . ." He looked down at his phone.

At the several text messages he'd sent in the past half hour, all of them left unread. And that didn't mean anything—Celadon had a big task in front of him. It was only that . . . Vehan couldn't shake the feeling that something was definitely wrong.

"Do you have Lethe's number?" he asked in a wild shot at hope. "Celadon isn't answering me."

Raising a brow at him, Aurelian snorted. "And you think *Lethe* will?"

"Well . . . all right, fair point, but still—"

"And what makes you think I have his number to begin with? It's not *my* brother he's fu—"

"Finally," Vehan cried in relief, sliding off Celadon's desk to rush over to the Egress. Its murky glass, which had been previously dark, began to glow with some inner light, a desert setting taking shape out of the fog.

Vehan watched in rapt fascination as the image sharpened into focus—then morphed to horror as blobs and smears clarified into a city on fire and a gargantuan monster of horns and flame and demonic death within, taking great swipes at buildings and people alike . . .

Similarly alarmed by what he saw, Aurelian came around the desk to join Vehan.

"They were too late . . ." he uttered in hushed, grim observation.

"They're coming through," Vehan said, sweeping a hand out to brush Aurelian back, making way for the two figures barreling straight at the glass.

All at once, Lethe and Celadon spilled through the portal onto the emerald carpet. Panting, covered in sand, smelling vaguely of smoke and char, Lethe scrambled to right himself from the tangled heap they'd arrived in. "Close it!" he urged. "Quickly, Celadon—close the portal before she sends it!"

"Sends what?" Vehan asked, coming over to help Lethe pull Celadon to his feet. "She?"

"Arlo," Celadon breathed, laboring to catch his breath.

And Vehan's gaze snapped to the glass.

Immediately, it sought out Arlo, wherever she was in all that sand—there, almost impossible to miss now that he was no longer absorbed in the Flaming City's demise. Arlo, with her fire-bright hair and night-black robes billowing against a backdrop of orange sand.

Arlo, standing with a hand in the air, amassing at her fingertips some dark power into an enormous, crackling orb.

"Close it!" Lethe pressed wildly.

"Wait!" Vehan said before he even registered speaking. Breathing heavily, fairly certain he was about to do something extremely foolish—something that might actually kill him, given how insistent Lethe was on closing the portal, so he was *really* banking on Arlo to pull through for him here—he rounded on Celadon, who'd already begun the process of closing off the mirror. "Give me permission to call on your Egress."

Celadon stared at him, perplexed. "What?"

"Your permission!" Vehan implored, eyes darting to the quickly fading image of UnSeelie Summer. He had to act now; he couldn't wait—if that Egress closed, there would be no way back through except that singular, tucked-away portal in Bangladesh. "Give me permission to open this back up once I go through—or else I'll have to use our mother's, and it's right back into Riadne's clutches, which I'm pretty sure none of us want."

Expression tight, golden eyes bright with disapproval, Aurelian took a step toward him. "Do you want to tell us *why* you want to go expressly where even *Lethe* doesn't want to be right now?"

He couldn't, really.

Honestly, Vehan didn't fully understand what compelled him at the moment.

All he knew was that the feeling that something was wrong had lingered after Celadon's return, and that black mass gathering in Arlo's hand looked an awful lot like the miasma in the bowels of the pits she'd been jumping through—a lot like maybe it could do more than just obliterate a Court.

Arlo, who was already so exhausted by her own admission . . . if she used that power to open her own rift between the realms, and Ruin threw her down another hole, she'd be forced to take control once more far before she was ready. If she didn't, Ruin would most definitely use this chance to wreak unfettered havoc in immortal territory, allowing them to grow stronger and claim ground in the war for Arlo's heart . . .

"PERMISSION!" he begged, ignoring Aurelian's question to make for the Egress as he spoke. He had to go; it was the one thing he knew for certain about any of this—Arlo had an easier time of holding on to herself when her friends were with her. "CELADON!"

"GRANTED!" Celadon hollered back, irritated, but slowly beginning to work out too what Vehan was on about. He shot forward as well, as though to follow Vehan right through the Egress, after his cousin.

Lethe *growled* out his name to stop him.

Aurelian expressed his opposition to Vehan's decision in a similar manner.

Unfortunately for Celadon, it was only Vehan who made it in time through the glass, jumping through it just as the image faded to closed-off black.

Vehan stumbled as soon as he hit the sand.

Skidding, sliding down the dune the Egress spat him out on, Vehan didn't spare a single second to pause and adjust to his new surroundings.

Morning climbed into the sky. Arid heat began to gather steadily in the air. His Bone Guard armor wasn't made for his body, stolen from the palace laundry as it had been, so it pulled and hindered as he hastened for Arlo—he had to reach her, had to, before that orb left her hand.

"Arlo!" he shouted. "ARLO!"

Craning her arm back, she prepared her strike, the orb groaning under such intense pressure of its immense mass—

And hurled it.

"ARLO!"

Arlo whipped around—but not in time.

The orb left her hand, streaking disproportionately fast for something of its size, arcing high into the sky to slam down on the Flaming City like a dark moon crashing from the heavens.

A blink was all the span of time Arlo had in which to act.

Vehan barely kept up with proceedings.

The orb set loose, Arlo lunged—crossed the distance between them with preternatural speed and gathered Vehan up in a fold to her chest.

The force of her knocked them flat to the sand; the force of the *orb* . . . Vehan was fairly certain he blacked out for a moment.

As though it had disrupted the very physics of this world, Vehan felt like he was being simultaneously stretched and compressed to nothing. As though every atom in his body had vibrated apart into singular, separate entities, and then, realizing it shouldn't be this way, snapped back together to reconfigure him completely anew.

Color bent.

Objects bled and swirled together.

It was day, then night; an inferno, then ice.

For the sliver of a second, Vehan knew everything. Every single answer to every single question the universe could pose, and his mind felt like it would splinter under all this knowledge—then, blessedly, finally, at last, like the release of a taut elastic band, the world snapped back to order . . . and silence that rang in his ears.

Blinking took effort, but eventually, Vehan opened his eyes.

Arlo's body was plastered on top of him, his face tucked protectively to her sternum. They were covered in sand but spared the worst of it thanks to what Vehan assumed was Ruin's self-preservation—waves upon waves of the heavy, fine granules had rippled outward from where the orb had struck . . .

"You absolute *idiot*, Vehan."

Arlo, hovering over him, *glaring* down at him, but still . . . it was her.

And Vehan was suddenly angry himself.

"If that's what caring about you makes me, fine. I'm an idiot—you're one too, if you actually think I'm going to let you do everything on your own. You're going through another pit, and I'm going with you."

Arlo's fury turned quickly to horror.

"*Vehan*, it would *kill* you."

"No, it won't," he insisted. "You won't let it."

The flash of red in Arlo's eyes told him that for at least a moment, it wasn't her he spoke to right now. "How very curious," Ruin replied in her stead. "How very *sentimental*. Do you know, this carelessness with your own safety is exactly how you died the last time."

That . . .

What?

Vehan stared. "Excuse me?"

Ruin pulled back, sand sliding off them in heaps. They peered down at Vehan, opened their mouth like they'd decided they might just reply . . . but Arlo pulled herself back into control to crane her head and gauge the damage behind her.

Lifting himself to his elbows, Vehan tilted his head to look around her at the destruction too.

There was simply nothing there.

Nothing at all—the Flaming City, Riadne's army, the massive demon . . . all of it, gone, annihilated, not even dust to blow on the breeze, just a great, gaping pit of throbbing darkness.

"So . . . *are* you going through?"

Arlo sighed. "I have to. Ruin is . . . insistently curious to see if they're right. They think this desert aligns with the vicinity of Urielle's palace."

"And you're . . . going to listen to them about that? It's quite soon after your last jump, you know."

Too soon.

Vehan could see the exhaustion dark under Arlo's eyes.

Unfurling back to standing, she offered Vehan a hand. "I'm aware."

Gods he missed how she used to be.

Talking to this Arlo, there were flickers of her personality, her former passion and emotions, all more consistent the longer her friends were around her.

But the stretches of near apathy in between . . . like Arlo was steadily hollowing out and filling back up with Ruin.

"I have to go. It's too soon, and that's exactly what Ruin is counting on. That in the least my defenses will weaken further in doing this. But the Flaming City is no more, which means no one remains to keep this location attached to its usual portal. Once we leave here today, it becomes just another patch of sand in some desert I have no idea where—not without a *lot* of time wasted on tracking my own trails of magic."

"All right." He drew a breath to clear his lungs, coughed out dust and sand; stretched his back, limbs, and body; gave her a brilliant smile. "I suppose it falls to me, then, to keep you tethered to all this *black*." He reached to tug on her robe as he spoke. "Nausicaä must be thrilled by your new palate preference."

"She's not," Arlo sighed wearily. "She's extremely offended that I make the better goth girlfriend." She sighed again, even heavier than before. "Fine, together it is. I don't have the energy or time to fight you on this. In the very least, please tell me Aurelian is okay with this?"

Grinning through a wince, Vehan replied, "Uh . . . that depends on your definition of 'okay,' I think."

"Lovely," she groaned, and turned for the portal.

CHAPTER 10

Nausicaä

~⌒~

NAUSICAÄ AWOKE, HIGHLY DISORIENTED, on the dark
emerald sofa of Arlo's bedroom as suddenly as she must
have fallen asleep. She hadn't intended on passing out
cold to the world when first sitting down here, but it had been a
long night thinking over Ruin's comments from earlier, and things
had been so stressy-depressy lately in . . . well, *every* area in her life,
that when she'd returned to the Luminous Palace to wait for Arlo, her
body—tired of the abuse Nausicaä put it through—must have made
the decision for her to get a bit of rest.

It could have at least let her succumb to weakness with dignity.
Her neck hurt like a bitch from the way it had just . . . fallen back
on the sofa, her mouth wide open, judging by the drool on her chin.

What time was it, even?

Had Arlo been back yet from Riadne's summons at all? The last
she'd seen her was in Disney World, and now the whole day had gone
past since.

Silver eyes scanned the dark bedroom—the firmly shut curtains
over floor-to-ceiling windows, the untouched, pristine bed, and none
of the usual evidence of Arlo's habitancy: a discarded article of clothing or an empty bag of Skittles, because apparently Ruin was devastation incarnate but also, thanks to a dare in Nausicaä's boredom, now
thoroughly addicted to chewy sugar coated in colorful candy.

"You aren't going to find her."

Nausicaä had a small—very small, not at all worth mentioning—
heart attack.

Jolting up from her seat, she whipped her focus to the young woman suddenly behind her, leaning against Arlo's dresser. Golden-brown, auburn-haired, eyes so deep a blue they gleamed black as ocean water at night . . . Nausicaä didn't know who this was at all, but she could hazard a guess based on how they were dressed, and it made her lip curl deeply and ugly over her teeth.

"So, which one are you, then?" Nausicaä drawled, doing a terrible job at effecting calm; her sneer drew even uglier. "New me, or new Tisiphone—I'm betting on the latter."

The untitled Erinys blinked slowly in reply.

Shoulders pinching slowly up toward her ears in her agitation, Nausicaä moved out from the sofa, a little bit closer to whoever this was. "You know what? I don't care—what do you mean, I won't find Arlo here? It's *her* bedroom. If you've done something to her, I swear—"

Finally, the Erinys spoke again.

"It's not *us* who has done anything." Straightening to full height, the Erinys matched the coolness in Nausicaä's glare with a touch of irritation. "Arlo Flamel is in the Infernal Realm with Urielle as we speak—she and Ruin and a mortal prince by the name of Vehan."

There it was again—just another minor, completely insignificant entire stoppage of her heart.

Nausicaä could *feel* her face drain pale.

"I'm sorry. I think I misheard you. *What?*"

"We don't have time for this," came the Erinys's brisk reply as she strode forward and, without so much as asking Nausicaä to dinner first, grabbed her by the elbow. "Your girlfriend is in the Immortal Realm. She poses a danger to Mother. I would like you to come get her and convince her to leave."

"Oh?" Nausicaä snorted, pretending she very much wasn't worried about the fact that Arlo had gone through a second rift in the span of twenty-four hours. "Listen, I don't know if you've heard, but word on the street is I've been exiled. Something about murdering eleven mortals and telling Mommy Dearest to go fuck herself and the law she loves so much, so damned important to her that she let it cost her two of her daughters. Arlo's in the Immortal Realm? Tough. Eat a whole fucking bag of dicks—she'll leave when she's damned well ready."

"I will escort you," the Erinys continued as though Nausicaä hadn't said a thing. "The Goddess Mother abstains from any move at the moment, so long as Arlo does, but also does she weigh the risk—to strike Ruin down now while they are mortal would clean this stain from the world before it sets in. Does she act? If she does not strike true, it will invite Ruin's destruction upon us. Does she do nothing? The Banished Titan walks among us, and many will take *in*action as sign of unforgiveable weakness. All of this, on top of the fact that Arlo Flamel is fatigued—if *she* is forced to act in any way, it may well be the end of her, which I do gather is something you're opposed to."

Damn it, damn it, *damn it.*

Contrary to what this Erinys and most likely everyone believed, Nausicaä didn't actually *want* to go back home. Back to that place that was a reminder of all she'd lost, all she'd suffered, all she and Tisiphone had bled themselves past breaking for.

But this was *Arlo.*

If there was anyone Nausicaä would walk back through hell for, it was her.

And of course Arlo was tired. This was *the second rift* she'd gone through in less than a day! It wasn't really a question; Nausicaä would go after her even if this Erinys hadn't offered to take her, exile be damned.

"Fine." Nausicaä glowered, folding her arms in a huff over her chest. Better to let this Erinys think she was doing them a favor. "I'll come collect my big, scary girlfriend. You didn't answer my question—which one are you?"

"Come."

Ignoring Nausicaä's question once again, the Erinys struck out a hand behind her and summoned from the void the same portal

Nausicaä had once been able to make. A portal she hadn't used in 117 years.

And still it felt like just yesterday when she followed the Erinys through.

Just like fucking yesterday.

Nausicaä walked out the other side of the Erinys's portal and back 117 years into the past. In the front courtyard of the Infernal Palace, she stood feeling both so out of place it made her skin crawl and like nothing had changed at all.

The sky was still that murky light of predawn, as it was perpetually until nightfall, when the realm would plunge to darkness unlike anything mortals knew.

The manicured lawn around her was still that spongy not-quite-grass, charcoal gray in shade, and the dozens of bloodvine willows that were indigenous to this region—enormous trees that grew in twists to form one giant mega-tree, the crimson leaves that dripped from their hanging branches like weeping tears of blood—creaked ominously as they swayed.

The fountain that stood center of it all rose in ornately carved cosmidian stone, which was more or less mortal moonstone, save for its sheen that gleamed like different swaths of the cosmos, depending on the angle you looked at it.

In the distance, Nausicaä could see a swarm of harpies circling in the air like vultures, diving in turns for the ground after whatever had the misfortune of becoming their morning meal. The distance to her right, a jagged range of mountains of pure, natural sapphire.

Behind her loomed the palace, and for a moment, Nausicaä could only stand and stare up at it, a rush of memories and emotions slamming her with tidal force as she took in the erebonite stone walls—a rock found only here, so black and gleaming it put obsidian to shame—the multilevel spires like dragon's teeth capping intricate adamant metalwork; the central five towers that pierced the sky, taller than anything else in the realm, and around which curled great streams of the five main elemental magics that Urielle commanded: a tower each for the hottest red Fire, the softest green Wind, the more vibrant blue Water, the purest white Light, and the richest amethyst Shadow.

"They are not expecting us," the Erinys said in the same placid tone she'd maintained this whole meeting. "Come, before your mitigation is pointless."

Tch—Nausicaä eyed the hand on her elbow attempting to tug her forward.

"Let's get something straight," she replied dryly, tugging herself free. "I'm *the* Alecto—the first and only made of Fire; defeater of the Titan Erebus; murderer, rebel, op of ops. The Dark fucking Star. You grew up on stories of my legend—I don't even know your name. So unless you have red hair and great boobs and your name starts with Arlo, you don't get to order me fucking anywhere. Understand? *Smashing.*"

Scowling, the Erinys followed *her* into the palace.

Nausicaä wished she could say it didn't affect her any, being here. Walking these erebonite halls that were once her beloved home, her greatest pride to call it such.

She wished she could say she felt only amusement when the palace denizens caught sight of her and stopped in their tracks in horrified awe, then took to whispering with their companions while leveling her with looks of distain and disgust.

The Fallen Fury—their greatest idol turned deepest disappointment.

Holding her head high through it all, Nausicaä kept her eyes trained forward and made quickly for the throne room, where Arlo waited. The guard on duty in their glinting adamant armor reached for their weapons upon spotting her but, at a look from the Erinys behind her, begrudgingly stepped aside to allow Nausicaä to place her palms on the enormous slabs of stone for doors and shove them open.

What an image.

Nausicaä was instantly transported back to the last time she was here—kneeling, broken, shaking with anger she could barely control. It was almost that night repeated, the way curious onlookers were gathered in the shadowy wings, the black granite floor smooth and sparkling like the night she'd wanted to sink and disappear into it. Urielle, presiding from her throne, that same look of barely restrained fury on her mother's face now as she'd worn for Nausicaä then when Nausicaä had all but told her to piss off—her and her Law she loved better than her own children.

Megaera, regal as ice, standing beside her.

The stark and almost mesmeric difference was, of course, Arlo.

Arlo, who stood in the midst of this all, looking the Goddess of the Elements in her tempest eyes and holding herself boldly; composed; vivid, the way those red flames for hair poured down her back.

Beside her, Vehan looked wholly out of place and not the least bit comfortable. Small and fragile and *mortal* here in the realm of the gods his own bloodline had disposed of.

On Nausicaä's entry, the whole room turned to look, and oh, but the déjà vu of it all made the hair stand up on the backs of her arms—especially the way Megaera's silver eyes narrowed into glaring outrage.

But Nausicaä had eyes only for her girlfriend. Not until she crossed the sea of black and stars, came up to Arlo—who was definitely still Arlo right now, if a little more red in the eyes than the last time they'd seen each other—and took her place by Arlo's side did she let her gaze wander, almost purposefully languid, up to her mother's throne.

Murmurs buzzed like an agitated hive of wasps.

Urielle, for her part, looked about to burst with her fury.

"Mockery," she sneered, rising to standing. "How *dare* you show yourself in my hall."

A moment passed.

Followed by two.

Slowly, Nausicaä brought her hand into the air, and as she closed her fist to raise her middle finger, the obscene sound of her blowing a raspberry shocked the whole room back to silence.

"I am overcome by your maturity," Arlo whispered, in that almost-her tone that relieved Nausicaä to hear more than she let on.

"I fell to exile, dramatically named myself *the Dark Star*, then got a neck tattoo to match. When did I ever give you the impression I was mature?"

"I'm really glad you guys are having a moment here, but . . ." Vehan cut in from Arlo's other side, shifting his gaze pointedly in the direction of Nausicaä's very angry mother.

But this was Arlo's show.

Nausicaä was here only for moral support, and to pull Arlo out the moment it looked like this was too much for her, or if her mother gave any indication she might launch an attack that would force Arlo to action she didn't have the capacity for right now.

Arlo watched Nausicaä fall to ease beside her, took her time in turning her attention back to Urielle. When she did, she cocked her head in a way that wasn't at all *her* Arlo and resumed control of the conversation, confident, poised—all those things Arlo had been convinced she lacked, but Nausicaä had assured her she already had, now emphasized by Ruin's influence.

"Your answer, Urielle," Arlo pressed. "Where is the entrance to—"

Her mother's eyes flashed indignantly to be addressed by her name instead of her title by someone she definitely considered far below her equal. But even goddesses, Nausicaä supposed, had to be wary of the way they spoke to the Titan of obliteration, because Urielle said nothing about the overfamiliarity. Rather, her ire focused even hotter on Nausicaä.

"How *dare* you show yourself here, Alecto-No-More. And in collusion with the enemy, I see—this *will* be your Destruction. My lenience will not be extended a second time to you—"

"Enough."

Nausicaä looked at Arlo, stunned and trying very hard to pretend she wasn't. It was just like when Arlo had slapped Megaera in the face, defending Nausicaä's honor against her older sister's misconduct.

Urielle's outrage grew wilder in her wide eyes. *"Excuse me?"*

"You heard me—*enough*. Nausicaä isn't your concern right now. All you should be worried about is answering my question," Arlo commanded, unflinching conviction layered beneath her tone, reminding all in the room that they were talking to more than just a pretty mortal girl.

Many in the shadows flattened further against the walls to put as much space between them and the person before them, Ruin beginning to seep into Arlo's edges. "Tell me where to go in the Mortal Realm to gain access to the Sacred Grove."

"I repeat," Urielle countered through clenched teeth and a voice like frost. "What will you give me in return for that information? We do not operate on favors alone here, and certainly not where *you* are concerned."

Nausicaä almost laughed.

She certainly wasn't the only person in the room able to see it, but it was so well concealed that, most likely, Megaera and whoever this new Erinys was would have been the only other ones to catch it—the way their mother was starting to flounder.

All the indication Nausicaä needed was right there in front of them: her mother actually acknowledged how dangerous a position she was truly in here, by conceding to turn the conversation back to negotiations.

She could weigh whatever she wanted, decide on any of the scenarios the Erinys who brought Nausicaä here had threatened, but it didn't change shit. No one person here could contend with Ruin, not when sealing them away the first time had required the unified power of all seven of the major deities.

If Ruin wanted, if *Arlo* wanted, Urielle could be snuffed completely out of existence at any given moment.

"What do you get?" Arlo repeated, head cocking in the opposite direction, and like sand trickling through cracked glass, Nausicaä's girlfriend began to drain away.

Leaving far more space for Ruin to surge into and fill.

Arlo lifted a hand out to her side, though it was definitely Ruin dictating the action.

Nausicaä watched.

Urielle watched.

Arlo waited until the entire room's attention was rapt on her and only her, and then, once it was, that hand began to close into a fist . . . and pulled from their audience a *gagging*.

It started as a wet choking off to the side, one of the gathered immortals spluttering and coughing into their hands. Then, like flame in a parched forest, it caught among the others.

Fanned even hotter as it spread and consumed.

Into a groaning.

A creaking.

A crunching and snapping and cracking and tearing, bodied collapsing in on themselves, breaking apart at the folds.

Everyone gathered along the far wall—every last one of them, fully immortal, and it hardly seemed to matter—hacked and wept and screamed at one another for help, begging the goddess who watched in pale horror as the coughing grew harsher and the bodies of her personal court began to *dry out* right before her eyes and age rapidly toward death.

And then, just when it seemed they would hollow out completely, Arlo reclaimed control from Ruin, and tore her hand back to her side.

The moment she did, the crowd began to revitalize.

It was clear to Nausicaä, during this distraction of gasping, alarmed courtiers, that Arlo was nearing her limits, waning fast, was barely holding on to consciousness, let alone control of her actions. Which Ruin had clearly gone and capitalized on, seizing their chance to inflict their own brand of destruction, exactly what Arlo feared would be turned on her friends if moments like this occurred around less attractive alternatives.

This was the reason she'd fought so hard to do this entire thing alone.

Nausicaä had to get them out of here before things turned even uglier—as it was seconds away from becoming, when that hand shifted from the still-recovering crowd, palm outward, directed now at Urielle.

"What do you get in return?" Arlo asked, mildly breathless.

She might have gotten better at stuffing down her feelings on Ruin using her body to conduct their atrocities, but Arlo had never enjoyed the waste of mortal life; she hated having to watch her hands take it from someone.

She'd fight as best as she could, to the very last shard of her, to ensure no one died who shouldn't.

"What you *get*," Arlo replied, putting her all into keeping up the command in her voice, "is a few more days to prepare yourself for my impending assault. Because I *will* be back, and I won't be leaving a second time without what I came for. But if you keep me here any longer tonight, it'll be Ruin you have to deal with, and they are far less interested in negotiation. Save yourself the trouble and tell us. *Where?*"

There was so much force inflicted on the command that Nausicaä could almost feel it.

Urielle, meanwhile, balked.

She squared her jaw.

Nausicaä couldn't believe it, but she was actually on the verge of warning her mother to save her ass here and comply. That Crown on her head—twists of elements writhing in a circle, but there visible just beneath were flickers of the bleached white bone of the Primordials it had come from. How much of Urielle was herself these days? Nausicaä had to admit, she'd been harsh on her execution of punishment back when Nausicaä had been banished, but her anger undimmed toward her now . . . *still* . . .

Standing here staring up at the goddess she hadn't seen in over one hundred years, Nausicaä almost couldn't recognize her at all.

What she did recognize was the glint of madness in her eyes that she saw daily, just the same, in Riadne's.

Thankfully, Urielle finally showed she still possessed a shred of humility and self-preservation. This was not a battle she could currently win, caught off guard as she'd been by this arrival, and so despite how Nausicaä could see just how much it grated against her pride to have to yield anything to a mortal's demands, she hissed through gritted teeth, "It is exactly where you think it is and haven't dared to go."

Not an answer at all, except it was.

Arlo didn't asked for clarity, and neither did it seem she needed it.

"Thank you," she replied, softer, with a little more feeling, a lot less like the void waiting to snap its teeth and devour whole.

And just like that, Arlo turned.

Hesitating a moment, with one last look of contemplation at the Crown on her mother's head, Nausicaä turned as well.

"Okay, so, we aren't going to take Urielle's Crown, after all that?" Vehan asked, rushing to keep pace beside them as they exited into the hall and made for the palace front doors.

"No," said Arlo, shaking her head. "I'm too tired for that right now. They kept us here for hours just to meet with your mother," she added for Nausicaä's benefit of explanation. "Made us wait in the dungeon hold. It wouldn't end well for me if, after all that, I declared war on the Goddess of the Elements. But I know how to get here now, and that's half the battle—it was more important I learn the location of Tellis's realm."

Vehan nodded in understanding. "And did you?"

"Yes."

"Where?"

Shaking her head, Arlo dismissed the conversation, too exhausted for even that.

Wrapping an arm around her girlfriend's shoulders, flicking her middle finger now at the Erinys who'd retrieved her and still stood waiting in the hallway, Nausicaä said gently, "Come on, Red. Let's get you home."

"Nausicaä—a moment?"

Somehow, the silken, deep pitch of Megaera's voice was the most surprising thing of this evening so far.

She stood in the courtyard in front of the portal that Arlo had torn back open in the air like punching through a sheet of paper. Arlo had already gone through to clear the way, Vehan in arm to help protect him. Nausicaä had just been about to follow when her sister called after her, and she turned, frowning at the sight of Megaera striding toward her in her black leather gear, the sheet of her long black hair unbound and shifting like water around her.

Frowning, Nausicaä folded her arms over her chest and regarded her sister's approach with as much cool disdain as wariness.

"If you're looking to get slapped around a little, I'm afraid you missed your chance; Arlo's already gone."

Megaera rolled her eyes. "I'll leave that for you to enjoy, thank you." She frosted ever so slightly; the flash in her eyes said she hadn't forgotten or forgiven Arlo for that particular grievance. "But what I have to say does pertain to . . . well, by reports, it seems the pair of you are promised? I suppose congratulations are in order."

"Promised?" Nausicaä raised a brow and snorted. "Deities, I'd forgotten how insufferable I sounded back when I was one of you. Yes, we're banging. Understandably, not so much of that these days, but the sentiment still stands."

This was clearly going just as difficultly as Megaera had anticipated, and still she had to bite the inside of her cheek to keep herself cordial. "*Nausicaä,*" she snapped, then sighed. "*Nausicaä,*" she repeated, softer. "I am tied numerous different ways in this regard—"

"Kinky."

"Shut *up*, Nausicaä."

"I'm sorry! You're making me nervous—I get sarcastic when I'm nervous, you *know* that about me, we've been sisters for hundreds of years!"

Reminder of that seemed to soften something in Megaera even further.

"Yes," she said, far gentler than anything else so far, and the silver in her eyes calmed to gray. "We have."

A moment passed, in which the pair of them merely stood staring at each other, Megaera lost in some memory or another, and Nausicaä growing distinctly uncomfortable.

"So. How's New Tisiphone doing?"

Megaera sighed. "Nausicaä . . ." she warned, and Nausicaä lifted her hands in surrender.

"What do you want, Meg? This portal won't stay open for long. I'm not standing here having a heart-to-heart with you on my girl-friend's dime."

Pulling herself together, Megaera recovered back into her usual glacial self. "It's the matter of your girlfriend I actually wish to dis-cuss. Like I said, I'm tied in what I can and cannot do in this, as my allegiance is first and foremost to our mother and our Law. She might have crafted you in much of her image—might have made you so like her in attempt to fill the void of her infertility, forced as she is to rely on element and stardust to give shape to the scraps of souls that Fate's pity allows her to recycle. You might have her appearance, but *I* am her most loyal. I have always stood by her. *Always*."

"There's a point to this besides bragging, right? 'Cause I'm leaving if there's not—"

"My *point*, Nausicaä, is that I know our goddess mother. I know her extremely well. You had Tisiphone, and friends, and so many pur-suits that you never truly paid attention to her—all I had was our mother. And I know that something is *wrong*."

That . . . hurt a little.

The reminder.

That as terribly as Megaera had treated her in all of this, Nausicaä

162

wasn't innocent in what had unraveled their relationship to get here. She'd known it that night, dragged before their mother for banishment, and she knew it now—she probably should have cherished Megaera a little better than she had, a little more like she'd cherished Tisiphone.

"Yeah," Nausicaä replied, the confrontation in her tone deflating. "There is. That Crown of hers is taking its toll. Immortals aren't so immune to it as we'd all like to believe. It's why Arlo's after them."

Megaera nodded. "Do you think she can do it?"

"I think she's going to damn well try."

Another moment spanned between them then, of silence heavy with whatever Megaera wanted to say but had to figure out how to phrase in a way that wouldn't make her *disloyal*—deities forbid.

Finally, she'd decided on her words. "You know that thing that people say when they care a great deal for someone? That they would know in their heart, despite great distance between them, if they were injured or in danger? That inkling you feel to reach out to someone dear you haven't spoken to in a while? You know how they say that to love someone is to give them a piece of yourself?"

"Yeaahhhh," Nausicaä drawled out, not exactly sure where she was going with this, but it was obviously another piece of this puzzle Nausicaä had been trying to work out on how to save Arlo from Ruin if Celadon's plan didn't pan out. "Okaaayyy. I get you're trying to hint at the whole 'Arlo and I are connected' thing, but could you be *any* more helpful with what that's supposed to do for us?"

"Arlo carries within her a piece of you," Megaera deadpanned. "You carry within yourself a piece of her—have done, for some time. A piece of you, missing, untouched by the Sin you allowed into your heart. A piece of her, that isn't you, no permission given to be thus defiled. There is a reason you were able to retain a sense of yourself under Lust's control, and I really cannot give you any more of a lead than this—but I can tell you something else." Another flash behind those very stern and very steel eyes, like this was about more than

163

Nausicaä and Arlo now. "There are other people who care for her too. Other people who feel her pain. Other people who also carry a piece of her heart, and she a piece of theirs. Don't allow your bullishness to cost her that help. She needs that mortal prince who followed her to these infernal depths for nothing more or less than love."

As abruptly as that, Megaera turned.

"I was a shit sister to you," Nausicaä said to her retreating back, whisper quiet, but Megaera heard. "You lost Tisiphone too."

Megaera paused in her stride back for the palace doors. Cocked her head just so to the side. "I, too, failed you deeply. Please, save our mother. Despite how she . . . should have saved you too, and didn't."

It was the closest Megaera had ever come to admitting that Nausicaä hadn't been wrong to feel the way she did.

And she was extremely proud that the unexpectedly profound relief of this didn't break her down into tears until later that night, all on her own, when Vehan had been restored back to Aurelian and Arlo had passed out in her bed.

Of all the versions Arlo had envisioned himself growing into as a child, not one of them matched the young man he'd become at the end of his time at the academy.

Five short years he'd walked these halls; shared every lesson and dormitory with his best friend, Hyperion, the pair of them top of every class; dazzled his professors with his keen wit and voracious appetite for knowledge, his talent in alchemy par with none, leagues superior than even the tutors brought in specially by the High King for his extracurricular study. Handsome (if still on the spectrum of pretty), confident, surrounded by people who liked him and sought his time and opinion . . . everything Phoebus Viridian had promised would happen if he'd chosen to follow this path had come to pass.

So why did it hurt as though none of that mattered, as he stood in the private study that had become his well-equipped laboratory here at the academy . . . holding the letter his mother had written back to his hope that she and his father would attend his graduation.

". . . I'm sorry, darling; you know how your father can be. If you'd only just put this business with the philosopher's stone from your ambitions, I know he would be most eager to come—"

Angrily Arlo crumpled the letter and pitched it into his fireplace.

Stop chasing the secrets of the philosopher's stone—every letter he wrote home was met with this condition.

At one point, Arlo had brought his concerns over this to Phoebus himself, because his father had never explained to him, beyond nebulous insinuations, the full story of why he'd left his position, king, and Court, but it did lead Arlo to wonder . . . because his father had never been an unreasonable man, before all this . . .

And Phoebus had actually told him. Plainly, that Nicholas had discovered that whatever the philosopher's stone's full potential was, it was far darker than what he was prepared to put into the hands of the Fae High Council.

He'd never trusted them all that much, I'm afraid, the High King had explained around a humored half smile. *And they certainly don't give anyone much reason to—goodness, even I am a little afraid of them, between you and me,* he'd teased. *I can assure you, though, that the Council has only ever had the Courts' best interests at heart. Whatever's to be discovered of these stones' true potential, it will not be they who abuse it.*

That had been well enough for Arlo.

He'd made considerable advancements in this field since that conversation, had figured out that the stone was a living thing once made, and required, by use of the animus rune used to craft it, anchoring to an equally living host in order to keep alive. Well beyond what his father had worked out before his paranoia got the better of him— clearly, the old man was envious on top of everything else. His son had made him obsolete, so now he employed cold distance and unflinching silence as punishment.

On his own head be it.

Nicholas didn't want to come to his graduation? Phoebus would be there, and he was more Arlo's father at this point than his own.

"I see you're brooding again."

Arlo brightened considerably. "Alecto!" he exclaimed, turning from his desk to greet her.

Five years the Erinys had been checking in on him, with growing frequency. Her claim being that the deeper he delved into the stone's alchemy, the closer an eye she was required to keep on him. But recently, Arlo had begun to suspect it was something else keeping her coming around . . . something he recognized in the boy he'd once been, and maybe still was, at his core—Alecto was lonely.

"Wonderful, I'm *so* glad you're here." He pushed off from his desk, his school robes fluttering around his legs. "There's something I've been wanting to show you—first, before even *Hyperion*."

"Oh, blessed fortune," Alecto replied in a tone so dry it could have been dust.

Still, for all she grumped and pretended to be extremely put-upon by his enthusiasm, she turned regardless to follow him out of his lab.

It was just after nightfall and well past curfew, but Arlo was a prefect and school darling besides—not to mention, it had been requested of him to plan the spectacle that would mark his graduation. No one was going to stop him from wandering after hours.

"How are your sisters?" he asked as they walked down the corridor, Alecto a silent, stalking shadow cast just off from his side.

She shrugged at the question. "Same as ever."

"They've not warmed up to you *any* more, even a little?"

Rolling her eyes, Alecto replied, "Fine. A little, perhaps. As much as they ever will, I think, toward a Hunter who took such a coveted role from their ranks."

It was Arlo's turn to roll his eyes. "You didn't 'take' anything, Alecto. Just because you were born into immortality and not made for the role like the others, doesn't mean it's any less rightfully yours. You fought in the same trials as all the other Furies; you *earned* your position fairly. The first Erinys to have *chosen* the duty—and the goddess Urielle wouldn't have yielded it to you if she didn't think you suitable."

They'd talked a lot, in these last five years.

Always begrudgingly—Alecto never gave anything to him without something of a fight, but Arlo had at least learned a little more about her than what he'd known their first meeting, that fateful night long ago.

Alecto, who'd been offered the position of Hunter for the battle prowess she'd shown during mortal life . . .

Oddly enough, it was Lethe who'd made her true desire possible, who'd pulled every string he could to release Alecto from her bonds to Cosmin in a way that would still afford her immortality so her service could be transferred instead to the Goddess of the Elements and Mother of the Erinyes.

It was all Alecto, though, who'd fought in and passed the vicious, grueling trials open only when an Erinys position needed filling—with exceptional scoring to boot.

The things Arlo had learned about the Immortal Realm through the course of their friendship . . . when Alecto felt like chatting, it was actually difficult to get her to *stop*.

"Yeah, well," Alecto replied. Short. Awkward. Arlo spotted the hint of blushing color in her cheeks and cracked a grin at her.

Reaching out, she smacked him up the back side of his head.

"What are you showing me?" she asked, changing the subject.

Which was fine with Arlo—they'd crossed out into the school grounds, were already descending the twisting flight of flagstone steps leading down a slope to the greenhouses.

Arlo merely winked at her, and the pair continued on in far more comfortable silence until they came at last to the farthest-back greenhouse, where Arlo had been storing and working on his project.

Inside, on a table, amid pots of dirt and gardening tools and trays of the wildest-looking faerie herbs Arlo had ever seen, was a beige cloth draped over something large and bulky and oddly shaped.

He ripped off the cover.

Alecto bent her head to peer down at what was revealed. "What . . . is it?"

And Arlo's grin only sharpened wider.

Collecting his project in his arms, he led Alecto back outside, behind the greenhouse, where it was a little more private—not that this would matter in a moment.

With a great thrust, he planted the spike of it deep in the soft, loamy earth and grabbed his flint and stone to strike a flame.

"Wouldn't it be easier to use alchemy to do that?" Alecto pressed.

"Yes," Arlo replied, "but some things are worth doing the long way."

In no time at all, he lit the wick that protruded from the object's bottom, then ushered Alecto quick steps back.

"It's not going to explode, is it?"

"Just you wait," Arlo replied, barely able to contain his excitement.

He'd been wanting to test his final model for days now—a few last tweaks from this run-through and his spectacle would be perfected. But he'd been waiting specifically for Alecto to show, and now that she was here . . .

The project went off with a *BANG*.

Alecto's hands lifted on instinct to her ears as the night caught on fire, sparking flame shooting from the object, which had taken momentary flight in its initial bursting.

Up and up that sparking, sparkling, vibrant flame rose, and together they watched it, Arlo sneaking glimpses of her face all the while and pleased to see the mild hints of awe.

But it wasn't until the streak of flame reached peak height that it truly *exploded*.

The night sky lit up, sparks and shimmering and ribbons and flame molding together to create a colossal phoenix that spread its wings and soared through the air overhead before burning out over the forest beyond them.

Arlo's gaze lowered from the heavens to size Alecto's reaction and found exactly what he'd hoped to see there, her face alight with open amazement and glowing color in the dimness of night. But more, and not for the first time . . . Arlo caught himself a little breathless, snagged by the sharp edge of her otherworldly beauty.

"Fireworks," he heard himself explain, as though his mouth needed something to say to distract him from his embarrassing thoughts. "In China, they used to throw bamboo stalks into flame to create a sort of crackling explosion. The practice has evolved with the ages, in various areas of the world—I simply added to existing experimentation exactly what humanity added to magic: metal. Among other things." He shrugged, turning back to the night.

"This is . . ."

Arlo beamed at her. "Incredible? Stupendous, genius?"

Alecto snorted but didn't drop her gaze from the sky, either. "You're quite full of yourself. Whatever happened to that shy boy hiding in his parents' loft?"

Not at all affected by this barb with no sting, Arlo folded his hands behind his head, at perfect ease. "You like me, admit it."

He didn't know why it struck him so—standing there, watching her; no smile on her face, but in this moment, she looked so happy, and something about knowing he'd been the cause of that made him happy too.

Alecto rolled her eyes. "We've a long way to go yet for 'like,' Red."

"Oh, clever," Arlo teased, scrunching his nose at her. Too pleased with his success this evening, both with Alecto and the firework going off without hitch, Arlo merely shook his head and turned his face to the dying embers of his display. "I'm going to do it, you know. I'm going to create a philosopher's stone. Become the greatest alchemist the world has ever seen—*will ever* see. I'm going to take this world by storm, and when my time here is up, there won't be a person in all the Mortal Realm who doesn't know my name."

He could feel the intensity of her gaze when Alecto finally lowered it to regard him.

It lingered on the side of his face a moment . . . two . . . then turned back to the darkening heavens as well. "I know," she replied so softly, Arlo might have missed it altogether. "That's what I'm afraid of."

CHAPTER 11

Celadon

N ENTIRE COURT, WIPED utterly from the map—without so much as batting an eye, Riadne had committed a genocide of the UnSeelie Summer folk in one swift strike. And worse was that if UnSeelie Autumn didn't yield itself to her either, they would suffer the exact same fate, Celadon just as powerless to prevent this as he'd been two days ago in that desert.

"Everyone wants to be king until they realize how heavy a crown can become," drawled Pallas Viridian, lounging in his high-backed, crushed-velvet armchair, a glass of the Faerie Ring's finest whisky held aloft for his study against the firelight.

"I didn't want to be one," Celadon reminded, drooping against the back of his own armchair to stare dejectedly into the fireplace beside them. "I wouldn't have chosen this for myself at all if it hadn't been for *her*."

It was quite late at night.

The Faerie Ring didn't sleep, and neither did Toronto, but here in the private lounge his many-greats-uncle kept—a small but comfortable space in various tones of deep, bloody red; of overstuffed bookcases, cabinets of imported alcohol, bizarre and fantastical trinkets, and the intimate setup of chairs around a stately mantel—it was just the two of them against a backdrop of soft crackling flame and the whisper-low lull of classical music playing in the far corner.

"What would you have done?" Pallas asked, his consideration transferred to Celadon. "Say your mother never put mind to satiate her grudge against your father; say your father met his natural end that awaits all who don Primordial Bone. What would Celadon

Fleur-Viridian Lysterne have been instead of what he is now, if the choice were up to him?"

A good question—and something Celadon had been at war with for a number of years before his world had overturned entirely and his personal desires no longer mattered.

Back when he'd had the luxury of being able to weigh things like purpose, he'd only just gotten ahold of his gender and sexuality—tenuous as it had been back then, and still a little confusing now, at times; still in a state of fluctuation, changing here and there to grow with the man he was becoming.

"What would *you* have been?" he countered.

Pallas raised a russet brow, so much of him similar to the way Azurean had looked in pictures of his prime. "If I hadn't become a vampire, you mean?"

It was the only reason they were able to even have this chat right now, when by all rights he should be long dead. Pallas and his cohort of sidhe fae had dabbled deeply in the darkest of blood magic back in their day, and it had cost them more than their jobs, their lives, and their respect in the community.

It had caused the birth of vampirism, and Pallas had suffered immensely ever since for his hubris, for his hand in the creation of this undead affliction.

"Hard to say," he continued stiffly. "I'd already wasted much of my life away on the boredom of royalty, and Phoebus cast quite the shadow as both Court Founder and High King; shade has never been known to allow much to grow under its pall. I existed in life to serve my brother—at least in death I was spared the tedium of his endless, vapid dinner parties." Frowning, he paused and reached for his side table to fetch his decanter of whisky. He spoke softly now as he refilled his glass. "I would have liked to have grown old with my partner, Noel."

Celadon had been coming to the Faerie Ring frequently these past few months.

He'd never had anything like a relationship with his great-great-great-grandfather's brother. Pallas Viridian hadn't been a name acceptably spoken within the palace walls after his fall to dark magic, and Celadon hadn't ever felt much motivation to seek him out for introductions.

But in the short span of time since Celadon's unveiling of the Night Court, because Pallas had responded to the invitation extended to him and had gone out of his way to attend that night, Celadon had been coming here . . . had been doing his best to forge not just an alliance with the vampire king but a personal relationship, too, with one of the few remaining Viridians he had left to him.

In so doing, he'd learned quite a lot about Pallas's story—his *tragedy*. About the love of his life, his soulmate, *Noel*, who'd taken so poorly to the magic in Pallas's bite—the first and only fae he'd ever attempted to turn—that his mind and soul had broken, emptying Noel out to darkness's terrible control. What had resulted had been quite a notable moment in vampire history, Noel abandoning Pallas to chase down a path of even darker magic, ending in the abduction of several humans for sacrificial slaughter, attempted necromancy, and the inevitable intervention of the Furies.

Yes, Celadon imagined there was quite a lot Pallas would do differently, if he could.

"And where are you keeping *your* affection tonight?" Pallas asked in a stronger voice, changing the subject so abruptly Celadon startled. "Lethe. I do remember that one. Phoebus would envy you deeply for the way you've tamed what he never could."

Celadon breathed a laugh, grabbing for his own glass now to throw back its fire-warmed contents. "I wouldn't so much call it 'taming' . . ."

"No." Pallas chuckled, replacing the crystal stopper on his decanter. "Perhaps not. He doesn't strike me as a thing to be collared. Very pretty, though, and oh, those teeth and *claws* . . . you've commendable taste, Many-Greats-Nephew. Though admittedly, age and predicament have somewhat altered mine."

He winked at him, and Celadon rolled his eyes, hiding the way he blushed beneath the rim of his glass.

Once he'd drained it completely, he set it down on the table between them.

"I should get going," he sighed, rising from his chair. "I didn't intend to spend nearly . . . gods, six hours?" It was almost two in the morning. He'd really only come for a change of scenery while Lethe had been otherwise occupied.

Pallas placed his glass on the table and stood as well. "Easy to lose track of time when you spend so much of it in the company of those for whom it has no meaning."

A snap of his fingers and the door to his lounge opened, admitting the two vampires who'd been on guard at his door since Celadon had arrived. "His coat, please," Pallas requested, and almost as soon as he finished speaking, one of the guards already had Celadon's black wool coat held up and open, waiting for him to slip in his arms.

"My men will see you home, should you require it?"

Wrapping the belt of his coat around his waist, Celadon shook his head. "No need. I'd like the fresh air, to be honest, and if anything untoward happens along the way, I will try to remember that I'm a king, whether I want it or not—I'm not entirely defenseless."

"Mmm," Pallas hummed through a frown. "But it's precisely that you *are* a king, and this is a time of war, that you should have an escort."

Celadon glanced up from his belt. "She is still my mother. I am still her son. If she does decide I need to die, Riadne Lysterne will be the one to deliver the blow. And I doubt she'll turn up downtown tonight."

"Death is not the only harm that can befall you, Nephew—not even the most permanent. Your untamed Lethe would be quite cross if you walked into trouble, I am sure of it. I would be, with Noel."

Smiling patiently, Celadon reassured, "I won't tell him if you don't. Though I promise to exercise the other perks that come with kingship and call immediately on my Egress to portal me to safety, should any-thing happen that I can't contend with. I'll be *fine*, Uncle." As he spoke, he pulled on his cashmere gloves. "I appreciate the concern, though."

Lifting his hands, Pallas sued for peace. "Very well, but take care. I've come to enjoy these evening visits and, more than this, would hate to have lived this long just to meet my end by gruesome eviscera-tion by your beloved for letting you leave here alone. Give my regards to Lethe. Do impress upon him to join one of these visits—I should very much like to speak with another who's known too much of this world."

"I will. Thank you, Uncle—and take care of yourself as well. Good night."

He took his leave.

Toronto in January was freezing, even this far into global warming. The wind was the worst of it—an irony that wasn't lost on Celadon, as a fae of this element. Funneled like a rushing current between the many buildings, gusts were a sudden and vicious assault that no amount of winter layers could fully guard against.

Tonight was one of the rare occasions that the air was actually still—as such, Celadon's first step out into the frosty night felt rather bracing.

He paused on the sidewalk, simply breathing in the chill as the Faerie Ring's entrance sealed shut behind him. Snow fell slowly from the sky in thick, fluffy flakes, dampening sound to a gentle hush. His breath crystalized in visible puffs before his face. The cold was a mild sting in his cheeks, but it served to chase away the fog of one too many whiskies better than anything else could.

For a moment—the first since the fiasco in the desert two days ago, and perhaps, if he were being honest, in the whole of the last four months—Celadon stood and merely . . . *existed*, in the quiet and calm and familiarity of night.

And for that moment—just a sliver of time—he felt so blessedly *normal* that it made him want to cry.

"And certainly *that's* the alcohol talking." He laughed in a breath to himself.

Tugging his coat tighter around his body, Celadon flipped the collar high over his neck and began the short enough stroll through Toronto's downtown to home.

People spilled out of one bar and carried on in boisterous groups to the next.

Though traffic was far less dense at this hour, there were still a number of cars that streaked by, most of them taxis and Ubers.

A war unlike anything the world had ever seen was so close to spilling over the horizon, and once the wave of it crashed ashore, nothing would be the same again, regardless of what resulted. Neither community that called the Mortal Realm home would be spared, so let them have this, he thought to himself, watching it all in passing.

A few more nights of happy ignorance.

Coming up to a crosswalk, he paused—his phone had vibrated in his pocket. Once, twice, four times now. Whatever it was, it was clearly urgent, because the text vibrations turned immediately to the longer insistence of a call.

"You know," Celadon said as he answered, his breath of laughter a crystalized cloud in the air. "I think this is the first time you've ever phoned me. Normally, it's—"

"Where are you?"

Slowly, Celadon replied, "Yonge Street, heading for Bloor. I'm on my way back to the palace—why?"

"You're walking?" There was a rush of irritated breath like a sigh, before Lethe growled, *"Never mind. Portal back. I've just received word from the Hunt that Riadne has gone after the Tsukino royal family. She's attacking UnSeelie Autumn. I'll—"*

Too many things were happening at once.

Lethe spoke, his words more chilling than the winter night's air, and Celadon tried to keep up. But simultaneously he noticed that the street's activity had lulled down to . . . nothing. Quite startlingly nothing, as though by some unnatural cue he'd missed in his distraction.

Doors snapped closed on the heels of new patrons whisked up off the streets; the final car sailed off down the road. Everyone installed at their next destination, Celadon found himself quite suddenly and very wholly alone in the weighted stillness—or rather . . . alone but one.

A man stood at the opposite side of the crossing, his own coat turned up against the wind much as Celadon's was.

Tall, with long black hair tangled up in bits of slick seaweed, and skin the pale mottled green of decaying flesh. He was very obviously one of the folk, and the way those clouded blue eyes locked unwaveringly on him as the man took a step off the curb to begin to cross the street, he could tell the man knew exactly who he was.

But Celadon's reassurance of Pallas's concern hadn't been bravado.

He was a king; a Celestial reborn; the son of two High Sovereigns and product of four Seasons—if this faerie meant him harm, he'd have to give it a hell of a go to render Celadon defenseless.

"Evening," Celadon greeted in a low, not-quite-threat, when this faerie reached his side of the street as he stood with his phone pressed to his ear, Lethe still on the other end.

"Celadon?"

"Evening, Your Majesty," the faerie man replied, his voice both a hauntingly lovely tune and . . . *uncomfortable*, the way it rubbed like the film of ooze over decomposition.

"Celadon, who's there, who are you speaking to?"

Lethe's panic—it should have cut through Celadon like a knife. It should have spurred him to abandon his pride and summon a portal to get himself away as quick as possible . . . but it didn't.

Those eyes . . .

Hells, he shouldn't have looked. It was such a basic rule of defense among the folk, not to directly meet the gaze of a faerie that you didn't know, for exactly this reason—that there was no telling how powerful their knack for mesmerization was.

It was the drink still warm in his veins to blame for this foolish mistake, but Celadon's sight locked with that of the faerie before him, and his brain had all of a *second* to realize what was happening before it smoothed to an unnaturally sedate calm.

There was something so *terribly* lovely about this faerie, was the thought in his head; the longer Celadon looked, the harder it was, he found, to do anything else.

Later, when recounting events, he'd berate himself quite firmly for falling so easily into this trap.

Later, when recalling this scene, he'd realize how very little control he'd actually had of this moment, the faerie's astoundingly strong compulsion be damned—all because of *her*.

The white-haired, silver-eyed, starlight-freckled goddess standing off to the shadowy sidelines. Goddess, clearly—Titan, he would even venture, because she radiated nothing less, and he would bet his life and entire fortune on which one she was.

What ill fate, after all, that there was so conveniently no one around to help in what happened next—

"Nothing personal," the faerie man said into his ear, but when had he come so close?

Celadon couldn't say—he couldn't do much, as a matter of fact.

The needle to the back of his neck made him drop his phone, which cracked on the pavement. Then, suddenly, a cloth was pressed over his face; fae weren't impervious to the effects of chloroform, though considerably more was needed to render them unconscious . . .

. . . as apparently the faerie had accounted for.

Celadon groaned, attempting to unstick his eyes.

When he'd passed out, he couldn't even recall, but waking made him want to vomit down the front of him.

"That would be the mercury you're feeling."

A hand gripped the top of Celadon's head, fingers winding painfully tight in his hair—they yanked his head back to bare his throat, harsh enough that Celadon cried out. He tried to lash back but discovered something else about his situation . . .

His wrists were chained together by thick iron links, strung up over his head, and fastened to . . . a warehouse ceiling?

Celadon's vision swam in and out of focus, rendering it impossible to make anything out in detail.

"Well, mercury and iron powder—a specialty blend of mine."

The floor felt like it was bobbing on waves.

Celadon tried to rip his head free from the man who held him in place, but the man only held tighter . . . tapped his nose with the end of the syringe he'd emptied into Celadon's veins . . .

"Hush, little king, I wouldn't struggle so much. That will only speed the spread of it through your system, and there's enough in you to cause serious damage if you don't give yourself time for your magic to recover."

Groaning, Celadon fell still, more because nausea swelled dangerously high again, and where had his coat gone?

Where was his shirt?

This faerie had stolen his clothes—his shoes, as well. His thoughts, besides. He wanted to vomit, and sleep, and *scream* for the feeling like razors in his veins, this poison in his fae blood that neutralized his magic, until his body could sort enough of it out to allow it to rekindle.

"As I said, it's nothing personal."

The faerie tossed the syringe aside, stalked somewhere out of sight—and then, quite suddenly, a *yanking*.

"It's simply politics."

From somewhere behind him, the faerie man tugged on the chain that bound Celadon, and slowly began to reel him up off the floor, just enough that his toes could only brush the cement, his entire weight suspended by his wrists . . .

"Your mother needed a favor, and I wanted something in return—ah, ah, ah, *stop struggling*—"

Heavens.

Cold crept through his limbs with the liquid metal he'd been injected with, making its way to his heart, where it clenched its icy fingers around the traitorously slowing organ as though to pull it down into the depths of . . . he could smell it: the water.

Were they still in Toronto?

Was this a warehouse on the harbor?

This faerie, he was almost as talented with his mesmer as his mother was; Celadon fell still again in an instant, merely at his word.

"Perhaps a little too much iron?" The faerie had come back into view, tilted in consideration of Celadon, though perhaps that was Celadon's brain, which felt like a melting forge. "No matter. I was tasked by your mother to pose a distraction, to buy her time should you again become aware of her business tonight. If you'd have simply carried on your way . . . if that phone call hadn't given up Her Majesty's game, you'd be safe and warm and comfortable at home right now, but here we are. Here *you* are, and . . . well, she'd be a little cross with me if my methods cost your life, but you won't go and die on me, will you, Your Highness? I have so much *fun* planned for us tonight once that injection wears off a little."

It took every ounce of strength Celadon could muster just to spit in the faerie's direction.

Which caused him to laugh. "So *feisty*—I like that. To be honest, I hadn't expected you to be such a pretty thing. I did hear the rumors, have seen the pictures, but they certainly pale in comparison to the real deal, I must say." Stalking forward, the man extended long, bony fingers to trace along the waist of Celadon's pants, making his skin *crawl*.

"You'd better hope . . . this *doesn't* wear off . . . even a little," Celadon threatened, like speaking around cotton stuffed into his mouth, and nausea roiled once more for the effort.

The faerie laughed.

"Good, yes, I like them even better with spirit." Leaning in, he snapped his teeth at Celadon's nose, and Celadon couldn't help himself—he flinched. Those teeth reeked of death . . . and flesh . . . and briny water . . .

Handsome . . . terrifying . . . carnivorous . . . faerie . . .

"Kelpie?" Celadon breathed out.

The faerie man frowned in disgust. "How offensive."

Ah.

"An each-uisge then."

Fuck.

There were flesh-eating water horses, and then there was *this*— similar concept, same family, dreadfully so much worse, and with the ability to take on human shape to prowl the land for their prey. Armed with glamour that could spin beauty so bewitching, very few who met their gaze could resist the draw of it, and powerful magic fed not by the Courts but the Wild, they were extremely dangerous predators—enough so that they'd earned a place on the list of species banned from living in the Courts.

"Call me Eanraig."

"Henry the *aughisky*?" Celadon forced a laugh, causing the each-uisge to glower. Over-anglicizing faerie names tended to piss them off—which probably wasn't something Celadon should be doing right now, given how awful this specific species was known to be. But in for a penny, as the saying went. "Is my mother . . . running so low on help . . . she had to resort to *you*?"

Nails scored trails of bleeding sapphire down Celadon's chest, curled over the waist of his pants to tug the pair of them closer. "Be careful, pretty king. I swore to your mother I wouldn't kill you—she made me seal no promise about not harming you . . ."

Eanraig released him to stalk a slow circle around him like the predator he was.

"It was almost *embarrassingly* easy to capture you, you know—how deeply afoul you must have run of Fate that she seemed to have paved my way clear to you."

Oh, if this faerie even knew the half of it.

Celadon laughed self-deprecatingly, though perhaps it was only in his head.

The each-uisge had no idea how spot-on this observation was—clearly couldn't see her the way Celadon could, for there she was again, the white-haired Titan looking on from the warehouse corner . . . like this was her approved design and she'd risked a great deal to be here to ensure it would be carried out to the letter.

"I could make you *want* me to hurt you," Eanraig fairly purred as he teased out his threats. "I would dearly love to hear you beg for it. I would love to hear you *gag* for it."

He leaned in, nose tracing feather light against the back of Celadon's neck—the mercury concoction still heavy in his veins, Celadon jerked, tried to kick out at the faerie behind him . . . earned only a slash of claws to his back, and Celadon had to bite his lip to restrain himself from satisfying the faerie with a cry.

"I could make your life quite miserable too," Eanraig soured.

Latching onto Celadon's hair once more, he yanked his head back as far as Celadon could bend, and the world began to spin. "And ah, but you would thank me for it too, as you *scraped* this floor to kiss my boot."

Again Celadon spit at his captor, and this time it managed to land, right in his eye.

Eanraig didn't seem to appreciate it as much as the first time; he'd appreciate it a lot less the moment Celadon could regain his physical strength, could call his magic to his aid.

Just a little longer—

Slap.

Eanraig struck him across the face, releasing him to pitch forward.

The faerie strode back to the front of him—*slam*; he rammed a knee up into Celadon's gut, forcing him to empty the contents of his stomach onto the ground.

"I could make you clean that with your tongue," the each-uisge gritted out, bending to speak once more at Celadon's ear. "I could make you do *anything* I wish, and you would comply, with memory of the degradation to haunt you forever after."

A hand slipped around, behind, down to caress the interior back of Celadon's thigh. "I could imprint such lovely horror on your body, Your Highness, that every time any lover touched you after, it would forever be through the ghost of me—*and you would plead for me to ruin you*—"

THUD.

A small price to pay, the splitting pain of whipping his head upright so forcefully that Celadon heard the crunch of breaking bone.

Eanraig cried out in pain—his hands flew to his nose, sapphire blood pouring through the cracks between his skeletal fingers.

Fury ignited in the gaze leveled now at Celadon.

Seconds were all he had to catch up with proceedings—one moment, Eanraig was building rage before him, puffing up and baring a collection of teeth that were a combination of blunt and sharp, meant for tearing meat and sinew and crunching through bone all alike.

The next . . .

How quickly the each-uisge circled back around him.

"You wish to deal in agony, do you?"

Celadon *screamed*, his body seizing tight.

Those brutal teeth had clamped down on his shoulder.

Blood poured thick and hot down his arm, his chest; flesh tore from bone in a sizable chunk as the each-uisge took a bite of him, chewing his mouthful right in Celadon's ear for him to hear himself be devoured.

His body felt like fire . . . it twitched and shuddered through the purest, sparking pain.

He both wanted to look and didn't at the state his shoulder was in . . . could see only the sapphire pooled ominously beneath him and the boots of the each-uisge as he curved back to the front of him.

His hand darted to grip Celadon's chin, and Celadon struggled, fought, tried to free himself of the hold as that bloody *mouth* began to lower to his . . .

To feed him his own gore?

To tear flesh next from Celadon's face?

Blessedly, he would only ever be able to guess what Eanraig Each-Uisge had in store for him, because that was the tip of a dagger suddenly at the soft of his captor's throat.

That was an arrow, applied to the other side.

They appeared out of nowhere, peeling from the dark to form shadowy figures in glittering black. One . . . two . . . the third just behind the each-uisge, adamant teeth glinting sharply in the slant of moonlight . . .

Yue.

Eris.

Vesper.

Fate in the corner, rage stark on her face as her plans for Celadon's demise shattered just as she did into dust, vanishing the very same moment as a fourth presence stepped out of the gloom to impose itself firmly at Celadon's back . . .

"You wish to deal in agony?"

Ah.

There he was.

Lethe's voice . . . Celadon had never heard it like this, soft but pitched in the purest, wildest fury.

"Eris. Yue. Vesper." He continued to speak in that frightening tone, like every bit of misfortune this world possessed had just fixed on the faerie between them, whose eyes began to widen, like he hadn't known, when he made threat of lovers, who Celadon kept in his bed. "Take him home. Address his wounds."

A claw-tipped hand reached up to slice so easily through Celadon's chains that it made him giggle breathlessly as he collapsed right into Lethe's arms—that could be the poisoning though, or the blood loss. A faerie had just taken a bite clean out of his shoulder, after all.

"Celadon?"

Far too gently, far too preciously for what this man embodied, Lethe maneuvered him about to face him.

To take stock of every injury this faerie would pay for.

"I'm okay," Celadon breathed, but his entire body began to shake. Adrenaline. *Poisoning.* It was worth mentioning twice that a faerie *had* just taken a bite clean out of his shoulder.

He sagged a little; gagged a little.

Lethe's hand came up to the side of his face, the other so dearly careful of . . . goodness, that was an actual gaping hole. Celadon could see his own bones. If he didn't get this metal out of his system soon, his magic wouldn't be able to heal him enough in time—what a ridiculous way for a fae king to go, *bleeding* to death.

"Take him home; fetch Aurelian. He needs lesidhe assistance, and I will have *no one* but his brother's mate in his vicinity right now. Keep all others out." Lethe spoke to the Hunt, a touch of hysteria wearing at the edges of his tone, making Celadon want to hug him. Funnily enough, the way Lethe's arms twitched, he might have wanted to hug Celadon, too.

Or . . . again . . . the poison talking . . .

"Come on, Celadon," said another gentle voice, with yet more gentle hands—Vesper, Celadon could only somewhat discern through the way his head was beginning to simultaneously fill with lead and float away like a balloon. "Come on, let's get you cleaned up, okay?"

"Yeah, all right." He went along easily, Lethe handing him off like he was breakable treasure. Vesper was nice; xe smelled a bit distinctly like Paris, and Celadon couldn't explain that, but Paris was nice too. "Is Lethe coming?"

Vesper smiled patiently, collecting him from Lethe's hold, and he must trust xem a lot. Must really like these people who were probably the most family he'd known in a very long time—Lethe *didn't* like when people took things from him; he liked it even less when Celadon was what was stolen.

"Won't be a moment, *aulea*," Lethe replied, his tone grown dark as death, and it wasn't until Celadon awoke the next morning to his boyfriend asleep on the bed—his arms wrapped possessively around Celadon's middle, and flecks of sapphire blood still under his nails—that he realized what *exactly* Lethe had said to him in parting.

No access to his magic meant no automatic translation of foreign languages, as most of the folk relied on, but Lethe had spoken in mer.

Which Celadon knew—quite a few dialects, as a matter of fact, his lifelong fascination with the folk of water making a lot more sense these days, but that was a digression . . .

Aulea, Lethe had called him.

Treasure, it translated to . . . most beloved, it meant . . . the most intimate term of endearment in mer language, as a matter of fact, and reserved only for their bonded partners.

"*I abhor the things I find I would do for you.*"

"*I rather think you love it.*"

"*Not the* task, *I don't.*"

Celadon leaned in, pressed his forehead to Lethe's, who still slumbered on. "I love you, too."

CHAPTER 12

Ruin

"SUCH A PITY."

Ruin watched as the fine point of the High Queen's rather deadly looking footwear pressed on the cheek of the corpse beneath it, turning its other cheek to the floor. It was not them she spoke to. Her words were for a man none but she could see—such was the toll of the Crown she wore, and Ruin was only far too happy to encourage this degradation of her sanity. The fae general she'd brought along with them on this mission, bent over another body and looting it of its valuables, didn't seem to mind all that much either that the one holding his reins was losing touch with reality.

"You know, I really did have much higher hopes for this Court, that our show in UnSeelie Summer would have made a better impression. To have the Death-Touched fae of UnSeelie Autumn on our side . . . *such* a pity."

That foot pressed even harder.

The sound of cracking bone—so lovely a thing to hear—cut sharply into the silence that lay over the UnSeelie Autumn palace's inner sanctum. Here, where the king and queen had fled with their young prince and infant princess after Ruin's slaughter of their entire guard.

It had almost been a satisfying battle.

The king had fought brave and honorably.

The queen had fought with a viciousness only a mother protecting her precious children could ascend to.

In the end, all fell to Ruin, but this had been the most fun they'd had in quite a while.

Riadne moved from the king she'd ground into the tile, the stark white of his silk kimono stained thickly with his sapphire blood.

She crossed the floor to the artful display of white-handled katanas on the back wall.

"Everything I have done for our son, yet he still shows me nothing but scorn. He mocks my efforts at every turn, has only grown more rebellious under the influence of that *Hunter* he's taken into his bed. I worry that, soon, he'll be beyond my care and guidance." Riadne paused, tilting her head as though the ghost she spoke to was speaking back. "No, I didn't think it would be easy, but to show such contempt for his own mother . . ."

Recovering herself, the High Queen turned as though she hadn't been absent in mind at all, snapped her fingers in the direction of the lifeless boy still clutching the cold body of his baby sister. "Him. You shall bring him with us—I want the eyes."

Now it was Ruin she spoke to.

Ah, he would perhaps miss this particular mortal.

It was such a pity indeed that she would also have to fall. That soon that Crown's weight would be inconsequential—she'd grow too weak to fend off the Sins that drained her, and then they would consume her. Ruin would be free of her shackles. All that would remain would be Arlo, and with how exhausted *she* had been since their return from their meeting with the goddess Urielle . . . that would be only a matter of time as well.

But Riadne Lysterne . . . he supposed this mortal *had* to be so unflinchingly ruthless, so deliciously cruel to have made all her dark ambitions a reality—to summon Ruin back into being.

With a clarity in her eyes that had been diminished mere moments ago, she began to stalk back across the room—along her way, she walked right across the queen Ruin had cut down, the heel of her shoe piercing the corpse's gut, and a gush of yet more sapphire joined the pool around her when that spike pulled out.

"Your High Majesty," said one of the Bone Guard, appearing in the sanctum's open doorway. He looked . . . distinctly uncomfortable, as though what he'd come to tell his queen was something she wouldn't be happy to hear.

Riadne pierced him with her gaze. "Go on, speak then, if you're to interrupt."

The guard floundered only a moment—how quaint, Ruin noted, that he seemed to be keeping his eyes from falling on the motionless children. Mortal weakness, to be so absorbed in their frail young.

"Y-your Hunt has arrived."

"Lovely of them to show at last when no longer needed." Riadne snorted. "Why was this a necessary announcement?"

"They've . . . ah . . . come with a faerie for you. A . . . uh . . . gift? From Lethe. I . . . feel it worth the forewarning that his *face* has been carved off. Among . . . other things."

Oh?

The true pity was that Ruin had come too late in this game. How terribly they would have liked to wage destruction at the side of Misfortune.

With a sound of disgust in the back of her throat, Riadne resumed for the door. "*Must* I do everything? Did I not *warn* him to restrain himself lest he attract the wrong attention?" Over her shoulder, she snapped at Ruin, "Put the body with the others. In the morning, I would like you to pay a visit to my ungrateful sons and invite them to join me for dinner tomorrow evening. They may bring their respective others—do assure them a cease-fire, in which all will be permitted to leave in the exact physical health they arrived in." She paused at the doorway. Turned her head just enough that Ruin could see her profile. "My invitation will not be declined."

Ruin frowned slightly. For all of Riadne's many attractive qualities, that she used Ruin so lowly as her personal messenger meant they would still rejoice in the day they were able to cut her down too.

Bending to retrieve the boy, breaking the babe from his stiff grip and discarding her to the floor, they swept to follow their master from the room.

CHAPTER 13

Aurelian

~~~

AURELIAN ENTERED HIS OFFICE breathless and drenched in sweat.

It was nearing noon when Elyas had come bounding out to fetch him in the arena, where he'd been training with Ivandril, as he'd taken to doing now every spare moment of his day after what Celadon and Lethe had faced in the desert drove home how *overwhelmingly* underprepared they were for the war on their horizon.

He almost didn't believe what he'd been sent for *twice* in a matter of hours. The first half of his night had been spent managing the flood of UnSeelie Autumn folk seeking refuge in the Market, fleeing their homes in the wake of Riadne's surprise attack on their royal family. The other half of his night had been spent at Celadon's side after being pulled from his duties by an emergency summons to find their allied king barely conscious, propped in a chair in his bedroom and bleeding out from an injury so horrific, even Aurelian's magic had barely been enough to see him through the worst of it.

And now another summons, another emergency.

He'd come straight here without even stopping to change out of his sparring outfit, his black shirt stuck uncomfortably to both his chest and back, because surely there had been some misunderstanding; Elyas had to have been mistaken.

There was no way that *Arlo* was here to see him, in the Market of all places—yet there she was when he opened the door, perched on the edge of his desk and looking into the massive fireplace behind it, watching the fledgling flames leap and flicker.

Vehan—whom Aurelian was still a little cross with for taking off through the Egress after Arlo only days before—stood by Aurelian's vacant chair.

Frozen warily just this side of Aurelian's private portal were Lethe and Celadon as well, the latter looking far better than the last time Aurelian had seen him, but still considerably poor: pale and green around the edges, exhaustion dark around his eyes, and trembling minutely as his body worked still to expel the last of the poison he'd been injected with.

Everyone watched Arlo with grim expressions etched in stony mistrust; Arlo looked at none of them in return.

"Arlo," Aurelian greeted hesitantly. "Not that I'm not happy to see you, but . . ."

"Don't worry," Arlo replied, still not looking away from the fire. "Ruin can't touch you."

Ruin couldn't touch them, yes, all right, the gate that guarded the Market ensured even Titans couldn't enter without permission. "But how can *you* be here, if you don't mind my asking?"

It seemed like a very large security flaw to leave exposed in the middle of war. Aurelian wouldn't mind knowing how it had happened.

"Oh," she replied a bit absently, still thoroughly entranced by the flames. "Because I'm not."

". . . What?"

It was then that Arlo flickered—the *image* of her—and everyone in the room startled. Cast from where, Aurelian had no idea, but suddenly it made a lot more sense that the fireplace should be so interesting to her. Wherever she was, something else stood in its place that they couldn't see.

Impressive magic, impressive *alchemy*, to be able to project herself so clearly from someplace else entirely, and Arlo was always welcome to be here—her, not Ruin—but Aurelian couldn't deny that he breathed a bit easier now that he knew she wasn't.

"Ah," was his delicate reply.

Aurelian hesitated only a moment longer before crossing the room to come to a halt in front of her. "Arlo?"

"Hmm?"

At last Arlo turned to face him.

How different she looked these days. So pallid she could be ice, her jade eyes taking on more and more of the red sheen that had occasionally flickered in Vehan's gaze back when Ruin had been *his* burden to bear.

Exhausted, eyes rimmed with similar dark circles to her cousin's, her cheeks grown sharper for how hollow they caved beneath.

Unwell.

Arlo looked unwell to him—a poisoning of a different sort—and it pulled at Aurelian's heart just as painfully as it would to see Harlan in this state.

He reached out.

Given her impermanence, he hadn't really expected his hand to meet solid flesh, but Arlo's magic was apparently so strong now that he could actually touch this illusion the same way he could her.

And so he lifted his other hand as well and placed it on her opposite shoulder.

"You and I," he began softly, holding her gaze all the while, "we haven't had much time for each other. Our significant others . . . are a little dramatic. They keep us very busy."

Vehan wisely remained silent.

"But I can't even begin to tell you what I owe you. How grateful I am for you in my life. How fortunate I count myself to call you my friend. I just want to tell you that I care about you. A lot. So that you know how personal and invested a place it comes from when I ask you: Are you all right?"

Arlo watched him now the way she'd been watching the fire.

A moment passed . . . another . . . "No," she replied, as sincerely as how simply the word had been spoken.

"Would . . . you like a hug?"

It felt so ridiculous to even ask it.

Nothing Arlo had gone through and was currently going through was anything that could be healed by affection. She had to be so far from okay that the word had lost meaning entirely, but the Arlo of before, who'd once been free to cry when she was overwhelmed and seek physical comfort from the people she cared about . . . Aurelian just wanted to give a piece of that back to her.

Arlo, for her part, examined him more closely. "No," she replied, again so simply. "But not because it's you. Not because I don't want it. I just . . ." She trailed off into a pause, seeming to consider her answer carefully. "I don't know, it's a bit like how I feel about crying. I want to, sometimes desperately. The things I have to do, the things I have to *watch* myself do. The people around me . . . Riadne . . . I can feel it building and building, pressing to burst against my seams, but when it finally feels like the tears might fall, everything just . . . stops. The tears won't come. The apathy settles back in to force everything back down. Like my body's forgotten how to do anything but suppress the great many things I'm feeling. Survival mode, I suppose you'd call it." She shrugged. "So no, I wouldn't *like* the hug. I think I'm forgetting how to like most things in general. But I'll take one still . . . if you're offering."

No further prompting needed, Aurelian folded her against his chest and hugged her tightly, resting his chin on top of her head.

No one spoke.

For a moment, it was almost nice. Things were almost like they would be if it weren't for . . . *everything*.

Then . . . "Riadne politely demands your attendance at dinner tonight."

Aurelian's eyes shot open wide.

He took a step back.

Examined Arlo very carefully. "She can't demand anything from us. She isn't our queen."

"True," Arlo replied. "But I would attend, regardless." Back to the fireplace her eyes drifted. Aurelian found himself suddenly, and with no real explanation as to why, not wanting to know at all what was there on her end. "Riadne isn't doing well. To not show will push her to breaking, one way or another—whether to war or to Ruin, neither's a very good outcome."

Her attention snapped back to him so abruptly, Aurelian took a step back. "Plus, I've been instructed not to take no for an answer, and I'd rather if you didn't make me force you. If it makes *you* feel any better, she promises no physical harm will come to any of you. You'll leave exactly as you came. It really is just dinner."

The silence resumed.

Aurelian looked over to Vehan, lost and searching for the right reply.

"I'm going," he said, like he'd already decided before Arlo even asked it.

"It sounds like we don't have much choice in the matter," Celadon mused, a touch of frustration to his illness-hoarse tone. "I don't like this. I know my mother. Whatever this is, it isn't *just dinner*. There's something not being said. Are you going to be there, Arlo?"

Arlo nodded, slowly and silently.

Pursing his lips, Vehan paused a moment in thought before asking the rest of them, "Is it better or worse for us that she is?"

"I don't know," Celadon huffed, folding his arms quite gingerly over his chest, and earning a rustle of unease from Lethe, whose hand shot out almost on instinct to steady on the low of Celadon's back. "Arlo, who *else* is going to be at dinner?"

It was then that Arlo straightened.

That red flashed brighter in her gaze.

She slid off the desk and stretched. "I'll inform Riadne that you accept her invitation. She'll be expecting you—formal attire, please. She also expects you all to look your best for this reunion."

It was the way she said it—*reunion* . . . Aurelian had a funny, sinking feeling that she did not mean it in context with Riadne.

...

Seated in the same room they'd dined in when Arlo and Celadon had first joined them last summer—the walls of electric waterfalls, the glass cabinets stocked full of wines and liquors and exquisite crystal, all exactly as they'd been half a year ago—Aurelian's funny, sinking feeling had turned rancid in his stomach.

All in their finery.

Riadne, her Bone Crown stark against her raven-black hair, commanded the head of the table in a rare dress, pieced together from thousands of tiny diamonds and a material that clung to her body as though poured.

No one else wore the Seelie colors of Summer.

Celadon had opted for a matte tailcoat suit as black as his hair, Lethe beside him in robes of matching gothic darkness, both of them heavy on the gray-and-kohl makeup.

Aurelian and Vehan, meanwhile, had gone with suits of red, brown, and black brocade and lavish silk from Celadon's private stores, because of course he played around in his scant spare time with actually *making* the outfits they all wore.

It was Nausicaä who'd been most transformed, though.

Of course she was there, if Arlo was. But in all the time he'd known her, he'd never seen her look so . . . soft.

Hair lightly curled, gentle sweeps of blush and eye shadow for makeup, a deep red velvet dress encrusted with crystals that dripped over her bosom.

She looked like an entirely different person, and maybe that was the goal? Because there was an air of . . . *unease* about her, about the way she kept darting glances to Arlo, who sat there beside her, examining her nails, not even the least bit interested in what Aurelian was certain the real Arlo would have been stunned by under normal circumstances.

But the version of Arlo here didn't seem to care at all.

Arlo was the only one in the room not dressed up in the least for the occasion, either. And the only one besides Riadne not concerned in the least about the two people the High Queen had seated on her left and right.

But Aurelian couldn't focus on what Arlo's lack of behavior in any regard meant, not right now, not when he was working so hard not to peel away from this table to vomit—Vehan looked even closer to doing so, his hand gone white around the fork he clutched to the point of bending.

"How *lovely* is this," Riadne gushed, leaning in over her plate as though sharing an intimate moment with them. "The whole family, together at last."

At least they now knew why Riadne had been collecting bodies.

She'd been *using* them.

For parts.

"You can't know how long I've been anticipating this," the High Queen continued, oblivious to the looks she and her . . . *additional guests* received. "My two handsome boys, my two handsome husbands, everyone happy and together at last."

Unable to hold her tongue any longer, apparently, Nausicaä tore her dismay from Arlo to burst out, "Okay, first and foremost, congratulations on going so *fully* around the fucking bend that you made it all the way home. Second of all . . . are they, like . . . alive?"

"Oh, quite!" Riadne exclaimed brightly. "I'm glad you asked, dear. It's a bit of genius I really can't help but to boast about—both of them, perfectly alive! It took some time gathering the right pieces. And Vadrien, the eyes I just couldn't get right, but an earlier appointment today provided the closest I'm going to get, I'm afraid." She turned to the *thing* beside her—the sewn-together, reanimated corpse that reminded Aurelian strongly of the cavum they'd battled in Aurum Industries . . . but he supposed that's where she got the idea, and ran with to a vastly higher degree of unhinged.

Vadrien Lysterne.

And on her right, Azurean Lazuli-Viridian.

"It's been long in the works," Riadne continued, unbothered by her rambling's reception. "I didn't know at the time exactly why I'd saved Vadrien's heart, only that it might prove useful later, but Azurean's was intentional. A bit of Lust to give them both purpose, and honestly, you'd never know they'd died at all."

That was *very* much not the case.

It wasn't only the faint rotting stench of them that Aurelian could smell all the way over here that gave Riadne's dolls away as reanimated dead. It wasn't only the mismatched limbs and features carefully sewn together to make one gruesome whole. Vadrien and Azurean, they both . . . just sat there, staring dead ahead, no light in their eyes to suggest even a flicker of self-awareness or mental activity in general. Neither touched the food on their plates, though really, only Riadne had eaten anything since it had been served. Neither moved an inch until their puppeteer commanded something from them.

And all Aurelian could do was stare.

All he could do was wonder how long until all those corrosive emotions swirling in Vehan, which he could feel like his own through their bond, ate through his boyfriend's composure. This was Vehan's *father*, after all, a man Vehan didn't have any solid memory of, as he'd been so little when his father died. So to have those precious few flashes and childhood impressions rewritten with *this* . . .

"For *goodness'* sake. I haven't poisoned the food, you know." Riadne leveled an electric-sharp stare at each of them in turn until utensils were reluctantly taken up and put to their first course of vibrant lobster bisque (Aurelian's she actually remembered to have made up vegetarian). "On that note, I do hope you're on the mend, Celadon, my love. That *awful* each-uisge—I specifically forbade him from taking things too far, had instructed him to your distraction only. All he'd wanted in exchange was a couple of the Bone Guard on loan to help him wrest control of the Swamps from his brother—and what do I care about Wild politics? It will all serve under my banner in the end, regardless. So I thought, what was the harm? But alas,

197

that's the last I trust your keeping to a *faerie*, I assure you. Water under the bridge, though, yes?"

Celadon blinked at her, a little incredulous.

It was Lethe who looked like he might lunge across the table and eviscerate the queen.

"Yes, water under the bridge," she answered, nodding to herself, and moved on as though that matter was settled.

Appeased that her guests were acting as they should, Riadne turned her attention next on Vehan. "As for you, my darling," she said, with more feeling for him than Aurelian had ever heard her apply. "Your nineteenth birthday is coming up soon—the end of the month, your mother doesn't forget these things. Regrettably, I've been a bit preoccupied, but there's still plenty of time to plan you a party befitting of a High Prince. Did you know your father was only nineteen when—"

SLAM.

Aurelian startled.

He wasn't the only to do so, though Vadrien and Azurean remained staring unblinkingly ahead, and Arlo's attention merely meandered over to where Vehan had shot to his feet, palms flat on the table.

Shaking.

Pale.

Vehan looked on the verge of shorting out completely.

"*Vehan,*" Riadne gasped. "This is an appalling display of manners in front of your father. We taught you better than—"

"That *thing* is not my father."

Riadne's expression darked perceptibly. "Vehan Lysterne," she snapped like a crack of lightning. "You will apologize for that comment this *instant.* We are having a *nice* family dinner, everyone together. I worked exceptionally hard to make this happen for you—for *us,* for my children, as ever I have done. *Always* for my children. I will not tolerate this disrespect, certainly not under the roof that raised you, so you will sit, and you will eat. We will discuss the terms of you and your brother dropping this *ridiculous* rebellion of yours.

You will cede the Courts you stole back to my power. And then, with all that settled, we will begin to plan you a party."

"I don't even know who you are anymore," was Vehan's whispered reply before he pushed off from the table and stalked out into the hall.

Riadne called after him, ordering his return with growing outrage.

Dropping his spoon, Aurelian pushed back from the table as well. Got to his feet. Didn't bother thanking Riadne for this horror show of an evening before taking off after his boyfriend.

"Vehan," Aurelian breathed out in the hall, quick strides carrying him to where Vehan stood bent over by a stained-glass window, clearly attempting to regulate his breathing between his knees. "It's . . . well, very far from okay, but come on, let's get you home. You don't need to be here, didn't need to see this. Damn your mother for even *thinking* this was acceptable to do to you—"

The dining room doors swung open again.

Far more frighteningly white than before and eyes even darker hollows, Celadon strode out to join them, Lethe slinking closely in his shadow and keeping his attention trained firmly on his boyfriend.

Behind them both . . . Nausicaä.

"So *that* was fucked," she said finally when everyone had gathered and no one had said a word.

Aurelian frowned.

Whatever Nausicaä thought she was doing right now, he was not about to let her inflict more injury on his shaken soulmate.

Four months Nausicaä had been taking her frustrations out on them, making everything harder for them by causing chaos and destruction wherever she went. The worst of her mood had been inflicted on Vehan, and Aurelian understood, to some extent. He wouldn't be all that happy either if Arlo hadn't made her switch and it was Vehan burdened by Ruin—in fact, Vehan would have been dead; another reason why he owed so much to her.

But he digressed.

If he had to fight Nausicaä right here in this hallway to preserve what little fortitude Vehan still possessed, he would.

"Like *really* supremely fucked—and Arlo didn't even seem to care at all." She sighed, eyeing Vehan, frowning a little herself as though she were weighing two evils to determine the lesser. Eventually, she landed on: "Listen. We . . . need to talk. And . . ." Her gaze cut to Aurelian, and he must have been wearing something deadly in his expression, because she sighed even harsher and rolled her eyes. "Thank you. For what you did in the desert. For going after Arlo and following her through that rift. She told me why you did it, that you risked obliteration just so that she'd have a better chance of surviving two jumps in one night, and I just . . ."

Her shoulders crept a little closer to her ears, her posture so tense that she might snap at the slightest of provocations—clearly, whatever this was, it went against everything she held dear, but there was also the air of resignation. "Arlo's *really* struggling to keep ahold of herself these days," she continued in a far quieter voice. "I know you guys know that, but at the same time, you really don't. You aren't around her like I am. And as fun as it's been to invent ways to throw her off guard, into remembering who she is, even for just a few moments"— she motioned to her dress—"that's starting to lose effect as well. Which means I'm getting real close to crunch time with dick-all figured out apart from the fact that if I want to better my chances of saving her from Ruin when *your* shitty plan backfires, we perhaps shouldn't be at *complete* odds. You carry a piece of her, just like I do; I'm told that's going to be . . . helpful."

Another glance at Aurelian.

She seemed to be picking her words based on his reaction to them, which was fairly in keeping with what he imagined of someone as powerful and exalted as Nausicaä had once been—in between the convolution, this *almost* sounded like a request for help.

"And it was maybe a little unfair of me to blame everything on you," she tacked on with a huff, glancing over at Vehan. "I'm . . . sorry."

It was the world's shittiest half apology, and if it were Aurelian, he would have laughed in her face. But Vehan, too unused to anyone showing contrition over their abuse of him, practically launched himself at Nausicaä, cutting her speech off with two arms flung around her shoulders and a complete breakdown into tears.

"I didn't m-mean for any of this t-to happen!"

"Yeah, I . . . know," Nausicaä said awkwardly.

"I l-love Arlo. I didn't w-want this for her."

"I . . . know that too," Nausicaä repeated, a little stronger.

"I l-love *you*, too, you enormous ass."

"Geez, do you kiss Aurelian with that filthy mouth?"

"Shut up." He hugged her tighter. Nausicaä relented just a little to let an arm wind around his shoulders in return, however loosely. "I'm sorry I couldn't save her," he breathed against her.

Nausicaä shook her head.

"Things are just kind of fucked all around," she replied. "I'm getting pretty over it. Pretty over losing people I care about; pretty over not having a home or family to go back to, *ever*."

Aurelian . . . deflated, just a little.

He couldn't imagine.

It was easy to forget, given Nausicaä's personality, but in immortal terms, she wasn't any older than they were, still just a teenager, and what it must feel like, to be cast aside by everyone she'd ever known and left all alone for over a century.

"I'm especially over that jackoff Titan squatting rent-free in my girlfriend," she added dryly. "I don't like that you all only decided on *one* fail-safe to protect her from them and then crossed your fingers and prayed to rainbows that everything would go without a hitch. Because it already hasn't, and I'm not going to hang my head and call it a loss if you can't sever her from Ruin with that sword in time. We need a backup plan. Megaera seems to think that plan should involve all the people who carry *pieces* of Arlo's heart in theirs."

Oh?

That was something that none of them had considered yet.

They knew that Arlo had an easier time remembering herself around people she had prior connections to, the more and deeper the better. But that this could actually be a method of saving her, even when all seemed lost . . .

"You know you're welcome to come with us back to the Market, Nausicaä."

Aurelian fixed her with a pointed look as he spoke; she looked at him back, her gaze just as unflinching.

They'd never gotten along all that famously, but they'd been through so much together, and just as she'd said, he was getting pretty over all the negativity in their lives. If they wanted to keep from failing Arlo *twice*, now, more than ever, they needed to come together.

They needed Nausicaä.

She needed them as well.

"A Dark and Hollow Star, isn't that the saying?" Vehan added, peeling back from his embrace to hold out a hand to her. "How wild would it be if the fortune teller Aurelian went to in the Forums Market back before we met meant *we* were the two stars that had to align!"

"I would go back and ask for a refund, if I were you," Nausicaä deadpanned.

CHAPTER 14

Celadon

~~~~~~~~

I T WAS CROWDED ON the TTC, as ever this time of day.

Celadon sat in a seat by the window, watching but not really seeing the tunnel's darkness streak by.

His entire body still felt wrung-out, overtaxed, coltish and bruised. His veins still itched like a poking of needles from the metal that had finally run its course.

His shoulder twinged *awfully* with every movement, but despite all this, here he was; from one end of the track to the other, and back to the start again, Celadon couldn't say how long he'd been riding this line today. He'd been too absorbed in his thoughts to care. But upon his third or fourth time pulling up to St. George Station, habit drew him out of his seat and led him to the platform.

Not until he stood facing the white stone pillars of the University of Toronto's front gate did he surface at last from his inner turmoil to even realize he'd made it from that platform outside—and further, that it was starting to rain freezing bits of slushy snow.

Just like you to remember to bring me *an umbrella and not one for yourself.*

Only a little over half a year ago, but it felt like so much time had passed since Arlo's eighteenth birthday. Since the last time he'd come here, just before his cousin's visit to the Good Vibes Only café, where this whole entire mess they were in had first begun.

Not that I don't love you and all, but if you're only here so you can shirk responsibility, you're going to have to deal. Everyone already thinks I'm too much of a distraction for you as is.

Shivering, he burrowed down into his coat, biting the inside of his cheek against laughter.

It was funny, because here he was, doing the same thing as back then, roaming around the city to avoid the serious decisions he'd have to make as soon as he returned to the palace.

Decisions that revolved around things like his mother and how obviously past the point of no return her sanity had sailed.

That stunt of hers at dinner, the callous lack of concern that her investment in that each-uisge had nearly cost him his life—that pretty much sealed it. Whatever still existed of the woman whose mind had been like a steel trap, Riadne was all but gone, slipping away at a rate even faster than Arlo was fading. Now Celadon was faced with the terrible reality that no matter what, even if they somehow managed to free his mother from Ruin's impending backlash, the Crown had claimed too much. Riadne would fall the moment they destroyed it. And they *had* to destroy it. Even if it hadn't been for Arlo's task, or what she'd conveyed to him about Coyote's request, in that he and many others would only believe the fae genuinely ready to make amends for the harm the Courts had done by seeing to the Crown's eradication. Letting that cursed object remain in this realm would only cause this cycle of misery and colonization and greed to repeat and repeat and repeat . . . and Celadon was so tired.

Gods, he missed his cousin.

So clingy. We need to find you a significant other. Or a cat.

"I do like cats . . ." he muttered under his breath, repeating what he'd told her back then, amused despite his dejection. Lethe would not be, to know that Celadon compared him to a feline.

Oh, look, there's my dad.

His memory of their last journey here together played on in his head. Celadon stood in place, looking up at the UNIVERSITY OF TORONTO signs as though they were a screen for his thoughts to play out on while he spiraled deeper into his sorrows . . .

"Celadon?"

Celadon startled.

His gaze snapped forward, falling from the signs to the collection of three people: a sidhe fae and an ironborn girl, a red-haired man sandwiched between them with an umbrella in one hand and a stack of books tucked under the arm of the other.

"Rory," he uttered in soft surprise. "Fyri. Theodore! What are you all doing here? I know my territory precludes you from the terms of Riadne's banishment, Theo, but you *should* still be careful about walking so casually out in public—and Rory! When did you get back from—"

"*Shhh,*" Rory cut in, looking furtively up and down the sidewalk as though worried they could be overheard.

And Celadon supposed that, yes, they shouldn't be chatting freely in the streets about the secret mission he'd sent Arlo's father on.

"Come here—goodness, you're soaking wet!" He waved Celadon over to him, fitting him under his umbrella alongside Fyri and Theo, shielding them all from the rain the best he could. "Did you come all this way looking for me?"

Celadon shook his head. "No, honestly, I was just sort of . . . wandering. Trying to clear my head."

"I take it a lot has happened in my absence?"

Wearily, Celadon breathed out a laugh. "You could say that, yes."

"Well," said Rory, tucking him in closer, and he pitched his voice low to keep his words between them. "It's a good thing I came back when I did, then. *These* two seemed to know almost the moment I did and were waiting for me at my apartment. I was going to message you then, but there were some materials I needed to collect from my office at the university first before reporting back to you. We were all on our way to the palace just now . . ."

Looking back up the street, back down again, he nodded with a jerk of his chin a little up the way. "Let's get somewhere dry, hmm? You look like a man who needs a change of scenery. We'll go back to my place and warm up, eh? And then I can show you what I found."

"Is it a requirement for all white, middle-aged Englishmen to collect more fancy teacups than they could ever drink out of in their lives, or do you just really like floral-printed china?"

Rory paused on his way back to the arrangement of armchairs in his living room, cutting a look to his side, where Theodore stood in front of a glass cabinet containing dozens of differently patterned cups of varying floral-print style.

He considered the cabinet a long, silent moment, before looking pointedly away. "Not particularly," he replied softly. "They were Thalo's. I used to buy them for her every time she was the one to come and check on me, back when I was still living in England and the Courts sent regular babysitters to make sure I wasn't getting up to . . . the great amount of trouble I got up to in those days, regardless." He paused again, a fond half smile in the corner of his mouth as he lingered on memories. "We weren't supposed to interact, much less become friendly. But from the first time I laid eyes on her, I thought she was the most beautiful woman in the entire world, and my mother, a human woman through and through, owned her own tea shop. It was a family love language of sorts, to leave fresh cups of tea waiting for one another. I used to leave one for Thalo on her doorstep every night before we started dating, and after. Until the Courts gave us permission to marry on the stipulation that I move here, and Thalo had insisted we bring with us every single one, and . . ."

He trailed off into silent reminiscence tinged with the hint of sadness.

From her armchair by the happily crackling fireplace, Fyri frowned at Theodore. "You're such an ass," she hissed at him.

"I didn't *know*!" Theodore rebutted, looking thoroughly uncomfortable.

Rory chuckled, shaking himself from his thoughts. "No harm, Theo," he assured. "Come sit. You have no idea how hard this was to track down . . ." Grinning now at Celadon, he set his tray of an afternoon tea blend on the coffee table between them, then immediately followed it with a nondescript, worn leather journal placed beside it.

Brightening considerably, Celadon straightened on the couch opposite the armchair Rory settled into. "The journal!" he exclaimed. "You found it!"

"An absolute nightmare," Rory replied with a shake of his head. But for all the wariness in his voice, there was excitement about his expression too. "I'd sent it back to England when Thalo and I decided to wipe our memories. To an old family friend I trusted to keep it safe for Arlo if she ever needed it. But then that friend passed, and their family had no idea what the journal was, sold it to a pawnshop that then sold it to some collector of curious things . . ."

Arlo Flamel's private journal.

If there was any hope of defeating Ruin should the worst come to pass, and Arlo fell to their might; if there was anything in the world that could possibly hold that answer, it had to be within the pages of notes copied down by history's *true* greatest alchemist, first of his vilified name.

Shifting a touch to the edge of his seat, Celadon reached for the journal to peruse it.

"And?" he asked eagerly. Honestly, this was the best news he'd received in a while—just finding it alone, when he'd been almost positive he'd sent Rory on a wild goose chase through England . . . "Have you had a chance to look through it yet? Is there *anything* in here that could be useful to us against Ruin or Riadne?"

Anything they could use to save Arlo in the event that Ruin won permanent control.

"Nausicaä seems to think that we can somehow use our connections to Arlo as a means to pull her back from oblivion. Is there anything in there that touches on that?"

"Mmm, not that I've yet read." Rory considered a moment before his expression darkened. "But as for whether or not there's anything useful in these pages . . ." he replied, far more serious than moments ago, "plenty. Plenty, too, that could make our plight so desperately worse. The things my ancestor got up to in the name of the Courts . . ." He paused to once again shake his head. "There may be something to Nausicaä's theory, but as for our other fail-safe . . . the one we've been searching for, in the event that Arlo should . . ."

That Arlo should die.

Celadon wilted, the journal suddenly far less a thrilling discovery in his hands, more a portent of his worst fears come true.

He'd already lost a father, a mother, siblings, and soon Riadne too.

Rory had lost his beloved wife.

Neither of them wanted Arlo to be the next on their list of losses, and Celadon would do *everything* in his power to help his cousin through her task. This journal, though . . . after what they'd faced in the desert, just a *taste* of what Riadne had at her disposal . . . they needed this journal.

They needed a plan B—or C, in case Nausicaä did manage to make good on her sister's hints.

Taking up his own cup of tea, Rory spent a quiet moment gathering himself and his thoughts. When he was ready, he added, "It's all there. Every detail we could possibly need. We *can* banish Ruin back to their prison, but it will come at the cost of defeating Riadne before she too falls to Ruin and claiming her stones so we can use alchemy to destroy them. It's complicated business. My daughter would be more than up to the task, but us . . . we'll need to gather a few more alchemists. Fyri and myself is an excellent start; Leda's gone into hiding, but I'm sure we could convince her to join us with these extra sureties on our side. A few more, and we might actually stand a chance of this, Celadon."

Nodding, Celadon replaced the journal on the coffee table. "Good," he said, firm and direct. "I'll leave you three to that, then: assembling the team we'll need, should needing them become necessary. Meanwhile, I'll continue to do the only thing I can and keep watch over my cousin."

"It was a fortunate day indeed that you and Arlo became best friends," Rory said, gentle and warm and so much like a father that Celadon felt his eyes sting. "She's going to survive this. And we will too."

Or we all die trying went left unsaid.

"Did you know he speaks *fifteen* different languages, fluently?"

"I hear he spent an entire summer living with actual *dragons*, and that they liked him so much they imparted some of their ancient magic to him."

"Well, I heard that the High Council practically *demanded* he marry the human girl he's engaged to, just to keep the iron in his bloodline strong, but that he's *actually* in love with someone else—do you think it could be someone we know? Someone in our *class*?"

A derisive snort and snickering from the group—"And wouldn't you just love it if it was you, Acacia."

Glowing warmly in the face, Acacia fired back, "As if *you* wouldn't!"

"Did you know, as *I've* heard," Arlo interrupted, "that Professor Flamel is secretly really three goblins in a greatcoat, and every night on the full moon, they divest of their guise, split apart, and run bare-bottomed through the fields in worship of the moon."

His addition to this conversation earned clicking of tongues and scoffs from the gaggle of girls collected in front of the door to his office. They turned in unison, wearing looks that suggested his outlandishly false comment was about to earn him a scathing evisceration, but their words froze on their tongues the moment they realized who'd spoken it.

And Arlo beamed at them.

Three girls—Acacia Sarkar, Yamada Chiyo, and Madi Pagenknopf from the Advanced Theoretical Alchemy class he taught here at the academy every Wednesday and Thursday—stood in such unmoving shock before him that Arlo couldn't help but feel a bit guilty.

He hadn't been able to help himself, in his poor defense.

It amused him to no end how enamored most of the female students here were with him; that small groups of them could often be found trailing him in the halls between classes; that his after-hours received dozens of them, swearing up and down how desperately they needed his help with some assignment or lesson, or whatever they could think up to secure the one-on-one sessions Arlo offered to any of his students.

No doubt this was what had drawn this particular group.

Their gossip was hardly the first he was hearing of what had spread through the school about him, and part of him was flattered, as always, that he should be held in such high regard—another part of him felt this eidolon they'd created needed knocking down a peg or six.

"Professor Flamel!" Acacia exclaimed, her brown cheeks flushing rosy with embarrassment. "W-we didn't see you there . . ."

Madi bowed deeply. "We're sorry," she apologized, as though they'd been kicking his dog in turns rather than trading adulations about him. "We didn't mean any offense!"

"None!" Chiyo promised, her eyes growing wide with the furious nod of her head.

Arlo laughed. "Nonsense, no offense was taken!" he assured. "It's always nice to know I'm in good enough graces that no one will chase me from the premises with a pitchfork yet. However"—his smile turned rueful—"you will have to excuse me today, if it's my time you've come for—if you recall, my after-hours have been canceled for the day. A man has a great deal he needs to prepare the night before his wedding! I only came to fetch a couple things I left behind."

Hyperion would have a heart attack purely out of spite if Arlo blew off the bachelor's party he'd been planning ever since the day he first told him the Council had chosen his bride.

Hearts broken but smiles strong, the girls gave more apologies and well-wishings, thanked him for his lessons this year, and imparted their hopes to see him again next year when he returned to work from his honeymoon.

By the time he was able to enter and close himself in his office, twenty minutes had already passed—which meant twenty minutes less to wrap up all the other things going on in his life. These lectures were more of a personal hobby, a way to inspect the new upcoming alchemists who might one day be working with him at his real job up at the Black Castle.

Phoebus Viridian's Head Alchemist, at long last—it had only cost him his father completely.

Sighing, Arlo began for his desk . . .

. . . and stopped one step into his course.

Arlo Flamel . . .

Concentrating as hard as he could, Arlo was absolutely certain he'd heard something.

A whisper?

A voice?

It was hard to say—and perhaps it was nothing at all but his frustrations and nerves; too much stress with too little time to manage it all, so much going on and now a new wife thrown into the mix.

He started forward once more.

Arlo Flamel . . .

There—again!

It *was* real; a whisper to be sure. It sounded as though it had come from his desk, so he closed the distance remaining, to look for what it could possibly be.

Arlo Flamel . . .

Whatever the whisper was saying, it was far too quiet for him to make out. But he scanned his desk—there was nothing here, not unless the voice was coming from his inkwell or the pile of essays he'd left for his assistant to start marking tomorrow.

Nothing, except . . .

Arlo Flamel . . .

The journal he'd forgotten. The very thing he'd returned to retrieve.

And as certainly as the voice was real, it was coming from its pages.

Arlo reached for it, cautious but not afraid—after all, it was his journal, and while it did contain research and ideas and starts of projects well beyond dangerous, knowledge had never done physical harm to him before; it wouldn't do so now.

Arlo Flamel...

"Arlo Flamel!" Hyperion entered his office so abruptly, the door banged against the table beside it, and Arlo jumped with a start, actually dropping the journal back to the desk.

Where it clattered open to a random page.

"Hyperion Lysterne!" Arlo replied, a lot less buoyantly, with a cutting glare to match. "*What* are you doing here?"

"Why, collecting you, of course, dear cousin!" Closing the door, Hyperion strode forward. "I had a feeling I'd find you here, hard at work as ever and always, when there's *whisky* to be had and ladies of sin to ravish."

Arlo rolled his eyes.

"What's this?" Hyperion asked, when he reached the desk and found Arlo's open journal. Picking it up, he examined what was drawn there.

Hyperion was his closest friend in all the world, the only one he'd ever shared this journal's contents with. He was the boy who'd followed Arlo's studies with supportive enthusiasm, who grew into the man who spent long hours in Arlo's laboratory just to keep him company.

He knew this journal almost as intimately as Arlo did.

Looking down at what had caught his attention, Arlo considered . . . then shrugged, unconcerned. "I have no idea, as a matter of fact."

"It's *your* journal; you had to be the one to copy it out—I've known you too well for too long, and you never let anyone else even touch this but me, and I sure as hells didn't do this."

Arlo continued to examine it.

He honestly hadn't a clue what it was.

This wasn't unheard of. Arlo had a tendency toward manic spells when truly engrossed in something, where he could spend whole days hyperfocused on some issue or another and, when he surfaced, had no recollection of what he'd done in that time. But as whatever he'd been working out had been solved by the end of it, this didn't overly concern him.

Arlo Flamel . . .

"Ah! Talking book!" Hyperion exclaimed, dropping the journal as though it had burned him.

Oh?

So this page specifically was where the voice had been coming from.

Interesting.

Arlo took the journal in hand.

"Uh . . . what are you doing?"

"You know what *we* have to do?"

Hyperion looked at him like he knew exactly where this was going. "Yes. We close the talking book and ignore the dangerous dark magic symbols trying to tempt you to an early grave."

"No, Hyperion," Arlo replied, already moving to collect some chalk. "The opposite. Obviously."

Hyperion sighed. "Obviously." He moved to join him. "This is why no one likes you, you know."

"Everybody likes me."

"This is why *I* don't like you."

Arlo tossed his friend a charming grin. "You like me the most."

Bending to the floor, he smoothed the journal out beside him and, right there on the stone, began to copy the array he had no memory of sketching in the first place.

It was perhaps the most difficult array he'd ever worked with, baring the one he was still piecing together for his philosopher's stone.

The runes and equations seemed to fight him every step of the way, the math he couldn't recall one bit having worked out in the fugue state that created this; it was almost beyond his comprehension now. And the *linework* connecting it all together—so fine and intricate! He had to switch and whittle down several pieces of chalk just to get the right thickness. Should he draw even one a point zero decimal wider or thinner than the array called for, it would disrupt the flow of energy, sending too much or too little where it was needed—fully qualified alchemists had died in fiery explosions all from the simple error of linework.

Two hours later.

The array had taken a full two hours to copy out, and that was only because Arlo was who he was—in all his humility, the greatest alchemist of the age.

"Is it done yet?" Hyperion moaned from the chair in which he'd been slumped over for the last half hour, flipping through one of Arlo's textbooks and adding no doubt obscene remarks along the margins.

Arlo dropped back on his folded legs and sighed in weary relief. "Done." He placed his piece of chalk in the bucket that contained the others and got to his feet just as Hyperion rushed over.

Whistling low under his breath, he stood beside Arlo to take it all in. Even Hyperion—a full-blooded sidhe fae—could appreciate the beauty of such a complex array, so much fit together in its exact place like an exquisite puzzle.

"All right," Arlo declared, rubbing his hands together. "The runes suggest this is a portal of some kind. I've no idea what we're summoning, but—"

"Uh . . . wait," Hyperion inserted, taking a step back. "We *definitely* shouldn't be trying to summon something in the middle of your office when we have no idea what will come through. Right? Shouldn't we have protections and such? There are children in this school."

Snorting, Arlo waved him off. "Hyperion, please, a little more faith than that. My office is exceptionally well warded, and the array is too.

215

See that there . . ." He pointed to the four matching runes along the outer ring, which was the thickest line of them all. "That's a barrier. Whatever we summon, it could be the devil himself and he won't be able to cross that to get us. Just make sure not to smudge it."

Hyperion took another hurried step back, as though he'd been anywhere close to doing just that.

"All right," Arlo repeated, eager and quiet. This was much more exciting to him than a bachelor party—he would have chosen this by way of celebration over anything else Hyperion had orchestrated for their evening.

Easing back down onto his knees, he placed his hands on the array.

Closing his eyes, he focused on the core of his power, drawing it forth to pour into the array beneath his fingertips. In his mind, the array etched itself in an exact replica and began to glow pale blue, inch by inch, as his magic trickled through the points of connection and down the lines.

As he understood it, no one else saw their alchemy like this.

Powering arrays was done all in the same way, but to actually be able to picture it activating, functioning in his mind . . . to bend his magic there with just a thought in a way that would physically repli- cate in the real one . . . that was uniquely him, and his father. He'd yet to encounter any other alchemist who could do this.

Finally, when the array was fully alight, Arlo opened his eyes.

At the center of the array, barely noticeable, but glowing faintly too, a line bisected the air. It lengthened, then widened, parting the space around it as one would open a curtain. Behind it, a shimmering, deep navy was revealed.

Hyperion, just behind him, considered the portal. "Pretty," he decided. "But who's it meant to—"

Crack—

Arlo startled, jerking back.

He looked down at where his hands still touched the outer ward of the array . . . at the *fissures* beginning to split through the stone it was etched on, breaking the wards apart, the *array* apart, above which the opening portal hovered.

Crack—CRACK—

The fissures spread.

"What's happening!" Hyperion panicked, pulling Arlo forcibly away from the array, which should have lost power the moment the breaking stone disrupted it. "Who's coming—Arlo, *who did you summon?*"

Arlo, meanwhile, could only gape.

An impression like darkness began to press on his vision to his left.

On his right, the impression of light.

A chill and a warmth, safety and fear . . .

"Arlo." It was the smooth voice that had been calling to him, the light on his left, and Arlo wanted to look, but some innate sense screamed at him not to.

"Arlo," a new voice poured like oil, the darkness on his right.

"Arlo Flamel, at long last you heed our summons," the voices both said together.

Scrambling even farther backward with Arlo in his grip, Hyperion hissed in his ear, "Close it! Close it, Arlo, something's not right—something's coming through!"

Something was, indeed.

All Arlo could do was gape—a hand that wasn't quite human, fingers long and skeletal, nails even longer and sharpened to needle-point severity at the ends.

The arm followed next—whoever this was, their being was enormous. It took nearly all of the portal just to produce the mottled, decrepit appendage.

"You may call me Moros, scion of the End—" the darkness on his right said as the hand from the portal stretched farther through, enough to latch onto the floor and sink its nails into the stone as though it were instead cotton.

Whatever that arm was attached to, Arlo could feel an odd

sensation of a great, hulking body heaving even closer.

"—And I Eos, scion of the Beginning—" the light on his left continued.

"—Together we serve the beings of unity. Balance. You have nothing to fear from us, Arlo Flamel, or from our progenitors. What we wish is only to talk."

The cracking didn't stop.

That hulking body might well be trying to break its way through to them.

Arlo didn't believe for a moment whoever this was speaking to him—there was more to them than what they seemed, more behind their words. They might only wish to talk, but as certain as starlight, Arlo had *everything* to fear from them.

"We only wish to warn you."

"The Crown the mortal Phoebus Viridian possesses, it is no friend to you. It will bring about unimaginable destruction if allowed to remain in this realm."

"Arlo!" Hyperion shook him, trying to break the transfixion Arlo had fallen to. "What's going on—what are you staring at?"

Could Hyperion not see? Could he not hear?

"It is not him we appeal to," the darkness said, speaking to Arlo's very thoughts.

"The only assistance we need for now is yours," said the light. "Arlo Flamel, Master Alchemist, first mortal to ever truly wield this status— your Courts are a lie; your High King does not control them. You should very much fear the Fae High Council your father warned you against, for they are a danger that, if left unchecked in their voracious pursuit of power, will lead this realm to utter destruction, and many others with it."

The hand from the portal had extended all that it would go.

Unsheathing its claws from the floor, it turned itself over, unfurling its palm to reveal a singular sheet of paper—an exact match to the pages that filled Arlo's journal.

"To you"—the darkness took over, its voice beginning to wrap around Arlo like cool silk—"and you alone, we yield what your Council is after."

Light—"To you, Arlo, we trust the philosopher's stone, perfected. The array, complete—the very thing that, should it fall into any other hands but yours, *will* condemn this world to ash."

"There is much at work here," the two opposing forces said, speaking as a unified one. "Much that you do not understand. That you will *never* understand and should never wish to. There is also a great deal still that needs uncovering. We leave to your capable research and discovery what's necessary to make it work—"

"—But in order to set things in motion in time—"

"—for the one who will assume your labor and bring this plot to its close—"

"—we will aid you this much, in what you seek—"

Together once more: "So that your Pride may act faster."

"Arlo," Hyperion tried again—hadn't stopped trying, in fact. Arlo had merely been too entranced by the paper held out to him to show he even heard him at all. "Arlo, I don't like this. I don't know what you're seeing that I'm not, but I think it's time to find a way to close this portal now—"

SLAM.

"ARLO!"

This time, Arlo startled and wheeled around in place, despite Hyperion's hold on him; his eyes widened on Alecto standing wildly in his office doorway.

"We beg of you, Master Alchemist," the darkness implored, fading. "We plead, beseech, entreat you—"

"—The Council *will* create the stone if you do not, and if they do, then all is lost. We beg of you, please, become the corruption in their stead. Become what you swore to reject. Take up the role of the villain before the ones you serve steal fate for their own . . ."

"Unleash your Pride, to save us all from certain doom."

"GET AWAY FROM HIM!" Alecto roared, flinging herself forward.

Arlo felt the air grow dense enough to choke, felt it began to draw and gather and shape into wings at Alecto's back—she hadn't been born a Fury, didn't come by these appendages naturally, but her stunning magic had been more than up to the task of compensating. *"Get away from him,"* she threatened like the death she was, but it was a rescue he hadn't needed in the end.

For all the dramatics, for everything that had just occurred, the light and darkness vanished in an instant.

The hand disappeared.

The portal—gone.

Almost as though nothing had happened at all, silence rang out across the room. The only evidence that this hadn't been some mental break Arlo had completely imagined were the cracks in the floor from the floating portal and an impression of the array used to summon it, scorched into the stone.

Looking furiously from Arlo to Alecto and back, Hyperion could hold his tongue for only so long. "Will *somebody* tell me what just happened?"

"Arlo?" Alecto breathed, and crossed the distance in a flash.

In the first show of genuine emotion, she took Arlo's face between her hands—how curious . . . that he should be so much taller than her now. He recalled first meeting her, how enormous she felt in presence and importance, untouchable, cold . . .

"Arlo, are you all right?"

Yes, he thought, a hand coming absently up to cover hers.

Alecto, who'd been his friend just as long as Hyperion—longer, even, if he counted the start of their relationship from that very first meeting tucked away in his loft.

"Arlo?"

He cleared his throat. "Of course," he replied, and took a step back. If his heart was beating just a little bit faster, that was surely because of what had just happened—not because it suddenly occurred to him how pretty a pearly white Alecto's eyes were this close.

"Of course," he repeated, and moved around her, bending to retrieve the only other thing that proved whoever had just been here had been real.

The piece of paper.

"And what in infernal hells is *that*?" Hyperion asked, like daring Arlo to tell him it was another mystery array to try out.

Which it was, exactly—though looking at it, not a mystery, no. It felt like . . .

"A challenge."

CHAPTER 15

Vehan

———◦~◦———

THE FOLK OF THE Market might not place their *full* trust in Vehan yet, but that hadn't stopped them from throwing him the best birthday party he'd ever experienced.

Perhaps it was because there was so little to celebrate these days that they'd poured themselves and their efforts so enthusiastically into tonight. Perhaps they wanted to make nice for Aurelian's sake. Even more likely, this wasn't about Vehan at all, but whatever the reason, he was grateful for this chance to unwind regardless.

For the music that poured through streets strung with hundreds of colorful paper lanterns; the foods that spiced the air with savory scents, wafting up from dozens of vendors littered here and there, all offering up their roasted and fried and simmered specialties free of charge.

He was grateful for the children weaving happy through the crowds, crackling sparklers in their hands and streamers trailing behind them with the echoes of their laughter.

He was particularly grateful for the center of it all, the enormous bonfire roaring high into the night. Folk danced, vibrant and spirited, around its massive, glowing body, most in varying states of intoxication, because the seemingly endless barrels of ale and whisky, courtesy of Celadon, were also complimentary.

For just one night, everyone who called the Market home could set aside their weariness, their pain and loss and fear and trauma. Nothing rationed, looming war far from all minds. The folk here were free to indulge in the moment, exist in cheer—and at the heart of the whole thing . . .

"I can't believe you orchestrated this," Vehan marveled, sitting at a table along the outer limits of the bonfire, watching dancers twist and spin in a circle around it.

Aurelian, opposite him, picked at his spear of roasted vegetables. "I can't believe you thought I wouldn't."

"I mean, it's a marked improvement on the eighteen years previous—my mother's stuffy galas; being forced into her choice of clothing and her choice of company, the majority bestowing their congratulations like condolences at my own funeral."

A grin quirked in the corner of Aurelian's mouth. It could be his ale talking, or just Vehan's overwhelming obsession emboldened by their soulbond, but tonight that mouth, which was so good at kissing, so good at *biting*, seemed even more inviting than ever. "The majority were rather put out that it was not, in fact, your funeral." He cut Vehan a look over his spear that was, for a moment, quite serious. "You have no idea how relieved I am that you're out of that place."

That place.

His home.

Except, less and less it felt like such; more and more, home was wherever he could be at Aurelian's side.

"Aurelian—hey!"

"Happy birthday, Vehan!"

Their conversation paused a moment for nods and waves and passing pleasantries.

So many people stopped to give thanks and greeting to Aurelian, to give their well-wishings to Vehan.

It was curious in one way, to be what Aurelian had been forced to be his entire life at the palace—the shadow, so to speak, to the sun he orbited. Vehan wasn't used to being the cursory glance, and it was strange at times—difficult at first to adjust to, in all honesty. But when it meant Aurelian finally got the attention Vehan had always felt he deserved, when it meant getting to see his talents praised, his personality bloom, his spirit soar and friendships grow beyond a singular, lonely little prince . . . Vehan would take the Market's complete disinterest or even their hatred if it meant his boyfriend could always enjoy this appreciation.

The revelers carried on.

Vehan and Aurelian were left alone once more.

"It wasn't so bad," Vehan replied mildly to Aurelian's unanswered statement.

Raising a brow, Aurelian studied him. "It was worse."

He really . . . couldn't argue. And didn't feel like it, not tonight. Aurelian was right, and Vehan had already confessed as much to him—in a conversation he never wanted to repeat, for the way it looked like Aurelian was breaking to tell him just the tip of Riadne's full abuse of him, both during Aurelian's occupation of, and after his flight from, the palace.

Tonight wasn't for those heavy thoughts.

Tonight, Vehan wanted to hold Aurelian close and dance with abandon around that fire, where Theodore and Fyri, and Celadon and Lethe, spun dizzily in their pairs as well.

He stood from the table, offered Aurelian his hand. Setting down the remains of his spear, Aurelian took his proposition gladly.

Long, warm fingers interlocked with his own—a hand that seemed so much bigger these days, and now deeply calloused from manual labor and weight lifting. Vehan shivered a little, when it clutched suddenly tighter and drew him close enough for a ghost of a kiss to the shell of his ear—a chuckle low and rich to puff against it after—and then they were off, Aurelian tugging him in the direction of the dancing faerie ring.

As soon as they reached it, the music changed.

It dipped into something slower, haunting and beautiful all at once—a song Vehan vaguely recognized but couldn't concentrate on for the way Aurelian's golden eyes *blazed* this close to the flame.

The way it waltzed shadows across his sun-browned skin and caught sharp light on his cheekbones . . . the lavender of his hair . . . the buckle of the leather belt he'd taken to wearing around those oh-so-narrow hips that Vehan immediately clasped with his free hand, twisting his fingers into the loops of Aurelian's jeans and anchoring himself even closer.

"I love you," he breathed, as they started to sway. "Quite desperately. You have no idea the relief *I* feel knowing you're out of my mother's reach as well."

There was no standing stationary in the ring—it swept them up almost instantly. Though the tune was slowed, and the movement now too, the circle still rotated, and it was Aurelian who pressed them on into action.

That hand still clutching Vehan's drew it up to trap over his heart; the other slipped just under the hem of Vehan's black shirt to spread a touch possessively at his bare waist.

"I would have suffered far worse far longer for you," Aurelian breathed back, his eyes so intense that Vehan couldn't look anywhere else but into them. "Since the day we first met, it was only you. It's only ever been you, Vehan—you are everything."

Dazedly, Vehan heard himself reply, "Some might suggest that's a bit unhealthy."

"I really don't care," Aurelian said back, his voice growing deeper, more intimate between them. "When it comes to you, I have no moderation. I'm selfish. Did you know that? You seem to think I'm such a great person, but I'm actually disgustingly selfish where you're concerned, because you're *mine*. I've never wanted you to belong to anyone else, even when I had to pretend that seeing anyone but me next to you didn't make my skin crawl."

The *things* Aurelian said sometimes.

Vehan felt himself start to warm in a way that had nothing to do with the now pale excuse for heat beside them.

"Oh?" he fairly gasped out—and then actually did, when Aurelian surprised him with a sudden spin, a dip, and then pulled him even closer than before so that their bodies were flush.

"Oh," he replied in answer. "Vehan?"

"Hmm?"

"I am really, *very* selfish."

Vehan curled a playful grin, leaning up and in. "Yes," he replied, speaking the word in the barest touch against his lips. "I seem to recall you mentioning. It's okay. I'm rather selfish when it comes to you, too—"

Something heavy and cool slid down his finger just then that cut Vehan off from words so completely, he almost forgot how to breathe as well.

He looked to the side.

At the hand Aurelian held aloft, just enough that Vehan could see around his ring finger a solid, polished black band.

"Selfish enough that, no matter what happens in the coming days, I want to face it with you as mine in *every* way possible."

Vehan *stared*.

"Aurelian," he spluttered, still unable to tear his eyes from his hand, as though what had just been placed there might vanish the moment he did. "Aurelian, are you . . ." His heart rate sped up. "Is this a . . ."

"Proposal?"

Vehan nodded, once again lost for words.

For the first time this evening, Aurelian's tone then wavered briefly into anxiety. "Yes, Vehan," he added in continued clarification. "Yes, I am proposing. I . . . actually had this planned out much differently—a lot more romantically, and privately too. But we're here and we're happy and I've never felt this way about anyone, and I know I don't want to spend one more second without you knowing that I *want* you—everything that entails. All of you. And that I want you to have me, too."

"Aurelian?" Vehan's voice cracked on emotion, but he managed all the same.

"Yes?"

"Come with me."

Vehan closed his fingers back around Aurelian's, and this time he was the one tugging the pair of them—away from the ring, back to the tavern only just beyond it, up the stairs, down the hall, and right back to their bedroom, where it was quiet and secluded . . .

"You're not about to tell me to pack my things and get out, are you?" Aurelian hedged in the open doorway. "Only because you haven't actually *answered* my proposal yet, and—Vehan!" It was his turn to splutter as Vehan reached down and, in one fluid motion, divested himself of his shirt and tossed it somewhere—anywhere; it was completely unimportant right now where it actually landed.

"Of course not," Vehan . . . not quite snapped, but there was definitely aggression in his voice, the sort that had nothing to do with anger. "Of course I'm not going to tell you to get out. Of course I'm going to damn well marry you! And if you don't get your selfishly toned butt inside this bedroom, of course I'm going to show you *how much* I agree to marry you right out there in that hall."

Aurelian, needing no further coaxing, entered and closed the door.

And he was on Vehan in an instant—snapped immediately from his moments-ago hesitation to being aggressively in charge.

With his grip on Vehan's jaw, he directed their mouths together, claiming Vehan's lips with a dominance that sparked brightest behind closed doors. Aurelian knew exactly what he was doing—kissed Vehan with a certainty each and every time, like he'd spent years imagining every wicked thing he'd do to him the moment Aurelian had him.

When his hand released his face, it traveled the cut of Vehan's jaw to the back of his neck, and those long, clever fingers of his sank into the fine hairs there, wound the strands tight to tug, just shy of sharp, but with control enough that electricity that had nothing to do with his magic danced hot across Vehan's skin.

Falling against him, Vehan tipped his head back at the unspoken command, for Aurelian to claim his mouth openly now, hungrily.

It was Vehan, though, who began to lead them stumbling backward, Aurelian too consumed with him to do anything but follow and run his free hand down the front of Vehan's bare chest.

Down and down those fingers traveled, dancing over Vehan's abdomen to follow the V of his muscle to where it dipped below his trousers.

Mission accomplished—Vehan gasped, allowing Aurelian to press his advantage and sweep his tongue across the expanse of Vehan's mouth, before retreating, for his teeth to catch on the soft of his lower lip.

A groan now, and the back of Vehan's knees hit the bed.

But instead of toppling, Aurelian hooked a thumb into a vacant belt loop and anchored the pair of them hip to hip, chest to chest, tongue to tongue, so close they could almost be one, so close Vehan could feel Aurelian's heartbeat echoing both against him and through the bond that *sang* right now between them.

It was an ungraceful, rough *yank* that tore Vehan's button from his pants and opened them; an ungraceful, wet sound that tore Aurelian's mouth from his.

Vehan whimpered slightly for the sudden loss, but hands planted firmly on his pectorals, distracting him—gave a sudden push.

He fell to the bed, laughing up at the ceiling. "So bossy in the bedroom," he said huskily, but his words quickly turned breathless as Aurelian's hands then skimmed down, down, down again, and gripped him by the thighs, *pulled* him abruptly to the edge of the mattress.

The pants went next—thrown across the room over Aurelian's shoulder.

When the heat of Aurelian's mouth swallowed the length of him, it drew a jagged cry from the deep of Vehan's chest that stole with it the air from his lungs completely.

After a torturous eternity that made stars burst in Vehan's darkening vision and heat like a liquid begin to pool in his core, Aurelian released him. He traversed his torso back to his lips, in less a kiss than a collision, a crashing of their mouths in which Vehan could taste himself on Aurelian's tongue, and the electric heat inside him only sparked hotter for it.

At some point, they devolved into whatever their mouths could taste, their fingers could touch, their lips could trace, and teeth could graze.

Aurelian bit a possessive mark into the juncture between Vehan's shoulder and neck, drawing a keening sound Vehan belatedly realized was *him*, and causing his blunt nails to score dark lines down Aurelian's suntanned back that he was almost sad would heal too quickly to remain visible come morning.

How long they spent purely on the sensation of each other— devout worship, as though they were each other's temple and god. As though they hadn't done this numerous times in the past few months, as though they might never have this again . . .

But then it was Aurelian, as always, leading Vehan back to himself, the tip of his nose ghosting lightly along the line of his jaw. Mindlessly Vehan swayed with it, until their mouths were again returned to each other, to seal together in a kiss Vehan could feel in the pool of heat low, low, low in his belly.

"I love you," Vehan whispered, ragged but heartfelt.

He was so far gone at this point, his electric magic began to crackle unchecked between their undulating bodies, their bond the only thing protecting Aurelian from how it would no doubt sting anyone else.

"I was made entirely for nothing but to love you back," Aurelian replied, ardent and difficultly, through panting breath and around his tongue chasing after an electric spark just to swallow it against Vehan's throat.

And then sank into Vehan like ownership.

Foreheads pressed together, sweat beading between them—one hand gripped tight enough to bruise Vehan's hip, the other splayed in devotion over his heart, their bodies rising and falling like the moon and tide.

Faster, harsher—their movements became erratic, their breaths began to stutter and break as they chased the completion building at Vehan's core.

It was always Vehan cresting the peak first—Aurelian made sure of this.

Back arching off the bed, magic crackling hot in his veins and over his skin, a cry so far from dignity poured, obscene and wanton, from his mouth as all that liquid heat gathered tight and tight and tighter and tightest, into a solidified ball . . .

That melted in a burst like gold submerged in a forge.

Aurelian picked up the pace after that, to a degree that had cracked their previous bedframe.

In and out and in until he sank and sank and *sank* as deep as he could go, and light sparked behind the lids of Vehan's fluttering eyes until he was left begging and an absolute wreck and Aurelian had taken and given and nothing was left, and neither of them could be any closer if their souls occupied one body instead of two.

Aurelian's breath hitched; his rhythm faltered . . .

"Vehan," he moaned, not so much his name as a prayer as he shuddered apart.

And Vehan pressed his mouth to Aurelian's already abused shoulder to whisper, "No one has ever said my name the way you do."

"I very sincerely hope not . . ." Aurelian gasped out.

After, the pair of them wrapped up in each other, their skin cooling slowly in the night air and the party outside flicking color and shadows through their window to dance across their skin, Aurelian added softly into Vehan's hair, *"Fiancé."*

CHAPTER 16

Nausicaä

A FIREWORK SHOOTING UP INTO the night paused Nausicaä's walk through the woods. For a moment, she stood in silence to watch it streak high in the air, burst apart into shimmering reds and yellows and whites that rained back down on the Market—and for some reason, the sight of this display made a mixture of sorrow and nostalgia tighten in her throat that had nothing to do with the reason for tonight's celebration.

Vehan's birthday.

It wasn't that Nausicaä didn't want to be there, enjoying the excuse for a party. But what she'd done to the Market the last time she'd been here . . . under Riadne's orders, Riadne's control, but that didn't change the fact that it had been Nausicaä's hands. That her fire had caused such utter destruction here, had even cost some lives.

For the most part, the folk had been gracious enough to recognize she hadn't been acting of her own free will, and since coming back, she'd been helping where she could with the finishing touches of their rebuild. But . . .

Still . . .

She felt she hadn't quite earned the right to indulge in tonight's cheer.

Turning from the revel's displays, she continued her aimless wandering.

The Hiraeth had changed quite a bit in these last few months. On the one hand, the demons that had been confined to haunting it before Ruin had been summoned were now free to terrorize other bits of this world as well. Their numbers here had thinned considerably, but replacing them was . . . everything else, it seemed.

Folk who couldn't or wouldn't flee to Celadon's newly formed Night Court; folk whose kind she hadn't seen in decades—ones she'd even assumed by now were extinct—had slunk from their hiding places, taking to this rare bastion against Riadne's world supremacy.

It was strange to walk through the forest, all this trembling fear and anxiety mixing with the Hiraeth's natural calm that still called to the immortal in her, eased her physical ailments and awakened her senses to a degree that it felt in comparison like she normally stumbled around with them closed off.

And she was strongly reminded of the last time she'd found herself poking around a forest full of terrified faeries—Darrington.

The start of everything.

Of the Reaper, and her first discovery of a failed stone—of Riadne's hideous crimes.

Of the plot that had led to her meeting Arlo.

"I know you're there," she said, coming to a halt in the midst of a clearing and speaking to the presence behind her that had been following her for a short ways now. Nausicaä didn't need her full, immortal senses restored to recognize the press of vile energy, twisted around that of the only aura that felt anything like safety and *home*. "Don't tell me you miss me already, Red."

She turned around just as Arlo stepped into the clearing—

—and felt her breath catch in her throat.

Iron-blood-red satin, the same as what Nausicaä had worn to that horror show of a meal Riadne had demanded she attend a little over a week ago. On Arlo, it had been cut into a straight-legged pantsuit, solid on the bottom, with elegant lace for the blouse, and draped in a voluminous, pleated, open-front skirt from her ample hips, to flow like the spill of the substance its color resembled.

Distantly, somewhere in the back of her head still capable of thought and personality, Nausicaä wondered if it was Ruin keeping those killer red stilettos of hers from sinking right through the earth as she strode forward, her mass of fire-red hair so wild around her it blazed at odds with the rest of her image.

"Uh . . ." Nausicaä began, attempting to unstick her tongue. "Not that I'm complaining, because . . . *damn*, Arlo. But . . . you might be just a touch overdressed if you've come for Vehan's party."

Still striding for Nausicaä one purposeful step at a time, Arlo shook her head but said nothing.

There was red in her eyes to match her outfit, but it was definitely Arlo that approached her—however altered by the parasite she carried. For a moment Nausicaä was transported back to the last time someone with that look in their eyes had ever gotten this close.

Noel. Pallas Viridian's vampire lover, whom she'd had to destroy with her own bare hands.

Deities—if there were any sympathy left for her in Fate's heart, please don't let her have to end this girl in a similar manner.

At last, Arlo reached nearly flush with Nausicaä's body.

Dark exhaustion paired with heavy mascara and a crimson lip she couldn't at all look away from, Nausicaä swallowed, felt her hands move of their own accord to place themselves on the flare of her girl-friend's hips.

To draw her even closer, to let herself have just this one moment to pretend like everything was fine, that Arlo was hers and nothing stood in the way of that.

"Why are you here, Arlo?" she whispered between them.

Distantly, she took note of how deathly still and quiet the forest around them had fallen.

"Can I not want to see you?" Arlo breathed, and something inside Nausicaä started breaking to be spoken to in such soft familiarity. "You looked so pretty at Riadne's dinner, and I was so *under*dressed."

Her hands came up to rest on Nausicaä's shoulders—to trace gently as shivers down the muscled lengths of her arms.

As they went, Nausicaä's own state of dress began to change, until she was once more back in that red satin dress, the perfect match on Arlo's arm.

"I didn't think you'd noticed."

"I always notice you, Nausicaä."

The comment made her face go warm. "You've gotten good at alchemy," she said instead of chasing that very tempting insinuation.

To which Arlo replied, in complete lack of modesty, "I've gotten good at a lot of things. Nos?"

How long had it been since she'd called her that?

Nausicaä felt heat sting in her eyes.

"Yeah?" she grunted thickly around constricting emotion.

But all Arlo did was lean in. As slow as a bloom unfurling to flower, she pressed her lips to Nausicaä's and kissed her—gentle, at first; deeper the longer it went.

Something not quite a groan or a whimper rose to Nausicaä's throat, and it was all Arlo needed—the small parting of lips for her to bend the kiss more passionate, to capture Nausicaä's mouth completely in a dominance that hadn't quite been her before, but then . . . they were still so new to this relationship. Perhaps this really was how Arlo would be if left to grow naturally more comfortable in this.

Right now, however . . .

Nausicaä wanted her girlfriend so badly, and hells, if she didn't find her so fucking hot in this moment—but this . . . there was something not quite right about whatever this was.

She very much wanted to surrender herself over to the soft give of Arlo's body, the heat beginning to curl at her core. Despite this, she disengaged, pushed Arlo back to stare down at her, a little breathless, a lot in regret. "Arlo," she sighed, and repeated again, slower this time, *"Why are you here?"*

That red flashed a little bit brighter; Arlo pulled back another step.

Nausicaä found herself missing her warmth immediately and had to hold herself back from reaching out and returning her to where she belonged.

"I love you—you know that, don't you?" Arlo said.

Why did that feel like her saying goodbye?

"Arlo—"

Arlo shook her head. "You're right. I *am* here for a reason." She took a step back, holding Nausicaä's gaze all the while. "I have to ask you to do something while I still care to ask it so that *I* can do something while I still have the control."

Heart rate speeding up to racing, Nausicaä merely stood in place, so afraid of what she was going to say.

And already knowing.

"You figured out how to get to Tellis."

Nodding, Arlo confirmed it.

"I know you want to come with me." Arlo spoke so softly now her words could almost be the breeze. "I know you want to follow me in this, to help me, to make sure I make it back out. And I *want* you to come with me. I want it so badly. I don't want to have to do this alone. But if I ask you to come with me, then so many people are going to die tonight, all the others that I love."

Oh . . . *shit*, of course it was here! Of course the entrance to the Sacred Grove would align with—

"The Market."

Again, Arlo nodded.

"It has to be tonight. Riadne has ordered it. I don't need to tell you she doesn't love the quest I'm on and is rather counting on all the errands she sends me on to exhaust me into failing before I can get to *her* Crown, but Ruin's told her where I need to go, what I have to do, and it aligns with a punishment she wishes to deliver."

Nausicaä stood horrified.

"She wants you to blow the fucking Market off the map with her sons and everyone still inside?"

"Vehan and Celadon I'm to get to safety first. But . . ." Another nod.

Nausicaä felt *ill*.

She already knew how little Riadne cared about innocent life—

child life—but this? This was completely unhinged, even for the High Queen.

"We have to warn them, Arlo. We have to at least give them a chance . . ."

Silently, Arlo reached into a pocket in her pants and extracted a stone in the shape of a heart that was dark and glassy and *screaming* negative energy.

And Nausicaä recognized it immediately.

A failed philosopher's stone.

"I can't do anything but what I've been tasked," Arlo said at last, soft and steady as she extended the stone between them. "The choice has to be yours. I took this from Riadne's personal store; there's enough power left in it that you *could* use it to follow me into the Immortal Realm and help me take down a goddess so easily that my own energy would be spared. Ruin would win no ground from me tonight, if that was the case." She paused, looking Nausicaä firmly in the eye, every bit as serious as this situation demanded . . . because Nausicaä understood already what she was being asked to do, and it felt like a breaking. "You could come, and you could save me from what might be my potential death. But every single person in that Market would die in result. *Or* you could take this stone and use it. Once, just once, that's all it would give, but I believe with this stone, someone like you would have no trouble finding a way to get Celadon and Vehan and all the other people in there to safety all in one go."

The Market or her.

Arlo was asking Nausicaä to choose between the Market or *her.*

The Nausicaä of even a year ago would have made this choice easily, would have picked her pretty girlfriend, her own selfish desires, to hell with the other people, the majority of who she didn't even know. To hell with the ones she did, who'd done nothing lately but provoke her temper.

The ones who'd put Arlo in the crosshairs of all this danger—who'd all but sentenced her to this painful, drawn-out death.

236

Nausicaä had condemned several mortals to death for a similar trespass. Vehan and the others, their reckless desire to outwit deities and play at heroes, they were the reason Arlo was in this at all, and just knowing that—just *feeling* that ache, a mere echo of what would come once Arlo was gone . . . it made her *so angry*.

And oh, the things she'd done out of anger.

Not to mention that the loss of so many folk who definitely still paid worship to the lesser deities would be a huge blow against the Immortal Realm, and she'd been so intent on punishing for so long . . .

It was just so tempting—and not at all who she was anymore.

If she chose Arlo, she wouldn't be able to live with herself after. If she chose Arlo, it would be letting her anger get the better of her instead of wielding the power of it responsibly. *If she chose Arlo*, the Market would be wiped completely from existence, along with so much innocent life. And more than that . . .

"The Goblin Market's the only thing pinning the Hiraeth to this realm."

Once again, Arlo nodded.

No matter what, after tonight, this place would be lost to the Mortal Realm for good. All the doors would close. The Hiraeth would be completely inaccessible, and every creature and faerie taking shelter here who didn't reside within the Market's walls would be forever unable to return. Nausicaä . . . if she chose to save even a few of these folk . . . she couldn't just coax them to flee. She would have to *teleport* them all to safety—every single one. All at once, Arlo said, because even with the stone to bolster her, the moment Nausicaä pushed her magic to such an unfathomable feat, *she* would be too exhausted to do anything else.

"Me, or our friends," Arlo summarized, as though it were that simple. "You can't save us both."

Nausicaä stared back at Arlo . . . then at the stone, as Arlo pressed it into her palm.

For a beating moment, they stood opposite each other in weighted silence. Her choice was already made, and she knew Arlo could tell.

"You know I love you too, don't you?" Nausicaä rasped.

This one time.

This *one time*, she couldn't choose Arlo—and the impossibility of such a concept made her eyes sting even hotter with tears she refused to let fall. "I'm sorry," she added in a whisper.

But Arlo only smiled.

That flat little scrunched-up Canadian quirk of hers. It was sad, but it was understanding—relieved, even, and the most Arlo of all her actions so far. "You don't have to apologize, Nos. You're doing the right thing."

"Yeah, well, it feels like shit."

"Which is probably the best indication it's what you're supposed to do." She shook her head, her smile fading as she took a step in withdraw. "I would get going . . ." Her attention finally broke from Nausicaä to wander skyward. Whatever she saw, it turned her expression grim. "It's almost time."

Shit.

Nausicaä grabbed her girlfriend by the shoulders. "Don't you *dare* die," she growled. "I swear on every fucking star that if you do, I'm going to be *so* pissed."

And pressed their lips together in what very much would *not be their last kiss*—but the edge of desperation to it made the stinging in her eyes turn wet.

"I love you."

"I love you, too."

Peeling away felt like tearing her limbs off with her bare hands, but Nausicaä went. "Promise me!" she called as she backed to the tree line. "You'd better promise!"

"I promise," Arlo called back in the clearest lie she'd ever spoke. "Good luck, Nausicaä. You'd better not die on me, either."

CHAPTER 17

Celadon

~~~~

CELADON WAS FAIRLY CERTAIN he'd never felt so wonderful in his life.

It had been far too long since he'd given in to unwinding in this manner—as a new king of a new Court and their entire world on the verge of war, there simply wasn't time to spare for things like parties and clubbing, which he'd indulged in quite frequently before. Even when he met with Pallas, he never drank more than what would leave him with a polite buzz, and really, this was all such a crime, because if there was anyone Celadon wanted to positively *waste* himself in excess with more than a hundreds-upon-hundreds-of-years-old vampire, it was the man he was currently leading away from the Market's celebratory bonfire to the collection of busy picnic tables stuffed into the sidelines.

"Sit," he commanded, with all the gravity of his title, as he manhandled Lethe down into a vacancy on one of the benches. "Thank you."

He proceeded to slip himself, sideways, into place in his lap.

"I feel like this is probably the truest indication that this poor man is absolutely *gone* on you," Theodore drawled from the opposite side of the table, looking up from the conversation he'd been engrossed in with Fyri at their arrival. "Lethe, may I ask what happened to the last unfortunate person who tried to push you around anywhere?"

Lethe's poison-green eyes narrowed on Celadon. "I cut off his hands and drowned him, his family, and entire kingdom all to the bottom of the sea. . . ."

This would be far more threatening if he hadn't also slid a hand up

Celadon's back while he spoke, to brace him with the flat of his palm while Celadon shifted into a more comfortable position.

"Hush," Celadon said, while dipping back to fling out a hand and snag one of the paper cups of green-apple cider from a passing tray. "You like it very much when I'm bossy," he added when fully righted once more.

Lethe rolled his eyes in response, but there was a squeeze to Celadon's inner thigh from the hand with his claws, and sharp adamantine sliced right through the thin fabric of Celadon's pants to drag across the sensitive skin there.

He liked the shiver that flared down his spine in response to this.

He liked it, because it was born from respect.

The more comfortable he and Lethe became as partners—the better Celadon got to know Lethe and Lethe him in return, the stronger the bond between them grew—the more he enjoyed these mild advances and slightly darker overtures. It helped a great deal that he knew Lethe would leave it entirely to him whether or not they would go any further; that there would be no guilt or sighs or put-out looks if they, more often than not, didn't; that he got to decide the pace when they *did*, and whether or not he wanted simply to give or receive as well.

And for Lethe, who still didn't confide in him all that easily but was slowly settling into this partnership, Celadon knew he appreciated in return being allowed his space when he needed it, that Celadon didn't force or expect him to fit into any specific model of what a romantic couple should be.

It was nice. It was *wonderful*. It was incredibly bizarre as well, that he should slot so well together with someone so vicious and morally gray, but so very good in all the ways that counted, especially to Celadon . . . and Arlo.

"You have that *look*," Lethe murmured, low and private and sinfully dangerous between them, brightest green softening under heavy, dark lashes tipped white as his hair.

Gods, but Celadon couldn't help the way this man drew him in. "Which one is that . . . ?"

Lethe turned thoughtful, his eyes darkening. "The one where I think I live in your head as a *far* better person than I actually am."

"What would *you* know?" Celadon said with an affronted sniff. "You're a terrible judge of character."

"Clearly," he replied, almost warm, almost teasing, before snapping his teeth at the tip of Celadon's nose.

"Speaking of disgusting!" Theodore chirped, earning a glare from Celadon and Lethe both. "Which you two are very publicly being . . ."

He cut a glance to Fyri, who'd engrossed herself in conversation with a pixie male on her other side. When she turned to look—a glare from her, too—Theodore wordlessly waggled his brows, tilted his head in their direction, and cast a pointed look at something she held below the table, and she shot him argumentative hesitance in return. Celadon had no idea what was going on, was very close to bidding them a pleasant evening and taking Lethe up on his promises, but then . . .

"Oh my gods," Fyri sighed in defeat. "Fine."

She lifted what she'd been holding concealed and slapped it on the table.

A bottle.

A very large, very distinctive, very ugly brown bottle, which Celadon snatched with wide eyes and a highly unbecoming screech. "Ogre Tears?" He gaped, at the bottle and Fyri in turn, then shook his head sadly. "Oh, Fyri. How very unbecoming of our future Head of Ironborn Relations."

He uncorked the bottle, and immediately his eyes began to water; his nose and throat burned like he'd just inhaled gasoline.

Which it wasn't far off from, really. Whatever went into making this, it was only the dwarven community that knew the recipe—a little bit of everything, Celadon had to assume, but certainly there had to be paint thinner. The name came from the insinuation that the smell and taste could bring even an ogre to tears, and it was *awful*, banned from sale within the Courts, strong enough that a bottle this size could wipe out an entire battalion of dwarves, so of course they'd invented a whole culture around it.

Of course the dwarves had developed the underground competition of who could take the most shots and stay conscious.

"I'm extremely disappointed in you," he added.

Fyri snorted. "Says the pretty fae prince who couldn't keep down a shot of that if they tried."

"I beg your pardon," Celadon gasped, fully offended, swinging himself around so that his legs slid properly under the table, and Lethe's hands fell to his waist to slot them flush together, that he could continue acting as his chair. "I have never suffered such insult in my life. Have you heard nothing of my drunken exploits? I spent the majority of my youth in these trenches. You have no idea who you're talking to."

He tossed back the cider he'd only just procured, earning a highly suggestive comment about his gag reflex from Theodore in the process. Slamming his empty paper cup on the table, he glared down Fyri's bright-eyed smugness as he poured himself a shot. "Give me your cup—we're settling this like gentlemen."

Again Fyri snorted, but she drained the rest of her cup as well and slid it over.

Theodore did the same.

"Lethe?" he asked, turning in place to look at his boyfriend. "I've never seen you drunk before. Actually, I don't think I've *ever* seen you drink."

Frowning, Lethe shook his head. "That's because I don't. But by all means, defend your honor, you vain creature."

"Ho, that's rich!" Celadon teased, but turned back around. Recorked the bottle. Grabbed his cup and raised it between them. "To the death, good lady and sir."

"You're so dramatic," Fyri muttered over the rim of her cup.

In unison, they threw back their shots.

"OH GODS!" Celadon flinched, moaned, doubled over and gagged on the fumes of the liquid that felt like it was eating a hole through his esophagus.

"*UGGH.*" Fyri practically vibrated, she shook her head so furiously, and had to force herself to swallow, slapping the table like encouragement the entire time.

"I'm going to be sick—" Theodore moaned, and immediately retched his shot back up onto the ground behind him. "Yeah, no, I'm out," he conceded. "That's extremely vile. My palate was made for far better things."

Perhaps Celadon commented back.

Perhaps his brain was melting through his ears.

All he knew was that suddenly, he was pouring another shot for him and Fyri, absorbed into what she and Theodore had been discussing upon Celadon and Lethe's arrival, of an idea Fyri was toying with for the inevitable war on their horizon.

"He's the Madam's grandson," Fyri said, curling in over the table in a poor attempt to keep secret what she had to shout anyway to be heard over the noise. "He might not be a full-blooded dragon, but the magic, the ancestry, the inheritance is all there! I'm absolutely *certain* that if I can fix the animus rune in the right way in the array, and anchor it to a singular aspect—the dragon in his blood—I could draw it out; I could force a shape-shift. We'd have a fucking *dragon* on our side."

Celadon blinked at her over the paper cup he was filling, then slowly shook his head.

"What a terrifying person you are, Fyri Eldraine. No wonder Arlo recommended you for this position." He passed her a cup. "Can you really do this? Is it actually possible to turn a man into a dragon using alchemy?"

"HAH!" Fyri laughed. "You don't even know the half of what this magic could do. *I* don't even! That's the beauty of alchemy: its limits are set only by the wielder's imagination. I've been bouncing this off Rory for a while now—he seems to think it's possible. A little more time, and I'll have the right array for sure."

Glancing at Theodore, who was too busy watching Fyri with a grin of pure admiration to notice Celadon's scrutiny, he raised his cup. "To the limits of imagination, then!"

One moment, they were toasting to their hopeful success.

The next, the bottle was half-gone, and Theodore had disappeared somewhere. Celadon and Fyri had abandoned the table as well and were linked arm in arm as they wandered the streets with Lethe like a mildly unamused shadow behind them. They stopped for food. Threw up a couple times. Stopped for more food, then challenged a group of goblins to another shot, then to a karaoke battle, then the whole lot of them adventured through a jungle together, which Celadon would recall later as merely being a bush they'd all fallen into and couldn't figure out how to get out of.

Eventually, Fyri admitted defeat, not because she couldn't handle any more shots—Celadon had a feeling he would have lost, if they'd gone for even one more—but because Theodore had resurfaced and propositioned her for a much better time, which made Celadon grin and wink at him, and call embarrassing encouragements at their retreating forms.

Then Celadon's party dwindled down to two, Lethe moving to hover above him with all the air of exasperation—when had he laid down on the ground? Even better question, how did he get up?

"All right, Your Majesty. Time, I think, to get you to a proper bed."

"I'm fine here," he was pretty sure he said, but judging by the look on Lethe's face, none of those words had come out right.

"Up we go," he coaxed gently, guiding Celadon back to his feet.

Through the haze of drink, which was beginning to layer thicker and thicker over his thoughts, Celadon had the distinct impression of wishing that Arlo could have been here too, to take his evening from wonderful to perfect.

It was right at that moment that Nausicaä appeared before them, serious and frowny and kind of blurred around the edges . . .

With zero preamble, and full sincerity, she said by way of greeting, "Ever look at over eight hundred drunk people and think to yourself, *Wow, I sure would love to try and wrangle them all into holding hands for a mass teleportation in under half an hour's time limit?* 'Cause if so, I'm about to make your fucking night, boys."

She held up a stone.

"What a weird thing to say," Celadon slurred. Unfortunately, whatever those words actually meant, Celadon's brain had decided it had had quite enough of tonight's abuse and traded in for a blackout.

CHAPTER 18

Ruin

ARE YOU SURE YOU *want to do this? It could very well be the end of you.*

Wouldn't you just love that.

Arlo stood outside the Goblin Market's front gate, far enough back in the tree line opposite to conceal herself in its shadows.

It was almost midnight.

Almost that time when the veil between the worlds was easiest to break though. This didn't normally matter, not with Ruin's power, but crossing into the Sacred Realm was going to take much more than her usual reserves of fortitude—and then she had to obtain a goddess's Crown. Anything she could do to make this whole ordeal simpler, she would.

> *Not to mention there's getting back out again.*
> *With the Market untethered,*
> *you won't be able to return to your realm,*
> *not from the Hiraeth.*
> *You'll have to create a second, new portal—*
> *and goodness,*
> *but what that will drain from you . . .*

Everything's coming up Ruin, isn't it.

They were right, though.

This was going to wear on her terribly.

This was the entire reason she'd snagged that stone from Riadne's store, and she was glad that Nausicaä had decided to use it toward rescuing all these people who would have otherwise died here tonight—a choice Arlo knew she would have made herself, before . . . but now, when so much of her had worn away to unrecognizableness . . . she hadn't trusted herself to do what was necessary with the temptation for even a *little* help that the stone would have provided . . .

> *And just to think, if you do survive the toll of this,*
> *there's still Urielle's Crown to gather from the*
> *Infernal Realm.*

Yes.

And in order to get back to the UnSeelie Summer graveyard, and the portal there that would let her out in the vicinity of the Infernal Palace, she would additionally have to pull on every tracking skill she possessed to follow the trail of her magic that had opened that portal to begin with.

Difficult work.

Tedious work.

Her magical signature was stamped all around this world by now, and with no telling how close or far she was from what she sought, it would require much trial and error, much personal energy spend on dead ends.

So the fact that tonight she would have to stamp *two* portals through the chaos that filled between realms—one into the Sacred Realm, and one back out into the mortal plane—wasn't about to do her any favors.

But needs must; Arlo had to do this.

At the very least, it wasn't going to come at the cost of Aurelian and Vehan, and Celadon and Lethe, and Theo and Fyri. Still, there were many people Nausicaä *couldn't* save, the ones who lived in the Hiraeth outside of the Market, because there just wasn't enough time for Nausicaä to teleport those additional thousands, not even for someone as powerful and determined as her girlfriend.

Ah well,

Ruin cooed in her mind, not at all sympathetic.

> *All wars produce casualties. Ending them does too.*
> *Perhaps, when this is all over, you can—*

Whatever they'd been about to say, Ruin was cut off by a curious sound—or rather, the sudden and impossibly loud lack of it.

Just moments ago, there'd been music. There'd been singing and laughter and voices and delight. There had been people, and then, in all of a snap, it was almost as though . . . there weren't.

Not anymore.

Not a single one.

Arlo took a step closer.

The fire still glowed warmly in the distance; she could hear its crackling if she listened hard enough. But that was it—that was all that remained to prove she hadn't imagined this village alight and alive.

"She's done it."

Arlo felt her heart sink.

What a curious feeling, this profound disappointment, when nothing much really affected her in that way anymore. . . . It was one thing to know she was doing this alone, and another thing to face the reality of it.

"At least this means I'm still *me* enough," she murmured to herself, to stand here missing Nausicaä and wishing they were doing this together—

POP.

Arlo *whipped* around.

"Gross, Nausicaä."

"Fuck you, Vehan—you ever teleport over eight hundred people all at once to the middle of some fuck-off random field?" She doubled back over to vomit again.

Arlo could only stare.

Nausicaä looked *horrible*, trembling and pale . . . and Arlo rushed forward without a second thought and took Nausicaä by the shoulders to straighten her and look up, up, up into those sharp steel eyes—just as she'd noticed during their first real acquaintance back in the Faerie Ring, Arlo couldn't help it again: Nausicaä was so *tall*.

"What are you doing here? You weren't supposed to come back! Nausicaä, you can't come with me, your magic—"

"Is completely drained along with the stone, yeah, yeah." She tried to laugh; it came out more of a wounded whimper. "The thing is, like cold fucking hells am I letting you take on a Great Goddess without me. I don't care if all I can do is throw up on her—which is a very real possibility and, personally, would be deeply demoralizing if someone did that to me, so I might be better help than you think. And, as you can see, there were two other people who also couldn't take a hint."

Almost as though on cue, Vehan stepped forward to jab Arlo's shoulder with the point of his finger. "I told you! You aren't doing this without me, either. And as I've had to learn, now so will you: the Bessels are something of a package deal."

That confused Arlo for a moment.

She studied Vehan, trying to figure out what he meant—until her gaze caught on a glint off a ring, innocuous and *everything* around his finger.

"Oh my gods, are you *engaged*?" Nausicaä remarked, playing up disgust. "Is *that* what I walked in on a few minutes ago . . ." She vomited again on the ground. Paused. Took a breath. Looked back up at Vehan and Aurelian. "Honest, that was just good timing. I'm actually very happy for you. Or whatever."

One thing at a time—Arlo's brain struggled to keep up with how quickly her thoughts snapped between points of focus. "Nausicaä, promise me you won't do anything stupid. You teleported over *eight hundred* people in *one* go—you're honestly lucky you didn't Surge or something and deplete your core altogether, even with that stone."

"Rude." Nausicaä frowned. "I don't recall ever, not even once, doing anything that could be considered *stupid*. Again, I'm not sitting out. If nothing else, I'm a master at vicious mockery, and besides, I'm already dressed for the occasion."

Yes.

She still wore the red satin glove she'd fit herself into at Riadne's dinner, to shock Arlo enough to remember herself, yes, but also definitely just a *little* for the way Riadne had been so irritated after that Nausicaä's beauty had outdone hers. It was no competition, but of course, Arlo was also a bit biased in that area.

Vehan and Aurelian, in their own party attire, were admittedly dressed better than what Nausicaä was still in. But that was definitely a tear in Aurelian's stretched collar, and Vehan's pants were missing their fasten, held up by a belt that screamed more Aurelian than him, and they both smelled like ale the Market had been serving—UnSeelie Spring's specialty, by the appley scent of it, which probably explained why Celadon wasn't here as well.

Sloshed.

The apple cider had always been his favorite.

So, here they were—Arlo's company. Not a one of the three of them were actually prepared for what they wanted to jump in on, existing purely on vibes and enthusiasm alone.

Arlo sighed. "None of you are going to listen to reason right now, are you?"

"Absolutely not."

"Not a chance."

Vehan and Nausicaä spoke in unison.

Aurelian stepped forward, drawing everyone in until the group resembled something close to a circle, and in the center of it, he placed his hand. "We started this together, Arlo. Back at Hieronymus Aurum's lab. The four of us then—the four of us now. We're all coming with you."

Arlo looked down at Aurelian's hand.

It had been months since she'd cried about anything—since she'd even felt the need to. She felt that familiar stinging build in her eyes now.

"Also, not to steal the show or anything, but . . ." Vehan reached into his pocket and pulled out an object he concealed in his palm. Placed his hand in the center as well, overtop his fiancé's. Unfurled it to reveal bright electric blue and gleaming gold. "Some redheaded alchemist gave me this cool die that I hear boosts luck or something. Can't hurt to have that on your side . . ."

How *badly* Arlo wanted to hold it.

That die had been hers. It no longer looked the same, but there was something about it at its core as familiar to her as her own magic.

Just last year, she'd hated it desperately. Right now she'd never been happier to see it.

"All right," she said, tone worn soft as she slowly reached her hand into the circle's center too. "The four of us."

Nausicaä's hand sealed the pact.

A long moment passed where they stood there simply staring down at their hands.

"Just so you know," Nausicaä said suddenly, breaking up the tension, "I am really very unhappy with you right now. How dare you."

She glared at Aurelian.

"How dare I what?"

"How dare you propose before I could!"

A look at Vehan. A look at Nausicaä. Aurelian frowned, confused. "To . . . Vehan?"

"No, you asshat—why would anyone want to marry Vehan?"

"What's wrong with Vehan!" Vehan pouted.

Arlo shook her head. "Oh my gods," she said beneath her breath, breaking from the group to step toward the gate in a stunning parallel of how they'd arrived at Aurum Industries.

These were her friends, for better or worse now.

She could almost feel it, the love she knew she held for each of them.

So very precious.
But ultimately useless.
Love has only ever been a weakness, Arlo Flamel;
I did think you'd learned that lesson already.

She ignored her parasite, more herself right now than she'd been in some time, thanks to the four people behind her. And wasn't that . . . curious, how Ruin almost seemed to be . . . afraid of them?

Arlo raised her hand.

"You're going to want to get behind me," she warned her friends, and they immediately complied as darkness began to gather at her palm.

CHAPTER 19

Nausicaä

~~~~~~

THE SACRED REALM—NAUSICAÄ HAD never been here, even before her exile. If the Hiraeth was magic's mortal throne, then this would be its immortal equivalent, and none but Tellis had ever been shown the path through the perilous maze that guarded it.

Of course, this only sharpened immortal interest in the place.

Speculation on what it looked like was something the denizens of both the Infernal and Cosmic Realms fell back on whenever other sources of gossip grew stale. There was at least one party a year that attempted to navigate the surrounding, ever-changing forest to find its legendary heart, but if the woods didn't spit them right back out upon entry, it devoured them gruesomely whole—at least, as reports from traumatized survivors went.

Arlo, Aurelian, Vehan, Nausicaä—the four of them stood where only one other being in all of eternity had been before, and it was *nothing* at all what Nausicaä had envisioned.

Open, clear sky the most vibrant shade of startling blue stretched on and on, as far as was visible in every direction. Beneath it, an endless, rugged expanse of rock. Ruby and quartz and amethyst and garnet; topaz, obsidian, aquamarine, and lapis. Silver, gold, platinum, adamant; gems and stones and precious metals, all swirled in glittering veins through craggy terrain the shade of terra-cotta. They jutted in enormous shards, clashed in a battle of sweeping arches and bold color, sprouted and rose in great fanning chunks that were shapes curiously similar to trees.

Everything dazzled and gleamed in the sunlight.

"The Sacred Realm is a Minecraft server," Nausicaä concluded, taking it all in. A comment that made Aurelian snort but went right over Vehan's head.

"I thought Tellis was the goddess of nature," Vehan said, confused. He bent to trace a thick vein of pyrite running beside his foot. "I know we call her Mother *Earth*, and that's more than just trees, but I *was* expecting more . . . green."

Honestly, Nausicaä had been too.

But Tellis had always been a bit of an eccentric, she'd gathered from all the rumors. It was a rare occasion when the goddess left the Sacred Realm, though, so nobody really knew all that much about her—or her domain.

"You're sure this is the right location?" Aurelian asked Arlo, moving a few steps forward to place himself beside Nausicaä.

Arlo nodded, still looking out over the rainbow-encrusted expanse. "I'm sure."

"All right . . ." Aurelian shot a skeptical look at Nausicaä. She merely shrugged in return. If Arlo said they were where they needed to be, they were where they needed to be. "Do you have any idea where we should start *looking* for the goddess, then?"

"No, but we don't need to."

Oh?

Nausicaä stiffened.

That caught her attention, and something that prickled against the back of her neck said she already knew what was coming next.

As fun as it would be to kick ass in heels and a formfitting dress, just this once she was going to leave those dramatics to her girlfriend. Arlo *had* at least altered her footwear, from their meeting in the Hiraeth clearing, to more practical burgundy boots, but the red of her skirt/pantsuit combo was so vivid in this setting that she fit right in with all these striking gems.

Nausicaä . . . she was already running on less than fumes, and this wasn't going to be some walk in the park. Tellis wasn't going to just

254

hand over her Crown, and Nausicaä didn't have Ruin's many advantages to make up for her exhaustion, not to mention the things her exile had stripped her of, the perks and amplifications to her power she'd enjoyed as an Erinys. If she was going to be any real use to Arlo, she would have to take this a little more seriously than her normal standards of irreverence for pretty much every situation.

And so, as Vehan stepped forward to her other side, Nausicaä dissolved the satin and red *she* wore in the smoky plumes of her magic.

Replacing it with her usual attire of a simple black tank, leather pants, and combat boots.

"We don't need to look for her?" Vehan repeated, wary, in a tone that said he already knew what Arlo meant too. "As in . . ."

"As in," Arlo replied, confirming his fears, her gaze remaining trained forward, "Tellis is already here."

What Nausicaä wouldn't give for her full, immortal senses returned.

Yeah, she could feel the presence of the goddess well enough to place her nearby as well—but whatever Arlo's sight was trained on, Ruin and her own natural ability revealed a far clearer picture.

She stepped toward Arlo, coming up beside her. There was nothing she could do right now to help, to protect. Her magic was so depleted, she couldn't even summon her sword from the void where she kept it, and exhaustion wore so heavily on her, she felt it like a physical pain.

But still . . . she wasn't going anywhere. "Which direction—just say the word, we're right beside you."

"There won't be any need for that either," Arlo replied with a shake of her head.

And no need to ask what she meant.

Because as soon as spoken, the ground began to rumble.

Began to tremble, began to quake, began to fissure and cave in places all around them, as something began to peel itself up from its surface.

Not something, but some*one*.

Nausicaä stumbled backward.

Vehan crashed into Aurelian, who caught him quickly and, in an even faster maneuver, pulled him out of the path of a crack that snaked directly for his footing.

Only Arlo stood perfectly unfazed, Ruin anchoring her firmly in place, a single goddess no match for a Titan, let alone one of their caliber. She watched without moving as Tellis amassed before them as a terrible colossus: two great arms lifting from the earth, a torso robed in those glittering gems, a rocky head set with adamant for teeth, and two cavernous holes for eyes that glowed like the infernal forges burned deep within.

The goddess of the earth was *enormous*.

Grew bigger and bigger and taller, until her shadow consumed them, until the debris crumbling from the crust of her skin on every grating movement fell to the ground large as boulders.

"Looks like she was expecting us!" Nausicaä yelled over the din.

"And a bit like we've already outstayed our welcome," Aurelian shouted back.

A fair assessment.

Once *finally* at full height, Tellis bared her teeth down at them.

She was more giant rock-monster than woman right now, so possibly, the lack of warmth in her limited set of expressions was hard to truly gauge. But Nausicaä would put her money with Aurelian's—she didn't look all that happy to see them.

Go back to your realm, child-puppet, Tellis thundered like a landslide down at Arlo. *Leave now, and I won't smear you across* my *realm for the audacity that brought you.*

In reply, Arlo held a hand out over the ground—right above a vein of adamant, where blue began to glow, began to etch itself into an array; where she pulled from the metal a wicked, double-bladed sword to twirl into the ready position.

Possibly, this was the hottest thing Nausicaä had ever witnessed her do.

So be it, the goddess said gratingly, and wound back a fist the size of a small moon.

"MOVE!" Nausicaä called out.

All four of them fanned into different directions as that fist descended like the heavens falling directly where they'd been standing.

Tellis didn't have time to change course, but Arlo was quick—riding out the shock wave of the blow's impact. Nausicaä watched as she darted closer, almost a blur of red for all those Titan-heightened reflexes she was utilizing right now, paired with her windborn fae magic.

With a great thrust, she buried her adamant blade into the goddess's forearm, and the ear-piercing shriek of pain that followed made everyone flinch.

The goddess retreated, pulling her hand free from the stone in an attempt to shake what had lodged there—Arlo, anchored and rising high into the air along with the appendage.

"Plan of attack?" Aurelian asked, surmounting an upturned plate of rock to close their ranks once more. "How do we defeat a *goddess*?"

Nausicaä turned a look on him, a fluttering in her vision like she was on the verge of passing out. Gritting her teeth, she shoved aside her fatigue and growled, "Listen to you! Are you the jacked general of a whole Wild army and soulbound to a Class Fuck-Off fae prince, or aren't you!"

It was so hard to keep her thoughts in order.

She could do very little in this situation—less and less by the second. In the very least, she should help the ground team formulate a battle plan, but her mind and body alike were beginning to scream at her for rest.

She'd just teleported over eight hundred people out of a pocket between realms—even with a second-rate philosopher's stone, that was no small feat—yet here she was . . . following her girlfriend to the ends of the earth, because no matter her level of desperate exhaustion, it was *nothing* to what Arlo would suffer for drawing so heavily on Ruin's powers to make up for lack of support.

Another sharp shriek of pain—Arlo, so high up now Nausicaä could make her out only by the glint of her sword, leaped from Tellis's forearm to her chest and plunged an end of her double-sided weapon deep into the goddess's shoulder.

Kicking off from that impaled shoulder, Arlo dropped with all her weight, the sword tearing downward too through rock, spilling ichor from the resulting wound.

Blood rained to the earth like molten gold and ate through stone and gem and metal all, as corrosive as acid.

"Pro tip: don't let that touch you," Nausicaä added in warning before propelling herself toward the goddess as well.

She couldn't use her magic.

Moments jumped forward in time as though she'd dozed through the ones in between.

But that was her girlfriend, and Nausicaä wasn't going to hang out on the sidelines while Arlo waged war against a superpowered goddess. Arlo wasn't going to do this alone, philosopher's stones be damned.

Unfurling her wings felt like cracking her ribs out through her back, but Nausicaä ignored this too, taking to the air. Up and up and up she soared. A giant stone arm swept in her direction as the goddess struggled to dislodge Arlo's blade. Nausicaä planted her boots on the limb to *run* up the length of it, tripping over her tired feet on more than one occasion.

Debris—crushingly huge rocks; deadly sharp, broken gems—was hurled at her from every direction as the goddess flailed . . .

Nausicaä dodged them all, at heavy cost. She could feel her fatigue down to her core, where it had begun to wind like razor wire, but all she could think as she pushed and pushed and pushed herself for the landing of the goddess's shoulder was that right now, Arlo most definitely felt worse.

This way, that—twice she was forced to flatten herself to the goddess's arm to avoid the larger boulders sailing her way.

Vehan's lightning was rendered more or less useless in this particular conflict, but no doubt that die of his boosted his odds of sending those bolts zipping past Nausicaä, with just enough force that they blew great chunks out of Tellis's body and aided in knocking debris from Nausicaä's path.

"Having fun?" Nausicaä shouted down at Arlo as soon as she reached the flare of Tellis's shoulder, but her heart wasn't really in the tease.

Not at the pale-as-paper white that Arlo's fatigue had already drained her complexion to.

Instead of answering, Arlo merely began to rock, holding tight to her sword embedded in Tellis like an anchor as she began to swing her body back and forth and build momentum. Once, twice, four times, five—back and forth she swayed, in wider and wider sweeps, until at last, the force of what she was doing began to drive a crack in the goddess's body.

As soon as it did, Arlo threw her entire weight into spreading it. With a tremendous lurch of her body, she swung herself so powerfully that her blade dislodged, following the fissure she'd created down under the goddess's arm.

Another great swing *hurled* her clear up Tellis's back and returned her to where Nausicaä stood on the shoulder . . .

Where Arlo drove her sword in deeper, one last time, and finally succeeded in splitting the entire appendage from Tellis's body.

The goddess roared.

Nausicaä widened her stance to keep her footing, but it was Arlo who planted her black blade in the stone of Tellis's shoulder, an arm around Nausicaä's middle to secure them both as the goddess *writhed*.

With a force she could feel all the way up here, that arm crashed to the ground—hopefully, Vehan and Aurelian had managed to get out from under its certain death. There was too much distance between them right now to check on them with a shout.

"Look out!" Arlo cried, pointing ahead.

Furious, Tellis brought her other hand sailing across her body in an attempt to grab them.

Arlo had only just enough time to yank her sword free before Nausicaä wound her arms around Arlo and took to the air, clutching her close.

Up and up they flew, higher into the air.

The ground was a patchwork quilt of color at this point, the goddess raging just below them. She slashed and clawed and swung and flailed after them—lost entirely in her moment of rampage for a few long minutes . . . until the pain eased enough that she could regather focus.

And gather . . .

And *gather* . . .

And—*"Shit."*

Out from the socket of her severed arm burst two to replace the one.

Three arms now, and each hand scraped the earth for ammunition.

"Hold tight, spider monkey!" Nausicaä yelled, black beginning to eat away at the edges of her vision, and the world beginning to take on a shimmery, dreamy quality. Clutching Arlo closer, she darted and dodged; shot higher, plummeted lower; swerved and wove as Tellis lobbed great fistfuls of rock at them—there was no time for passing out. She had to get them *away*.

One of the hands found one of the crystals that grew from the earth like a tree.

Wielding it like a club, Tellis threw her rubble and batted the air. Her misses were growing more and more narrow, and the current generated by each swipe of that tree harder and harder to keep from getting sucked into like an inescapable, gravitational pull.

"You can't keep this up!" Arlo yelled. "Nausicaä, take me back to her shoulder. I have an idea—"

Suddenly, the goddess stiffened.

Her attack on them froze as well.

For a moment, she seemed to . . . teeter.

Then nothing.

Then *CRASH*—Tellis sank, hit the ground on her knees, fell further still, onto her hands.

Nausicaä descended for a closer look.

"Oh good," she cried, not far at all from the ground now, close enough to make out Vehan and Aurelian clear as the bright blue rope of lesidhe magic tangled around the goddess's legs. "The boys have started being useful."

"Her back, her back," Arlo urged, patting Nausicaä's arm. "Set me on her back!"

Nausicaä moved as commanded, setting Arlo down on the uneven, broad expanse.

There was no hesitation.

Arlo streaked forward.

Palm to her heart, she pulled a ball of throbbing, inky black from her chest—Ruin's raw power, and Arlo's own life force for all that it would cost her to use this a second time when she'd already done enough damage drawing on it to open the portal here.

Smearing that power down the length of that blade, just as Arlo had done to Tellis's arm, she did to the goddess's neck—but this time, she drove in the blade, used her weight to propel its course down and around and back up to where she'd begun, tearing open a bleeding gold wound.

There was screaming, and gagging, and strangled shrieks—then nothing but echoes . . . as Tellis's head was severed as well and tumbled like a quaking to the ground below.

The body shuddered.

"Up we go!"

In a heap, it collapsed, and as it did, the gust kicked up began to build.

Not really fancying being blown clear across the realm, Nausicaä landed, held Arlo close, and reached out to signal Aurelian and Vehan to the shelter of her immortal weight, which anchored them in place.

The breeze turned to wind—the goddess to dust, along with the arena she'd cast.

The gems, the stones, the not-trees, the body, all of it crumbled and was ground down to fine sand, then blown away by the wind, and beneath was revealed all the lush grass, the fragrant flora, the ancient trees and gentle calm, the Sacred Grove of legend.

In the midst of it all . . . Tellis kneeled before them.

Dwindled down to the milder form of soft brown flesh and sewn-petal dress, earthen-brown hair, and verdant eyes that watched them closely—or rather, Arlo.

"What a terrible mission you undertake, Twice Flamel. The First Ones mean you no kindness in tasking you to it."

Deathly pale and trembling with the effort it took to keep herself upright, Arlo extracted herself from Nausicaä and made her approach of the goddess.

"Your Crown, please," her voice rasped.

She held out a hand, the one she'd used to wield Ruin's magic, and it filled Nausicaä with a horrible nausea to see how the veins there had gone an ashy black.

"What would you do with it?" Tellis eyed her almost curiously. "Would you keep it for yourself or return it from whence it came? Twice Flamel, I do not advise that. There's a reason we fought such impossible odds to reduce them to what they are now."

Standing as firm as she could, Arlo repeated, "Your Crown, please. You fell, we won—it belongs to me."

"It does, yes," Tellis said too simply for all the weight of her reservations behind her tone. Regardless, she reached up and removed her Crown, then held it out for Arlo's taking. "Do you understand what you're asking for, I wonder? What these Crowns are?"

"They're the bones of the First Ones, the source of your power, and they're driving your realm to corruption—yes, I know," Arlo replied distractedly as she took a step toward what Tellis offered.

Nausicaä frowned and caught herself just barely from the instinct to reach forward to stop Arlo from getting too close.

Tellis, meanwhile, watched Arlo's advance—the want that no doubt had begun to darken in her eyes—with a glint in her own like some point of hers was about to be proven.

"They are so much more than bone, child-puppet. The First Ones would have you seek them, caring little what it would do to you to merely *touch* them."

Arlo paused. The goddess looked down, considering the object she held, bone twisted into a circle.

"Three Crowns, made of the First Ones we sundered—Urielle, Cosmin, and myself the generals who led this war. They were meant to help us keep order, to bolster our powers and set us apart from those we commanded; to create clear hierarchy we'd felt then was necessary to ensure our realm and people flourished."

Nausicaä knew a lot about the lore of the Crowns, most recently from Eos and Moros, but the majority of her knowledge had come—for the most part—from gossip. From stories told in taverns and whispered at Temple and traded like currency in the markets. Urielle had been extremely tight-lipped about the part she'd played in the Primordial War, and even for a Fury, Lord Cosmin was a frightening figure to approach—giving maddening riddles for answers to anyone (like her) who'd sought him out regardless.

This was the first she'd ever heard this stuff from the source, so even though her head was beginning to spin, and her veins felt like the blood within had turned to knives, and her body was so incredibly *heavy* and light both at the same time . . . she couldn't help her interest, and took a step closer as well just to listen even better.

"It was Cosmin who foresaw how this would turn against us. How this stolen power would corrupt even immortal hearts. Urielle and I, we wanted to think ourselves better than this weakness, that we were strong enough to resist its pull. Our brother knew better—had sent his Crown to the Mortal Realm, not in punishment to your people as he allowed our kin to think, but in hope. The Lord of Death is a strangely optimistic fool." Snorting half to herself, she lifted her gaze, her hands extending to put her Crown on full offer to Arlo, unmoving before it. "He really did think that, for all the woe it would cause, eventually, there would come a mortal capable of the one thing we immortals fare even worse at than you."

"Oh?" Arlo said, in a soft rush of breath. "And what's that?"

Tellis smiled. "Resisting the call of temptation."

It was strange, the sudden swell of relief in Nausicaä. There was so much that floated around about the different immortals, gods and goddesses and deities alike. After a while, it left a girl with the inclination to assume the worst of them all.

She was . . . happy, she realized—or, in the very least, pleased—to know that Cosmin, who'd always struck her as one of the better examples of who they could be, had managed to live up to her hopes of him.

"Set it on the ground, please," said Arlo, again in soft, breathy words. "If you don't mind. Sorry."

Sorry—bless. Nausicaä wished she didn't feel like crying every time Arlo proved that pieces of *her* still remained, despite everything.

Tellis placed the Crown on the ground, and as soon as her fingers left it, Arlo amassed another ball of Ruin's dark power. Shot it at the Crown.

Obliterated it.

The Crown was just . . . gone. By the power that would destroy even the magic that clung to it, the first step in her promise to Moros and Eos fulfilled.

Nausicaä stared.

Tellis did too.

Arlo wavered slightly on her feet, and her entire being seemed to drain a shade or two duller for what this had cost her. But otherwise, the five of them existed in such unmoving silence, until finally, Tellis gasped a sharp, sudden breath, the sound of which startled all.

A moment passed in which the goddess had gone worryingly stiff, every muscle in her body tense.

Then, with a release of air through her nose, Tellis smiled; her body relaxed; the tension eased, and Nausicaä could see the beginnings of a golden blush returning to her cheeks . . . the flowers in her curling hair taking on brighter bloom.

She straightened, and only then did Nausicaä realize the physical and mental toll the Crown's weight had held over her aunt—lifted now, thanks to one mortal.

"Perhaps we were wrong in fearing what you'd do with Ruin," Tellis mused, half to herself, half to Arlo, then began to get to her feet.

She stepped toward Arlo, and Arlo could protect herself—she'd proven that a millionfold, having just slain a power-buffed goddess— but Nausicaä still felt herself stiffen.

For nothing, it seemed. Tellis halted an arm's length away.

"That does not change your predicament. That even though you may have it in you to accomplish what you set out to do—to obliterate all three of the Bone Crowns and, in so doing, contain the Primordial Ones in permanence—if you do manage rebirth into immortality, there's very few you will find who are friend to you here. Urielle will not be so easily conquered, besides, if you seek to complete what you're after. But for my part . . ." Her gaze cast off to the side—down at the patch of blackened earth where moments ago had been grass . . . and a Crown.

The gaze returned.

"Thank you," she said. "You have lifted a terrible burden from me that I could not, myself. These Crowns, while it might take much longer for immortal hearts to feel the effects, they warp us just as surely as they do you mortals. I have not been myself in quite some time. My sister neither. I will forever be indebted to you for the return of my health and autonomy. If you make it to the afterlife that awaits you, I should be honored to be counted an ally."

A goddess's favor, her allyship—*forever*. Those words weren't spoken lightly. Tellis knew exactly what she'd just promised to Arlo. But Nausicaä was more caught up, at the moment, in the *other* thing she'd mentioned . . .

Something that hadn't exactly occurred to Nausicaä until just now, hearing from Tellis how no matter what immortals liked to boast about their fortitude, they were no stronger against these Crowns.

She'd already known, from what Eos and Moros had revealed, that Urielle, too, hadn't been herself in some time either, but the connection that just forged itself in Nausicaä's brain . . . seeing how changed Tellis was from what they'd battled only minutes ago . . .

What did this mean . . . on the matter of what had happened with Tisiphone, and Nausicaä's banishment after?

Ignorant to the minor crisis Nausicaä was going through, Tellis extended a hand.

In the air appeared a portal. "Allow me to ease a burden for you. This will take you back to your realm, preserve you just a little longer, enough to seek the rest and recovery you desperately need right now, I fear. Go with care, Arlo Flamel—and do try to survive what it is you've undertaken. I think I should like to witness what you make of immortality."

"Phoebus!" Arlo stood quickly from the armchair he'd been sitting in, a tiny bundle carefully cradled in his arms. "You needn't have—"

Smiling congenially, the High King entered the nursery with a hand raised to wave off the unnecessary humility. "Please. Twenty years now I have cared for you like my own blood, have I not? What father wouldn't want to meet their son's firstborn child?"

What father, indeed.

Quashing a swell of angry indignation—because Nicholas hadn't so much as sent a single word of congratulations on the birth of his only grandchild; in fact, it had been that same span of twenty years since last his father had spoken to him at all—Arlo moved to meet Phoebus halfway through the room.

"A beautiful boy," the High King decreed, taking the child in arm. "He's his father's son, through and through, looks every bit like you, Arlo. Ah, what tremendous fortune, to be so blessed—I remember well the feeling of holding one's legacy for the very first time. You must be bursting with pride." Smiling down at the babe, he brushed a hand over the fire-bright fluff of hair on his head—the newest Flamel didn't stir from his sleep at all. "What name have you decided on?"

"Apollo."

The High King looked at him, long and quiet; the brief softness that smoothed his features said he understood the significance.

The High King had been named after the Greek god of music and law and blazing sun—for the strongest light, it was often said, cast the darkest shadows; the UnSeelie loved to play on those terms.

Pallas—Athena . . . Phoebus—Apollo . . .

Arlo's son had been named for *him*.

"A lovely name for a lovely boy." Phoebus handed the sleeping babe back.

Taking him up, Arlo carried him over and placed his son into his crib—a gorgeous piece of richly stained furniture outfitted in fine emerald silks and black draping lace, a gift from Phoebus.

This entire nursery—the whole wing of the Black Castle in which Arlo and his wife, Ghislaine, lived—had been courtesy of his High King. The Flamels wanted for *nothing*, had excessive excess to spare on top of that. Phoebus was owed more than a namesake for all that he'd done for Arlo, but he seemed quite happy with it, joining Arlo at Apollo's crib to stare down at the child.

A moment of silence passed, in which the two of them stood, watching rose-warmed cheeks and tiny fingers flexing in sleep.

Then—"The Council tells me the report on your research is long overdue."

Arlo winced, but his gaze didn't lift from his child. "I'm aware," he replied, as quiet as Phoebus. "To be perfectly honest, I haven't decided if I'll turn one in at all."

He could feel the High King's gaze on him, sharp and considering. "Do you lack the materials necessary to continue?"

Arlo shook his head.

"Then you find yourself at an impasse and require time to work through the problem?" Phoebus tilted his head to cast him a humored, knowing look. "You've just had a child, Arlo—it's understandable that your mind's been a bit preoccupied with other things. All genius needs a challenge, or else it becomes complacent. I'll speak to the Council—I'm sure, with ample flattery, I'll be able to coax out a few more weeks of their patience—"

"No, Your Majesty," Arlo sighed, lifting his eyes from his son at last. "I am in need of nothing such. It isn't time or resources that will sway my decision. It's—"

"The matter of what must be done."

Considering the High King a long moment, Arlo nodded slowly.

He wasn't sure how much of his quarterly reports Phoebus read himself.

Everything Arlo did was submitted to the High Council for examination and approval, and it was only ever what was currently at hand when Phoebus visited that they talked about.

But it had been two years since Arlo had been given the template of the array he needed to create a stone.

The particulars surrounding this, he'd kept to himself—as far as both the High King and the Council were aware, he'd simply had a tremendous breakthrough, inspired by the joy of his impending nuptials. Two years, and Arlo had spent nearly every moment he could spare on dissecting his "gift": taking that array apart to study it piece by intricate piece, for a close examination of the language that made it—the art, the runes, the math, the lines.

Two years.

It had taken quite some time.

Eventually, though—as he knew he would—he'd figured out his puzzle, familiarized himself with what each of the pieces were . . . and what each of them would cost to activate . . .

What he'd learned about what was required to create even one of these hideous objects . . .

"Six times over the stone can be propagated," he recited dully, from a passage of his withheld report that he felt to his bones shouldn't fall into the High Council's hands. "Once will it be called. Seven stones and not one more, beginning first with pride surrendered. Innocence, to the rest."

"How very poetic," Phoebus said lightly.

Poetic?

"Not at all," Arlo grunted. "The philosopher's stones can be made only using hearts pulled beating out of innocent ironborn children. That's the terrible secret at the core of this gruesome work. Every stone but one must be made within a living host, cultivated until ripe, then ripped from their chest while alive. The initial stone *must* come willing, and direct from the alchemist who powers the array for the first time."

"Ah." The High King regarded him, expression betraying nothing. "So that's what this is about." He sighed. Turned his gaze back to Arlo's son. "It's a terrible predicament we're in, isn't it? The Courts are content—the people think that what we Founders did was enough to secure them an eternity's peace. But I can assure you, the gods are not so complacent. They lick their wounds tucked away in their banishment and plot among themselves the best way to inflict their revenge. Mark you, they *are* coming for us, and once they do, we must already be prepared to meet them. We *need* these stones—myself and Cenavy are all who remain of your original protectors, and we are getting old."

Reaching into his black-and-emerald robes, the High King extracted a pouch heavy with what sounded to be coin; he weighed it in his hand as he spoke.

"I refuse to leave unguarded what I fought so hard to build, Arlo. You have reached the limit of what you're willing to sacrifice for the good of our people—in morality, I understand. Disappointing as it is to learn this weakness of your character, your squeamishness is not unfathomable to me. Many the warrior has cowered in the face of his own demise, and you have a new child and wife to look out for."

He cut his gaze to Arlo now, fixing him with a look grown just as hard and incomprehensible to Arlo as his words.

"You do remember your contract is a geas, do you not? You have forged an unbreakable bond with me. Your father I released from his obligation, at a cost of tremendous agony to us both, because it was clear to me then that he did not have what it would take to unravel the philosopher's stone's mysteries. For all his knowledge, he knew nothing of what would make him useful to me. *You*, on the other hand . . ." He angled a rueful smile at Arlo, and nothing about it was at all recognizable, a glint of madness settling into his jade eyes and pitching them fever-bright. "Oh, there are other alchemists—

nowhere near your brilliance, but with the work all but done, many would consider it an honor to see through that which we must do. It's the principal of the matter, you see. I simply *will not* allow your fears to cost you the glory you are so close to achieving—"

"Phoebus, it isn't *fear*, it's—"

"*Pah,*" he said dismissively, flicking a hand in irritation at Arlo. "There will be no further talk of this. I will not release you from your contract. You are a Viridian in all but name, and I will not see any son of mine hold himself back from *legend* so nearly in his grasp. No. You will submit your report to the Council. You *will* create the first of the stones. And I will remind you that you signed the Flamel name to what you promised me—all who wear it will pay the price should you choose to abandon your geas."

Arlo felt his face drain pale.

Do this, create this first stone, and his life would be forfeit—he'd have to use his own heart as vessel for the magic the stone required. He wouldn't get to see his son grow up. Would be responsible for not only bringing what felt like a great evil into this world but the hideous knowledge of how to create *more*.

What was worse, the creation of the other six stones required the death of at *least* six other children, depending on how long it took to find the right one.

But if he didn't do this, not only would he die anyway—the price of a geas to a king, for the comfort and wealth and status Arlo had wanted more than anything back in his foolish youth—but his family . . . his *son* . . . they would all die with him.

It was so hard to reconcile this . . . *monster* beside him with the charming, benevolent man he'd known the majority of his life.

Arlo almost couldn't believe it was really him.

Almost.

This revelation brought to mind their long-ago meeting back in his family cabin, when Arlo had accidently murdered a girl with magic, and Phoebus had been all dangerous smiles in response, striking a chord of fear and warning in Arlo he hadn't understood back then.

It made far more sense to him now.

Phoebus tossed his bag in the air, caught it on the way down. He transformed in an instant, his expression sailing back into calmer waters, that hint of madness fading from his eyes . . .

"You need no incentive to make the right choice," Phoebus said in a pragmatic tone. "I know you, Arlo, as good as my blood, dear as a son. I know what you will choose. Not for the fame or the money, though perhaps you *are* due for a raise—" He set down the pouch on Apollo's crib's ledge. "You will do this for your family. You will do this because you're a better man than Nicholas ever was. And yes, you will die, as we all must die, but unlike the vast majority, myself perhaps included, your death will etch your name into history more lasting than immortality. There will be no one after who doesn't know it, and your every ancestor will wear it with *pride*."

Arlo wanted to be *sick*.

With a nod of his head, and one last look down at Apollo, Phoebus retreated back to the door.

Gaze trained on his son's sleeping face, Arlo heard himself call almost distantly, almost as though it were someone else speaking, "Would it be enough, to just have *me*?"

He couldn't see; his entire body felt numb to the soul. But he could *feel* the High King pause.

"You're right, Phoebus." He swallowed, attempting to inject some normalcy back into this conversation, as though he could possibly return to the boy who'd looked so starry-eyed and fond up to the stranger who now stood behind him. "You and this Court, you've been very generous to this family over the many years, and I did promise you a stone. Would it be enough, would you and the Council swear not to take this any further, if I performed my duty? If I used my heart to summon Pride and give myself over to legend?"

No death required but his own. Eos and Moros would be satisfied, and Alecto had assured him this much wouldn't earn immortal interference. Phoebus would have his stone . . . and Arlo would have his word that no further Sins would be created.

No children sacrificed to this terrible *evil*—beautiful, perfect, innocent souls like the one slumbering beneath his gaze . . .

Again, Arlo couldn't see. Again, he could only feel the way Phoebus studied his back.

A moment of silence . . .

Wore into two . . .

"I'll tell the Council you'll have your report handed in by the end of the month," came the High King's reply at last—a grim answer, in the question's utter dismissal. "Take a few weeks to sort yourself out. Be with your child. Then remember who you are—you didn't work this hard just to disappear into ignominy like your father."

And then he left.

Arlo stood by his newborn son, looking down at the dark leather satchel of coins.

"How long have you been there?" He spoke to the room, and from the far corner, the room replied: "Long enough."

Alecto stepped forward.

She crossed the floor.

Silently, she came up beside him, placing her palms on Apollo's crib and staring down at the babe. "So," she said, and then, despite everything she could possibly comment on, added, ". . . this is your son."

The urge to vomit turned into a heat that stung at his eyes.

"Alecto, meet . . . Apollo," he replied in a watery voice—had to clear his throat twice just to restore it to normal. "Much as now I regret my choice of namesake."

Alecto, meanwhile, frowned down at his son—the only legacy Arlo would ever feel proud of.

A moment longer of weighted silence, then, "I don't think I really like children all that much."

Unable to help himself, and perhaps owing to nerves, Arlo burst into laughter, loud enough to make Apollo's tiny face scrunch up, his small little hands flail in that newborn startle reflex; he began to stir . . . to fuss . . . but eventually settled once more.

"You know," Arlo replied, placing his hand on the crib now too, so close to Alecto's it could almost be touching, "I don't think I'm surprised by that."

"You're going to make that man a philosopher's stone," she said next without preamble.

"I don't have a choice."

Sobering, Arlo bent himself until his chin rested on the back of his hands, propped on Apollo's crib. "It is what they wanted, after all," he mused aloud between them. "Eos and Moros. Create the stone, become Pride, start the process that will see such horrific sorrow and suffering and war claw into this realm . . . seven stones, and a Titan returned, all heaped at the feet of some poor future wretch who won't thank me at all, when all's said and done, my glorious legend be damned."

"Learn all that from a single array, did you?"

Softly, Arlo snorted.

"There's always a choice, Arlo," Alecto said next, bending her chin to her hands, exactly as Arlo had done. "And there's no magic in existence that can't be undone—a geas included. You would never have listened before, and I don't think I need to tell you now that Phoebus Viridian is a dangerous man. That he means nothing good in his quest for this power, and making that stone for him won't satiate his thirst in the least. He all but guaranteed you that they won't stop at the creation of one stone."

You did not work this hard for this long just to become your father . . .

Arlo's thoughts turned to the desk in his office.

To the letter he kept in its center drawer.

The only one he'd received from the person he suspected it to have come from, arriving by owl so late at night it was nearly morning, and at first Arlo had thought it was someone playing a prank on him. He'd thought it was their attempt to unnerve him in the hopes it would vacate his then newly won position.

It didn't take long for his suspicion to bend in a different direction, though.

For the letter hadn't been signed . . .

And it had been a number of years . . .

But there was no mistaking that handwriting—his entire child-hood had been taught by it.

> Phoebus Viridian is not your friend.
> The Crown he wears has changed him.
> He's a Gifted Silvertongue—will promise you the
> world, but it's that very world he means to use
> your knowledge and talents to win for his own.
> Do not make the same mistake as your
> predecessor in placing your absolute trust in him—
> for every luxury he will gild your life with, in the
> years to come, he will also weave beneath your
> feet an inescapable web, and when you're well
> and truly caught it in, he only has to tug a thread
> to bind you to his madness.

Phoebus was right about one thing—he hadn't worked this hard just to quit now, or to become his father, who might have sent that letter in warning, but had done nothing further to rescue his son from a situation no boy who'd just had everything stripped from him could possibly resist.

There could be a way out of this geas, but was that the path he was meant to take? The danger his family would still be in if he won his freedom aside, what Eos and Moros had charged him with . . . to become Pride, become the villain, in order to set things right? To destroy the Bone Crown . . . this suddenly seemed a far more impera-tive task than he'd originally understood. The evidence was all in that *look* in Phoebus's eyes, his insistence on chasing power, no matter the cost.

"You've made up your mind about something," Alecto mused, studying his face. "You have the look."

Arlo frowned. "I'm not sure. This sort of magic . . . what needs to be done . . ." He looked down at Apollo, and despite all his options, his hesitancies, his questions, he had a feeling he already knew what he would do. It just needed discussing with someone very specific first.

Someone who'd dabbled in the darkest of magics, and had . . . *somewhat* lived to tell the tale.

"I need to speak to Pallas Viridian."

CHAPTER 20

Celadon

‿⟡‿

D ESTROYED.

The Goblin Market had been *completely destroyed*, and even if Celadon hadn't been beyond intoxicated that night, there was nothing he could have done to stop it.

He was reeling.

The Hiraeth—gone. Their weapons stores and training facilities and base of operations—gone. The Wild's refuge; all those homes and livelihoods and schools and memories; the first and oldest of all the markets, a famous last remnant of faerie history; the UnSeelie Summer Court; the UnSeelie Autumn Court—everything gone, gone, gone, *gone*.

Thank Cosmin Nausicaä had arrived when she did.

There were entire species of folk in those woods that were now wholly extinct to this realm, with the Hiraeth so suddenly untethered from it, families and friends and lovers so used to moving between the two Wild spaces now forever and cruelly separated. But if it hadn't been for Nausicaä's quick action, her alarming display of power even Lethe had been in quiet awe of to witness, the casualties would have been so much higher.

In the very least, the well over eight hundred folk residing within the Market's walls had been transported to safety.

Three days later, and Celadon was currently experiencing the worst migraine of his life so far, trying to figure out where that vast number was going to go—many of the folk had been sentenced to exile by one sovereign or another, so it had to be somewhere in *his* territory they fit them. But since he was already trying to adjust Night's boundaries to lessen the impact of his Court on the Indigenous folk without displacing multiple generations of faeries and fae that called here home too now . . . it was a lot.

"This looks . . . cozy."

Celadon looked up from the spread of papers over his desk to find Theodore Reynolds standing in the doorway.

As much as Theodore claimed to prefer the comforts of palace life, it was clear these days (and growing clearer) how profoundly house arrest was wearing on his Hiraeth-raised sense of freedom. Theodore, who was normally so carefully groomed, every curl in its exact place and expensive clothing pressed and pristine, had a *wildness* about him now. A look in his eyes like he might start snapping his teeth at things for fun; a way of moving, like a panther pent up far too long in its far-too-small cage.

His clothing was tighter, less gaudy and more practical, as though he might take off at any moment, tearing through the streets of Toronto in a reckless burst of energy that would get him killed if he wasn't careful—Riadne hadn't just exiled Theodore; she'd placed him under Mark. Come nightfall, wherever he was, the Wild Hunt—which now technically included Arlo, if she was feeling particularly sour that day—would snatch him up the moment he left Celadon's immediate protection.

Without the Hiraeth for an outlet, Theodore was well and truly trapped until he died or their war was over—and a panic behind his deep brown eyes said as much had occurred to him, too.

"If you're going for shut-in academic in the middle of a manic episode, you're doing a very good job . . ." Theodore looked around, at the piles of books stacked anywhere Celadon could set them, with other random things stacked on top of them like vases of withered flowers, a bowl of soup he'd long forgotten, and about twenty cups of half-consumed tea that were maybe beginning to turn a bit sour, judging by the way his nose pinched at the bridge. "Perhaps we should . . . open a window?"

"Later," Celadon said dismissively as he straightened and ran a hand through disheveled hair like combing it would reorder his thoughts. "Since you're here, there's something I'd like to ask you— and Fyri. Please tell me Fyri made it out of the Goblin Market too?"

Nodding, Theodore entered the room.

Picked his way carefully through the mess to an armchair Lethe particularly favored and removed the stack of books there (capped with an old bit of toast) to seat himself on the cushion. "What can I do for you, Your Highness?" he asked, through no small amount of boredom, by now too used to his tasks being confined to things he could do around the palace and the Hiraeth, which was no more. "Was there something that needed researching in the library again— provided there's anything left there. All the devils are *here*, by the looks of it."

Already moving to gather materials, Celadon shook his head. "No," he replied absently. "No, I want you and Fyri to go with Rory to help him persuade a few more alchemists to our cause—Fyri is our hopeful ironborn ambassador, after all, and Rory is well respected from . . . past *infractions*. But neither of them are quite so good at personal relations as you are."

Theodore straightened, a spark of hope in his suddenly far sharper attentiveness. "Oh? You want *me* to go with them? As in, I get to leave the palace, and Toronto too?"

"It's entirely up to you, Theodore," Celadon replied, finally locating the paper he was after and snatching it from its pile. "I'm not keeping you here against your will. It's your only safety against Riadne and the Wild Hunt—" No Hunter would dare enter Lethe's territory, Riadne's Mark be damned. "But you aren't a prisoner. If you want to leave, the choice is yours. And Rory—good, Rory, you're here."

Theodore's head snapped to the side, only just now noticing their newest visitor, but Celadon was already crossing his office to hand Rory his sheet of paper. "There. That's all I have for you and Fyri, I'm afraid, but more than nothing to get on with. Every alchemist the High Council was keeping watch on."

Rory took the sheet of paper with his free hand, a quiet reservation about him that Celadon was going to ask after—until he realized what it was.

With the Hiraeth no more, this was the first time Rory had come to Celadon instead of the other way around; the first time standing in the place he'd once come with frequency back when his family had been whole.

"I . . ." he began, a little at a loss for what to say, but wanting to comment *something*. After all, Celadon understood: he had to stand every day in the halls his own family had once occupied. It was part of the reason he'd had the entire place gutted and redesigned.

But Rory merely shook his head, cleared his throat, turned to Theodore, and held up his other hand—the one that carried a peculiar-looking lantern, of thick, looping gold framing shimmery panes of frosted glass.

Brows drawing together in contemplation, Theodore studied what was held before him. "A lantern? A very pretty lantern, but—"

"It's called a Sunray lantern," Rory supplied, his melancholy giving way to excitement. "I found the array and specifics in Arlo's journal—not my Arlo, Nicholas's boy, but never mind that." He raised the lantern higher to show off the underneath. "You see here, on the bottom? Once activated, this seal will generate inside the walls of this sky-forged glass what is essentially a miniature, trapped sun, providing the one who carries it with genuine, constant sunlight."

Lowering the lantern once more, he tapped its array, and in all the span of a moment, just as he claimed, a tiny ball of brilliance began to grow within.

"I added some features—you can adjust the brightness like a touch lamp, anywhere up here." He pressed and held a finger to the lantern's hood; the sun grew brighter and brighter, until both Celadon and Theodore had to wince and turn away from it. Then Rory lifted his finger, applied it again; a moment later, the light grew dim down to an ember. "It will also stay lit now, rather than having to hand it back to me constantly to activate when needed, and should last until either the array is broken or the sun runs its natural life span. Which is about ten billion years, so . . ."

He handed it over to Theodore.

Sunlight in a jar.

When Rory had told Celadon he'd be able to make one no problem, so long as he could get his hands on the exceptionally rare glass, Celadon had requested one immediately and ensured Rory had everything he could need. Because with this, the Wild Hunt could follow Theodore all they liked, but its design had been for the exact purpose they needed it for now—none could touch him within sunlight's circle; the Wild Hunt, as beings of night, were vastly diminished by its counterpart and couldn't snatch away anyone who wasn't touching night's shadow.

"Like I said . . ." Celadon continued his speech from before Rory's arrival. "You aren't a prisoner here, and now armed with that, you should be more or less safe for small spells of time. I wouldn't press your luck, but . . ."

Shooting to his feet, Theodore could only stare at his gift.

A moment.

Two.

Then—"Oh, thank *gods*. It's only been days since the Hiraeth was unmoored, and if I had to spend even one more cooped up with you and your overprotective nightmare of a husband glaring at me any time I so much as breathe in your direction, I was contemplating throwing myself out one of your windows."

"Celadon!" Rory chimed. "I didn't know you'd gotten married—congratulations!"

"I did *not* get married," Celadon said sourly. "And don't call Lethe a—"

Theodore scrunched his nose. "Jeesh. You're *both* overprotective."

"Uh . . . is this a bad time?"

Celadon, Rory, and Theodore turned all in unison to Vehan, the next to fill Celadon's threshold.

He'd almost forgotten he'd summoned him too. Celadon hadn't seen his brother since his birthday party, though they'd been in constant contact since his return from the Sacred Realm.

In his slim-fit black cargo pants and tight, black, long-sleeved top that was the standard uniform of the tactical unit he was part of with Aurelian, Vehan looked so different to him these days. Older. Deadlier. Paired with his Class Four, possibly *Five* lightning ability and Luck's magic in his palm, he supposed "deadlier" was exactly what he was.

"UM, EXCUSE ME, *VEHAN'S* MARRIED THOUGH!" Theodore shouted so suddenly Celadon startled.

The dragon prince darted forward, grabbed Vehan's hand, and tugged him into the room by the wrist to thrust the appendage into closer view. "*Look*—oh my gods, Vehan. Who would want to marry *you?*"

"Why is this the *second* time someone's said this to me?"

"Vehan!" Celadon gasped, far less appalled than Theodore, more . . . surprised. "You never mentioned Aurelian proposed to you. When did this happen?"

He looked to Vehan's sapphire-flushing face. "Uh, really recently. At my birthday. There's . . . kind of been other stuff going on. I *was* going to tell you."

"Hey," he said softly, and closed their distance to hug him tightly. "Congratulations, little brother. I really am very happy for you. It's about time we had some *good* news."

Slowly, Vehan raised his hands to hug him back, and his face sank into Celadon's shoulder. "Thanks," he muttered against him.

A comfortable hush fell over the room, to give the two brothers this moment. Celadon was grateful—they didn't have many opportunities to be gentle with each other these days.

"Remember when you used to fantasize about marrying Celadon?" Theodore supplied when the silence wore longer than he apparently liked. "Remember when you use to—"

He started to perform an obscene motion up and down with his hand, but blessedly, Rory stepped in.

"All right, boys! Prince Reynolds and I must track down our Fyri and prepare ourselves for departure. Say goodbye, Theodore."

But Rory didn't give him the chance to so much as utter a syllable. He took him by the shoulders and steered him out the door, leaving Celadon and Vehan alone with each other.

Celadon cleared his throat. "I *am* happy for you."

Vehan's head dipped a little in embarrassment, but his repeated, quiet, "Thanks," was heartfelt. "What did you want to see me about?" he added, a little stronger. "I'm afraid I still haven't heard from Arlo since the Hiraeth. Have you?"

Shaking his head, Celadon straightened and waved his brother to his desk. "No, nothing from Arlo. I finally got a text from Nausicaä last night, though. My cousin is . . . not doing all that well. That fight with Tellis drained quite a lot from her. Nausicaä tells me that yesterday was the worst she's seen Arlo yet—not once did she surface from Ruin until nightfall, and even then . . . Arlo was very noticeably subdued."

He sighed.

Things were getting dire in every corner of his board.

Punching a hole through the Market, her fight with Tellis, and breaking her Crown all in quick succession? It had taken a heavy toll.

How much longer did they have before Celadon was forced to take action? If he cut her off mid-task, if Arlo missed destroying even one Crown, everything she'd been doing would be for nothing. Lethe was the only other immortal with a Titan's power that could and was willing to take over where she left off, but the whole reason they'd all needed Arlo to do this to begin with was because Lethe wasn't a recognized Greater God yet. Riadne aside, there was also still the Crown that Urielle possessed that needed destroying, and no way to reach it until Lethe was free from the restrictions that bound him in the minor role of a Hunter, and strong enough to strike against a fellow Greater immortal.

Did Arlo have it in her to last another battle against an amplified goddess?

"Which is why I have a request of you," Celadon added, choosing his next words carefully. "A dangerous request—the only type, it seems, that I've been making lately. But with everything going on, and Arlo where she is . . . I'm extremely worried about her. We need a way to check on her for ourselves, more than what Nausicaä is able to provide. And I feel like, additionally, we could use a pair of eyes on the inside to scope out what's building to march on us."

"You want me to sneak back into the palace."

Celadon nodded. "Yes. As I hear it, you were still popping in on Mother on occasion—don't worry, I'm not upset with you, although it was exceptionally risky to do that all alone, not telling anyone . . ." He paused to fix Vehan with an older brother's admonishing glare. "But that die of yours makes you better equipped than anyone else for this bit of infiltration. You can disguise yourself, where Nausicaä would only put up everyone's guard. And you know your way around the palace better than anyone. *And* . . ." He paused again, failed. His heart clenched in his chest to even speak it, but they were running out of time, and a reality would soon have to be faced that he didn't think he would ever be ready for. "You also know Arlo. You know what to look for. You know how to gauge if enough is enough, and we need to step in or risk losing her for good."

Vehan nodded—agreement, just like that. "Of course I'll go. When would you like?"

"As soon as possible. Tonight, if you can manage."

"I'll talk to Aurelian, then. Let him know."

"Thank you," Celadon breathed out in relief, and finally retook his seat behind his desk—it was back to more damned planning after this, and his temples were starting to pound.

It was the thoughtful hum low in Vehan's throat that alerted him his brother hadn't taken his leave yet.

Looking back up from where his gaze had dropped to endless books and papers, he braced himself. "Is there something *you* needed to discuss?"

"Celadon . . ." Vehan sighed, relaxing his posture a little on the word. The look he gave Celadon now was obvious in its concern. "Have you had *any* rest at all these past four months? I mean, you've been running yourself ragged taking everything onto your shoulders. Rebuilding your Court, contending with Mother, meeting with the other Courts and your generals and who knows who else on your own time, keeping track of Arlo . . . then the battle with the ifrit, and that assassination attempt on the harbor, and now over eight hundred people displaced and in need of a home. I know you're *basically* a god, but . . ."

Snorting, Celadon waved a hand. "It's fine, Vehan. I'm fine, don't worry. Of course I'm tired—who isn't, these days? This is simply the burden that comes with a crown—something you'll find out for yourself, if you accept what we've discussed?"

It wasn't something he overly wanted to broach right now, with everything else going on, but he *was* curious—had Vehan made any sort of decision, one way or another, in the matter of becoming King of Day if they won out over their mother? It wasn't that he didn't know Theodore would do splendidly in this position, and very much wanted it, but this was his *brother*—the trust and connection between them was something no one else would be able to replicate.

Vehan gave him a rueful little half smile and shook his head. "I think you already know that isn't where my heart is anymore."

Yes.

Celadon figured as much.

And with Theodore so interested in the position, with the proper training and pedigree to boot, it wasn't a complete loss that Vehan was going to abdicate the Seelie throne when this was all over.

But still, it would have been nice to rule together, brother with brother.

"I simply won't put Aurelian through that again," Vehan explained, firm if also apologetic. "For years he stood by my side in a place he hated, among people who hated *him*. Everything Aurelian's ever done has, for the most part, been for me, and now that he's finally where *he* wants to be . . . it's my turn to stand beside him."

Nodding, Celadon leaned back in his chair. "I do understand, Vehan. I get it. I—"

He had someone of his very own he'd give up quite a lot for if it meant protecting him from trauma relived.

A someone who stood, silent as shadow, in the open expanse of his office doorway, wearing concern in his expression too.

Confusion flexed across Vehan's face, and he turned around, spotted Lethe behind him, and stiffened a little . . . "I'll leave you two to it, then," he replied, looking back to Celadon. "Make sure you get some rest."

"I will, Vehan. And good luck with tonight."

Nodding, Vehan left, and silence swelled in his wake.

"What's the matter?" Celadon hedged when Lethe made no move to enter farther into the room and that look on his face didn't smooth away. "If something else has happened, please, I'm begging you to keep it to yourself for just . . . an hour? A year?"

Lethe shook his head. "No," he replied. "Nothing has happened. I was merely . . . thinking."

"Ah," said Celadon, unable to help himself. "Yes, I can see how that would be a cause for all that concern."

Lethe lifted a brow, a glint of something playful striking through his bright green eyes, but other than this, he didn't bite. For once. "Did you know," he said instead, "that souls tend to stick together? That each time a person is reborn, it's in some way, shape, or fashion with the souls it collected as important to them in their previous lives? There are exceptions, of course. Additions and subtractions depending on the choices you make, but ultimately—essentially—you know your *truest* friendships through every lifetime."

Oh?

Celadon hadn't known that, in fact.

But where was this coming from? Why had Lethe focused on that particular piece of obscure information now, of all times.

And as ever, as though Lethe could read his thoughts—and maybe he could, in a fashion, with how close they'd grown over the last few months—his Hunter shook his head. "I'm struck by it, on occasion. How very long I've been alive. How very similar certain people are to the ones they were before." He frowned now, down at the carpet, as he did when truly absorbed in his thoughts. "The Vehan of this incarnation . . . I can't say for certain, but given what I know, I believe that Fate withholding you so long from reincarnation forced the universe to fill a void. I believe, given the strength of your attachment to our Arlo, that *you* were meant to be *his* companion, back when Arlo was Nicholas's boy. I believe, given the strength of *Vehan's* attachment to Arlo as well, that he became your placeholder. Whoever he was meant to be, originally, before Fate's meddling forced his path in a new direction . . ."

That acid gaze lifted, much clearer than before.

"I can't decide the use of that information, though. Like I said, the occurrence of this thought is fleeting—the princeling strikes it, here and there. I rarely saw the first Arlo Flamel without Hyperion Lysterne."

"You like Arlo," Celadon observed, so suddenly it almost startled him to realize he'd been the one to speak it. "Genuinely."

Lethe cocked his head in Celadon's direction. "Of course I do."

"Why?"

They'd never really spoken about it—his gravitation to Arlo. Yes, Lethe needed her because of her destiny, if he was to lay claim to his, but it struck Celadon as a little bit more than this when the matter of Arlo arose.

But again Lethe merely peered at him as though Celadon were being obtuse on purpose. "Because she is yours," he replied slowly, again as though it were obvious. "A soul *can* know more than one bond, and certainly more than romantic attachment. Why shouldn't I like Arlo Flamel, when you *love* her, and I love—"

The sudden

ringing

silence.

Lethe caught himself just before he could finish his statement, and if Celadon had been holding anything, it would have shattered on the ground.

Slowly, he rose to standing.

Circled his desk to cross the room and approach Lethe, who looked to be debating whether or not to flee through the door.

"At the harbor," Celadon began, low and careful, like speaking too loudly might break whatever spell held Lethe in place.

At the mention of that night, anger flexed across Lethe's face. "One night I left you to see to my Hunt, and Fate took full advantage. It should have been *her* face I carved off and fed to the water she stole me from."

"Lethe," Celadon soothed, drawing closer—enough that he could place his hand on the sharp bone of Lethe's hip. Those black training joggers Lethe taken to wearing for practice lessons . . . the absurdity of how normal it made him look . . . how *appealing* . . . "I'm all right," he reminded him. "You arrived in time. And Aurelian worked wonders on my shoulder."

"Mmm," Lethe hummed through a hint of lingering agitation . . . and a flash of . . . was that jealousy?

He snorted. "I feel like I should clarify that never, not once, despite the rumors I'm assuming you heard, did I ever actually kiss Aurelian Bessel—"

Lethe swept in—claimed a kiss of his own that bit Celadon's lips, sudden and only *just* verging on rough.

Unable to help himself, Celadon leaned into it, opened his mouth against the flash-fire of Lethe's consuming need. With little coaxing, Lethe deepened his possessive display, danced long fingers up the curve of Celadon's lower back, only to splay them just so and *push* the two of them flush at the snap of their hips.

He angled his head . . .

Opened his mouth wider . . .

When one of his teeth caught on Celadon's lower lip, it spilled a pinprick of warm blood between their tongues. The delighted moan that rumbled in the depths of Lethe's throat when he tasted it . . .

"Jealous," Celadon gasped out in breaks of their lips. "Of *Aurelian*. He'll be thrilled to know it."

"By all means," Lethe growled, pulling back, irritation spurring his possessive streak, to snap teeth at Celadon's mouth. "Do keep saying his name as you pant against me. It only endears him to me more."

Breathing out a soft laugh, Celadon dropped his forehead to Lethe's chin—rested it there, while he gathered himself. It wasn't often Lethe initiated these things, but there were occasions when his desires got the better of him, and Celadon . . . didn't mind.

He liked kissing Lethe very much, he discovered.

Almost as much as he liked to be the one to unravel him.

But nowhere near as much as it pleased him to hear what Lethe had just about uttered twice now.

"You called me *aulea* back at the harbor, Lethe. Do you remember?"

Hands drew up Celadon's back to hold him, light but secure against him.

Lethe sighed. "*Treasure*. Yes." Those arms held fast, but Celadon could feel the way Lethe's heart raced in his chest—nervously.

"I won't make you say it," Celadon consoled, dipping inward to press a kiss to the soft of Lethe's throat. "It makes you uncomfortable. But I want you to know that—"

"I love you."

Silence again.

Perfectly still in Lethe's hold, Celadon could only breathe, his own heart racing now.

Had he really just said it? Or had Celadon misheard—invented the sound of those words in that voice he so longed to hear, but understood why Lethe had reservations about them. Not that he didn't care about Celadon, but Lethe had so little practice with the feeling. Much like Celadon with desire, that emotion simply didn't exist to him without profound and lengthy connection.

"I have told you before, you may wish I did not, and it will never be the simpering romance that others attach to the meaning. But I do. Irrevocably. And if you ever terrify me the way you did that night you turned down Pallas's escort home . . ."

"Lethe . . ." Celadon whispered, so overcome with emotion he could barely lend sound to the word.

What he'd been about to say . . .

I love you, too.

We're at war, Lethe, against a woman who oscillates between wanting to cage me and kill me. I fear there are far more ways for me to terrify you before the end of this . . .

He didn't get the chance to find out.

The palace *shuddered*, as harshly as though an earthquake had just rocked beneath them, sending Celadon toppling against Lethe and forcing Lethe to scramble to catch him before he crashed to the ground . . .

Along with the room's books.

Along with Celadon's trinkets and collectables and decorations.

A painting on the far wall clattered loudly to the floor; a mirror wobbled off a cabinet and shattered to pieces on the carpet.

One quake . . .

Two . . .

The second hit even harder than the first, and almost exactly the moment it was done, like the earth was trying to crack itself apart down to its very core.

"What the *hells* is going on?" he yelled over the din.

CHAPTER 21

Aurelian

❦

"HOLLLLLYYYYYY *FUCK*," ROSALIE BREATHED, stepping toward the wall of glass that separated them from the city.

Three days, and they'd had to scramble to find a new location to establish their base of operations. The palace would have done in a pinch, there was quite a lot of room, but most of Aurelian's units were composed of the Wild folk, and as much as the Wild was willing to join forces with a sidhe fae king, they did prefer to have their own space dedicated to training and surveillance.

Their new headquarters was an enormous shard of a building not far from Celadon's House of Night, as his teams had taken to calling it. Eighty-six floors including the rooftop—enough to house those displaced from the Market *and* run Aurelian's operations, at least until more suitable accommodations could be secured.

They'd been deep in the middle of sorting through the nine separate reports of demon activity that had come in this morning—twenty-three in total the day before, sixteen before that. All of them urgent, all of them requesting immediate backup and supplies, with portals popping up clear across the world to spill out their monsters in such density the independent rebel outfits couldn't keep up on their own.

But Aurelian didn't have that many units to spare.

Even if he parsed them down to pairs, he wouldn't be able to answer all the desperate pleas for assistance—he and Ivandril, and a few of the goblins who'd been high in the ranks of the Market's Watch, had been debating the order of who to answer when the first shock wave rocked through their building.

Ceiling tiles rattled.

Computer monitors flickered.

Supplies and cups and trays and books clattered to the floor.

Aurelian had braced himself firmly on the table they'd been bent over, planning, but Rosalie, with absolutely no sense of self-preservation, had wandered over to the full-paneled wall of windows.

The shock wave hadn't lasted long.

Did Toronto get many earthquakes?

He tried to think on the answer to this, but his brain kept circling unhelpfully to where Vehan was right now, and whether he was all right.

Pushing a swell of concern through their bond, he relaxed slightly when, quickly, a pulse of reassurance was sent back in return.

"Aurelian . . ." Ten now. They'd moved to join their girlfriend once the tremor passed. "Boss? You, ah . . . you want to come see this?"

No.

No, he did not.

Whatever it was, with everything that had happened at the Market; the proceeding battle with a goddess in the Immortal Realm; attempting to relocate over eight hundred folk; and now all these damned demon reports keeping them running morning and night, Aurelian did *not* want even one more thing heaped on top of this, like the tone of Ten's voice suggested would happen the moment he joined them.

"Woooooow." Tiffin.

"Gods." Jaxon.

Leaf, Aurelian's steadfast woodsprite, who seemed to like only their wolf-boy faerie, landed on Jaxon's shoulder, delicate wings drooping as she gaped at the scene outside.

A look shared quickly with Ivandril, Aurelian straightened and crossed the room as well.

"If that's a fucking portal, I am tendering my resignation. Which I hope is fancy lingo for 'I quit,' because . . ." Even Rosalie had run out of words for what this was. Because . . .

Aurelian tore away from the glass.

"I want every news station in Intelligence on those monitors," he commanded to one of the goblins as he fled, making for the stairwell.

"Aurelian!" Theodore called, racing up the staircase toward him, Rory Flamel and Fyri both hot on his heels. "Aurelian, what the hells just happened—what was that?"

The prince had probably been on his way to see them when the shock wave hit. Celadon must have already apprised him of what he'd wanted the three of them to do, and no doubt they'd stopped here first to gather whatever equipment they'd need.

But Aurelian didn't have time to pause.

He took the flights two steps at a time.

Rosalie, Ten, Jaxon, Tiffin, Leaf . . . they'd followed him right out to the hall, up and up the stairs as well, collecting Theodore and his troop, the mass of them speeding up to the roof.

Aurelian wanted a better look at this.

He needed to see with his own two eyes how far this damage stretched.

Out on the slab of concrete boxed in by a waist-high wall, Aurelian threw himself at the north side of the building, exactly where they'd just been inside.

The winter wind was biting—made his eyes water, his skin prickle with cold, his breath seal tight in his throat . . . or perhaps that last one was a reaction to the gravity of their situation, laid full and clear down below them.

"Cosmin's *balls* . . ."

Yeah.

Aurelian very much echoed Ten's statement.

The crack that had just opened in the pavement, the rock, the earth, was a line that wrapped entirely around the heart of Toronto with the House of Night caught in its fold.

It curved down around the CN Tower and up toward Simon & Schuster, then arched up and through St. James Town, around Casa

Loma, through Little Italy and—perhaps most devastating to Celadon when he learned it—the Fashion District too, all to connect full circle back again at the CN Tower.

Smoke and dust and tiny fires, sparking wires and blown transfuser boxes . . . sirens and screams and panic and cries . . .

The crack was a crevice that looked from this distance to be Aurelian's width four times over, and who could even say how deep.

It crossed through buildings, though streets, through homes . . . The only reason they hadn't felt more than the nearest building's collapse was thanks to the powerful enchantments and wards he, Celadon, Ivandril, and several others of his Wild company had woven over both this building and the palace as extra protection—half the city could blow up and none of them would even know if no one bothered to look out the window.

"Aurelian, what the fuck do we do?" Rosalie panicked.

"This can't be a portal," Jaxon said, eyes grown wide. "Aurelian, it's wrapped clear around us! We're trapped!"

"We can't take on that many demons—we just sent half our forces abroad!"

"Aurelian—"

Aurelian, Aurelian, Aurelian, *Aurelian*—their fears echoed in his head, and Aurelian had no answers. His mind was numb. He couldn't move, couldn't think beyond the dread rising up inside him.

Riadne.

This had to be Riadne.

She'd called start to their battle, and followed through—*was* this a portal? Nothing had poked up or come through so far, but any moment . . . any minute . . . any second now, it could . . .

What were they going to do?

What was *he* going to do?

Rosalie, Ten, Jaxon, Tiffin, Leaf . . . his people were all depending on *him*, and Aurelian had no answers to give.

You're okay.

It's okay.

Take a deep breath, Aurelian, and focus.

Vehan.

It was Vehan, as always, as ever would be—his best friend, his first love, his soulmate, his soon-to-be husband.

Not so much words—these were feelings he sent, picking up on Aurelian's distress and sending back exactly what Aurelian needed to center himself.

Aurelian swallowed.

A hand—gentle, the hint of electric warmth at the fingertips—slipped onto his shoulder.

"Aurelian?"

He turned his head to meet Theodore's gaze, and he couldn't explain it . . . something about Theodore had changed from the last time he'd looked at him.

This was Theodore almost as he'd never seen him before and, at the same time, as he'd always known him: tall, regal, with an ease of confidence straight in his back, his intelligent brown eyes bright with focus. Every cut of him was sharper, his airs carried suddenly far studier weight, and his magic against Aurelian's was at once invigorating and soothing.

"What's the one thing every *good* king knows? And I don't mean a benevolent king; I mean an effective one."

It was hard to school his panic-unraveled thoughts, but the longer he stared into Theodore's steady gaze, the calmer he felt himself becoming.

"I . . ." he began, searching for an answer. "Don't know. When to strike?" he guessed, but what did he strike at? If this was Riadne making her move, what did he do to contend with it? How was he meant to hit back?

But Theodore shook his head. "The very opposite. A good king is an *alive* king, Aurelian. He knows how and when to *delegate*." The hand slipped from Aurelian's shoulder to clasp wrists behind his back, and Aurelian could see it.

He'd always known Theodore would do well with a throne, but this was the first time he actually saw him in this role.

"You and all your pretty muscles are very good at action. But that's not where your energy needs to be right now. Where it should be is . . ."

He held Theodore's gaze one good minute longer . . . then turned to Rosalie.

"We need to call an emergency meeting," he said, waving her to him as he pushed from the ledge to make back for the stairs. "Theodore's right: we need to strategize. I want every power, every general, every leader under Celadon's banner in our war room in half an hour, by any means necessary. Video call, astral projection, a bargain with the human devil himself, it doesn't matter; I just want them there. Tell them Riadne's got her board up and running—we're going to do the exact fucking same."

"Do you mind if I sit here?"

Bright crimson eyes regarded him sharply over a goblet of viscous red liquid as Arlo stood with his hands on the back of a vacant chair at Pallas Viridian's private, tucked-away table.

It hadn't been easy to locate Phoebus's younger brother, even through use of magical means. Given the little Arlo knew of the man, from rumor of what he'd been like—social, vain, and more than a little delinquent—before he'd become *this*, he'd had his misgivings at first that the *king of vampires* was actually here . . . some hole-in-the-wall, shabby human tavern whose patrons all seemed of the roguish sort, to phrase it mildly.

Yet here Pallas was.

In a simple, cheap tunic, no adornments or jewels or otherwise indication of the station he'd been stripped of upon his fall from grace. Beautiful in hints, startling on the whole—paper-thin skin that had been sunny golden in every portrait Arlo had seen of him, now drained to the pallor of death; russet hair that gleamed bright as brass against it; sharp bones and cutting features and incisors elongated to fangs, currently bared at Arlo's request.

"Arlo Flamel—my darling brother's prized possession, come to waste himself with the dregs?"

This surprised him.

Given that his entanglement with dark magic had happened slightly before Arlo's birth, he hadn't assumed Pallas would know him at all.

"Oh, please," Pallas drawled, leaning back in his chair, his expression morphing into cool disdain in response to the shock on Arlo's face. "You do rather announce yourself. Who, in our world, does not know the High King's young, red-haired alchemist? You're nearly as famous as he is—and I'm sure that disagrees with him terribly." He pursed his bloodless lips, pale gray as stone. "Regardless, I'm in no such mood to entertain whatever it is he's sent you for. Lovely as you are, tonight is for wallowing and brooding self-reflection; I shan't be dissuaded from it by any pretty face."

Unable to help the grin on his face, Arlo shook his head.

"You mistake my presence. I've not been sent on your brother's behalf, though what brings me does concern him. The matter is quite . . . delicate, and you're the only person I know who can truly appreciate the predicament. Five minutes of your time—this is all I ask. Allow me to explain myself, and if after you want nothing further to do with this conversation, I will take my troubles and go."

Pallas lifted his goblet back to his lips.

It couldn't be blood, though it looked a great deal like it. This wasn't a faerie space, and besides, no creature apart from what Pallas had become was sustained by such a diet; it wouldn't be stocked, either way.

"I have not been a part of Court politics in some time," he said quietly, over the rim of his cup. "Whatever you think I can illuminate for you—"

Arlo slapped a piece of paper on the table, face up to reveal the wholly complete and perfected philosopher's stone array.

Pallas looked down at it, awareness beginning to weigh heavy, heavy, heavier on his brow the longer he looked, the more he understood.

"Five minutes," Arlo repeated. "You are the only soul in existence that has survived the cost of the magic in which I may be forced to deal myself. Our descents into darkness differ. Alchemy did not deliver you to those fangs, but you recognize evil; you've seen this before, exactly as it is here. *Five minutes*—allow me to confide in you the whole ugliness of my story. I have come only for advice, but if you wish not to give it at the end of what I have to say, I *will* leave you be—on my word. Please."

Red eyes traveling up from the paper, Pallas frowned even deeper—but the slightest brush of his hand manipulated the air to push Arlo's chair out in invitation.

"To defy the geas that binds you would be foolish," Pallas said, after far longer than five minutes, and with a great deal of gravity in his voice. "Should you somehow survive the toll of such a betrayal, there would be no reaches of this earth where you could flee to with your family that would save you from my brother's ire. It is no option."

Arlo pressed his lips flat together. "It's not. I must make this stone. Which is what the scions want, but then, they *don't* want the rest of the stones to be made, or the Sins' power to fall into the Council's hands. Which it will, if I make the first stone, so you can see my confusion here."

Nodding, Pallas toyed with the edge of the paper between them. "Have you tried asking for clarification?"

"Yes." Arlo huffed a derisive laugh. "I've called on the scions many times in attempt to speak with them again. The array that brought them the first time simply will not power, no matter what I do. I can only assume it means they cannot impart any more than they have."

"They do not wish to run afoul of Fate."

Arlo looked at him quizzically.

With a sigh, Pallas eased himself into a more comfortable sprawl in his chair. "They have put this task to you. I suspect it was not something they were supposed to do, but it has been done, and is now part of your destiny. Which means the path they wish you to take will be a natural occurrence, if you work out how to get there—any further tampering on their part to nudge you along the way could earn them grounds for Destruction."

It was easy to forget.

Pallas looked so much younger than Phoebus, despite the fact they were so close in age—and especially for the hundreds of years that had passed in their lives so far. The curse of his dark magic preserved him as he'd been when he'd committed his sin, but Pallas had been alive for the First Great War against the gods. He understood them a little better than anyone born after, such as Arlo.

Swallowing down his surprise with a gulp of ale from his own tankard, Arlo shuddered, then . . . not exactly pouted, but it was far too sulking to be labeled a frown. "My only hint is that I must become the villain. But when Phoebus claims to ensure my name goes down in honor and glory, I don't see how that's possible. I create the stone and bring this evil into the world, but if everyone sees it as a tool of protection . . ."

"Perhaps that is the issue," Pallas mused, drawing the array toward him once more. "*Perception.* It is not, I think, the *world* you must turn against you. You're a Lysterne; cunning is in your blood—so put it to use, boy. How does one deliver to the Council what they *want*, and yet foil all their plans in the delivery?"

. . . Oh.

Arlo was a little ashamed of himself—to have prided himself for so long on his cognitive prowess, and still he'd missed it. The glaringly obvious solution to his problem. "I have to become a villain to the *Council.*"

"And no doubt, once you do, they will happily smear your name through history on your behalf, far better than you could on your own."

"I have to make them the stone," Arlo continued, unable to stop now that he'd pushed past this block. "And I have to do it in a way that renders it useless to them after, along with all my research . . ."

But how?

. . . *Oh.*

Yes . . . that would work.

Arlo surfaced from his thoughts to meet Pallas's gaze. "I don't actually know how to thank you for this. This has been . . . tremendously helpful."

Pallas merely shook his head.

A look came over him—thoughtful, nostalgic, sad. "Thanks enough will be your success," he replied after a long moment. "What you do is supposed to result in the correction of imbalance. That Crown, I think . . . the one he wears." The Bone Crown, he must mean, but Arlo didn't dare interrupt for clarification, not when Pallas's expression had worn down to such exhaustion. "You will do this. You will succeed. It may not be in time to rescue my brother from the clutches of that power that has changed him so—you see it now; I saw it long ago, almost the minute that offensive object touched his head. For the ones who will inherit it after . . . yes, success will be thanks enough."

Swallowing, wordless, Arlo nodded.

CHAPTER 22

Vehan

NOT ONCE IN HIS lifetime had the Luminous Palace ever entered a state of emergency. Dressed now as it was for war, Vehan hardly recognized the space when he stepped through Celadon's Egress and into the Endless Corridor as he'd never seen it before.

Every door but one was barred with slabs of iron, so dense they made his skin itch just to stand in their proximity.

The lighting had dimmed considerably, to divert power to the Head of the Court, pulling great swaths of shadow across ceiling and floor.

The tiny gold suns inlaid in the marble walls had sunken down behind the clouds etched around them, which had grown dark and stormy, and crackled with sparks of real electricity—a safety feature that would have been initiated clear through the palace. It was meant to give the sovereign stores to pull from wherever they were, should conflict breech the grounds.

What surprised him, though, wasn't the gloomy transformation of his home.

Both he and Celadon had been highly suspicious when Vehan laid out the terms for his venture here tonight and his die asked for only a two to secure them—the lowest number he could roll other than critical failure.

And true enough, here he stood, not a single person—guard or otherwise—in sight to make him.

Where was everyone?

Riadne had to know there'd been at least *some* form of espionage at some point, given that Celadon had found out about her planned attack on Unseelie Summer. And between Nausicaä and Lethe both able to teleport wherever they wished now and glamour themselves with immortal magic, it would be foolish of his mother to assume they wouldn't use that to their advantage—and his mother was many things, but a fool certainly wasn't one.

This door left unbarred was no oversight in security.

Perhaps it was merely entry and exit narrowed to one for ease of patrol. Or perhaps his mother wanted to funnel anyone who dared come through here uninvited to a particular place in the palace.

Whatever the reason, Vehan made for it regardless. He had his die, luck in his favor, and fairly decent camouflage with this Bone Guard general armor. So long as Ruin had kept to themselves that Vehan had been caught sneaking in here, there was little reason for his mother to anticipate *him*, and no cause for close examination from anyone else—provided he play his part.

Eyes forward, back straight, leisurely confidence in his gait—no one would suspect him for an imposter. He'd spent his entire life around these people and could mimic their mannerisms to the mildest quirk of the brow.

The halls of the palace were just as deserted, everything quiet and still, nothing and no one on the other side of the doors he passed, at least the ones that weren't locked or otherwise barred to his investigation.

Jewels and gilt glinted darkly in their shadowed corners, catching the fissures-like threads of lightning in the walls. Gloom clung thickly in the spaces between windows looking out over chilly night, where fat flakes of snow drifted lazily from the sky and melted to icy water on the slick palace grounds.

Vehan's breath formed crystals in the air as he walked. Wherever he was being led, he hoped it was a little warmer there. Why his mother had let it grow this cold in the palace to begin with . . . She was a fae with Winter in her blood, yes, but she was Summer through and through, had always preferred the warmer climates.

"What are you doing?"

Vehan froze—it had nothing to do with the temperature.

He couldn't say how he knew what he would find when he turned around. The voice was completely unrecognizable to him. Perhaps close as possible to the genuine sound—his mother had never been known to skimp on details—but even if it was, Vehan had no memory of how his father's voice had actually sounded . . . but it was him all the same standing behind him. Vehan's mouth flooded with the sour-saliva threat of nausea.

Vadrien looked at him.

Vehan stared back, trying his best to control his breathing, the hysteria he felt every time his thoughts even crept toward what his mother had done building like ice in his chest.

There was no flicker of recognition in those disturbingly cloudy eyes, no sign that he was cognizant of himself or his surroundings at all. And the way he held his stance, so stiff and awkward, like every movement fought against the body's varying stages of rigor mortis . . .

It was horrendous to look at.

Unconscionable, that his mother had thought in any stretch of sanity that this was not only okay but something that would have appealed to her sons.

"All generals of the Bone Guard are to assemble at the throne."

For a moment longer, all Vehan could do was continue to stare at this man, who, as an assembled whole, looked close enough—so damned close—to the Vadrien in every picture he had of him that the part of Vehan desperately disassociating from reality was actually fairly impressed.

Then he realized what this thing had just said.

"Uh . . . what?"

"All generals of the Bone Guard are to assemble at the throne."

This took a moment to land.

There'd been a reason he'd chosen this uniform, specifically. He hadn't done so lightly. There would be far more suspicion surrounding the disappearance of a general's uniform, for one, and a far better chance at being caught out when this pool of faces was so much smaller, for another. But the extra protection this rank afforded him . . . no one would stop to ask a general what they were doing. As executors of Riadne's deadliest assignments, they'd earned a certain reputation that trailed fear wherever they went. If someone did look closer at him, they would be less inclined to ask for proof of who he was lest that proof come in the form of their own head.

Tonight, though . . . had his choice worked in or against his favor?

"Um . . . right. I'm . . . ah, I was just on my way."

Thank goodness this thing he refused to call his father didn't really seem to understand him. Most likely, if Vehan had argued the point or revealed himself as an imposter, he'd learn very quickly how skilled it doubtlessly would be in exterminating him.

For now it merely stared at him.

Cocked its head.

Turned abruptly and started off back down the hall, didn't so much as look to see if Vehan followed, but he got the impression it was expected he did.

There was something so disturbing about the way it moved, as though the limbs were controlled by strings Vehan couldn't see, as though they fought against the unnatural life that compelled them.

And the way it dipped in and out of the shadows, between the streams of moonlight through the windows . . . like it was vanishing and reappearing farther on ahead.

Silently, Vehan trailed the creature.

He didn't like his chances of passing unrecognized a second time in his mother's presence, but hopefully since the die had asked so little from his luck, he would be able to sink into the ranks of the other generals without incident and observe whatever was going on.

At last, they came to the doors to his mother's throne room.

It was strange to see it completely unguarded, no one lined up outside waiting in hope for an audience. Vehan had almost gotten used to the increased activity as the new head Court. To see this space now quiet and completely empty . . . oddly, it filled him with more dread than anything else tonight.

So when the creature pushed open the doors and light spilled in a flood at his feet, he very nearly hesitated, had to fight the compulsion to turn and run back to the Egress. Back to Aurelian and Celadon and familiarity and . . . well, *relative* safety, because they weren't quite sure yet what the circle cracked open around the House of Night meant, but probably nothing good.

But his Not Father crossed into the room, one disjointed, awkward step in front of the other, and if Vehan wanted to keep his cover, he'd have to remain close in the shield of his shadow.

Head tucked down, he followed into the very worst place he could be.

"—it's the numbers I care about, not years of experience."

"The Vor'Urc have numbers aplenty, Your Majesty."

Vehan nearly stumbled on his way to file himself behind the group of Bone Guard warriors, off to the left of the surprisingly crowded room.

The *Vor'Urc.*

He couldn't see who stood ground level at Riadne's platform, not over the numerous heads in front of him, but it was bad enough that even *one* of the Vor'Urc was present.

The orc tribes were all notoriously dangerous, however dwindled the count of them.

It was the Vor'Urc that stood as worst, though. They'd been the ones to join up with the goblins during the war and very nearly turned the tides in their favor.

Orcs were vicious, bloodthirsty, enormous juggernauts of thick muscle and gruesome features, with peculiar magic that could send them into a berserker sort of rage during battle that made them unhinged levels of dangerous.

In the same family and genus as ogres, adding insult to injury was that they were also unfathomably intelligent on top of this. So when the Vor'Urc had declared themselves allies of the goblin cause, that one tribe alone had been such a formidable threat to the Courts that they'd pulled out *everything* in their arsenal to combat it—even permitting alchemists to enlist as soldiers.

And even then, the only reason they'd won was because the Courts had been fighting as a unified front.

More and more, this hopeless feeling like a vise in his chest tightened further and further—how were they expected to win this new war when *orcs* were among the least of their concerns?

"They will be ready for the morning?"

Morning.

Vehan sucked in an involuntary breath.

They were preparing to strike *tomorrow morning*—that was hours away! Not the days they'd been hoping, but *hours*.

"Of course, Your Majesty. We've haste aplenty too, when the situation calls for it. You may count my ax among your allies."

Hells.

Vehan *had* to survive this—if only because he had to warn Celadon what was coming, and when. An army of demons and ifrit and Vor'Urc orcs, Ruin and Riadne and her Bone Crown at the helm of it all . . .

"Raibeart Each-Uisge," Riadne said next. Seated up high on her throne, she presided over this meeting resplendent in her enchanted glass-shard battle gear, her Sins worn across her waist like a jeweled belt.

Vehan had no idea what or who Raibeart was, but an each-uisge . . . they were water-horse faeries of the Wild, often mistaken for kelpies, but so much deadlier. The force of their compulsion was almost as strong as Riadne's Magnetism, and this paired with the ability to shape-shift into handsome men, among other forms, made their hunt for human flesh far too easy.

The Bone Guard in front of Vehan shifted uncomfortably at the mere mention of the one that apparently stood among them, and a couple of Riadne's advisors took a step back in the crowd.

"King of Swamps. As you are no doubt aware, your brother, Eanraig, recently ran afoul of my son and his *paramour*, and very deeply disgraced me," Riadne continued imperiously. "Her Highness Alanthe has quite the distaste for working with those of us on land. Some trite excuse, some poor little boy she lost to us eons ago. Hardly worth the fuss she's struck up over it, the *moping*—displeased though I am with your late kin, I do hope *our* relationship hasn't become tarnished in result? I trust that you and the forces you've promised to my army possess no such ridiculous reservations as the Sea Queen's?"

"No such reservations at all," replied the each-uisge—Raibeart . . . and apparently, royalty. His voice made Vehan's skin crawl, struck him with the sensation of slimy seaweed against his skin, and was at the same time almost impossible to ignore, there was such a haunting quality to its depths. "And as for my brother, one can hardly mourn the inconsequential; it does sound as though he rather got what was coming to him. My true brethren and ilk—those of us who cling to the fringes, lurking in the murky depths, the mer of the Mire—we are yours to command, however you see fit. As we speak, they already begin to spill to your front lines."

"*Lovely*. And how does—"

An echoing gasp from the collection of onlookers interrupted whatever Riadne was going to ask next.

Fae scattered, parting like spooked fish right down to where Vehan stood, clearing his view to the center of the room.

He could see without obstruction now, the hulking, blue-green body of the Vor'Urc war general, black hair shaved on the sides and groomed down the middle to stand like the helmet of an ancient Roman soldier.

The each-uisge he could see now as well, a tall, awkwardly shaped man, whose warpedness reminded him strongly of Lethe, like his real body had been forced into the shell of a human he presented—long black hair, tangled with seaweed, that dripped and dripped in a puddle at his feet; skin the pale, mottled green of decaying flesh; clouded blue eyes . . .

He was extraordinarily handsome, in such a false way that Vehan suspected what laid beneath was a horror he never wanted to see.

And he was staring directly at Vehan . . .

But it was neither of these foul folk the crowd backed away from.

It was *Ruin* that sent them scattering, shuffling back, pressing themselves to the walls and shadows as they turned sharply on their heels, from the company they stood with, and stalked purposefully toward where Vehan stood rooted to the spot.

He couldn't move.

"Spy," Ruin announced like a silken threat, and Vehan's heart leaped into his throat.

He couldn't move.

His feet wouldn't work.

He was *terrified*, and the whole room was watching, looking too closely! With Ruin clearly still in control, this was going to end very badly for him, he could already see it—would his own mother feed him to her carnivorous water-horse?

A hand shot out.

Ruin's red, glinting eyes locked firmly with his, but it wasn't his face they grabbed by the jaw and *yanked* from beside him.

This could be you, that look seemed to warn; Ruin definitely knew he was there. Vehan felt lightheaded.

"NO!" The guard who'd been just ahead of him, the one that had shifted uncomfortably when the each-uisge had been introduced, thrashed and clawed and growled and raged.

He fought Ruin every step of the way, though their grip on him had been firm enough to bruise as they dragged him by his face to the middle of the room and threw him to the floor.

Then their hand went to the back of his head, sank fingers into his hair, and *pulled*.

"And who are you?" Riadne asked—and only because Vehan was so well acquainted with it by now did he hear the layers of Magnetism in her voice. She'd applied her compulsion so strongly even Vehan felt like announcing himself.

"My name is Kyle. I'm the leader of one of the southern rebel groups, and I'm here to kill you, *Your Majesty*."

Kyle!

No.

He knew this fae, had worked with him multiple times—the one Rosalie and Ten liked so much, with the rocket launcher and the normally colorful hair, and party-boy outfits, all of it traded now for a Bone Guard's garb just the same as Vehan. . . . Oh gods . . . they were going to *eviscerate* him, and all Vehan could think in his terror was how easily he could be next.

It all depended on Ruin's mood . . .

Please, Arlo, he thought in a fervent prayer to her. *Please, I know you're tired, but* please *resurface. . . . I need you.*

Laughter broke out across the room, starting first with Riadne.

The others joined; now that they'd deemed themselves safe from the Titan they feared more than anything else gathered here, they were quick to close up their ranks once more, but Vehan pushed his way to the front.

The part of him that wasn't frozen in terror was already trying to think up ways to rescue Kyle from this extremely poor decision of his.

"You're here to kill me. A nothing fae man who fancies himself the storybook hero . . ." Riadne's head tipped back with her laughter. "Oh, how delightful. Please, Ruin, do let him make his attempt—"

But the queen's amusement was interrupted.

The crowd gasped afresh, and *everyone* shot once more for the safety of the walls as Ruin pulled that grip in Kyle's hair so hard his entire body was wrenched backward—and painfully, by the sound of his cry.

"Ruin," Riadne commanded, not at all happy to be ignored in this manner, but Ruin either didn't care or was too preoccupied with their study to notice.

The way they looked down at Kyle . . . as though he were something mildly curious they just couldn't figure out . . .

Arlo, please . . .

I need you, I need you, I need you to be you *right now!*

"What are you waiting for, *parasite*?" Kyle ground out, squaring his jaw in defiance. "I'm not afraid of you."

"No," Ruin fairly whispered. They sounded so unlike Arlo that if Vehan wasn't looking directly at her body they possessed, he would have sworn it was someone else speaking. "No, you aren't."

"Come on—*do it*. Or can't you act without your master's *permission*? Just a yappy little dog on a leash. Who would be afraid of you?"

"*Ruin*. Unhand him this instant. I did not give this order—you will obey!"

"*DO IT*."

Vehan watched, struck aghast, as Ruin's free hand moved to seal over Kyle's face, the full of it now, smothered in their palm . . .

And then they *crushed* it in their grip.

Crumpled the bone like the body of a soda can, a horrific crunching, and then . . . nothing.

Kyle didn't even have the chance to scream his pain.

Vehan couldn't look away—stared at the brain matter squeezing out from between the cracks . . . at the bone that had punctured through the eye from the underside . . .

"Absol*utely* unacceptable," Riadne snarled, tearing herself from her throne to descend the steps. "Your impatience gets the better of you, Ruin. Do try to contain yourself a *little* bit longer."

The each-uisge looked bemusedly down at the carnage on the floor.

"Come," she continued to command, this time to her guests. "We'll adjourn to the war room; Ruin will join us when they finish *cleaning up this mess*."

Ruin merely stood staring down at the body at their feet.

The room began to filter out, everyone following Riadne into the hall, many so quickly they stumbled over one another just to get away from Ruin.

They were all thinking it.

They were all afraid.

Riadne had given an order, and Ruin had disobeyed. She was losing control . . . which meant that she was *weakening*.

The room had cleared out—until all that remained were the Titan and Vehan.

"Ruin?" he said hesitantly, taking a slow step forward. There was no use pretending they didn't know he was here, and something in Vehan's gut told him *this* was where he was meant to be, not trailing after his mother.

Ruin lowered themselves to a crouch, peering closer down at Kyle.

"What are you doing?" he heard himself ask, despite how his brain and body alike screamed at him to make his escape and run the other way. Instead, he only drew closer. Somehow he knew that this, right here, right now, was the reason his die had wanted him to come.

At first Ruin gave no indication they'd heard him.

Then . . . "Wondering."

". . . Wondering what?"

Ruin cocked their head. "Wondering what it will feel like to die a permanent death."

This . . . struck Vehan as something odd to say, when all along they'd been so sure they would win over Arlo.

In his pocket, he could feel his die grow warmer. Almost as though it could . . . sense its original . . . owner.

Ruin turned their gaze to look Vehan dead in the eye.

Vehan looked at them.

And looked at them.

And suddenly, it clicked, what they'd just said. Who it was staring back at him.

"... *Arlo?*"

Ruin hadn't disobeyed Riadne. Ruin hadn't been in control here at all. This had been *Arlo*, Arlo all along.

Arlo had been the one to kill Kyle.

A mercy, perhaps—what Riadne would have done to him, had it been left up to her cruelty, would have put him through *far* more suffering than this ultimately quick death . . . however gruesome.

Yes, it was a mercy, what she'd done, but something didn't sit right with Vehan about it. Mercy or not, it had been Arlo's hands to deliver it, which she'd *always* tried to abstain from before.

"Do you know, it doesn't even bother me at all?" Arlo continued to muse in that worryingly detached tone. "I thought it would. It should, shouldn't it? That's a bit frightening, and I suppose if I think that, there's some *me* left in here, after all. But *I* killed this boy—I only wanted to see—and there's this . . . nothing inside me. The remorse is all wrong." Abruptly, she stood. "Which pretty much means we're out of time."

Still stunned, still reeling, still desperately wishing he'd misheard her somehow, misunderstood what the words she said meant, Vehan moved with her.

No.

They couldn't be out of time.

No.

"I need you to deliver a message to Celadon for me. I would like him to meet me at these specific coordinates just before sunrise." She pressed something into his hand—a shred of paper. Vehan couldn't focus to read it, merely stared down at it blankly.

They couldn't be out of time.

No.

"You're afraid."

He looked up at her. Swallowed against something lodged in his throat that felt too much like his heart attempting to squeeze its way through.

314

"Don't be afraid. There's still *some* of me left for this to work—seeing you now, it helped. If you can get Celadon to meet me there, that will help as well. I'd tell him to bring his sword, though."

Bring the sword . . .

His heart clenched in his chest to realize it was finally time.

Not *all* was lost, but they'd have to act fast. Arlo was only threads of herself and, judging by the tonelessness to her, fading quickly. She wanted to complete her mission—they *needed* her to complete her mission, but more than that . . . Vehan would do anything to help her carry out her last wishes.

By the sounds of things, though, what Arlo needed most of all, more than him or Celadon or anyone else . . . what she *needed* was a hells of a lot of . . .

"I'll tell him." Vehan's voice cracked on the words. He held the paper close to his chest as though it were a priceless jewel. "He'll be there. I'll tell him. Arlo?"

She looked at him.

That not-her look of hers that was so much Ruin, she might as well not be part of the mix at all.

Dipping his hand into his pocket, he pulled out his die and held it between them.

This was the reason he was here—*she* was the reason he was here— and now he knew what the die had been after in sending him here and paving his way with ease.

He closed his fingers around the object, and time stopped all around them—for everyone but the two of them . . .

Arlo looked at him, confusion breaking through her apathetic calm.

"One last wish," he reminded her, as the die's options assembled out of a golden shimmering in the air. "And I'm going to use it."

The glittering number one burst apart into dust that fell from the air.

"Because I made you a promise not to leave you alone, and now I know how to ensure that."

He took his die and pressed it over his heart—completely unnecessary, but as Aurelian assured it, he *could* at times be just a touch dramatic.

"You're going after Urielle's Crown."

Arlo stared at him, considering. Then she nodded her head.

"And then you're going to have Celadon kill you."

Again, a nod.

"All right, then, it's decided." He closed his eyes and took a breath. "Arlo, I wish to give you back your luck."

The die in his hand glowed sapphire bright, brighter, then started to change . . . to darker gold numbers . . . and green like stunning jade.

CHAPTER 23

Ruin

*W*E KNOW WHAT YOU ARE DOING.

Arlo stood at the edge of all that was left of UnSeelie Summer.

It hadn't been easy to track down this location. Worlds were a lot like the human body and went to immediate work as soon as they were injured in an attempt to heal themselves. Which meant as soon as the rifts she and the demons had been opening all over were no longer in use, they began to seal closed again, at least enough to shut out the creeping consumption of the void below.

*WE CAN FEEL THE ABSENCE OF WHAT
YOU'VE DESTROYED.*

In normal circumstances, all Arlo would need to do to keep the portal open was to continuously tear the wound anew. But this place had been concealed to her the last time she was here—finding it again had meant retracing steps and following trails of her own magical residue in the hopes that one would lead to the little that remained imprinted here.

*MORTAL INGRATE, IF YOU CONTINUE
DOWN THIS PATH
YOU HAD BETTER SEE IT THROUGH.
LEAVE EVEN ONE CROWN,
AND WE SHALL SET OUR VENGENCE
AGAINST ALL THAT YOU HOLD DEAR.*

On top of everything else, Arlo didn't actually know the last time she'd properly slept. Well before her attack on the Market. She found she didn't exactly need it anymore but still felt the lack of it, and was simultaneously so tired that she was half convinced if she closed her eyes, she might never wake up again.

That . . . and the End and the Beginning had finally grown wise to what she was doing. She was certain it cost them a great deal to speak their threats to her themselves using the link already forged between her and their scions, but oh, they were *livid* . . . making it even more imperative to do what needed doing *now*.

"You're early. I told Vehan to send you just before dawn," Arlo said, gaze trained on the palm of her hand, and the jade die there cradled.

Slotting himself into place beside her, Celadon peered over the ledge only a shuffle away, into the shallow depths of a sandy crater, wide as the Flaming City had been.

Quietly, he replied, "When have I ever been good at doing what I was told?"

Arlo snorted.

Folding her fingers over her die, she turned her head at last to appraise him.

When was the last time she'd taken a good, long look at this young man Celadon Fleur Viridian-Lysterne had become? When was the last time she'd cared enough to do so and feel anything more than this strange weight in her chest? Ruin grew heavier the more that Arlo faded, and who was to say which one of them this body had ever belonged to?

There were moments now, whole days now, when Arlo lost touch with reality so profoundly that she wasn't even sure *she* had ever been real at all.

"You stand taller," she observed blandly. Something of her memories lingered, burning away like flame ate at film, but she could still recall the Celadon this person had been in comparison to who he was now.

She'd never noticed it then, but kingship . . . Lethe . . . the things in her cousin's life now, they'd given him a reason to stand with his back straighter, his head held a little higher. "And you dyed your hair black."

"You know," he said, smiling gently at her, "you're the first person other than Lethe to comment on it in the four months that it's been like this. I was beginning to think no one noticed."

"I always notice you, Cel."

She didn't know what made her say it.

There wasn't even any sort of feeling behind the words.

Except that deep down, the spark of her that still remained enough to know its name was Arlo wanted so desperately to speak them, and it meant something. To that spark—to *her*. That he was here now with her at the very end, just as he'd been the very first person, apart from her parents, to stand beside her in this world.

The same something that compelled her to speak made her turn toward Celadon then. Quickly enough to startle him and make Lethe, standing a few paces back, arm himself at the ready with her mother's sword, she threw her arms around him in a tight hug.

It took him a moment.

To recover from the shock of it and return the hug with arms wound tightly around her shoulders, his face pressed into her hair.

"Are you certain I can't come with you?"

Arlo shook her head. "I need you here. If this goes badly and Ruin takes over, you'll be trapped."

Trapped with Ruin. Trapped with Urielle. Trapped where it would be so easy for the End and Beginning to send their scions after him to make good on their threats.

Humming dismay, but also understanding, Celadon whispered instead of argument, "Do you know how fiercely proud I am of you?"

She could feel something wet trickle down between the strands, but Celadon only hugged her tighter; she couldn't pull back to see.

"Do you know how proud I've *always* been of you?"

319

Arlo nodded.

The spark insider her flared heat against surroundings that felt like a wasteland of cold.

"I'm sorry I have to ask you to do this," she said, peeking around his arm at Lethe, at the sword he carried—the weapon that would be her end.

"I wouldn't trade this privilege for *anything*." Pushing back from her, Celadon looked at her; took her chin in hand; tilted her face and pressed a kiss to her brow, then stepped fully away. "I'll be waiting right here for you—me and Lethe both. So you go in there, you do what you need to do to win a Crown from a goddess, and then you bring yourself back, okay? You bring yourself back to me, Arlo Flamel."

Another nod.

How nice, in the end, to feel *warm* again, even just one last time.

"Go stand with Lethe," she ordered softly, turning back to the crater. "He'll keep you safe until I get back." From whoever she came back as, she didn't say. Pausing for a moment, she drew a breath, lifted her head, and looked over at her cousin, already making for Lethe's side. "Celadon?"

"Yes, Arlo?"

"I hope you know how very proud I am of you, as well."

Water welled up once more in his gaze. Arlo turned away. "I love you," she breathed, quiet, to herself. For the spark and the warmth, and she had to be imagining it, surely—the *I love you, too*, that flooded back through a bond stronger than any fate that waited to greet her once this was done.

With one hand she cast an array at her cousin's and his lover's feet, a ward springing up around them—in the other hand, she drew on more of Ruin's power and summoned the force she would thankfully, blessedly, never need to call on again, to blow open wide this pit . . .

> *Finally.*
> *I was trying to give you your moment of goodbye,*
> *but I half feared we'd be here all night,*
> *trading these useless emotions.*

Not useless.

She pressed back, and stepped over the ledge, into her portal—one last time.

CHAPTER 24

Ruin

~⌒~

URIELLE—GODDESS OF THE ELEMENTS, Shaper of Worlds. She'd been expecting Arlo's visit, this much was obvious, because Arlo stood where the pit expelled her, on some invisible platform, in a vast expanse of nothingness that shimmered and swirled like the void that had brought her here—which wasn't at all how this space had looked upon her first visit. She'd gotten the coordinates right, she didn't doubt that for a minute—this *was* the Infernal Realm, but it had been redecorated into this endless, sprawling arena to receive her.

"So, you have come."

The voice spoke from behind her.

Arlo turned, entirely unconcerned—but was met with a sight that struck her still.

Legends about the deities were many; there was always something about each that carried from one story to the next, though. Urielle was famous in all her tales for a form that would not be defined. None who looked on her could speak on it after, could say with any clarity what she looked like, apart from the elements she commanded, which swirled and seethed and whipped and churned around her—before, like fine robes; currently, like armor.

But there was distinction to her now.

Steel-sharp eyes.

Hair so hot it flowed like white flame.

A face that was . . . goodness, did Nausicaä know? Was she precluded from the magic that warped all memory of what her own mother looked like? *Did she know* how stunningly similarly

Urielle had crafted her daughter of Fire in her image?

"I thought perhaps you wouldn't. I thought you'd know better—you are so *weak* now, child. But then, perhaps you came for me to put you out of your misery."

Distance here meant something different than it did in the Mortal Realm, as did the laws of physics in general.

Urielle walked—it seemed to take her ages to close any space between them, despite the fact that Arlo would swear she could reach out and touch her skin.

"If it's mercy you long for, I shall oblige."

Careful, Arlo . . .

That voice!

> *Dearest sibling—how joyous an occasion,*
> *that we should speak again,*
> *after all this time.*

It was probably the most shocking thing of the day so far—that voice, the one Ruin jumped to respond to . . .

Luck.

It had been so long since the last time she'd heard them, the last time she'd seen them, and Arlo cared almost nothing about it now . . . save for *everything*, in the briefest of flashes: happiness . . . nostalgia . . . *relief* that here at the end of the line, she wasn't alone after all . . .

That warmth she'd thought had finally guttered out, spent on farewell to Celadon, flared in the pit of her like a cooling ember catching its last bit of oxygen.

Urielle is by far the strongest of the children who wear my progenitors' bones. Those claws of hers are designed to Destroy—you will not survive, body or soul, should they deliver a fatal blow.

Arlo's gaze lowered to Urielle's hands—to the claws Luck mentioned: a long black talon on the end of each finger, wicked and curved, like that of a raptor.

"I don't want mercy," Arlo returned to the goddess, and threw out a hand beside her. "I'm here to deliver it." Ruin's darkness gathered again in her palm, lengthened and shaped itself into a weapon, hardened and transformed until the shadows that made it yielded to a cruel cut of heavy iron. "Unless you'd like to make this easier for the both of us and hand over your Crown right now?"

Urielle chuckled—it was low and dark and echoed around Arlo from every direction. "I think, instead, I would like to see . . ."

Ah, but this is so exhilarating.
This last clash of Titans—it's almost poetic.

". . . who of us will emerge victorious—primitive Destruction or equitable Creation." She smiled obscenely, and Arlo found another piece of her that yet lived in the way that expression reminded her of Nausicaä.

The action showed off double sets of razor teeth.

"Do give this all you can, sweet girl," Urielle continued. "No afterlife waits to receive you, should you and all that soft flesh run afoul of my claws."

Hand clenched firmly over her die, jaw squared at the goddess, Arlo replied, "All right—if you think you can keep up . . ."

Urielle *lunged.*

Again the laws of space and physics seemed to alter to suit the goddess's whim.

It wasn't so much Urielle flying toward her as their arena pulling itself around Arlo, speeding *her* toward those lethal claws as though on a conveyor belt.

Arlo ducked—timed just right, holding her ground, she rode out the momentum until the very last second. With Urielle so much larger than an ordinary mortal, than even the standard immortal, Arlo was able to sail right between Urielle's legs and slide out the other side.

She didn't pause to reorient herself.

Instead, with a flick of her wrist, she re-angled her sword, and it was Arlo now who lunged for Urielle's back.

Just before the point of her blade could connect with flesh, the goddess spun about—crossing her claws before her like a trap that caught Arlo's sword between them.

With a firm twist, she hurled Arlo off to her right—where again the world around her moved separate from the physics she was bound to, to rush past her . . .

And *slam* her with bone-shattering force against a pillar Urielle pulled from their transparent platform.

My, that did seem to hurt . . .

Arlo choked out a groan.

"Hurt" was an understatement—it felt like every bone in her body had broken at once. Normally, in these last four months, any time she sustained injury, Ruin's magic flooded so quickly through her to repair it, she barely had time to notice the pain.

Right now, though . . .

You're not going to make this easy on me at all, are you? she snapped at the parasite inside her.

*I do seem to recall a stalwart fae king with
a very sharp sword,
awaiting your survival to forestall mine.*

Of course.

The singular most difficult battle Arlo would ever face down, and the Titan she shared her body with was going to fight her all the way, just to wear her out even faster, just to ensure that this place would become her grave, one way or another.

Urielle rushed toward her, arena and preternatural speed working in tandem to close the distance at an alarming rate.

She couldn't *move.*

Couldn't arm herself.

Could only sit in her crumpled, broken heap of shooting agony . . .

Arlo as herself would have felt incredibly panicked right now, unable to do anything but watch impending death draw closer and closer, Urielle's claws extended outward as though to spear directly into her on arrival.

A benefit to her erasure, then. Her unmooring.

Ruin would make this difficult, yes, but they wouldn't allow Arlo's body to die before her soul could—that would only kill them, too.

All she had to do was sit. . . . All she had to do was nothing. . . .

Closer.

Closer.

Closer Urielle flew, but Arlo merely waited, and without the panic, it wasn't even hard.

Sure enough—the points of those claws came within narrowed focus; in a flash, just before they could connect with Arlo's chest, her body was restored.

A *second* was all the time Ruin had left her to pitch herself to the side.

Claws embedded in the pillar behind her, equally transparent as the flooring, but somewhat glassy, just enough to see a shape defined in the air; Urielle shrieked in outrage, before slicing right through it, and the pillar shattered, raining jagged shards over her head.

No time—Arlo rolled.

The pieces of the pillar sliced her, embedded in her flesh and hair and clothing.

She grabbed for her sword and pushed to her feet.

Urielle had the advantage here—this was her territory. She knew how to manipulate this space to her benefit, and if Arlo continued to let her chase her around it, she was only going to lose.

It was time to remember she was more than just Ruin. Time to start fighting back with the *other* tools at her disposal.

About-facing to zero back in on where Arlo had withdrawn,

Urielle continued her onslaught, hurling herself with unrelenting force in this new direction.

A flash of blue light—Arlo's hand extended, and in the quick-fire draw of less than a second, she pulled her own column of their glassy platform up and directly in Urielle's path.

SLAM.

There was no vibration from the impact, but the sound of it echoed through their arena.

Snarling, Urielle peeled herself off its surface and flung herself around the pillar back in Arlo's direction—

SLAM.

Another flash of blue light—another pillar.

Snarl—SLAM.

Snarl—SLAM.

Sn—SLAM. SLAM. SLAM.

The faster Urielle tried to recover, the faster Arlo pulled on her alchemy. After every collision, Arlo pitched herself to a new place on their suspended board. This on its own wasn't much of an impediment, but—there. Arlo caught it, only just: the wince of disorientation.

Urielle might be able to crash her way through this obstacle course, but doing so and constantly having to readjust her target afterward . . . it *was* beginning to have an effect. The goddess was slowing down, draining, dizzy.

Arlo pressed her advantage.

Again it was easy, to give herself over completely to her task, detached as she was from her usual emotions.

She'd made a wish back when challenging Lethe. A wish for incomparable swordsmanship. With Urielle worn down just enough, all Arlo had to do now was place her trust in her blade, and it would take over, would rain down assault on Urielle faster and more artfully than she could contend with.

It was really that—

A dark chuckle inside her head . . .

Ruin resurfaced to impede her once more.

SLAM—but this time, it was Arlo, and the force was a surge of power inside her, so immense and immediate that her mortal body had no idea what to do with it.

With a scream, she dropped to the ground, curling in on herself, in turns writhing and shaking uncontrollably—

And just like that.

As soon as it came, the power drained away.

And away, and away, and *away*, leaving Arlo's magical core so empty she felt she might be sick on the floor; might pass out, like her veins were dust and her bones were brittle, and peeling herself up off the glass just in time to *slouch* out of Urielle's way—recovered and hurtling toward her—was all she had within her to do.

Skidding to a stop, Urielle turned.

Arlo could barely move; her arms trembled to try and support her as she pushed up from the ground, tried to take to her feet, tried to pull herself through Ruin tampering with her power levels and ride out the wave of it until they stopped.

Scenting weakness, Urielle grinned—that infuriating grin of hers that drew a flare of anger in Arlo, that grin that was Nausicaä's, not hers! Regardless, the goddess leaned in, and her arena shot her forward.

And it cost Arlo far more than she really had to give to heave herself upright just in time . . .

To meet the momentum of Urielle's flight with a guttural cry . . . and sweep of her sword.

Clean in two—the blade caught the goddess of elements right through the middle and halved her over the flat of its iron.

The pieces of her dropped to the ground behind Arlo—a dull thud and wet squelch as they rolled a little, rocking to a stop . . .

Panting, Arlo took a minute to regroup.

Everything in her stung from overexertion and exhaustion. Starbursting black began to eat at the corners of her vision, like the film of her life was nearing the end of its reel. Pain radiated like an alarm in her head, and Ruin sat like a leaden weight inside her, Arlo so ragged and thinned . . . her parasite so substantial and smug.

She had to get back.

She needed to collect her Crown and get back to Celadon, while she still had enough of her left to do so.

This had taken . . . all of her, but she'd done it. She'd finally done it. And now it was time to—

The sound of trickling water—at first Arlo didn't register it as anything worth noting, but then her sluggish, failing brain caught up with her.

Urielle.

The goddess of *elements*.

Arlo turned.

The pieces of the goddess had liquified into twin pools of crystal-clear water. Arlo watched as the pools rejoined into one, as it spread wider, thinner, and became almost a portal of sorts, for a claw-tipped hand to shoot up from and plant itself on the platform.

"It was a very good effort . . ."

She didn't need to look to her side to see who was speaking, but did so anyhow.

"I think there isn't a soul in this lifetime, or any other, who's ever managed to defeat Urielle, even in her first form."

Shamrock-green hair . . . obsidian-black horns . . . glittering void eyes, golden shimmering skin, flowing robes of silk and gauze and emerald cosmos . . .

"First form?" Arlo clarified, looking up at the towering figure of Luck beside her. "As in, more than one?"

The hand that had planted on the platform dug its claws into the glass, anchoring itself to begin to heave, and another hand shot up to join it, followed by a head . . . shoulders . . . a torso . . .

"Unfortunately," said Luck.

Arlo breathed a laugh.

She felt slightly manic.

And yet . . .

Luck stood beside her. As they'd done in the Faerie Ring. As they'd done in Aurum Industries. As they'd done this entire journey, all the way here to the end . . . where she was about to go out blazing in an epic, Final Fantasy–style boss battle.

She cracked a smile—it felt like a flare of her usual self, a sliver of Arlo *Jarsdel*, had just revived.

"Boy oh boy . . ." she quoted to herself, one of the most iconic lines from the series, because it felt . . . extremely fitting, given what she was about to do, and again she felt like laughing. As she gripped her sword tighter, lifted it to the ready . . .

As Urielle pulled herself from the pool and to her feet, rolled her shoulders . . . for wings neither leather nor feather to burst wide from her back . . .

As Luck reached over to ruffle her head. "Good luck," they blessed fondly. "I'll be right here with you." And dissolved into a burst of green glitter.

"Boy oh boy," Arlo repeated. "The price of freedom sure is steep."

Urielle took to the air.

Almost as though on the thought alone, Arlo's die materialized in her palm. Hot to the touch, ready for action. She clenched her first around it and called—"Boost to my windborn Gift."

No time to stop here, and she didn't need it, regardless.

Arlo was a Hollow Star—she was *the* Hollow Star, and she knew exactly what she was doing.

Numbers appeared in the air, and she pitched her die up as high as it would go and flew forward, trusting the die and Luck's blessing to roll what she needed.

Sure enough, the air began to rush around her—Arlo seized onto it, willed it to build around her shoulders . . . take shape at the blades of her back . . .

Urielle tore upward into the sky. She thought she had the advantage.

It was mildly satisfying to that revived Arlo-sliver that, when she righted herself, another flare of her wings to stabilize her in midair, Urielle's eyes widened in shock—and she had to dart quickly to the side to avoid the way Arlo shot toward her like a javelin on the wings she'd fashioned from the wind.

Around the boundless, cosmic arena they darted, streaking after each other.

Arlo slashed in great sweeps with her two-handed blade . . .

Urielle rained down furious swipes of her claws . . .

"She misses!" Arlo called, when the goddess's maneuvering led her to a blow she couldn't block.

"It lands!" she commanded, balling up bits of the air into a solid, violent force, to volley at the goddess when she sailed too quickly out of reach.

"Show me her current trajectory!" And again the die rolled in her mind's eye, responded flawlessly to mark Urielle's current foreseeable path of attack in a trail of golden-dust shamrocks.

Sweep—*parry*.

Lunge—*clash*.

Urielle was growing furious, and Arlo knew that the moment she settled, the amount she was using this die would exact such a heavy toll on her that she might fade to Ruin as soon as she landed.

But it was this or die speared on the end of Urielle's claws.

It was this or cede herself over to Ruin here and now—for they weren't making this any easier, still.

Arlo tried to balance her assault with her alchemy—blue light pulled more of the platform below into spears that pierced the air after Urielle, chasing her around. Fashioned the ground into wicked spikes to meet the goddess when Arlo managed to land a kick that hit so hard, Urielle fell from the sky.

The more of herself that Arlo spent, the more Ruin had to play against her.

At one point, she lost her vision entirely—Ruin seizing control of the nerves to blot her sight completely black, and she was forced then to rely on her die more than ever.

Whatever Ruin took, they returned at the very last, crucial second.

Clearly, their game was hoping Arlo either wore herself out trying to keep up or begged them to take over.

Arlo did neither.

She lunged and slashed and sliced and swept.

She tossed herself around the arena, summoned her alchemy in ways she'd never before used it—to wield the minerals in Urielle's ichor like knives turned against her, whenever her blade struck true enough to wound; to latch onto her hair and force it to grow and tangle around the goddess; even once, at great cost to her energy, to take over control of the bone in Urielle's arm and attempt to turn those claws against her . . .

When Ruin surged up to impede her, she reached for her die.

When Urielle took advantage of her failing energy—again, for her die.

But this wouldn't last.

Arlo had to end this, now.

The bigger the ask, the greater the toll, so she had to wait until the perfect moment—the surest timing, where what she asked would have no chance of failure and optimal effect.

When Urielle sank down, down, down below Arlo just to shoot herself back up with bullet speed, that time finally came.

Arlo waited . . . and waited . . . and then spun in the last second—"Strength boost!" she called as she turned, and as soon as she completed the full rotation, the die had already rolled and responded.

Urielle streaked by—then was snagged by the ankle in Arlo's grasp.

Arlo, who continued to turn, and dragged the goddess with her.

To turn and turn and spin and turn, building and building and building momentum, and Urielle whipped around with her, unable to free herself.

Gathering all her bolstered strength, Arlo *flung* her to the ground below—where the goddess connected . . .

With a complete and loud shattering of her entire body.

Finally. Arlo descended.

Or rather, didn't so much descend as the wind of her wings began to dispel, her fortitude, her magic, her life force . . . all weakened past the ability to sustain her.

She touched the ground not far from the broken goddess.

In a pool of ichor, and bleeding profusely, Urielle held herself barely aloft, bone jutting through skin. Her massive wings lay drooped around her, her entire aura fatigued.

Which was surely nothing to how Arlo felt as she dropped with a dull thud to her hands and knees.

The wear of the die . . . Ruin's purposeful inconsistence . . . the spark of her, it was no longer warm, barely a glow at this point.

"You think you have won?" Urielle rasped; gold spilled from her lips. Her steel eyes blazed with fury. With great difficulty, and sickening cracks, the goddess's body began to reknit itself so she could pull herself up to standing . . .

So she could heave her great wings unfurled in the air.

"You think you have defeated me? *You*, a mere mortal playing at power that I've wielded since the dawn of your pitiful world?"

Yet again, her form began to change.

As she spoke, she gained in limbs.

They peeled from her back, three additional arms on each side, each one with a blade made of the purest elements, until eight in total aimed their points at Arlo.

"This is your end, girl. *This* is what you've sewn. You have not bested me—none ever shall. I am justice, law, duty. I am the birth and weight of your entire realm. You will *bend* to me in supplication when this is over, as it will be soon. And then I shall give you the oblivion you do not deserve—that is how this battle ends. This is how it was always meant to end—with you, who are *nothing*, at my heel. . . ."

Turn back now.

Arlo could turn back now—preserve herself, because Ruin would not allow Urielle to Destroy them, but this fight had worn on long enough that staying to defeat this goddess would be the last of what she could do.

If Arlo left—through the portal still open for the time being, but slowly starting to close—and returned herself to Celadon as promised, he would end her life by the blade he'd brought. She'd be free of Ruin, sent to Cosmin, and rescued and restored back to her friends by Lethe.

How badly she wanted to take that option—how loudly it screamed at her to do so.

> *And in the doing, you'd condemn your world*
> *to a cycle never-ending.*
> *The Bone Crowns would remain at two.*
> *Urielle Fallen would alone command the realms,*
> *consumed by her Crown's weight.*
> *Violence and death on endless repeat, until*
> *both realms succeeded in their own ruination . . .*
> *better than even I could inflict.*

> *Provided, of course, they managed to defeat me,*
> *and buy themselves time to die.*

> *Slowly.*
> *Painfully.*

Her other option.

The only one there'd ever truly been . . .

We simply ask she chooses villain too.
She could give herself over to Ruin, completely.

> *Allow me to sweeten this choice for you,*
> *my first and last Flamel.*
> *Do what you were meant to do.*
> *Become the villain you were meant to become.*
> *Grant this body to me,*
> *And when the spark of your soul gutters out,*
> *I shall complete your mission.*
> *I will win you this battle and destroy the Crown*
> *your sacrifice earns.*

> *This I do solemnly vow to you.*
> *Let me shatter to dust, should these words I betray.*

Shaking, and with great difficulty, Arlo pulled herself to standing too.
Go back, and live.
Die, and save the world.
What did she choose?
It's heroes who are the stuff of tragedies—isn't that what you once told me?
Luck spoke to her, with all the reverence of a deathbed.
They threw words from so long ago at her, and Arlo could only barely remember. Could hardly reconcile the person she was right now with the flashes of who she'd once been—that timid thing, so afraid to stand her ground, so easy to push around and walk over.
She frowned in concentration, trying to hold on to those long-ago memories, trying to make sense of what Luck was saying—useless Titan, constantly speaking to her in riddles. How desperately she wanted to sleep; how dangerously close she was to snuffing out . . .
"You do not yield? It is death you choose in the end." Urielle lifted into the air. "I do not commend you on this defiance—it is a stain my wrath shall cleanse from your soul. . . ."

Heroes are the stuff of tragedy. Reversely, Luck purred, and Arlo was struck with the impression of a large black cat trailing her into a building. *Did you know—every story about a villain . . . they all begin and end in hope.*

Well, Arlo?
What do you choose?

What indeed.
Boy oh boy.
Back tall, head held high, Arlo took up her sword.

"You're certain you want to do this, Arlo?"

In the depths of his lab, in the bowels of the Black Castle, Arlo and Alecto stood bent over a table—between them, too innocuous for what it was, lay the array Arlo had just finished carving into an iron brand, an exact replica of the image on the sheet of paper beside it.

Alecto looked up at him, mouth downturned. "There's still another way. We can still dissolve the geas that binds you. . . . I can help you hide with your family, conceal you from Phoebus and the Council, and you can live out the rest of your days happy, healthy . . . and very much not a *Sin*."

With a hint of a rueful smile on his lips, Arlo traced a finger along the edge of the iron slab.

"It would be no life, Alecto," he replied after a moment, soft and thoughtful, his mind a whir with everything that had to go exactly right for this to work . . . "Even if you could free me from the backlash of betrayal, I won't make my son and wife fugitives. I won't bring that shame on my family name; my pride is far too strong for that." He shook his head, that rueful smile growing wider. "No, I'm certain. This is what I want to do. What I *must* do. I did the job properly—I examined every inch of this array, delved into knowledge none but myself have been permitted to even know exists. The runes, the snippets of lore recovered from the libraries the gods once kept, burned by their own hands as the tides turned in our favor to keep such knowings out of our heads. There are things that remain yet beyond my ken, I admit . . ." Finger halting, gaze lifting, he turned his examination now on Alecto. "But it's enough. I've made up my mind. To set into motion what the scions want . . . to protect the Courts, the *world*, from what the Council would do if left to continue unchecked . . . to eradicate that which has caused such harm to a man I so admired . . . I will do this."

Pausing, he frowned in deeper thought, considering what was perhaps the most volatile aspect of his plan, the part of it least in his control. "How long, do you think, will I remain once it's summoned? Pride—will it consume me entirely the moment the philosopher's stone is made, or will it take some time for my soul to die?"

Still armed with a frown of her own, Alecto seemed to consider his question—or perhaps rather, what she was willing to reply to it.

Her silence wore on quite a while.

Arlo had been just about to change the subject, when finally she said, "Who can say; I've never known anyone to attempt what you're about to do. The Sins weren't even meant for mortal harm. They were born of the long-ago conflict between the deities and Titans. But . . ."

Again, she paused.

Again, she seemed to be trying to work out the words to say.

"There's this belief among immortals that if you could hold a soul cupped in your hands and lift it to your ear, you'd be able to hear this very quiet sort of . . . humming from it, like a song. It's believed that there are many variations of this song, and some don't harmonize well at all, but others . . . others combine to make the most perfect melody, and it's those souls yours was meant to find." Shrugging, Alecto played up nonchalance, but there was something about the defensive hunch of her demeanor that told Arlo these weren't just words to her. "Who's to say if any of that's true. I can tell you one thing for certain: you spend your whole life giving pieces of your heart away to the people you care for and love—family . . . friends. . . . Pride can make their best attempt at taking what's left over, but a part of you will *always* remain, as long as . . ."

"As long as I have you."

Alecto's mouth closed.

It opened.

And shut again, her gaze dipped to the side.

Sapphire color bled into her face, just enough to give it that blush of magic so curious to Arlo, even now, who'd been born to a half-fae, half-human father and a fully fae mother, yet his blood still ran the purest red.

"They won't be able to use it," he blurted, perhaps in an attempt to fill the silence; perhaps in an attempt to make her see that her trust in him all these years hadn't been misplaced. "My research. I've branded it all—every sheet of paper, every note, even the ones that the Council has. And the brand is my *name*, Alecto, my signature; anything I put it on will become illegible to anyone but my own blood the moment I become Pride. I put the same marking on me."

He held out an arm, rolled up his sleeve, revealed to her what he'd branded with scarring permanence on his wrist—his signature.

"As soon as I active this, it all takes effect. With this, when I'm gone, Pride won't be able to reveal any of my secrets. They won't be able to make sense of my thoughts to even utilize my alchemy. What I do here tonight begins and dies the moment that I do. The Council will be pissed; Phoebus may be furious. But this is the only way I have of ensuring they don't take any more than what was promised."

Relief flexed across Alecto's face—replaced quickly with a sinking grief.

"We did this all wrong, you know," she sighed, her gaze dropping to the floor. "I didn't like you one bit at first. In the beginning, I was fairly certain I would end up Destroying you, and that didn't bother me a mote."

Yes, Arlo remembered it well, the disdain on her face, that first-ever meeting with the two of them flat on their stomachs, watching everything change between wooden bars.

Looking at him once more, those pale eyes of hers pinned Arlo in place so that he couldn't move even if he should wish to. "And now here we are, these many years later, and you're about to do something so phenomenally asinine, which is just you all over, Arlo Flamel. Who can say how it will end, but chances are, I'll have to Destroy you, and all I can feel about that is . . ."

"You are the most incredible woman I have ever met in my life," Arlo cut in when Alecto's words died, barely able to contain himself from speaking what felt like a rising in his chest that had been building for quite a while. "And by far the most beautiful thing I have ever laid eyes on. Of everything I've ever done, earning your friendship is what I consider the greatest of my accomplishments."

Alecto considered him.

The space between them had dwindled to all of a breath.

"Sad," she said, choosing the words at last, and barely above a whisper. "All I can feel is sad."

Smiling softly, Arlo dipped in and placed the lightest kiss to Alecto's temple. "This will not be goodbye—of that, I am firmly certain. Our story doesn't end here. I'd say it's really just beginning. Will you do me two favors, though? For the Arlo of *this* lifetime."

"Go on, then," Alecto bid, pretending at dismissal. "What can I do for you, O Arlo Flamel, greatest alchemist of all time?"

He was *really* going to miss her.

"Make *sure* that it's you," he asked of her softly. "I'm counting entirely on your Destruction to pull the rest of this off. I need you to be the one to end it once my purpose is served. Once the stone is made, and Pride claims my body, and the things that need to be set in motion are underway, I would like it to be your hand that delivers my demise . . . and in so doing, Pride will fall to *you*."

He paused to allow her a moment to work out what he was asking.

"Whoever kills the stone's current owner becomes its master . . ." Alecto said in breathless understanding. "You want *me* to be the one to guard it?"

"Please?"

A moment passed . . .

Followed by two . . .

"I'll make sure that it's safe," Alecto finally replied—tightly, around a great deal of emotion she was clearly trying to swallow down.

Perhaps she had something else to say. She had the look, like all her walls were shattering for feeling to seep through, and whatever it was, Arlo knew in that moment it would change everything between them . . . and nothing at all.

But the door to his laboratory swung open then, and Alecto peeled away just as Phoebus poured into the room, trailing his entourage of High Councillors.

"Arlo!" he boomed, in a far better mood than the last time they'd spoken, at Apollo's crib. Hands in the air, he greeted Arlo as though he were a soldier returning from war. "My boy—I came the *moment* I received your summons. Is it true, what your messenger tells me? Have you finally embraced your chance for glory, ripe for plucking?"

How hadn't he seen it until now?

Phoebus was old.

He'd aged quite a lot in the time between Arlo's childhood and where they stood today—far more than he ought to have in such a short span of time, relative to what he'd already lived.

There were lines in his face, there was salt in his hair. His proud stance had begun to hunch a little under the weight of not only years but that thing on his head—that twist of bone that looked, if not to Arlo's imagination, as though it had somehow improved the more its possessor began to fail.

The look of madness was near constant in that clouding jade gaze, and his *obsession* with greatness . . . Arlo had been too close to realize what was right in front of his face.

The Bone Crown was no prize but a curse.

His resolve to do what the scions had requested only hardened for this knowledge.

Smiling tightly, Arlo turned to face the man he considered as good as his father, grabbing from his desk behind him the philosopher's stone array carved into the iron brand.

"I will make the stone, Phoebus," he began in grave tones.

If Phoebus was able to pick up on Arlo's hesitance, he simply didn't care, too caught up in his hunger, in the longing with which he stared at what Arlo held. . . . The Council fanned out to his sides to examine the iron poker as well, with all the keenness of vultures.

"I will use this brand to anchor this magic to my body and mark it for Pride's vessel. Then I will step into the matching array, just over there, and initiate the summons." He waved off to the far end of the room, where the philosopher's stone array had been drawn out to a much larger scale on the flagstone floor.

With a raised brow, Phoebus considered this. "Must it be a brand? Surely there's no need for such barbarism—would it not suffice to merely draw it out on your skin and save you a little pain?"

Arlo snorted. "This magic is not *kind*, Phoebus. A brand, a knife—whatever the tool, what carves it must cause pain, to demonstrate the resilience of the host; it will not respond to anything less, and will cause far greater agony once activated."

"Very well," Phoebus replied, his gaze hardening. "Have you chosen a date for this necessary evil? We are not unreasonable." He cut a glance around at his Council. "We wouldn't have you make this ultimate sacrifice, for the good of the Courts, and not allow you time to put your affairs in order . . . to make your goodbyes."

"No need," Arlo replied, clipped and dismissive.

It would have been nice—to have more time. Arlo was young; he loved his son; he had a happy family. He didn't want to die, but the longer Phoebus had to ponder what was coming next, the greater the risk it wouldn't go to plan.

Crossing the room, he approached his fireplace and put his hand to the array he'd etched into it, and the hearth flamed to life in an instant.

Brand held out toward the fire, he turned once more to the High King.

"I'm prepared to begin this here and now. Everything you've

wanted—security for the Courts, the fame of having been guide and support to the alchemist who made this possible. I'll make this stone, but on one condition, first."

The *longing* on his face—but Phoebus blinked and surfaced from it quickly. He might be ailing, his mind might be dulling, his faculties slowly beginning to betray him, but he was still an intelligent fae, and right to suspect what Arlo would ask.

"Oh? And what is that?"

Heart starting to race, Arlo sent a silent prayer to whatever luck was on his side that he hadn't misjudged the High King's desire.

"You must swear me a geas," he said, doing his best to keep his tone calm and ignore the way the Council began to ruffle. "You must swear it in the capacity of the High Sovereign, so that all that come after you must abide by this promise too. The Fae High Council must do the same. And it *will* be a geas—I won't do this for anything less, no matter what you threaten; no matter how you rail. You must all swear on magic's name that if I make this stone, at no point will you undertake or seek another alchemist to create the rest. I will be the one to do it. Pride will still have access to my alchemic ability. This glory will remain mine alone and won't be shared with any other—on terms of Destruction, should this geas be betrayed."

Never mind that Arlo had no intention of creating the rest.

Never mind that Pride would be born knowing this plan, that the moment he created another stone, it would put him in transgression against Law and permit a Fury to Destroy him.

So much Arlo was relying on to go just right—but he'd done it, he was sure. He'd found a way to the path the scions wanted. It *had* to go right from there; Pride would have to fear too much losing their host to pursue the rest.

Buying Alecto enough time to fulfill her promise and Destroy him regardless before the Council could figure out a way to dissolve what was sworn.

And if they did, there was the fail-safe in place with the distortion of his notes. Surely, this was every base covered? Surely, this was enough.

It was all such a risk . . .

But there was no other way.

All he needed was Phoebus to agree.

"Everything you've wanted," Arlo reminded. "Exactly how you wanted it."

"Sire . . ."

"I must protest these terms, Your Majesty."

"Let us convene the Council and discuss it first—"

"Here and now," Arlo pressed, "or I won't do it at all."

Phoebus's eyes flashed—awareness and desperation at war with each other. He understood what was happening, on some level; it made Arlo both relieved and wretched to see that despite this, he couldn't escape the grip of his unquenchable thirst for fame.

Softly, sadly, he added the final nail in his coffin. "Please, Father? Let me become a son to be proud of. Let me bring honor to my true Viridian name."

"I accept your terms," Phoebus said, resolute, with a flicker of grief like he might know, deep down, what he'd just helped lock into place.

CHAPTER 25

Celadon

———◦⌒◦———

"WHAT THE ABSOLUTE *FUCK*, Celadon?" Nausicaä growled, detaching from Vehan and Aurelian to barrel toward him the moment he stepped out of his private office, incandescent with the outrage that propelled her. "Vehan says Arlo went off after Urielle's Crown, that she gave your shit-ass plan the green light for when she got back with it, and *nobody* thought, hey, maybe Nausicaä would like to be there when we *off her fucking girlfriend*?"

Windswept.

Sandy.

Exhausted down to the marrow in his bones—Celadon could only stand there, unable to process the words blasting him.

"Well?"

Nausicaä jabbed a finger into his shoulder, and he felt his body tilt with the impact, but couldn't process *that*, either.

"How. Did. It. Go?" Nausicaä pressed, her irritation mounting the longer Celadon did nothing but stand there . . . silent to each of her very valid questions . . .

Hands came up to brace his shoulders from behind.

"Nausicaä," a cool voice half warned, half attempted to assuage her anger.

But Nausicaä would not be consoled. "And what the fuck is *he* doing here?" she cried, her ire still building as she glared down Lethe, who'd pressed closer to Celadon's back for support. "You're supposed to be *up there* with her, aren't you? I thought that was the plan—Arlo gives her life for the cause and *you* go with her to make sure she isn't,

I don't know, tied down to Cosmin or whatever. That she remembers who she is and who we are, and I swear to fucking gods if neither of you cuts in soon to tell me everything's okay, I'm going to—"

"She did it," Celadon croaked, his throat as parched as the desert they'd just left behind in the Egress . . . along with his heart. "She was successful. Arlo defeated the Goddess of the Elements, and her Crown was destroyed. Your mother is free. Only one Crown remains; they paused on their way back out to assure me of that much."

He could see it in her face, how hard she was working to piece together all the hints of the terrible truth he couldn't say.

Because of course this should be unfathomable to her—he had a hard enough time believing it himself. In what world, what miserable time-line, should he exist—should they *all* exist—but Arlo Jarsdel Flamel, his cousin, sister, soulmate, was . . . *gone.*

Lifting her gaze, Nausicaä studied Celadon, closer this time, more than the cursory glance she'd given his discomposure before her temper took over.

"*They,*" she repeated slowly.

Celadon nodded.

They, not *she*—Arlo had been the one to go in, but the one to come out had been . . . "Ruin," he said, in a voice that was breaking, a heart that was shattered, a purpose completely unmoored. "Arlo succeeded, but it cost her her life. We failed, Nausicaä. *I* failed to save her. By the time they returned, she was already g—"

Gone.

Gone.

"Celadon?"

"I'm sorry, Nausicaä." *Gone.* "I'm sorry! I failed. I *failed* you. I failed everyone. I failed *her,* and now she's g—"

Gone.

Gone.

Gone. Gone. Gone. Gone. Gone. Gone. Gone. Gone. Gone. Gone. Gone—

It grew harder and harder to make out the shock on the faces beyond. Vehan, draining so pale at the news of Arlo's fate that he could be mistaken for dead as well. Aurelian, aghast . . .

How was Celadon going to tell Rory what happened to his daughter?

That he'd left things too long, had let his love and respect for his cousin override his responsibility—Arlo hadn't been in her right mind at all; he should have interceded, should have ended this well before tonight. Arlo never should have had to be the one to shoulder all that burden alone.

His vision swam.

His mind reeled.

His body felt as though it might tremble to pieces.

She stepped toward him, and Celadon braced himself for the strike he knew was coming. She'd been furious with Vehan when he'd merely done her wrong by proximity—Celadon deserved far more than her fist in punishment; hoped for it, in fact . . .

But what he received instead was worse.

"Celadon," she breathed into his hair as two strong arms slid around him and eased him out of Lethe's hold—into hers, tucked against her chest. "You didn't fail her. You didn't. You're probably the one person in this entire world that actually did her *right*. You let her choose the path she wanted—I don't think I could have done the same. There's a reason she didn't ask me to come with you."

Belatedly, Celadon realized that the reason he couldn't see was for crying.

"I let her go . . ." he choked into her shoulder.

"You let her take charge of her life."

"I didn't want any of this!"

"None of us did."

"She's *gone*, Nausicaä!"

Gone. Gone. Gone. GONE! Nausicaä was taking this far too calmly—didn't she understand? Arlo was gone, would never come

347

back, wouldn't ever be reborn, for what she'd willingly welcomed into her.

"Mmm, no. You're wrong about that, too."

Hesitant—against all hope—Celadon . . . paused. Pulled back from Nausicaä's embrace to study the grim determination in her face. "What do you mean? I saw it myself; it was Ruin and Ruin alone who came back—"

Nausicaä shook her head. "No. I don't believe that."

"Whether or not you believe it, Nausicaä, it's still the truth," Celadon replied hotly, anger sparking inside him now to have to repeatedly say the words that felt like a cleaving in two . . . "She's *gone!*"

"*Listen to me,*" Nausicaä rebutted, heated now too . . . not but unkind. "Celadon, listen. There's something I think I've pieced together from my time spent in the thrall of a Sin. When Lust had my heart and I wasn't supposed to feel anything but still somehow managed to care about—" Nausicaä paused.

She looked down at her wrist.

At the bracelet she wore still, at Celadon's insistence. Each of them wore one since Arlo's switch to ensure that if the situation ever became dire enough, Celadon could transport these people he cared so deeply about to the safety that still stood in downtown Toronto, even if the Court had changed.

Celadon was still a Viridian—the protection still applied.

And come to think of it, his own bracelet was feeling considerably warmer than usual.

"Uh . . . what's going on?" Nausicaä lifted her head. She looked to Celadon, to Lethe, then behind her at the others. "Is everyone feeling this?"

Warmer, and warmer, as though something was activating its magic—or rather, someone, but who? It shouldn't be possible. An individual could whisk themselves to safety with the spoken command, but to connect to each bracelet like this . . . Celadon was the only one who remained who had that power.

A hand fisted the back of his shirt. "Celadon . . ." Lethe began, alarm creeping into his whisper tone. "Did you know that it's perfectly possible to hijack the runes that etch your protective circle downtown? All it would require is a talented enough alchemist . . . with Viridian blood to allow them to bypass its security measures."

A talented alchemist of Viridian blood.

Celadon looked at his wrist again . . .

Then finally realized what Lethe meant. "Take them off," he said, panicked, clawing at his bracelet. "TAKE OFF THE BRACELETS! TAKE THEM OFF BEFORE THEY—"

But it was already too late—the bracelets flared uncomfortably hot, and all of a sudden, in a whisking sensation of wind and fragrant spring, Celadon felt himself transported.

"Ah, there we are," said a voice so wholly foreign to Celadon, it made him physically flinch to hear it, wrapped in the one sound he knew better than the beating of his own heart. "How nice of you all to join me at last to witness the beginning of your end."

CHAPTER 26

Nausicaä

❦

BREAKING FROM THE OTHERS, still gathering themselves and their wits, Nausicaä stalked for the city square's center, smoke forging Erebus in her hand.

It was the deep of night, and just like the first time Alecto had come to this middle-of-nowhere cabin, she didn't want to be here at all.

In the strangest sense of déjà vu, she could almost swear she'd lived this moment before. Her wings unfurled as she made her approach; her glamour faded with every step. Molten steel eyes *burned* on the figure that watched with a mocking grin her steady progress toward them, and she couldn't, couldn't, *couldn't* shake this overwhelming feeling . . . as though something in her had ignited, come to life, like a sliver of whoever it was who'd owned this soul first was *remembering* things that weren't Nausicaä's to know.

Doing her best to shake this off, she pressed forward.

In the encircling midst of towering glass and stone and metal, buildings gathered like an austere audience around them, a Fury began to take monstrous shape. Hair began to lengthen, to pour like white-hot flame around a hollowing face; limbs and torso began to thin, enlarge, forge a skeletal figure with overlong fingers tipped in glittering black talons.

Pride had eked out far more time than Alecto had thought them capable of.

In the manner that he had summoned them, Arlo hadn't committed a sin against unflinching Law, hadn't earned the Destruction that would cut this Sin down before they could cause overmuch harm.

The plan had been to wait the natural course for Pride to cross that forbidden line. Alecto, who didn't have permission to take a life that hadn't transgressed the Three Principal Rules of Magic, would cut Arlo down the moment Pride ran afoul of Law, extract his heart, and hide it somewhere secret and safe, where no one would be able to find it.

But lo, a flaw in their plan—they hadn't accounted for Pride taking such careful measures to observe what bound them to safety, to the very letter.

It hid behind the Flamel Order—used the cult of worshippers that had sprung up around them in the mere two years they had been here at large to commit every deed that would have earned a Fury's intercession.

Two years, and here they stood at the end of it all—Alecto in a loft that had once belonged to a curious boy, a talented boy, whose only sin had been wanting a friend . . .

That boy now a man, staring up at her from down below.

It was hard for Nausicaä to see anything of Arlo in the person she stalked a path toward.

Ruin was a contrast of bloody reds and stark-death whites, in wicked armor of black and gold that made them up like some legendary battle priestess. Nausicaä was tempted to envy the look, but just as many people had once flinched from her in her Furious glory as they now did Ruin.

She was a legend to behold herself, and the flicker of wariness beneath bold invitation was all she needed to know that Ruin was keenly aware of this.

"My darkest shadow," Ruin said, their voice almost grating to Nausicaä's ear to hear how very *un*-Arlo the sound was in that mouth. "I cannot tell you how *pleased* I am that you should offer yourself up first to demise; how many nights I tortured your pretty little girlfriend with thoughts of the way I'd mangle your body, once hers belonged to me. . . ."

Tch—this bastard; what a brave face they put on.

But all magic had a price, including what made this Titan so devastatingly strong.

"Some might call that an obsession, Ruin," Nausicaä drawled, coming to a halt just far enough back that nothing would touch, should either extend a hand. "I'm flattered to be what you think about when you're alone at night, but I'm already spoken for." She smiled, revealing all the razor-sharp teeth in the black hole of her widened mouth.

Tipping their head back, Ruin laughed. "Yes. You are, aren't you—or rather, you *were*. Poor, darling, naive Arlo. My only regret is that I could not make her watch what I have planned for you."

"Promises, promises, and you haven't even dined me yet." A flick of her wrist—she armed herself at the ready, Erebus extended point down to the pavement. "You know what, I would spend a little less time in fantasy murder land, if I were you, and a little more time being very concerned that the Dark Star has you all figured out—*I know what your secret is*," she taunted in a singsong voice.

And there—the flicker of apprehension beneath that calm facade.

"You know, I almost didn't come," said Pride in a voice that made Alecto's nails score into the loft's wooden banister.

Arlo's voice.

She hated every time she had to hear it devoid of his warmth.

But not much longer—this ended tonight.

"It's becoming rather tedious," Pride continued, in that mixture of insufferable haughtiness and cold dispassion. "Batting aside your attempts to rouse me. This is another trick of yours, I assume—somehow, you hope to use this disgustingly idyllic shack to move me to murder and register this body for Destruction. But who, I found myself wondering, has the patron Fury of wrongful death selected for sacrificial slaughter?"

They laughed at the idea . . . then narrowed their gaze on her in thought . . . only for their eyes to widen and amusement to break from their throat once more. "Oh! How quaint—you intend me to kill you!"

Snorting, Alecto made for the stairs that carried down to the cabin's main floor. "You couldn't even if I allowed it."

That rankled their ego—Pride's amusement died. "I am a Sin, love. I'm older even than you, and far more powerful."

"Maybe once." Alecto nodded, descending the last step and curving toward them. "But it has been a very long time since you've had a proper container, and you're all alone. None of the other Sins are here to bolster you—the folly of pride is that it requires an audience. Without one, you're just an impotent, irrelevant, bygone immortal."

Pride bared their teeth in a hiss of displeasure.

"You know what, girl?" Ruin sniped in reply. "I know a secret of yours as well."

They slunk a step closer, pulled themselves as tall as their five-foot-four frame could extend.

Nausicaä raised a brow. "Oh yeah? You don't say. That's not as impressive as you want it to be—*everything's* a secret when you work as hard as I do to avoid self-reflection. No one's more mystified by me than me."

"Ah, but you do *love* the sound of your own voice. Do you ever cease speaking?"

"Ah." Grinning even wider, Nausicaä lowered her center of gravity to match the sudden widening of Ruin's stance. "Meaner *baddies* than you have tried to make me—but I'm still here; *they* are not."

Ruin ignored her comment, their expression sliding back into condescension. "Do you not want to know what *your* secret is, Nausicaä Kraken?"

They were trying to ruffle her, that much was plainly obvious, to buy themselves time to assess what Nausicaä knew about them.

"Probably not?" Nausicaä shrugged, making a show of her lack of concern. "Again, the whole 'avoiding self-reflection keeps me young' thing. But go on. *Dazzle* me—you obviously want to share."

"Nausicaä, watch out!" Vehan called suddenly from behind her.

And Celadon, beside him, warned, "Ruin's done something to the circle—none of us can move. Nausicaä, be careful, they want *you* specifically!"

Oh, she knew.

Because deep down, less deep the longer they stood here taunting each other, Ruin knew that *she* knew *exactly* what they were trying to hide.

But it happened that fast.

One moment Ruin stood imposing before her—the next, they were gone, wicked completely out of existence, until a shadow pressed in against Nausicaä's back, and a voice that made the hair on the back of Nausicaä's neck stand on end whispered in her ear, "The truth you work so hard to conceal . . ."

Nausicaä jerked her shoulder in an attempt to dislodge them.

"You're *glad* that Arlo Flamel is gone," they slid to whisper in her opposite ear.

The very suggestion made Nausicaä ram an elbow backward, but Ruin had already wicked out again, chilling laughter all that remained in the place they'd been previously standing.

"You said it yourself, you abhor self-reflection . . ."

Nausicaä swung her arm to the side—struck through nothing but air.

"And no one has made you look harder at yourself and your actions than *she* . . ."

She whipped forward, sliced with her blade in the place they'd appeared, but Ruin had already vanished again to slink right back behind her.

"No one has made you feel more broken," they taunted, "more monstrous, more woefully childish. No one has reminded you better than the paragon of goodness *she* stood as beside you that you are nothing but an ugly, miserable, belligerent wretch too pusillanimous to do the world a favor and take your own life. You had to try and get

354

others to do it—and even then, you held back out of fear."

"Shut the *fuck* up," Nausicaä snarled, and this time, she was quick enough. This time, the edge of her steel met Ruin's throat, but all they did was smile.

"Strike a nerve, did I? Such a strong reaction—has what I said echoed down the pit of your heart to where you keep all that bitter resentment?"

It was Nausicaä's turn to laugh, and if it weren't for the fact that this was Arlo's face looking back at her, she'd spit at them.

"Yeah, see, that's the thing. You talk real big about hearts and shit . . . but you don't understand them at all. Know how I know that?"

"Oh," Ruin purred, "I'm sure you'll enlighten me. . . ."

And held out a hand.

Pulled from the very buildings around them, bars and sheets and pieces of iron *snapped* apart from their surroundings; melted as they flew through the air toward them; pooled together and then reforged into a lethal blade that slotted into Ruin's waiting palm.

Arlo's alchemy . . .

The wish she'd cast to boost her prowess with a blade . . .

Viridian protection within this circle . . . Ruin must have been *ecstatic* when they'd woken to find themselves in the best living weapon the Mortal Realm could give.

"Throw every taunt you wish at me—I won't be taking your life."
Pride narrowed their gaze again, stepped forward to meet Alecto halfway,
glared down into her face.

"Again," she purred, "you really couldn't. But don't worry, it isn't me
you will face tonight. Someone else volunteered."

It was a ball of Ruin's dark miasma they hurled at her first, but a great pump of Nausicaä's wings sent her quickly out of its path.

Instead, it struck the massive plasma screen above the Eaton Centre, and Nausicaä froze to watch as that screen began to creak . . .

To tremble . . .

To bend forward and snap off its hinges and tethers before falling like the heavens. But before it could manage to crash over the square, Ruin's magic had eaten away at so much of it that it had practically dissolved it in midair. It was only scrap that rained down around her.

Screaming ensued—the humans and folk who'd been unable to flee, or simply refused to, when Riadne's portal carved itself clear around the House of Night . . . scrambled to clear the sidewalks; streaked to the windows of the buildings they'd sought shelter in and pressed themselves against the glass to watch.

They were unable to see Nausicaä and Ruin and everyone gathered within the Viridian circle, but a massive television suddenly peeling away from its foundations was warning enough to evacuate the area.

"All right, so, note to self—avoid the black balls of acid death."

Ruin sneered at her, "You are absolutely charming."

"That's very nice of you to say." Nausicaä blinked at them. "Gosh, you might make me blush."

With a quiet snarl for a reply, Ruin lunged, a streak of motion across the square.

Nausicaä had time enough only to leap a few paces back, narrowly avoiding the heavy, two-handed sword they swung like it weighed no more than a paper clip.

Missing its mark, it struck down on one of the spouts in the pavement that normally fountained water when it wasn't the dead of winter. The force of the swing had been so great that it cracked through the pavement to the piping below, which immediately began to spray and flood the surroundings.

"Come now." Ruin slipped back into drawling, picking themselves and their sword up from the pavement. "I do enjoy a spot of exercise, but if all you intend is to evade my assault, let us put this to an end. I will send you on to join your girlfriend—for Ruin can be merciful too."

"No need," Nausicaä said through gritted teeth. "You can keep your mercy. My girlfriend hasn't gone anywhere."

Ruin lobbed another ball of miasma at her, and again she could only dodge, whisking out of the way just in time—the second digital advertisement it hit behind her shattered glass and sparking live wires across the pavement.

The *wet* pavement.

This arena was quickly growing more dangerous by the second—it needed to move.

"You truly do believe that, don't you?" Ruin sneered, flying at her in another blur of slices and blows and sweeps of their blade. "Arlo Flamel, still somehow alive, clinging on to the edge of existence . . . my, how love deludes. What a terrible weakness to indulge, that which corrodes common sense in a creature such as you, famed for your reason and rigidity . . ."

Nausicaä blocked as best she could, tried to dodge, but this was skill even greater than Lethe's, and she'd only ever lasted mere minutes against *him*—and he hadn't been genuinely trying to kill her.

She was fairly sure.

"You truly do believe *that*, don't you?" she snarled back at them, teleporting herself from the spot their blade pierced a hair of a second later; reappearing airborne directly behind them. "Like I said, Ruin," she called over her shoulder, already turning for the building rooftops. "All magic comes at a price, and I know what yours is."

With a pump of her wings, she flew off for the nearest, tallest building, streaming through the freezing air.

Temperature didn't bother her overmuch—she was still a being of Fire—but the snowflakes beginning to swirl in the air, the frost and chill and ice, none of it was overly helpful to her flight.

A flash of blue light—then suddenly stone arched through the air alarmingly close beside her.

It extended from the pavement to the building she'd been making for. Quicker than she could fly, Ruin was already running up its length to the rooftop it had crashed into.

Three more balls of miasma in quick succession—Nausicaä swooped and dodged and wove around them.

They sailed off into the faces of the buildings opposite, corroding on impact and eliciting more screams, more panic, more humans fleeing . . .

Chancing a glance below, she saw that Celadon and the others still struggled with whatever held them firmly in place. It didn't seem like any of them could utilize their magic, either, but that was . . . fine.

Considering who was missing . . .

And what their absence meant.

"Distractions, distractions . . ." Ruin sang at her.

Nausicaä looked back just in time to spot the metal spike that alchemy hurled at her.

Again she teleported; when she reappeared a safe distance away, she shot her own magic back at Ruin—Fire, the purest form of it, in compact balls just like the Titan's, and they incinerated those spikes to dust as soon as touching them.

Which caused Ruin all of zero injury; only seemed to piss them off.

But Nausicaä hadn't been trying to inflict a severe wound, regardless.

"FIGHT ME!" Ruin roared, taking to the air again on the back of more arching stone.

It sailed them right up to where Nausicaä hovered.

Again she teleported.

Again Ruin changed course, with yet another arch.

Teleport, arch. Teleport, arch—a ball of miasma, a ball of Fire shot back. Nothing devastating on her end; Nausicaä very much needed Arlo's body *un*burned to a crisp, and it was just as Ruin said, only a *distraction*, only time bought minute by minute . . .

Because Theodore and Fyri weren't down in that huddle . . .

Which meant they'd managed just in time to remove the bracelets they wore as well.

And if *they* had done so, no doubt the man with them had been the one to instruct them . . . the man who would have recognized immediately that what heated it wasn't the usual magic. Would have known it was alchemy, would have been quicker than they were to act.

Surely . . . hopefully . . . her entire plan hinged on him behaving how he should—that he would know and, with Arlo's life on the line, *had* to be on his way to help . . .

Arch, teleport. Arch, teleport.

"How pathetic the infamous Dark Star turns out to be—such astounding cowardice!" Ruin was not impressed. They weren't wearing down; that wasn't what she was after, regardless, but it would have made things easier. Instead, the short fuse of their temper only made them more aggressive. "How fortunate that Arlo did not survive long enough to see this. What she endured for your spinelessness—the aching despair, slowly drowning in the darkness and negativity consuming her heart. The *anger* . . . until all that remained in the end was the many terrible things she'd done in her life, her agony and hurt and pain and loneliness . . . all for the Dark Star to *not fight back*."

Ruin raised a hand and drew it closed into a fist. Debris and trash began to shift from the ground to fly up and orbit their hand, to twist and warp together into a solid, singular unit like a meteor.

A meteor that kept growing . . . and growing . . .

"If you will not fight, I will not linger. Come, my darkest fallen star. Allow me to deliver you unto death—you, and your companions. Let me give you *ruin*."

They wanted a fight?

Fine.

Nausicaä shot for Ruin, so sudden and swift it was them leaping back now just to dodge her assault.

Above, the meteor continued to build, drawing now from the buildings, the pavement, the earth ripping open to yield pieces of the subway system below.

Slash.

Swipe.

Jab.

Nausicaä threw her everything into the blows she delivered, because *everything* was what it would take just to keep Ruin occupied. There was no chance that anything she could do would actually touch them, harm Arlo's body.

This was all about buying time.

Thrust.

Slice.

Swing.

Crash.

Ruin met every blow with a force that vibrated pain through her arms.

Miasmic balls hurled through the air.

Fire sailed to knock them off course, catching on their surroundings to turn their arena into an inferno.

Ruin lunged at her, leaping off one arch onto another pulled quickly from the earth to catch them.

They knocked into objects, into people, into buildings.

Nausicaä's Fire spread farther and quicker, Toronto being set ablaze in the wake of their battle and fanned so hot that the light began to tinge the early dawn a violent red.

Miasma corroded.

Yonge and Dundas turned into a flaming war zone, and overhead that deadly ball of metal only continued to build and tear at the city's seams . . . and it was all Nausicaä could do to keep alive, to keep their attacks from landing on the others trapped below . . .

Another glance down—her fatal mistake.

A powerful boot aimed at her chest sent her careening into the side of a building and tumbling down to hit painfully against the ground.

Ruin was there before she could shake her head to dispel her disorientation, the tip of the iron blade at her throat. "The immortal belief that the soul's a song—how beautiful, is it not? What a charming fairy tale, that two people in perfect synchronicity will always be able to find each other, led true by that unique tune."

A malicious grin tugged at the corner of Ruin's mouth as that blade tip pressed a little harder against her flesh.

"But ah, how rage corrupts, down to even this fundamental level. How it *warps* that song into something so deliciously wild and ruined—discordant, never to find its harmony again. You know all about that, Former Alecto—it's why your very aura hangs in tatters."

Just a bit harder, that sword pressed to her throat, welling a bead of blue around it . . .

"And now your Arlo knows it too. A casualty of the chaos I embody . . . the despair, the hopelessness, the *anger* . . . That is how utterly you have failed this girl, in leaving her so long to my influence. You have lost her completely. You will never have her back. Not in this life, nor any other. It is important to me that you know that, here at your end, as well," they added with a sneer.

Nausicaä opened her mouth.

Perhaps Ruin expected her to grieve? To cry out. To bite back some retort—anything other than laugh in their face, she gathered by their stark confusion.

"A Dark and Hollow Star," she replied. "A Wild and Ruined Song—sounds to me, Ruin, like all you've done is brought us back together. There's absolutely no version of Arlo I don't belong with; we were made for each other, right down to our stardust, and that's how I know, without a doubt, you're absolutely *fucked*."

And just in time, a thunderous *crack* split through the air, making her smile.

Blue light flooded the circle—began to unwind the seething ball of metal above and direct its debris safely to the sidelines, began to dissolve what Ruin had done to warp the circle into a trap.

Celadon, Vehan, Lethe, Aurelian were freed . . . and there was Theodore, Fyri now too . . . everyone rushing immediately for her.

But Ruin merely peeled away and stalked in deadly calm back to their arena's center, the point of their sword scoring a deep line in the pavement behind them as they went.

A man stepped into the Viridian Circle.

"Took your time, old man," Nausicaä called across the way.

"Apologies," said Rory Flamel. "You wouldn't believe the traffic right now."

Ruin's lip curled to bare their teeth.

Stab, stab, stab, stab—Pride skipped back, and back and back, deftly avoiding each of the enormous spikes of dirt Nicholas pulled from the earth and hurled at them in quick succession.

Keeping to the sidelines, Alecto looked on as the Mortal Realm's greatest powers pitted themselves against each other, here in the dark of the countryside where no one but her could bear witness.

Armed with all of Arlo's power, amplified by their own, Pride gave back as good as they got—better, even, for Arlo had long ago surpassed his father in his craft.

Blue light crackled; black light snapped back.

Earth and stone and wood bent into terrible, unnatural weapons.

Nicholas Flamel had been a wonder in his youth, but he was now a very old man. Nowhere near as agile as the Sin was; he couldn't evade with the same precision.

A spear forged of compact soil sailed directly for Nicholas, and Arlo's father tried his best to dart out of its path, but it still caught his shoulder, piercing it cleanly through.

Alecto grinned.

In the face of the man Arlo loved and hated in equal ardency, and with Arlo's heart as Pride's core, the Sin was forgetting themselves, riled by Nicholas, just as Alecto had anticipated—that spear was proof; it had been backed by a force perilously close to fatal.

Just a little bit longer . . .

Pride was so close to sealing their fate . . . to making their kill and earning Destruction before their ridiculous cult could help Phoebus and the Council find a way to circumvent Arlo's safety measures, before they could find a way to create the other stones, which would act as shield for

362

them too—Pride, the core component to every summon that allowed them
into the world.

"*That was almost impressive!*" Nicholas boomed, his long white beard swaying with his mocking laughter. He reached up, dissolved the spear back into earth for it to crumble away from the wound. "*No wonder Phoebus chose my son for my second-rate replacement. Good show!*"

Pride snarled. "*You—*"

"—useless old man," Ruin growled. "Foolish; *obsolete*. You fancy yourself my caliber for a simple show of parlor tricks?" They flicked their wrist, and their sword flew up and at the ready. "How I will enjoy cutting you down—as Arlo would have enjoyed it too, for all that you put your own flesh and blood through."

Nausicaä couldn't help another grin.

This was all unfolding just a little too nicely—Ruin playing right into her hand.

It had been a spur-of-the-moment, wild guess, a plan born in the span of seconds, all on the flash of a memory that *wasn't hers*, bold in the fore of her mind the moment she'd found herself in this ring.

The Sins were their own individual entities, but they'd been born of Ruin's power, in the original conflict against the Primordial Ones. They were connected in ways even Nausicaä didn't fully understand, but she did know this much—Ruin's core was Pride, the first of the requirements to summon them. And Pride's core was the original Arlo, and Nausicaä had put a lot on the bet that *probably*, fathers were still something of an *issue* for them . . .

"I will—"

"—destroy *you.*" *Pride seethed.*

Extending a hand, they called another weapon—pulled it not from the earth this time but Nicholas's own spilled blood. Bending the iron within it, Pride molded the liquid into three small but exceptionally sharp daggers.

Hovering just above his hand, the points aimed true, trained on the elder Flamel.

Ruin lunged.

Nausicaä had borne witness to a great many things in her numerous years. She'd seen countries rise, Courts fall, numerous battles and wars—nothing quite compared to watching the last of alchemy's greatest line pitted against each other.

It was almost funny; Rory had claimed to be no great wielder of the art that was basically synonymous with his name, had always lauded Arlo has his better, and she was. That was clearly evident in the rapid-fire way Ruin was able to pull and warp and bend and shape the elements of the world around them.

But *goodness*, could Rory Flamel fucking *fight*.

Nausicaä understood a little bit better now why the illustrious Thalo Viridian-Verdell had chosen him for her husband.

It was a little unbelievable.

Ruin *whipped* around their arena, leaped and bounced and spun and dove, over objects, around fixtures, and Rory chased them all the way.

He pulled great blockades up from the earth, evaded every miasmic ball.

Every blow Ruin aimed at him, Rory met with a blade of his own—simple stone, nothing flashy, just as this man had been in Nausicaä's estimation of him up until this point.

Vaguely, she wondered who'd he been in his previous life—the one before he became husband, father, tired old professor—but whoever, *whatever*, it certainly played in his favor now.

And Ruin was fucking *livid* for it.

"KICK HIS ASS, DADDY FLAMEL!" Nausicaä cheered, and Theo did too. Celadon watched like he . . . knew. Something. Like he usually did. Private information he would never tell, that explained maybe why Arlo's father and the Grim Brotherhood's Madam had once been friends of sorts.

Rory didn't have time to call back—he folded himself in another narrow evasion, but finally, Ruin slipped into the upper hand.

"RORY—"

"—NO!"

*Alecto startled; whirled around; caught just in time the blur of something streaking from the tree line—some*one. *She flew toward them, snagged them up in her arms before they could interfere with what was happening, ruin this one chance they had to fulfill what needed doing.*

"Let me go—"

"—Nausicaä!"

"Hyperion—stop! You can't get involved! You don't understand. This is important—stop fighting me!"

He swung at her, struggled enough to win freedom from her grasp. "That's Arlo's father," *he rasped at her. "That's Arlo's father. I won't let that thing* kill him! *It's the very least we owe him after what* you *let happen!" He swung at her again, his words more of a blow than his actual fist, and streaked off across the grass—*

"HYPERION! LISTEN TO ME!"

"Vehan, *stop,* don't get in between this!" Nausicaä snapped, both she and Aurelian grabbing for an arm each to keep him from darting into the fray. "Rory knows what he's doing, he—"

A cry of pain—in the *moment* Nausicaä had looked away, Ruin had managed to knock Arlo's father to the ground.

He lay there, sprawled and winded, a heavy boot pressing with what looked like rib-cracking force to keep him pinned to the ground.

"That's Arlo's *father,*" Vehan rasped. "She can't lose him too, I won't allow it!" And he capitalized on their momentary distraction to break himself free of their hold.

Tore off across the pavement . . .

"VEHAN! STOP!"

Barreled straight into—

—Pride, who was knocked over sideways, and the pair of them tumbled. Rolled.

"I won't let you kill him!" Hyperion cried. "I won't let you use Arlo's body to do this! I—"

Alecto acted on instinct. She tried. *Hyperion meant everything to Arlo, was his dearest friend. He'd never forgive her if she allowed something to happen to him—it was all that ran through her head as she shot wind like a javelin, spearing right through Pride's chest . . .*

But it wasn't Pride's *fatal injury that drained Nicholas to pale horror.*

"Your Highness . . ." he gasped in shock as Hyperion sank to the ground along with Pride.

They tussled like schoolboys fighting in the street, Vehan and deities-damned *Ruin.*

Nausicaä and Aurelian both shot forward; her heart felt like it was lodged in the back of her throat, but she ran for all she was worth— just in time for Ruin to flip them.

For Vehan to be the one pinned beneath.

A flash of metal—Ruin drew back their sword, point angled directly over Vehan's heart . . .

"VEHAN!" Aurelian cried desperately.

The sword plunged . . .

"ARLO, STOP!"

A dull thud.

Hyperion sank backward, slid off Pride to the earth.

Three daggers were pierced deep into his heart, sapphire already begin-ning to spill from the wound.

"No . . ." Pride gasped as they pressed their hand over their gushing

wound. But to Alecto, for the merest flicker of a moment, the agony on their face looked more for Hyperion than themselves, and more as though it belonged to the last fragment that existed of—

"Arlo," Vehan gasped.

Everyone halted . . .

. . . Including Ruin, their sword point touched to Vehan's breast, and not an inch closer.

Because once again, Nausicaä was right.

"Do you get it now, Ruin?" she panted, half in exhaustion, half in rushing adrenaline. "Did you guess it? The price your power demands." She took a single, careful step forward, not wanting to break the fragile force holding Ruin at bay. "You can stuff her down. You can smother her with everything you have. You can do your very worst to break her, but the truth is—your *secret* is—you can't ever fully claim a heart. A piece of its original owner will always remain, because everyone has *someone* to guard it for them. And with all the people Arlo cares for standing here around her . . ." She paused to snort. "*Tch*—she's not going to let you do *shit* to that boy beneath you."

A smirk unwound on Ruin's face.

Which was so, one-hundred-percent *Arlo's* expression that Nausicaä had to blink back tears.

"See?" Nausicaä choked out, so fucking relieved, so incredibly, deities-fucking *relieved*. "There she is—that's my girl. You know what this means, right, *Ruin*?"

She lifted her gaze.

Searched out Lethe . . . and the sword he should still be wearing, strapped to his back . . .

Shiink—

Nausicaä's eyes snapped back to Ruin—wide with alarm, terrified that she would find Vehan skewered after all.

But instead she found . . .

"They'll condemn him for this, too," Nicholas whispered, staring down at the body he cradled. "My boy, my son . . . this is all my fault. . . . This fate should never have been yours to bear. What have I done to you?"

Hyperion, dead in Alecto's arms, Arlo's heart in her palm. Pride's transgression would have been all the permission she needed to wrench the wretched thing from their chest . . . if only she'd held out just a little longer.

If only Hyperion had been the first to die.

Yes, the Courts were certainly going to use this to vilify Arlo far worse than they'd already done. Hyperion was a prince, a beloved, direct relative of Founder blood. . . . There would be consequences. The Council would exact their revenge for his withheld knowledge in the monster they'd paint him, for Pride's actions.

Consequences . . . just as there would be for what Alecto had done in ending Pride's life before it qualified for death.

"I need you to take this," she said, handing Pride's stone to Nicholas.

With great difficulty, the old alchemist peeled his sorrow away from his son's snowy face to gaze dully at what Alecto extended. "I don't want it. I want nothing to do with it."

"I'm sure," said Alecto. "Consider it your penance. You're going to take this stone to Phoebus, and he's going to tuck it away for safekeeping, because he won't want anyone else to have it or steal it away from him."

"But won't he be able to use it, then?"

Alecto shook her head. "I'm the one who killed Pride; the stone will only answer to me, until I die. And you're going to tell him that. You're going to bring him this stone and win back his confidence and tell him it's useless to him, and for a while it will be, so he ought to believe you. He'll tuck it away in his palace vaults and go back to obsessing over a way to negate Arlo's measures against him, because he's going to have you to make him a new stone as soon as he does. And you're going to spend the rest of your life ensuring that he doesn't."

A trembling, veined hand plucked the stone from her palm.

Nicholas held it as though it weighed the world.

His son's heart.

"You aren't expected to return with it?"

"Oh, yes," Alecto said darkly. "I very much am. But I don't want to risk leaving the stone in immortal care after . . . well, after my punishment. Because Arlo was as good as dead the moment Pride entered his body, but I did just go against Law and take what was left of his life. My kin will send me to the Starpool, especially once they realize what I've kept from them, and I will be all but erased, my soul ground up to dust and scattered—which means this is goodbye, old man. I won't see you again, in any version, unless Fate decides to grant me a touch of mercy and use a bit of my soul for some new creation . . . but Fate is a fickle mother. I don't foresee that happening. So you'd better not let me die in vain, either—do what you have to do with that stone."

"I will." Nicholas nodded. "I owe my son that much, for all he's been through in my stead."

. . . Rory.

Rory, standing over his daughter, his wife's sword plunged through her heart from the back.

Tears in his eyes, emotion weighing down his words to a whisper: "I'm sorry, Arlo. I'm so sorry you had bear so much, all alone, for so long. I'm sorry you had to bear so much for *me*. For everything you've been through in my stead." He shook his head in dismay at himself. "This one last thing . . . it's finally time I do something for *you*."

For a moment, Ruin just gaped.

Then, "Thanks, Dad," Arlo breathed out on her last exhale, before sliding down the sword's blade to collapse onto Vehan's chest.

Just like that.

How quietly Ruin died.

Nausicaä almost . . . couldn't fathom it.

She stood in stunned silence with the others around Vehan, who held Arlo's motionless body in his arms . . . until Lethe stepped forward.

"And this would be *my* cue," he said gently, lowering onto his

369

haunches. "My last act as a Hunter, how surreal." He reached out with his clawed hand to brush through Arlo's hair.

A glowing began in her body, starting in her veins. Not at all like the ghastly glow of the Sins that had started this, but instead a warm light that shimmered like gold.

Brighter it grew, and brighter still, until the shimmering took over, and Arlo collapsed into a pile of sparkling dust so light that a passing breeze caught it up in a swirl.

Lethe stood.

"Excuse us, if you will. Arlo and I have a pressing appointment, immortal order to upset; you understand. Try not to have too much fun while we're gone. *You*—" He rounded on Celadon, and in the span of an eternal, weighted moment, the two regarded each other in silence.

Then . . .

"Bring her back," Celadon whispered fervently.

"Keep yourself alive," Lethe whispered back.

And as abruptly as Arlo had died, Lethe vanished.

Again, all Nausicaä could do was stare.

At the place where her girlfriend had just been.

Please bring her back, she prayed up to the deities, who didn't like her very much, but they owed her. They owed her *this.*

Fire crackled behind them.

Somewhere in the distance, a sign fell from the face of a building and crashed into a car, triggering its alarm.

"So . . ." said Theodore, watching the spot Arlo had been as well, everyone still trying to process and collect themselves. "That was a hell of a warm-up. Can't help but notice it's morning—who's ready to go to war?"

CHAPTER 27

S HE AWOKE TO STARS—AN endless expanse of them.

To pinks and blues and purples, cotton-candy whisps of galaxies; sweeping, churning, deepest black, planets like the throw of colorful dice. The cosmos glittered vastly overhead and felt a little as though if she reached out a hand, she could touch the glinting edges of all those silver-fire souls, so far away, so much closer than they'd ever been before.

Strangely, the sight was reassuring.

Staring up at it, she felt nothing but calm, the truest sense of peace.

"It *is* quite the sight—even for one such as myself."

Belatedly, she realized that those words hadn't been in her head. Someone was speaking—and to *her*.

She sat upright, and more things began to occur to her sluggish awareness. That she'd been lying on the smooth-rock summit of a steep peak, protruding out over water below that effused the dark of space around it with a silvery halo-glow of light. Behind her, the cliff sloped into a staircase winding down this mountain and out of sight, and between her and the first of its steps stood four people.

One wearing impossible robes of rot and bone and glittering dust, with hair the exact night of the heavens above from certain angles, whiter than the hottest stars from others.

One with that same star-white hair, half of which had been shaved to his skin; driftwood warped and tall, with eyes like acid and silver for freckles and glinting claws on one hand.

Another with white hair, this one a woman. Her eyes a startling shade of pale, her skin, her lips, her wardrobe to match, not a glimmer of color anywhere on her save for what seemed to be threads wound up and down the lengths of her arms, the boldest and most vibrant *red*.

The last stood out quite starkly among the others. With shamrock-green hair and elaborate robes of emeralds and limes and forest and poison . . . and a smile of such fondness, fixed confusingly on her.

Which one had spoken?

She didn't know.

Couldn't find it within herself to feel bothered, either, to figure it out.

But then the one wearing rot and bone and space stepped forward from the group and approached her. He extended his hand, and she took it without hesitation and was helped to her feet with a gentle strength, and now she could see off to her sides that the water below wasn't just glowing silver but *was* silver—some unusual form of the substance, at least; it churned and rocked and rippled like molten metal, and yet somehow gave the impression of fluid water.

"Do you like it here?"

She looked back up at the man before her, so impossibly tall— larger than life, a formidable figure, but smiling down at her with almost paternal care.

His question—she didn't know that, either.

Did she like it?

"It's relaxing . . ." she heard herself reply.

The man chuckled, low and humored. "I am certain, after what you endured and gave your life for."

Still staring at the man, she considered his words. "Am I dead, then?"

"You are. In a way. Though I think I have not received a soul with so much possibility for what you still could be, besides."

The man drew back a step, at the same time as the one behind him with the half-shaved hair and the impossibly bright eyes stepped forward.

"Death is but the least concern of your current situation," the first

372

man continued, drawing himself even larger, leaning a little more into the imposing figure she knew he could be. Serious. Magisterial. "You stand on the cusp of the Starpool, soul. You do so nameless and unburdened by memory, as all who come here must. For the choice you will make, you shall do by heart alone." Taller he drew, and the blacks of him consumed to be even darker; the whites of him burned even brighter. "You have died with the darkest of magic in your veins and murder on your hands. But Law was never meant to be heedless of circumstance. The Starpool will take into consideration the *why*, and the good you have done, should you choose to give yourself over to its waters. To be Destroyed or Reborn."

Had she committed such a terrible sin? Had she really dabbled in dark magic and *killed* someone, besides? She had no idea who she was, but something about that statement seemed incongruous with another something, equally impossible to define, that burned like a flame inside her.

But the man wasn't finished. "The other option *I* have to offer would preserve you in your current incarnation. Would take your body and reforge it immortal, with none of the memory of who you were in mortality, but eons of a brand-new life to discover in the position you won, by fair rights, as one of my Wild Hunt."

She had no idea, either, what a Wild Hunt was.

It was clear to her, by the hint of pride in the man's black eyes, that a place in it was a coveted thing. But again that incongruity, with this burning inside her—others might long to belong to this group, but she didn't think she much wished it for herself.

"You would live, soul, in the greatest of glory. Held high in immortal esteem, a champion among deities. You would roam any realm you wished, hunt legendary prey, know greatest honor in guiding other souls to this peak and the best of them to my ranks."

Glory . . . honor . . . legend . . . *champion* . . .

These things that made a hero.

That burning flared indignant, repulsed by the very term.

"You could also choose *me*," said the second man, with the white hair and the green eyes and a grin that began like a mocking smirk . . . an aura that smelled like decaying flowers. He seemed at once both perfectly ordinary, *familiar*, and far more frightening than even the god of death beside him. "You could choose to become my scion—my very first patron, Misfortune's general. You would be in charge of keeping my temple, my myth, my worship, my name, and in return I would keep *you*. Immortality is the gift all first and fiercest worshippers receive on death from the god they served well, and as a scion, you would be just as free as any Hunter to roam the realms in spread of your god's awareness."

The smirk deepened.

"Free to spend as much time as you wish with your mortal ties. And with all the memory that death stole from you, because *unfortunately*, I do not play by standard immortal rules."

"You would be rejected, though," the first man cut in to clarify. "Disliked. Feared. Excluded by the rest of immortal society. Not only for the slights your mortal form committed against my kin, but also because Misfortune is not yet a god consecrated. No immortal yet recognizes his claim to a temple. To become such, he must have a following, and such are the circumstances of his birth that even once this privilege is secured, it will not be looked on favorably. For all intents and purposes, soul, should you chose to tie your lot to Misfortune, you may very well spend the rest of your life in the eyes of your peers, a—"

"Villain," she finished for him, and something about that . . . made her breathe a laugh.

The black-eyed man nodded, though not without a flicker of his own private amusement. "Only so that you are aware. For a choice to carry weight, it must be made with fair education."

Looking between them, she considered a moment what each had said to her.

It seemed like quite a lot they were asking of someone who didn't

374

even remember their own name, let alone what their old self would have considered the right decision.

Then her gaze traveled past the two before her to the two off to the sides behind. "And who are they?" she asked, jerking her chin in their direction. "What do they want?"

"We are only here as witness," the green-haired one replied softly. "I have already orchestrated all I could to ensure all the right pieces found their way onto this board at the same time. Now the choice is entirely up to you; whatever you will make: To become a Hunter will return you to the path Fate had in mind for you. To become instead my son's scion and legacy would put you on a more . . . *unexpected* path. You would become part of the family that had been so cruelly robbed from him, family that also includes my son's soulbound, which my dearest Fate was most aggrieved with me for restoring without her permission . . ." They trailed off on a look at the green-eyed man, who suddenly seemed . . . furious? Confused? Surprised? Like something had occurred to him—something *touching*—that he absolutely detested to know. "The first time we met, I presented you with a choice to make as well, and there were so many things you could have become in diverging from your predetermined set of destinies . . . but only one in particular I'd hoped for."

All attention turned next to the last of them. The white-haired woman—Fate, she assumed—who rolled her eyes and curled a sneer like a pout, not the least bit happy to be here.

"If it were up to me, Hollow One, I would slate you for Destruction and start over. I had such high hopes in creating you. . . . You were meant to be someone quite different." She paused a moment to fix her gaze on Arlo, her pale eyes glowing faintly with disdain. "Regardless," she continued when that moment passed, a little stony, but with the air of resignation. "Your options now are thus: Become a Hunter and live an immortal life of blessing alongside the best the Lord of Death can afford. Which does come at the cost of your loved ones, whom you will never again remember, and will greatly delay Misfortune's ascension,

375

so I must confess to a personal bias that this is the option you choose. Or . . ." At this, she heaved a sigh. "*Or* become his scion, and you will keep your friends, your family, the life that shaped you, and every memory that goes with it, but consequently, your immortality will be far from easy."

I will ensure it seemed very heavily implied.

She bit her lip.

Stared down the panel of beings standing before her.

Felt in some strange way that she'd stood in a similar predicament, once upon a time . . .

Should you choose it, the Council will reconvene this hearing on the day that marks the start of your twenty-sixth year.

However, if Maturity has not found you by this time, your choices shall revert to what they are now: human, or common magical citizen.

What if . . .

What if . . .

What is Arlo's decision?

She looked at the green-eyed man—Misfortune.

The something inside her burned hot, beating fiercely and speeding faster at the sound of these words, which echoed in her head . . . words that seemed an awful lot like *memory*—just one, returned in private.

And why had Misfortune chosen this one, of everything he could have snuck back to her to help his case?

Arlo . . . was that her name?

What if . . .

What if . . .

What does Arlo choose?

This Arlo, the one in that memory . . . she didn't know much about her, but felt all the same like most of her life, she'd struggled with making choices. With standing firm in what she wanted. Afraid that if she did, it would somehow blow up in her face and disappoint the ones she loved.

"Well, dear soul?" the god with black eyes prompted. "We do ask a lot. It's no small thing you must decide with very little time to think. Regardless, the choice *must* be made, here and now. What do you choose to do?"

What if . . .

What if . . .

What if she was no longer that girl?

What if her choice was really quite simple—and in fact, she had already made it?

That one thing this god of death had left her . . . Arlo knew in her heart what she wanted to do, what she refused to lose, for any promise of any glory.

And she somehow knew that she'd always had a soft spot for what others perceived as the *monster.*

"I choose the scary one with claws, thanks."

"That's my girl . . ." the green-eyed man drawled, and there was no missing the flicker of his relief or the way the green-haired one beamed.

CHAPTER 28

Vehan

"GOOD OF YOU TO make it!" Ivandril greeted, his tone jaunty, but the harrowed look on his face spoke volumes of a vastly different sentiment.

Vehan followed close behind Celadon and Aurelian as they made their approach of the lookout, where the lesidhe Autumn general stood.

Nausicaä, Theodore, Fyri, and Rory had all gone directly to join the front lines, but his brother and his fiancé had wanted to check in first with intelligence, and Vehan wasn't doing anything without Aurelian where he could keep an eye on him.

The rush of answering protectiveness through the bond they shared told him Aurelian felt very much the same.

"Has she been spotted yet?" Aurelian asked, direct and to the point.

He prowled the room to the enchantment-reinforced glass enclosing Celadon's palace rooftop. From way up here, all of Toronto unfurled itself to their surveillance. Vehan didn't need to press his nose to the window to get a good view of what made Ivandril so distressed—he could see quite plainly before he even reached Ivandril's side; rather, he couldn't help himself.

Riadne's forces had been busy during their showdown with Ruin.

On the cusp of the rift that had opened between their armies, hundreds upon thousands of demons paced, the sound of their snapping, their shrieking, their growling audible even all the way up here.

Behind the demons were rows several layers deep of the Vor'Urc, orcs of every shape and size, but all of them mean to the bone. Behind *them*, the towering, flaming figures of hundreds of ifrit and, littered in between their colossal bodies, all the fae warriors of the Courts that had chosen Riadne's side, all the creeping crawlies that had ever been shunned to the sidelines, packed in the spaces with crude but highly effective weapons—it would hurt just as much to be clubbed by a nail-bat as it would to be impaled on anyone's sword.

This side of the rift, which stretched farther than Vehan's eyes could see, stood the opposition to this nightmare.

The armies of Seelie Spring and Autumn; the hundreds of folk from the Wild, most of them doing this for their loved ones, not for a system they abhorred—the Courts that had swooped in to colonize and displace, they wanted nothing to do with.

It was . . . nowhere near enough, but how Celadon had ever managed to unite so *many* of the outlying folk . . . There were banners from different royal houses; from different Wild tribes. There were brightly burning torches with flames of every color, weapons being thrust into the air; chants and songs and taunts and war cries, a veritable sea. The folk of the world were collected here in the middle of a human city.

Thankfully, *hopefully*, they'd managed to evacuate as many humans from the area as they could, but this was their home too—and what probably shocked Vehan both most and least was that some had even joined the battle.

These humans had no idea what they were up against, to be sure.

No idea what they were fighting for, apart from clearing their city of every nightmare brought to life.

But they were there, some in tactical gear, many with weapons, others standing back from it all with their mobile phones held high, broadcasting the sight all over the world . . .

There was no going back to hiding after this.

Unless Lethe felt moved to mass-wipe the entire planet of all memory of this event, Celadon was going to have more than the folk to forge a new relationship with.

But that was provided they survived this first.

Which Vehan rather hoped they did.

He would like to actually attend his wedding to Aurelian, an event he'd been planning in his head since his early preteen years.

"You'll let us know when and where Riadne makes an appearance?" Aurelian asked the goblins, busy at work on their computers, connected all over Toronto, with eyes and ears in every corner.

He recalled his stereotypical first impression of this race back in the desert, nearly a year ago now, caught in the midst of a goblin turf war—these folk, they weren't at all the collective joke sidhe fae had tried to turn them into after the Great War.

How sharply intelligent they were, how fierce and determined and dedicated to protecting not just the Wild but their cities, too—in trading their magic, they'd grown an affinity for these human spaces that Vehan would never fully be able to appreciate himself.

The goblin nearest nodded his head. "As soon as we know, you'll know."

"We might as well get down there too, then," Aurelian announced, turning to Celadon. "Your Highness, if you'll follow me, we'll get you someplace—"

Celadon glowered. "Absolutely not."

Both Ivandril and Aurelian opened their mouths to argue this obstinance, but he silenced them with a raised hand.

"I am not sitting cloistered away while my people and my family lay their lives down for my war."

Pursing his lips, Aurelian folded his arms over a chest that had grown so broad lately . . . "This isn't only *your* war, Celadon. We're fighting for more than you."

"I know that, but—"

"We'll be fighting *because* of you though—namely with Lethe, when he comes back here and learns that we let you anywhere near that battlefield without him."

Vehan nodded apologetically. "He's right, Lethe would murder us. You know how he's been around you these past few months."

"*No.*" Celadon growled, pulling himself up to full, regal height. "This is my fight. This is my mother—I have every right to be down there, just as Vehan does. Would you have him sit this out as well?"

"Oh, one hundred percent, absolutely I would," Aurelian declared sourly, turning a glare next on Vehan, who pretended to find his boots very interesting indeed. "But it seems neither of you is going to listen to reason." He sighed, relenting, but still didn't look all that convinced that this was what they should be doing. "Just remember that if you die, Celadon, you're basically condemning this world to the destruction we've worked so hard to prevent. Your mother, her Crown, her Sins, her Ruin—I'd rather face every single one of them again and again on endless repeat than Lethe if he lost you."

Frowning, Celadon muttered something that sounded a lot like, "I promise to be careful."

Aurelian was unable to argue the point any further—Celadon was free to make his own decisions, after all. This statement was the matter settled.

Together, they made for the elevator that led down to the main reception and crossed the sea of black marble for the revolving glass doors that would take them outside.

They had just about made it to the exit when Vehan felt it, and immediately he paused.

It was Ivandril who first noticed that he'd stopped.

Followed closely by Aurelian, just ahead.

Then Celadon, and everyone turned . . . to regard Vehan with confusion and concern.

Had he lost his nerve, it seemed like they wondered. Was there something he had to say?

Vehan's heart sped up to racing in his chest.

Adrenaline rushed to his core.

Magic sparked in a sudden flood through his system, leaving him jittery and even further on edge, but he tried his best to look wholly unaffected—perfectly calm and unafraid.

Aurelian's brow quirked. "Vehan?" He hesitated. "Is everything okay?"

"Yes!" Vehan replied, perhaps a touch too brightly for the way his fiancé's brow dove next into a furrow. Vehan shook his head, clamped down tighter on his panicked emotions . . . "It's all fine. I was just . . ." He paused, somewhat for effect, more because a swell of *everything* he felt had risen to his throat, rendering speech a touch difficult. Swallowing it down the best he could, he jerked his head toward the door. "You guys go on ahead of me. There's something I need to do quick first."

It was difficult to close off just enough of their bond that only a little of his feelings slipped through.

This was still so new to him—Aurelian's gaze narrowed on his face, like attempting to read both his expression and whatever their bond betrayed. Luckily, it was perfectly normal for Vehan to be feeling a little fear and apprehension right now, giddy and sick to his stomach all at once.

The trick was keeping the ocean of that just a trickling stream down the bond.

Eventually, though—just when Vehan thought he couldn't hold it back any longer—the press of Aurelian's searching aura relented.

"What's the matter, Vehan? Is there something you need before we—"

Vehan shook his head, hard enough that his hair flopped across his eye. "I really just need to do something personal, very quick! It won't take long. And then I'll meet you all out at the front lines."

Pursing his lips, Aurelian stared him down a moment longer . . . then sighed. "Yeah, all right, but unless you're changing your mind and want to hang out here away from the danger—which again, I am perfectly fine with—try and be quick. I don't like the thought of you being on your own when there aren't any eyes or tabs on your mother."

"Noted." Vehan laughed in a gush of breathlessness.

And the group turned for the door.

They began to filter out, first Ivandril, then Celadon . . .

"You really will be quick?" Aurelian pressed one last time.

"Quickest as possible," Vehan replied.

Terror . . .

Grief . . .

Was this the last time he might ever see him? This boy he'd loved body, heart, and soul, since their very first meeting.

How hard it was to try and keep his heart from constricting at the very thought.

"Aurelian?" he called, unable to stop himself when Aurelian turned for the door, and he panicked, because it was one thing to send his boyfriend away . . . another to watch him go.

Aurelian turned.

Terror . . .

Grief . . .

I love you. Endlessly.

"Make sure you save some demons for me."

With a snort, Aurelian rolled his eyes, then turned back for the door. "Maybe just the one," he called as he walked . . . and walked . . . and through the revolving door he vanished, out onto the street.

Leaving Vehan in the foyer, which had begun to pulse with his heartbeat in its absolute, dreadful silence.

Click.

Click.

Click.

Heels across marble.

Vehan swallowed.

Pulled his shoulders back, straightened his spine, conducted himself in perfect confidence, as he turned to face an offshooting hall, drenched in shadow, and a figure appearing from its gloom to stalk forward.

On the hallways' threshold, the figure paused . . .

"That *weakness* we talked about . . . giving your life to buy your inferiors time."

From behind her, two other figures appeared: puppets on invisible strings; the cobbled-together corpses of kings.

"We've a very different definition of 'weakness,'" Vehan replied stonily, and at the sound of the monstrous parodies of Vadrien and Azurean drawing their blades from heavy sheaths, he squared his jaw. "Hello, Mother."

CHAPTER 29

Vehan

———〜〜〜———

"HELLO, MY SON."

She stepped from the doorway toward him, her horrible dolls trailing in flank.

The glass and diamond and gold of her armor glinted in the dim lighting, glittering darkly. Her Bone Crown snug atop her glossy black head, her seven philosopher's stones studding her waist like a belt, Riadne looked both exquisite . . . and exceptionally unwell.

Fatigue had stamped dark circles around sunken eyes.

Stress and strain had thinned her body to unhealthily gaunt and bony.

Still she radiated brilliant light, but against this palace's night, this made her more wraith than woman.

"Vehan, *Vehan*," she sighed his name with a shake of her head, despairing. "I'll give you one last chance to make the right choice. To return to where you belong. Where you will be worshipped as a god in the aftermath of my new order." Pausing before him, she extended a hand. "Vehan, my dearest. My only for so long . . . You were always my fiercest protector; would you truly pit yourself against me to the death? Don't force a mother to extinguish the child her body bore . . ."

Vehan . . . took a step back.

Then another . . .

Then another . . .

"I'm sorry," he whispered, because this weighed so much heavier on him then he could ever put to words. But Riadne had chosen her path. Every opportunity, and she'd stayed true to what *she* wanted, not what was best for her sons. "If you force my hand, this is what I must do. I'm *sorry*, Mother. I will not join you."

Electric-ice eyes flared violent blue.

"So be it," she hissed—and from behind her, her dolls sprang to action.

Unnaturally fast they flew toward him. Vehan had only enough time to lunge a step back before their heavy blades struck the marble where he'd just been standing, hard enough to crack several inches through.

They heaved out their blades . . .

Skated around Vehan to opposite sides . . .

Flung themselves at him in a pincher move, and it was all so quick—this was the former High King of legendary battle, and his *father*, who'd trained with the greatest of champions. Regardless of the fact that Riadne couldn't tether a soul to her scavenged creations, it was clear that the dark magic giving them life had drawn inspiration from the originals they blasphemed.

They closed in on him—Vehan leaped back.

Skidded across the starry-black marble with the momentum, hand bent to the ground to slow himself.

In his other hand, he called on his magic, the fizzling, crackling, sparking, hot lightning he'd thankfully been keeping himself primed with these days, and it was another testament to how far gone his mother truly was that she hadn't noticed until that lightning forged a violent, buzzing blade in his hand, so much stronger, so much brighter . . . real and natural electricity . . .

"You've been holding back on me," she mused across this makeshift arena, and sounded both appalled with herself and . . . proud? Excited, that he should finally prove himself better than her estimation of him. "Oh Vehan, what a secret you've been guarding!"

She didn't know the half of it.

Vadrien and Azurean lunged from their opposite sides of the room, and in a deft sweep of movement, Vehan caught the pair of their blades—parried them both with quick, angry *zips* of his crackling Class Five weapon.

It was a flurry of blows he contended with next.

A simultaneous assault, where Vadrien would swing at him from one side, slice at him, jab at him, *heave*, and Azurean would jab at him from the other, slice at him, heave at him, *swing*.

Thank goodness they couldn't use the magic that had made them even more formidable in life, but such was the strength of the darkness that powered them that Vehan was already beginning to tire, catching and returning every attack.

And then—a foolish mistake . . .

The quick footwork he'd been forced to dance, combined with the tension and urgency and reality of this moment, caught him on his own ankle.

He tripped and crashed to the ground but managed at least to turn himself so that he landed on his back and blocked the blow that rained down on him.

Vadrien's massive sword stopped barely an inch from his head.

"It is not too late to surrender, Vehan . . ." Riadne called from her sidelines, where she'd kept her whole life, an austere judge.

Gritting his teeth, Vehan channeled his entire strength into pushing back against the blade that, any moment now, could break through his defense, and his skull quickly after.

He pushed . . . and he pushed . . .

And Vadrien pushed back.

Soullessly—there was nothing in those eyes like emotion; he didn't recognize Vehan at all. This wasn't his father, he had to remind himself, and held on to that thought as a hand let go from his sword to *reach* . . .

And closed over the monster's face.

"I could say the same to you," Vehan growled back at his mother and, with a surge of all the power he could pour into his palm, seared lightning through the creature hot enough to fry him, in a *flash* of a second, from the inside out.

Charred to a crisp . . . motionless . . . smoking . . . the monster that wasn't his father teetered, then collapsed in a crumbling heap at Vehan's side.

Unfeeling, undeterred by his partner's demise, Azurean launched himself once more at Vehan.

But Vehan was quicker—finally; this once.

On his knees in an instant, and his mother's last remaining doll hadn't even been able to swing his blade in Vehan's direction before a thick bolt of lightning shot from Vehan's hand to incinerate all that hollow flesh and bone as well.

Panting, Vehan got to his feet.

Riadne watched him, furious.

"Commendable," she snapped. "You managed to deceive me. You're a far stronger wielder of your element than you'd led me to believe—well done."

But her tone suggested the very opposite, and as she spoke, it began to thunder.

Electricity crackled at her fingers, then wrapped like a flowing sheet around her arms and torso and legs. "But you are far from my equal, son. If it's a fight you want, a fight I shall give you."

The room began to tremble.

Vehan widened his stance to keep his balance.

Drawing on the power of her stones, Riadne began to grow—twice, thrice, four times her size.

Her lightning shaped itself into a long and lashing whip; her other hand unsheathed her infamous sword from her back. Her eyes stayed that haunting, too-vibrant blue . . . "Give me your all, then, my clever little snake," she purred, the Magnetism in her voice so powerful Vehan couldn't ignore it, even if his all hadn't been his intention. "Lay your worst at my feet. SHOW ME THE MIGHT OF THE LYSTERNE LEGACY—and I shall show you the strength of what made it."

Vehan lunged.

Meeting him at the foyer's center, Riadne caught his blade with the vicious crack of her own—and flung him away as easily as flicking a fly.

Stumbling, he managed to right himself before he could tumble backward, but nearly too late to parry her next assault.

Riadne came at him, utilizing his distraction to inflict an endless, alternating barrage of strikes and lashes and blows.

Vehan jumped, he dodged, he leaped out of the way; he swung, he slashed and parried every deadly swing of her sword.

Only because he'd trained so long and hard with Aurelian, with Lethe, and at times even with his mother, was he able to keep pace with her.

"I've taught you well," Riadne breathed in mocking laughter as she caught the thread of electricity Vehan had attempted to lash back at her with and began to wrap it around her wrist. "How unfortunate that I will have wasted all that effort by destroying you."

One of the stones at Riadne's waist gleamed as she summoned its gift. That thread of lightning in her grasp began to turn to a heavy gold that clattered to the floor when they both released the end they held.

And giving him no inch . . .

"Come *here*, Vehan," she pressed with her enhanced Magnetism, and Vehan could feel it . . . the slight haze that had often come over him through the years, that left him so easily compelled . . .

He took a step forward—

"Vehan, *STOP!*"

The voice was . . . Celadon?

Vehan resurfaced from the fog that had settled over him, and sure enough, there was his brother, closing great strides across the room, wind *billowing* around his body in anger to match his livid expression.

With the sweep of a hand, he shot a blast of ice at Riadne's chest to knock her back—vines burst up from the ground at her feet to tangle up the length of her legs.

And at last, Vehan remember himself.

Pulled lightning hot and seething from inside him—from a core that had trained itself to endure under Ruin's duress, under his mother's impossible standards. That had learned the scorch of his mother's power, only to be remade anew by Arlo's.

He pulled on his element and threw all that he was worth in his mother's direction.

An electricborn fae she may be, bolstered and protected by her stones and Crown, but Vehan wasn't a Class Five wielder for nothing.

Hit directly on the chest, Riadne *blew* the rest of the way backward— screamed out in an agony that pierced Vehan with guilt, but he didn't relent. He kept her down.

Down . . .

Down . . .

Until Riadne snarled and threw out a hand, and another stone gleamed a vibrant green.

Envy.

But what could it do?

Riadne hurled back a matching force of lightning in his direction, and Vehan dove to the side.

"Envy copies powers!" Celadon called. "She can literally learn any-thing we use against her and turn it against *us*!"

"Because that's fair!" Vehan growled, floundering a little. How did they defeat this? What could they do when Riadne could simply throw it all back in their faces? Also, what the hells was Celadon doing here?

There was no time to sulk or ponder their situation—Riadne got quickly back to her feet and threw herself into her next assault.

Sword and whip working in tandem, her weapons pinwheeled as she flew across the black marble for them—*slash*, she cut at Vehan; *crack*, she lashed at Celadon.

Celadon, who'd trained his whole life with Azurean, then after with *Lethe*.

Celadon, who'd inherited not only Spring and Summer but Winter and Autumn too.

He dove and dodged and leaped, hurled lightning at their mother, snagged her in more vines; threw sheets of ice to slick the floor; thrust his hands against the ground to awaken great quaking below the earth.

And none of it compared to what he could do with his own airy whip, flicking and snapping at her in return, quick as a cat's tail.

Instead of tiring, though, Riadne only seemed to grow stronger the longer this battle wore on.

Wrath's influence, most likely—they *had* to figure out a way to end this before it became impossible. Maybe it already was.

If they could just get at the stones . . . but then, how to destroy them?

Slice.

Cut.

Jab.

Parry.

"Mother!" Vehan cried, when a blow knocked him back against the wall and the length of her blade crossed his throat. "Mother," he said, softer. "It's not too late; you don't have to do this. I *love* you—I loved you when you were nothing but my mother, no Crown, no Sins, no world at your feet. . . ."

Tears welled up in his eyes.

Behind them, Celadon gathered . . . was that light in his hands?

What sort of power was *this* that he'd inherited—Summer's radiance? Or was it something else . . .

"Please," Vehan begged. "*Please*. I don't want to have to do this."

If there was anything left of his mother in the woman who stood before him, she wasn't listening.

Power had consumed her. He could see it in the steady darkening of the blue in her eyes; in the color beginning to leech from her hair, all that bold black draining to gray . . . bleaching to white . . .

"Please . . ."

Riadne angled her sword on its bite, prepared to cut clean through his throat. Vehan closed his eyes against it so that the *her* that was still in there wouldn't have to see his light die a second time by her hand—

Riadne *screamed*.

A beam of *moonlight* had shot from Celadon's hands and burned a hole into her side. Large enough, painful enough, that their mother dropped back in shrieking agony . . .

Then rounded on Celadon instead.

"How *dare* you?" She seethed, throwing aside her blade.

She advanced on Celadon, her anger making her *wild*, and Vehan scrambled. Tried to find something to protect him with, because Envy had a beam of moonlight already building in her now free hand.

"How dare you?" she raged, whisper quite in her terrible ire. "YOU THINK YOURSELF MY BETTER? YOU INSIGNIFICANT WORM, YOU THANKLESS LEECH—EMBARASSMENT OF MY WOMB! I BROUGHT YOU INTO THIS WORLD; I SHALL TAKE YOU RIGHT OUT OF IT—"

Her words cut off.

Riadne looked down.

Celadon looked down.

Vehan, behind them, looked not at the point of the sword sticking out of his mother's chest from her back—a fatal blow, if it weren't for the stones still preserving her life—but at the person who'd driven it there.

Red hair, jade-green eyes. Still in all that black-and-gold armor, but Arlo was herself again—herself, though distinctly otherworldly. *Immortal.* Everything about her seemed both softer and sharper all at once.

"To UnSeelie Spring's protection," Arlo uttered softly—and goodness, Vehan wanted to cry all over again, to hear so much emotion back in her voice, to hear *Arlo*, at long last. "That's what my great-uncle made me vow my service to last summer, in agreeing to let you teach me alchemy. Celadon might be something else now, but he's still UnSeelie Spring where it counts."

Arlo, returned, and just as Lethe promised—with all her memories intact.

Riadne stumbled.

She turned around.

She made to strike at Arlo next, but Arlo now was so much quicker—in one deft movement, she snatched up a stone from Riadne's belt . . . the black one, the first one. Riadne's Pride.

And tossed it back over her shoulder.

For a hand to appear out of sudden blackness and snatch it from the air.

A man formed next out of the cloud, appearing in robes of glittering black and swirling purples and brightest poison greens. His long white hair shone bright as starlight. He was lovely and terrible both at once, a sort of compulsion in his air that made one want to never stop *looking* at him, but hinted at disaster should they fall for that trap.

"Lethe?" Vehan breathed.

"Misfortune," Celadon corrected, relief in his face if not in his tone, which only reflected the boredom of a king who knew his knight would show eventually. "You certainly took your time."

"My deepest apologies," Lethe—*Misfortune*—said, in that same cool creaking Vehan had come to know, and yet . . . smoother. More enticing, like certain death wrapped in satin. "It does take a moment to establish one's godhood."

The hand holding Pride clenched, long fingers firm around the stone, that godhood bolstering him just enough to manage . . . an echoing *crack*.

The stone split in two.

For a moment, Riadne stared.

Then—"NO!" she screamed. "NO! NO! NO! NO!"

Pride destroyed, the others seemed unable to exist without it—all six of them began to crack as well, to crumble and grind themselves down, dissolving into tiny heaps of colorful sand on the floor.

Riadne sank to her knees. "NO!" she continued to shriek, clawing at the sand, scooping it up to cradle it between her palms. "I GAVE *EVERYTHING* FOR THIS! NO! YOU WRETCHED, AWFUL, HIDEOUS GIRL—THIS IS YOUR FAULT, I'LL—"

Vehan moved, almost without thinking.

Flung himself down at his mother, his arms slipping from behind to wrap around her middle.

"Mother," he said against her back, his voice heavy with sorrow . . . but with determination, too. "You did give everything."

Riadne *looked* down at the clasp of his hands around her.

"You gave so much more than everything for this. And so much of what you did . . . I won't ever be able to forgive you for. But . . ." It was so hard to see his mother reduced to the scraping creature before him. Riadne, possibly the greatest fae of their age, and all she'd ever wanted was for that age to take her seriously. "I'm so sorry," he said like a prayer. "I'm sorry you had to suffer so much. I'm sorry that you deserved far more than what you were given. I'm sorry that I couldn't save you."

"Vehan," she rasped.

"Please." Vehan begged one last thing of whatever was left of the woman who'd raised him the best that she could. "Mother, if you can hear me—not this woman you've become, but the one I once knew. Do you know what the goddess Tellis said? When we came for her Crown, and she handed it over?"

He swallowed.

He shook.

This was the last time he'd ever hold his mother like this, the last thing he'd ever ask of her.

"She told us that Lord Cosmin had given that Crown to the Mortal Realm, hoping that there would come someone here who was strong enough to do what immortals couldn't. That they could resist the temptation of the Crown to choose its destruction. Tellis . . . she was certain that person was Arlo. And I thought so too . . . at first." He shook, and he shook, and he tried too hard to hold back his tears.

"But the *more* I thought on it, the more I started to understand. It's easy enough to resist temptation of a thing you've never known. It's so much harder to yield something you've tasted. That person we were waiting for? For centuries. For strength. For someone who was the very best example of what mortality could be . . . it wasn't Arlo. I had my suspicions, but now I'm certain: it was always meant to be *you*."

He hugged her tight, this woman who'd been his everything—just the two of them for so long.

"Please. Just this once—please choose to do the *right* thing. For us. For *me*. The Crown must be utterly destroyed to save us all; all you have to do is choose to hand it over. *Please*."

And Riadne . . .

. . .

. . .

. . .

reached.

First for the clasp of Vehan's hands.

Then for the Crown on her head.

She removed it. Looked down at it. Trembled just as noticeably as Vehan, as though fighting the impulse to put it back on her head and finish what she'd begun.

"My whole life, Mother. I have loved you my whole life. *You*, not your Crown or your stones or your Court."

"I hope that in our next life," she said, in a voice so thin and quiet even Vehan wasn't sure she had spoken at all, "I get the chance to try again. To be the family you deserved. The *both* of you. My boys."

Slowly, the Crown between her hands—that simple, brittle twist of bone—she handed it over to Lethe.

There was a sighing of sorts, the moment Lethe used every ounce of the power he'd inherited from his Titan progenitor and wielded his misfortune against the Primordial Ones to dissolve the last of their bones, magic and all.

A releasing, not of the First Ones' magic, which Arlo had explained the bones contained and had just been fully destroyed as well. No . . . it was something different. Something Vehan would hazard to guess was the souls that the Crown had devoured over the years allowed at last to pass into their afterlife.

Meanwhile, Riadne shuddered.

She groaned and fell to the floor to writhe in pain—to age right before their eyes—and Vehan held her through it. As her body shriveled, drained of vibrancy . . . until finally, she moved no more, the Bone Crown exacting the toll of its use, if no longer able to imprison her in eternity.

Silence filled the room. Celadon, Vehan, Arlo, and Lethe stood somber, staring down at Riadne's body.

CRACK.

"Hey assholes, I don't know what's holding everyone up, but some wild shit is going—" Nausicaä, teleporting into their midst, stopped when she realized who stood right in front of her. ". . . Red. Hey."

"Hey," Arlo teased, then launched herself at her girlfriend, arms wrapping tightly around her middle. "Oh my gosh, I'd forgotten how *good* it feels."

"Uh . . ." Nausicaä really seemed to be faltering, at a complete loss in trying to come up to speed with what she'd just . . . teleported in on. "What does?"

"Hugging you!" Arlo laughed, and wound herself even tighter. "You have no idea how weird it was to not care about things like that. Or . . . well, maybe you do. Wow. It's been a bit, hasn't it? Since we've both been *us.*"

Peeling back a fraction, she leaned up on the tips of her feet and pressed a kiss to Nausicaä's mouth.

And Nausicaä dissolved into tears.

For a moment, the two of them stood there, hugging. Crying. So relieved to have each other back, and Vehan . . . he lifted to standing. Pushed down his grief over losing his mother for the last time.

Crossed over to them.

"Arlo . . ." he began, soft, unsure. Swallowed back another swell of emotion—different from sorrow, but it still made his eyes sting. "Are you okay? You did just die and come back to life—I know a little about what that's like."

Untangling herself from her girlfriend, she latched onto Vehan, pulling him in, and that seemed to be the trigger for Celadon to remember he wanted to hug her too.

The three of them converged—collapsed to the floor in a tightly knit huddle.

"If anyone's interested," Lethe drawled, frowning down at the huddle. "I do seem to recall Nausicaä's very *urgent* reminder that we're still very much at *war*."

Their showdown with Ruin.

Their defeat of the High Queen.

Vehan couldn't help but laugh, which probably sounded fairly manic, but he felt in this situation it would be forgiven. "All right," he managed in breaths between. "On to battleground number three we go!"

CHAPTER 30

Celadon

~⟡~

I T HAD BEEN AURELIAN who'd stopped him just as they'd reached the crowd of their ranks gathered at the cusp of the rift. Aurelian, who hadn't been fooled for a *moment* by Vehan's show of nonchalance in the foyer, and Celadon wondered if his brother knew just how deeply his fiancé loved him, to have known *all along* what Vehan was doing—how very dangerous and likely to result in his death—yet Aurelian had recognized how important it was that he, more than anyone, be allowed to confront his mother on his terms.

You need to go back; Riadne was in that foyer, Celadon. It's reckless as all hells, and Lethe might eviscerate me for sending you to your likely death, but much as Vehan deserves this chance for closure, as another of the sons she's wronged, you deserve it too.

And of course he'd known—Aurelian was lesidhe, so much better attuned to magical auras, and to have spent so long in Riadne's company . . . there was no way he hadn't recognized *hers*, when it appeared back in that foyer. In fact, it was likely through the bond that connected them that Vehan had recognized his mother's as well.

Right, Celadon had replied. *Thank you, Aurelian, for letting me know.*

Mmm, Aurelian had grunted, because as much as he respected his fiancé, Celadon could see in the tightness around his eyes, the barely perceptible shaking in his body, how much it cost him not to be there too. *Just try to bring yourselves* both *back alive.*

Celadon was extremely glad he wouldn't have to report failure on that front.

Together, they ran—Celadon, Lethe, Vehan, Nausicaä, and Arlo resurrected. Out the palace's front entrance, and the magic they'd woven to protect his seat of power had apparently been impeccable, because he hadn't felt it at all . . . the *tremors*—

"*Shit,*" Nausicaä swore, latching onto Arlo to help keep her steady the moment they spilled out onto the street, and a shudder rocked through the earth below them.

"What's going on?" Celadon called over the audible groaning of stone and steel, Lethe's arm around his waist, the other clutched tightly under Vehan's arm, to anchor the both of them upright too. "Is the rift tearing *wider?*"

Yelling back over the din, Nausicaä shook her head and replied, "No, it's closing!"

Without Ruin's power feeding it to keep it open, like all the other rifts that had opened up around the world, this one had finally burned through its fuel.

"The demons?" he asked next, pressing his luck for another bit of good news—with Riadne gone, and her stones along with her, might they be fortunate enough that without Wrath to sustain them, her infernal forces had retreated back to the pits of hell they'd come from?

The tremor passed; the street fell still.

Nausicaä took a moment to assess herself and Arlo before giving him another shake of her head.

"Sorry. Still *very* fucked on that front, the last I checked—come on, as soon as that rift seals over completely, there's nothing between us and the whole of Riadne's vicious army still angling for a fight."

Of course they were.

The Courts had been so awfully poisoned and warped for so long, controlled by the power-hungry, racist fascism of the High Council, that he hadn't had much difficultly in rallying its subjects—and the folk that it had maligned—to take up arms for change.

But there would always be those frigid souls who sought chaos for the warmth of its flames; who didn't care what they were fighting for so long as they were promised violence.

And Riadne had been an expert in wielding others' passions for her gain.

Their flight resumed.

Celadon taking lead, Lethe right behind him, the five of them tore down the streets toward his army—his *vastly outnumbered* army, short on weaponry thanks to what they'd lost in the Hiraeth. And now they were also losing the only barrier between them and unhindered, frontal assault.

They ran.

Tremors struck with increasing frequency, forcing them to stop and stand their ground; to dart out of the way of the pieces of the buildings around them breaking away from their whole.

The closer they drew to their battleground, the more obstacles they had to dodge and weave around. Huge chunks of debris. Cars abandoned in the streets. Panicked humans finally remembering sense to flee the scene.

But he could finally see it, just up ahead—the back lines of their forces.

"Nearly there!" Celadon shouted, pushing through the latest tremor, one that hit so hard that an entire building not far to his right collapsed with a thunderous moan.

More screaming—more humans fleeing.

A wave of dust and air crashed against them, and it was only his and Arlo's natural proclivity to the element that protected them from being blasted sideways with most of what was around them.

At last they reached the army.

All around them folk were hunkered down, fastened to the others around them, sheltering the best they could, and holding their ground as the earth knit itself back together up ahead.

Celadon pushed through their ranks, carving a path for the others to follow, heading for the front, where, doubtless, Aurelian would be found.

Almost there . . . when suddenly, the earth gave another groan, and there was barely enough time for warning—"HOLD ON!" Celadon roared over the swell of commotion, everyone around them scrambling for anchor. He reached back for Lethe, who reached back for Vehan, who reached back for Arlo . . . who caught Nausicaä by the hand just in time for another tremor to *slam* through the earth.

And then . . . stillness.

A quieting down to absolute silence.

Celadon looked around them, at the folk slowly raising their heads, getting back to their feet, assessing their surroundings as well.

Wordlessly, he plunged the rest of the way forward—and barreled almost directly into Aurelian's back.

"*Aurelian.* What—"

He shushed Celadon with an urgent swat behind him, eyes not peeling a moment from the scene just ahead.

Celadon peered around him . . . and saw.

The rift had closed, sealed over completely, bringing the front lines of Riadne's army all the closer.

The demons stood with their heads cocked, their mouths open, their cloudy eyes trained forward . . . the giant ifrit just behind them, flaming in their places . . . the orcs and the darker corners of the Wild, the sidhe warriors, and the best of the High Council's private forces . . .

Everything stood.

Perfectly still.

As though frozen under a spell.

Who would strike first? Celadon wondered. Who *should* strike first, in this instance? How long did they wait out this boon of a reprieve, his army picking itself up from the ground just to fall to this strange, enchantment-like trance.

Waiting . . . on Celadon to decide what they should do.

Aurelian looked to him.

Celadon looked back.

He opened his mouth—but before he could issue his order to arm their ranks at the ready, it was another who broke their silence first.

Another . . . by way of a *roaring*.

Such a terrible, piercing, deafening sound that Celadon and the whole of his army clasped their ears in an attempt to block it; winced and folded up smaller in desperate attempt to just get away from it.

But worse was when the creature the sound had come from unfolded great wings to take to the air—a massive, ruby body; a tail that lashed like a whip; formidable talons and even deadlier teeth; and a chest glowing hot with a burning core . . .

Celadon recognized this creature at once—not only what it was but *who*.

"A DRAGON!" someone in the ranks behind him shouted out in fear, and there were answering screams, even more cowering.

Not just a dragon, no.

It was so much worse than that.

"Melora," Celadon gasped. The Madam. The Madam, and at her command, three more hulking bodies took to the air as well; the dragons Celadon had hoped she'd content herself in community with after his defeat of her.

But no.

This was the Madam, and this was personal. Riadne had sought her out most likely the *moment* she'd learned of the Madam's disgrace, and played on that passion . . . on that grudge she no doubt harbored.

And now, without Riadne to lead them, without doubt this had become the Madam's show.

Her new and absolute reign to claim, should Celadon fall.

"*Fuck,*" he swore, and rounded on his forces. "AERIAL, AT THE READY."

But nobody listened.

They were too caught up in actual *dragons*, like this was the last straw in what they were willing to pit themselves against. The ifrit they'd been prepared to contend with, but dragons on top of this . . .

What were they going to do?

If this panic fanned any hotter, his entire army might disband, and then they were well and truly done for.

He needed to do *something*, quick, needed a way to snap them out of their terror, to remind them that this battle wasn't hopeless, wasn't—

Another roar.

His army froze.

So too did their opposing force.

Everyone's attention zeroed in on the row of buildings at his army's back—at the . . .

"FUCK YEAH!" shouted someone else. "WE GOT DRAGONS, TOO!"

. . . *Cosmin.*

Fyri had done it. She'd actually done it! Celadon's recollection of their conversation during Vehan's birthday was thin at best, but that vibrant gold and burgundy-accented dragon, with teeth and claws and fire to match, just as lethal as the Madam's . . . who *screamed* another echoing, answering roar and then launched from the top of the building he'd transformed on to take to the air as well . . .

Was Theodore.

Fyri had actually managed to bend her alchemy to draw out his dragon form, just as she'd told him she could in the Market.

And there—on the ledge of where he'd just been, there she was. There they all were: Fyri, Rory, Arlo's former tutor, Leda, and the handful of other alchemists they'd apparently managed to collect just in time.

Each of them holding aloft . . . what looked from here to be a stick?

Theodore circled high into the air above them—loosed another terrible cry, then dove back down and, in a single sweep, blew fire to light the alchemists' *torches.*

They'd been holding torches, all now burning, and as soon as the torches caught fire, they were immediately thrown down onto. . . . It had to be an array at their feet, because the moment they bent to place their hands to whatever was there, the dragon fire sprang roaring, flaming Theodore copies.

Celadon could almost cry in relief as finally his army remembered themselves, and their own fire began to rouse.

"AERIAL," he cried, and this time, they listened—the folk of the air, the faeries with wings, the sidhe fae stationed in the buildings, the alchemists crowned, with their elements primed at their fingertips . . .

"ARMS," Aurelian commanded next. The goblins and Wild and lesidhe forces, blue sparking magic in one hand, glinting iron blades in the other; Aurelian's own tactical team at his back . . .

Screech!—Theodore roared another piercing sound, and his flaming duplicates rose to the air, directed by the alchemists.

Nausicaä's wings unfurled behind her—"Bet I can bag more orcs than you, Legolas," she said, and smirked at Aurelian as she stepped up beside him.

"You can certainly *try.*" Aurelian smirked back, lifting a fist for her to knock her own against, their challenge sealed.

"We're mostly going to spend this battle covering their backs, aren't we," Arlo sighed to Vehan, who nodded his head despairingly—before startling a little when Arlo whipped out a hand to her side, and much as Nausicaä pulled her various weapons out of nowhere, a burst of air materialized her mother's sword in her hand.

An immortal talent—Celadon wondered what else his cousin could do now, how else Arlo had changed apart from the flush of health to her softy glowing moonlight complexion and the almost acidic brightening of her jade eyes.

Fingers at his chin tilted Celadon's consideration elsewhere, though—up, up, up to meet Lethe's gaze. Misfortune. His lover more a god now than ever, and goodness, he hoped there'd be time later for him to examine all these little changes.

The flecks of cosmic black in that poison stare; his own moonlight flush of life; still all those beautiful starlight freckles and that set of

404

impossibly thick lashes capped with the barest brush of white. But there was a silvery quality to his hair now too, and depth to his voice, rounding it a touch deeper, and—*focus*.

They were about to launch a war.

"Does one wish the god of ill fortune luck?" Celadon asked, breathy between them.

And Lethe smirked down at him.

Stooped to lower his mouth to Celadon's . . .

"From you I'll let it pass," he murmured, then *smeared* a kiss across his lips.

When Celadon righted back around, faced again the snapping, snarling agitation of their sea of opposition, he felt a little more hopeful now too about their odds of survival. Riadne's army might have numbers, but *their* folk fought with heart. For loved ones . . . for freedom . . .

Lifting his hand into the air, he locked his gaze on the Madam's, who watched him with burning prejudice, just waiting for Celadon to make his first move before issuing direction of her own.

He opened his mouth.

Nearly shouted commencement of attack.

When—*boom*.

Two figures appeared in the scarred stretch of land between the two armies, the first from a burst of smoking darkness, the other from a blooming of flora.

Cosmin and Tellis. Two of the Great Three, and both of them dressed for battle.

Celadon startled, and he wasn't the only to do so.

With the Bone Crown destroyed, the terms that had contained the gods to their realm had been rendered obsolete. He hadn't expected immortals to begin turning up in this realm again already, but there they were, two of the strongest . . . and then in further flashes of light, bursts of color and shadow and element, others began to assemble.

Gods and goddesses and deities he knew—so many others he didn't.

For a moment, he froze in terror.

They couldn't fight a war on two fronts. If the Immortal Realm had chosen now to lay siege to this one, they were utterly done for.

"Nausicaä," said a voice behind him, and everyone in the vicinity turned.

To watch a woman, who looked . . . remarkably like a far older version of the Dark Star, all grown up, as she approached Nausicaä, another, younger woman with pitch-black hair and Nausicaä's silver eyes trailing close behind.

White fire for hair, golden light for eyes, crackling electricity for armor—Urielle, the Goddess of the Elements and Creation, strode through the ranks, which parted like fish to make way for her . . . and dropped to a knee in front of her exiled Fury. "My daughter," she continued, in a voice that brimmed with motherly affection. "I cannot change what I allowed to pass; I cannot undo how I failed you . . . and your sister. But I can lend my strength to the protection of your loved ones and the home that cared for you when I could not."

She looked up at her daughter, imploring.

Nausicaä looked down, visibly awkward and pale.

"Will you allow us to fight with you, Aristos Alecto?"

Best of the Alectos.

A moment . . .

Two . . .

Swallowing thickly, Nausicaä nodded, and Celadon couldn't be certain, but he'd swear he caught the glimmer of tears in her eyes.

He felt a little like mirroring the sentiment.

The Immortal Realm—they weren't here to fight them; they were here to fight *for* them.

Turning back *again* to their opposition, he could tell clear as daylight that they weren't as keen to contend with his army now. In fact, some of the enemy forces were beginning to *flee*.

Celadon matched the Madam's furious stare with a smirk he'd definitely honed on Lethe's influence—but it was Aurelian's hand that rose into the air, and slowly, all eyes turned to him.

"HERE WE STAND," he called to the legion at his back, never once breaking gaze from the army that writhed adjacent. "HERE WE WILL FIGHT." Slowly, so slowly, but one by one, the folk around them began to recognize the speech he was making.

The few simple words—so very Aurelian, and oh, how they *resonated* with the Wild, for what they echoed . . . all those years ago . . . when the Courts had first come and *squeezed* them out of their lands and their lives and their home . . .

"AND IF HERE WE SHOULD DIE, THEN WE DIE BRINGING AS MANY OF THOSE BASTARDS AS WE CAN WITH US. OUR ANCESTORS ARE WATCHING—LET'S MAKE *THEIRS* FUCKING CRINGE!"

The crowd behind him roared to life.

Like the volley of a catapult, Aurelian whipped his hand from the air and launched them into war.

EPILOGUE

Arlo

————— ⌒ ⌒ —————

"AFTERNOON, GENERAL MISFORTUNE," the doorman greeted as Arlo approached the House of Night and stepped through to the foyer.

It was common knowledge in the palace that Arlo was scion of the king's godly lover and right hand to the pair of them. With the treaty between the Immortal and Mortal Realms in the process of redesign, it wasn't unusual for her immortal kin to come and go in Celadon's territory.

Not everyone was pleased about it, mortal and immortal both, but even without their Crowns, the Great Three were such that no one wished to cross them—not at the moment, not when their attempt at upheaval here was still a fresh wound that Celadon wasn't about to let them forget any time soon.

And Arlo?

Well, somehow or other, she'd fallen into the role.

Her mother's shield, her mother's cloak she'd always adored—with her alchemy and her immortal powers and the small green die she carried in her pocket . . . it had sort of just happened: *general* of the House of Night's private guard.

Her, and—"Arlo! Hey, birthday girl—over here!"

Nausicaä waved at her from across the packed room, bouncing up and down on the balls of her feet, as though anyone could miss the six-foot-two Fury, resplendent in the best black leather Celadon's money and eye for fashion could afford.

It was a busy day at the palace.

It was *always* busy, now, with Toronto to rebuild, among other things.

Riadne's war had cost them a great deal in many ways, more than the lives lost on both sides. It was unarguably thanks to their immortal reinforcements that Celadon's army won—and even then, it had been a close call, such had been the volume of what the late High Queen had amassed.

A few months later, Toronto was still in the process of piecing itself back together.

There was no going back after what had occurred here.

Too much of their world had been exposed for too long—Misfortune couldn't wipe human memory of it without causing significant mental damage, and Celadon hadn't been willing to sacrifice that for secrecy they'd outgrown.

Time to start working *together*, he'd decided—and together indeed they'd been steadily rebuilding, not only their city, but their relationship, too. It had been a long time since humans and folk had knowingly coexisted. A lot of hurt between both to make amends for, but here was a decent place to begin.

And still this wasn't all that was going on. Not with the Market they were busy reestablishing off in Germany as well. With terms to work out with the Wild and their pantheons, in an attempt to divide land and wealth and resources fairly among those who'd come first and those who'd been here so long, this was just as much their home now too. With newly established Night and Day Courts, Theodore fielding the tatters of the Seelie fae; Fyri and Rory and Leda working united to establish a community for the ironborn, with Arlo lending aid on occasion, whenever she could spare the time. Even the mer had begun to surface from their waters to meet with the king their long-ago, besotted prince had finally reunited with.

Celadon . . . free of Fate's wrath, with Lethe's godhood now to protect him.

Celadon . . . who had summoned them all from the things that were keeping them busy, busy, *busy* . . .

All for a promise Arlo had made to a certain young prince a year ago now in a random, nearby park when she'd first confided in anyone what Luck had given her in the Faerie Ring.

"Okay, okay, everyone, calm down!" Elyas called from the head of the table as everyone gathered and settled into place. "We'll start out simple, go around the circle, and everyone can introduce the characters they chose—you all *did* choose your characters, right?"

Arlo looked around the House of Night's dining room—the one she'd never been welcomed at when she'd been a girl and it had been only her and Celadon against the whole world.

And it was still her and Celadon, and things still had a long way to go before she could call them perfect.

But . . .

Now it was them, and also Nausicaä.

"Obviously I'm a Tiefling sorcerer on a never-ending quest to save my girlfriend, who keeps getting kidnapped to random castles."

Now it was them, and Aurelian, too.

"I'm the Dragonborn rogue who keeps stealing her."

"What! Fuck you—why are you trying to steal my girlfriend? You have your own toys—leave mine alone!"

And now there was Vehan, as well.

"Okaaay, well, I want to be a gnome and bard. I have no idea what my Dragonborn husband is doing, running around kidnapping girls and sticking them in towers—"

"Just one girl, and just to piss Nausicaä off."

"Excuse me, my Tiefling's name is *Shazam*."

"I'm not calling you that."

"I'm also a bard!" Celadon called happily. "We should form a band. Can we form bands, Elyas? Lethe's going to be in it too."

Misfortune frowned—he was Lethe only to Celadon and Arlo alone now, though Nausicaä took many liberties. "I wanted to be a monk."

"What, why?"

"To observe a vow of silence and solitude, and sit out this ridiculous game?"

Celadon clucked his tongue and shook his head. "Overruled by decree of your king. Lethe's going to be a bard. This is going to be a *family* band. Vehan is my gnome half brother. Which I guess makes me also part gnome? Lethe, would you like to be a gnome as well?"

"I quite physically loathe you and this entire table."

Elyas nodded, ignoring Lethe's objections to look eagerly over the notebook he couldn't stop beaming at in between glances, hard as he'd worked on this campaign they were about to embark on. "Arlo? Who did you choose?"

Arlo smiled, small and private, very happy to be in this moment . . . at the end of everything, with so many new people to care for, and to care for her in return.

"Oh, I don't know," she replied. "It might be fun to play a half-elf cleric with a shadowy, overpowered past, that they'll conveniently remember only once we get to the end of this journey."

Nausicaä rolled her eyes fondly.

Celadon snorted in humor.

Arlo reached into her pocket, pulled out the die within, set it on the table, and said in an echo of what she'd told the last person who invite her to play a similar game, "All right, Dungeon Master, you have your DnD party—read us the rules."

ACKNOWLEDGMENTS

Here we are at the end of this adventure, and what an experience it has been.

I've said from the beginning this is the story I *needed* to write, for the child I was, going through so much, and who would have deeply appreciated finding something like this in the bookstore. What started as a personal journey became words that resonated with so many more people than I could ever have imagined, and so my first and greatest thanks this time around goes out to you, dear readers. You who took these characters and loved them just as fiercely as I do; you who sent me messages of thanks, for representation that still doesn't get a whole lot of spotlight; you who filled this undertaking with excitement and joy with your anticipation and fandom. I will forever adore the community that has come together around this ♥

Thank you next—in a massive, extremely heartfelt way—to Sarah McCabe. I couldn't have asked for a better editor to see these characters from their humble, chaotic beginnings all the way through to their end. You gave this story life and shape in a way I would never have been able to do on my own, in a way no one else could. It has been my immense pleasure working with you on this. Thank you, thank you, with all that I am, for taking that chance on me six years ago now.

Thank you, as ever, to my agent Mandy Hubbard, this story's first believer. This finish line would never have been reached without you. Here's to many more ♥

Thank you to the whole of Simon & Schuster, both Canada and US. To the Margaret K. McElderry team, and everyone who had

413

even the smallest part in helping to make any of this possible. So much work goes into making a book a reality, as I've learned over the years—I am in awe of, and immensely grateful for, the many things you all do to bring these stories to life.

Thank you to my incredibly supportive family ♥ To Laura, Jee, Kyle, Jess, Jeryn, Colleen, Shana, and Juli; to Liselle Sambury, K. M. Enright, Priyanka Taslim, Nicki Pau Preto, Brittany Evans, and Xiran Jay Zhao; to the Toronto Writers Crew; to all the bookstagrammers and booktokers, booksellers and influencers, who loved and gave their time and effort to promoting and spreading awareness of this series, including (but not limited to): AJ Elford, Rosa, Zeal, Star, Kate, J.J. Fryer, Amy, Isabella, Chloe, Meg, Theresa, Katie, Angelina, Kyla, and Tae. Thank you to Desiree Duplessis; to the entirety of the audiobook team and the voice actors who effing killed it with these characters, including Neo, Imani, Michael, Vikas, Natalie, and Mizuo.

Thank you to my partner, Kade; my cat, Zack; and my darling son, Nyx.

To Turns & Tales for always hosting such lovely events for me and these books.

To Miss Rachel for watching that darling son when I needed to work during the day.

To Final Fantasy VIIR, XV, and XVI—I can't believe this series spanned three FF games.

I have been exceptionally lucky to have so many wonderful people standing behind these books. It's very rare anymore that authors get to write anything more than a trilogy, and to be one of the first to traditionally publish a longer fantasy series featuring a queer main cast has been a tremendous honor. It is a thing I wouldn't have been able to do without my queer predecessors, so my last thank you goes to the LGBTQ+ community—to the ones who paved the way, and the ones who will come after ♥ We are necessary, valid, beautiful, and loved; thank you for giving us a place to belong.

I hope this story continues to find its way into the hands and hearts of the people who need it. I am by no means at the end of my career—only getting started, with so many more worlds to explore, characters to meet, and lives to ruin ☺ Let's meet again, in whatever comes next ❤

ASHLEY SHUTTLEWORTH is a young adult fantasy author with a degree in English literature and a slight obsession with *The Legend of Zelda*, *Kingdom Hearts*, and *Final Fantasy*. They currently live in Ontario, Canada, with their cat, named Zack, and a growing collection of cosplay swords. You can find them online at AshleyShuttleworth.com.